MY SWEET V

Annie Groves lives in the nort............................. has done so all her life. She is the author of the Pride family series, *Ellie Pride, Connie's Courage* and *Hettie of Hope Street,* for which she drew upon her own family's history, picked up from listening to her grandmother's stories when she was a child. Her next set of novels was the World War II series *Goodnight Sweetheart, Some Sunny Day, The Grafton Girls* and *As Time Goes By.* These were followed by the Campion series, *Across the Mersey, Daughters of Liverpool, The Heart of the Family, Where the Heart Is* and *When the Lights Go on Again,* which are also based on recollections from members of her family, who come from the city of Liverpool. *My Sweet Valentine* follows on from *Home for Christmas* and *London Belles* and is the third in this series, which introduces a set of glorious characters who live in Holborn.

For more on all of Annie's books, www.anniegroves.co.uk has further details.

Annie Groves also writes under the name Penny Jordan, and is an international bestselling author of over 170 novels with sales of over 84 million copies.

Also by Annie Groves

The Pride family series

Ellie Pride
Connie's Courage
Hettie of Hope Street

The WWII series

Goodnight Sweetheart
Some Sunny Day
The Grafton Girls
As Time Goes By

The Campion series

Across the Mersey
Daughters of Liverpool
The Heart of the Family
Where the Heart Is
When the Lights Go on Again

The Article Row Series

London Belles
Home for Christmas

ANNIE GROVES

My Sweet Valentine

HARPER

Harper
An imprint of HarperCollins*Publishers*
77–85 Fulham Palace Road,
Hammersmith, London W6 8JB

www.harpercollins.co.uk

This paperback edition 2012
1

First published in Great Britain by
HarperCollins 2012

A catalogue record for this book is available from the British Library

ISBN: 978-0-00-736153-3

Set in Sabon by Palimpsest Book Production Limited,
Falkirk, Stirlingshire

MIX
Paper from
responsible sources

FSC
www.fsc.org

FSC™ C007454

FSC™ is a non-profit international organisation established to promote
the responsible management of the world's forests. Products carrying the
FSC label are independently certified to assure consumers that they come
from forests that are managed to meet the social, economic and
ecological needs of present and future generations,
and other controlled sources.

Find out more about HarperCollins and the environment at
www.harpercollins.co.uk/green

For Annie Groves' readers

Acknowledgements

To everyone at HarperCollins who worked on
My Sweet Valentine.
An acknowledgement to Yvonne Holland,
and one to my Agent Teresa Chris.

ONE

'Tilly, no! Stop! Don't go any further. It's too dangerous.'

'I'm all right,' Tilly Robbins assured her boyfriend, Drew, as the crowd surging towards St Paul's Cathedral parted them. All around, the air was thick with smoke and the dusty aftermath of the previous night's heavy bombing. Buildings were still burning, the acrid smell stinging the throats and the eyes of the onlookers. Even now, hoses were still being directed at the most intense fires.

The general noise of the Londoners, coming to see for themselves that St Paul's was still standing, added to the rattle of fire engines' wheels on cobbled road and the roar of persistent fires, made it almost impossible to hear oneself think, never mind hold a conversation, Tilly thought. Her earlier sense of adventure had been a little dissipated as the crowd swept her away from Drew and carried her along with it. Of course, she would never want Drew to think she was the helpless kind who couldn't look after herself, but already she was missing

1

his protective presence at her side and the warmth of his hand in hers. Soon, however, she managed to battle her way out of the crowd to stand in the shelter of a doorway whilst she waited for Drew to catch up with her. Turning, she waved and smiled at him. Relieved to see that Tilly was waiting for him, Drew waved back.

Then suddenly, a shower of burning sparks fell onto the crowd, followed by a piece of smouldering timber from a building. People started panicking, pushing and elbowing others to try to escape. Trapped in her doorway by the crush of bodies, Tilly couldn't move. Several bricks fell to the ground nearby, one of them hitting her arm, whilst Drew struggled helplessly to get to her against the surge of the crowd moving the other way.

'Watch out, the whole building's going to go,' Tilly heard someone yell.

People scattered in every direction. Frightened herself now, Tilly too started to push forward, trying to escape. Her chest was pounding; the air she was trying to breath was thick with dust and heat. Her nose was stinging from the burning smell. She had no idea where to run for safety as the bricks showered down. Right next to her a man was hit on the head by one of the bricks, staggering and then falling to the ground, blood pouring from his forehead. Automatically Tilly crouched down to try to help him.

Drew had been fixing his gaze on her as he fought to get to her side. Her sudden disappearance from sight had his heart slamming into his chest, until the crowd parted and he could see the cream knitted beret she was wearing on her dark curls.

'Drew!' Tilly knew she was trembling with relief as

Drew reached her and pulled her close. Another fall of bricks had her ducking her head into his shoulder whilst he raised his arm protectively around her.

'Come on, we've got to get out of here before the whole building goes,' he urged her.

The man who had fallen was being helped to his feet by his friends. Drew was right, they needed to get away, but still Tilly hesitated, wanting to make sure the injured man was all right.

She had just pulled a couple of yards away from Drew when she heard him yelling frantically, 'Tilly, no!'

The thunder of the fresh fall of bricks was terrifying. It held her paralysed where she was, right in their path. They were going to hit her. She was going to die, but still she couldn't move. A terrible sense of the ice-cold inevitability of her fate gripped her. This was it. This was her time. It was no good trying to avoid it. She couldn't escape.

She could hear Drew crying out, 'Tilly! *Tilly!*', his anguish making her heart beat faster but he was too far away to reach her.

Tilly looked towards him, all her love for him in her eyes.

Drew knew only that he had to save her. Miraculously, by some superhuman power he hadn't known he possessed, he reached out for her, somehow finding the strength to pull her bodily out of the path of the falling debris, and away to safety. His grip on her was so hard that Tilly could feel the sharp pain of the force he had used right through her shoulder.

It wasn't that pain, though, that was making her cry, as Drew held her tightly, whilst the bricks thudded down onto the pavement behind them. It was relief, Tilly recognised.

Drew had just saved her life.

She was trembling so much in the aftermath of her shock that she knew she was incapable of standing by herself. As he held her, she could feel his heart thudding, and hear his harsh straining for breath.

'Oh, Drew, you saved me. You saved my life. You put your own life at risk for me,' Tilly whispered, unable to hold back her tears.

'My life is nothing without you in it, Tilly,' Drew whispered back. If he'd lost her . . . It didn't bear thinking about. He loved her so much. She was everything to him, this pretty little Londoner who had stolen his heart so completely.

Thankfully they clung together, both aware how close to death Tilly had been, silently sharing their own small miracle, looking at one another with all that they felt for each other in their eyes. There was no need for words. They were together, they were safe. At least for now. Held tight in Drew's arms, Tilly felt vulnerable for the first time. Suddenly she was anxious to claim every second of life she could – to spend that time with Drew; to be with Drew. To be married to Drew, and soon, though she knew that her mother did not want that for her. Until this moment she had been relatively happy to accept her mother's plans for her, but now that she had come face to face with the reality of loss and death, now when she was still shaking inside with the fear of what could have been lost, Tilly knew that somehow she must find a way to change her mother's mind.

The incident, so potentially fatal for Tilly and Drew,

was just another everyday wartime event in the lives of London's citizens. A salvage team was already piling out of the truck that had pulled up close to the unstable building. Men were cordoning off the pavement and getting to work to make the building safe. The brief moments of panic and danger were over.

'Come on,' Drew said gruffly against Tilly's ear. 'Let's get out of here.'

'I still want to see St Paul's,' Tilly told him. 'We said we'd meet the others there, and Mum will worry if we don't turn up.'

'She'd worry even more if she knew what I know,' Drew told her grimly.

Tilly was right, though. Olive, her mother, *would* worry if they didn't meet up, and then Olive wouldn't trust him to take care of Tilly, and that was the last thing Drew wanted. He knew already that Tilly's mother thought she was too young for a steady boyfriend, and he could understand why. It was up to him to prove Olive wrong and to show her that Tilly would be quite safe with him.

But there were things about him that Tilly still didn't know. Things he hadn't been able to bear to tell her in case they changed how she felt about him. He hated keeping secrets from her. He wanted her to know everything, but with every day that passed since they had declared their love for one another it got harder both to tell her and to not tell her. His guilt was an increasingly heavy burden on his conscience. He guessed exactly how Tilly's mother would feel if she knew the truth about him. She would not like it at all.

'Come on, then,' he agreed, making himself focus on the present as he gave in to Tilly's insistent tug on the sleeve of his sturdy Burberry mackintosh – a staple in the wardrobe of all serious Fleet Street newshounds. 'But this time you stay right here at my side, and to make sure that you do . . .'

Drew took hold of Tilly's hand and held it tightly in his own, earning himself a speaking look of tenderness and love.

Darling Drew. She was so lucky to have met him, Tilly thought happily. Her American was the most wonderful man, the most wonderful boyfriend . . . he would be the most wonderful husband. Tilly tried to squeeze down the happiness and excitement she felt at the thought of Drew as her husband . . . and herself as his wife. And they *would* be husband and wife, just as soon as she could convince her mother that she wasn't too young to get married. Just because her mother had married young during the last war, and had then been widowed when Tilly had been a baby, that did not mean that the same thing was going to happen to her. She understood why her mother wanted to protect her, but she wasn't a girl any more, she was a woman now. A woman who was deeply in love and desperate to spend every minute she could with the man she loved. Life was so precious. How strongly that had been brought home to her. They had so much to look forward to: their love, and the life they would share, the book that Drew planned to write about Londoners living through the war, the children they would have . . . She couldn't wait for her life with him to start.

Standing waiting anxiously at the bottom of the street, with her back to St Paul's, Olive spotted the young couple from several yards away. The sight of them openly holding

6

hands caused her heart to sink. It wasn't that she didn't like Drew Coleman – she did – but Tilly was so young, too young, in Olive's eyes, for the pain that she knew could come from loving someone in wartime if that love turned to loss. Drew might not be in uniform but in his job he was often out and in the thick of it, reporting on the air raids on London.

Initially Tilly had respected Olive's wishes about not getting too involved with Drew, but since Christmas something had changed, and every day – or so it seemed to Olive, watching Tilly so anxiously – Tilly was making it plainer that she considered Drew and herself to be a courting couple. Olive only had to look at her now, openly holding Drew's hand in the street, where she knew that Olive would see her, to know that.

It wasn't that she couldn't see that Tilly thought herself in love. It was just that she wanted to protect her from the pain that that love could bring if it was lost to her, and war brought the prospect of that kind of loss so much closer.

Now that mother and daughter had found one another in the crowd, Olive's pretty face, so like her daughter's, was creased with anxiety.

'I don't think we should have come,' she told Tilly. 'It's so dangerous out here with all these buildings still burning and unsafe.'

'We had to, Mum. We couldn't not do,' Tilly protested. 'We all want to see for ourselves that St Paul's is really still standing. We all said the same thing, even you.'

'That was before I realised just how dangerous it was going to be,' Olive Robbins replied.

Tilly's 'all' referred to the three girls who lodged at

Olive's house in Holborn, and Olive's friend Audrey, whose husband was the vicar at the church they attended.

'And at least they didn't get St Paul's.' Tilly looked towards the cathedral, her heart filled with a rush of pride and love. There was something so special, even mystical, about the sight of Wren's masterpiece rising above the pall of smoke that must surely touch every Londoner's heart. It was a wonder that the cathedral had been spared whilst so much had been destroyed and damaged around it. Fire crews had fought all night to save it, and Londoners had come out in their thousands to pay their own often silent tributes to its endurance and the bravery of their fellow citizens.

There was no need to say anything to her mother about what had happened earlier, of course, Tilly reflected. She worried so much about her as it was.

Hearing the note of determined cheerfulness in Tilly's voice, Drew tucked her gloved hand into the pocket of his raincoat and held it firmly in his own, giving it a small private squeeze. In return Tilly looked at him with eyes luminous with emotion. Witnessing their small exchange Olive's heart sank even further.

Drew was a good man; he would listen to maternal reason, she felt sure, but Tilly was a different matter. Olive was normally proud of her daughter's spirited independence. She knew from her own experience of life that a woman sometimes needed to be independent, but Tilly could be very strong-willed and fearless. She had the courage that came from never having had to face the really bitter cruelties of life. Olive wanted her to keep that courage. She wanted to protect her from the pain of life's cruelties. Marriage at eighteen in the middle of a world war would do the opposite of protecting her. Not that Tilly had said anything to her directly about marrying Drew, but Olive suspected that it was only a matter of time before she did. And when she did Olive knew that she was going to have to stand firm and refuse her permission.

Marriage . . . a child . . . widowhood – Olive knew for herself all about the pain and loneliness that brought.

Loneliness? She hadn't been lonely in her widowhood. She had had her mother-in-law and father-in-law to live with and then later to care for. She had had Tilly to love and cherish. She had had a busy life and one that now, with the war and her WVS work, was even busier. Indeed, it was thanks to the WVS that she had made what was turning out to be such a good growing friendship with Audrey Windle, the vicar's wife.

It was a life without the kind of love that came from having a husband, though; a man to turn to, to share things with, to laugh with, to love . . .

Olive could feel her face starting to burn at the dangerous direction of her private thoughts.

Mother and daughter looked at one another, Tilly's chin lifting with determination – which to Olive looked like defiance – before she deliberately moved closer to Drew and nestled into his side.

Once, not so very long ago, it would have been *her* side that her daughter would have run to, Olive reflected.

Standing with Drew, Tilly surveyed the scene. Whilst the Germans hadn't managed to destroy St Paul's, the fires resulting from the bombing raid had damaged much of the heart of the city. Those streets with their ancient religious names – Pasternoster Row and Curie Street – the solid guildhalls built by its rich merchants, its learned seats of justice, all had suffered damage.

Initially it had been the photograph in the *Daily Mail* of St Paul's seeming to float above the smoke of the fires that had drawn Olive and Tilly, along with so many other Londoners, to come to see for themselves that the cathedral was indeed still standing and not a just a mirage.

In the dull light of the grey day Tilly could still see the fairer tips of Drew's mid-brown hair, a legacy of the outdoor life at American summer camps during his growing-up years, Drew had told her. They had lived such different lives; grown up in such different circumstances. She was an only child; Drew had four sisters. She had only her mother; Drew had both his parents. But the differences between them didn't matter. What mattered was how they felt about one another. Their love was still new enough for Tilly to feel almost giddy with a mixture of joy that they had met and horror at the unimaginable awfulness of them never having met at all.

'At least Article Row has escaped being bombed,' Drew offered comfortingly now.

'Yes, thank heavens,' Tilly agreed. She didn't know by what good fortune her own home at number 13, and in fact the whole of Article Row, had been spared the conflagration. She was just glad that they had.

Prior to the start of the war Article Row had been an immaculately neat-looking and well-cared-for row of houses that wound its way between closely interweaving streets. Chancery Lane lay to the west of the Row, Farringdon Road to the east, Fleet Street to the south and High Holborn and Holborn Viaduct to the north.

The residents of Article Row still did their best to keep it looking as it should, of course, especially Nancy Black, Tilly's mother's next-door neighbour, and the sharp-tongued busybody of the Row, but Hitler's bombs had destroyed so much of the city that even those buildings that weren't damaged had been afflicted by brick dust and greasy smuts, making everywhere look careworn and down at heel.

Article Row comprised only fifty houses, built by the grateful eighteenth-century client of a firm of lawyers in the nearby Inns of Court, whose fortune had been saved by the prompt action of a young clerk articled to those lawyers. The three-storey houses curved down one side of the Row facing the rear of the ivy-clad windowless walls of the business premises that backed onto Article Row, making it something of a quietly genteel backwater, its status much prized by those residents, such as Mrs Black, to whom such things were important.

It wouldn't have taken much for the flames of nearby burning buildings to be driven towards Article Row, and to consume the buildings there as they had done so much else, Tilly reflected. She gave a small shiver at the thought of suffering the loss of her home. She knew how much number 13 meant to her mother. There was something special about Article Row and the small close-knit community who lived there. Tilly felt even more fond of it now, with Drew living there as well, lodging as he did with one of the neighbours, Ian Simpson. Ian's wife and their children had evacuated to the country at the start of the war. Ian was a print setter, working for the *Daily Express* on nearby Fleet Street, which was how he had originally come to meet Drew.

This new bombing raid on the city was a dreadful end to a dreadful year, and by all accounts they had an even bleaker new year ahead of them as wartime hardship bit ever deeper into their lives.

It had been trying to snow slightly on and off all day, forlorn white flakes outnumbered by the soot and cinders still raining down from the sky. Now one of them landed on Tilly's face to lie there for a second before it was washed away by the tears she barely knew she was weeping.

'That's right, missie, if they'd hit St Paul's it would have taken the heart out of everyone in London, and not just the city itself,' said an elderly man emotionally, leaning heavily on his walking stick, medals from another war barely gleaming on his chest in the grey late afternoon light.

It was that kind of day: the kind when complete strangers spoke and turned to one another in comfort and in hope that somehow, like St Paul's itself, they would be saved – delivered from the awfulness of war.

A heavy pall of smoke and the darkening sky combined to create the illusion that even those buildings still standing were as fragile as cardboard, shifting on every shocked breath of the onlookers. Watchers and workers alike were pulling scarves up round their noses and mouths to block out the raw throat-burning smell and taste of smoke-filled air.

'I shall never forget this as long as I live,' Tilly told Drew. 'And not just the way everything looks, but the awful, acrid, destructive smell too. I'll remember it for ever. First Coventry's cathedral and now this. Do you think Hitler is deliberately targeting our cathedrals?'

'I think he's getting desperate enough to know that the only way he's going to win this war is to destroy the spirit of the British people,' Drew told her, his arm tightening round her when she moved closer to him.

Tilly reached up to touch the chain hidden beneath her plum-coloured polo-necked sweater, from which hung the ring Dew had secretly given her on Christmas Eve – Drew's own graduation ring from his American university. She might only be eighteen, Tilly thought rebelliously as she felt the comforting weight of Drew's ring against her skin, but the war meant that people her age were growing up fast. Surveying the full horror of the aftermath of the air raid, Tilly's heart ached for those whose lives would be changed for ever. The very thought of anything happening to her Drew made her heart pound with anxiety.

In an attempt to distract herself she asked him, 'Will you write about this in one of your newspaper articles?'

'Yes,' he confirmed. 'And about how brave you all are.'

'You're brave too, because you're here with us when you don't need to be, when you could be safe in America,' Tilly reminded him.

'No,' Drew said softly, shaking his head. 'There is only one place I can be, Tilly – only one place I want to be – and that is here with you.'

'Oh, Drew.'

For a few precious seconds the intensity of their love wrapped a protective coat around them that excluded everyone and everything else. Within that protection Tilly gave Drew a look of burningly passionate love that made his heart turn over – with male desire for her, yes, but also with a need to protect her from that desire.

To distract herself from her anxiety over Tilly, Olive turned towards her friend Audrey Windle, who had stood back when Tilly and Drew had first appeared. She had seen the look on Olive's face and guessed she was anxious about her young daughter and the handsome American reporter.

Now as they stood side by side in their WVS uniforms, Olive asked Audrey with genuine concern, 'Have you had any news from your nephew?'

'Yes, thank heavens,' the vicar's wife responded. 'His plane was shot down over the Channel, as you know, Olive, but we heard only this morning that, miraculously, a naval vessel saw his parachute and was able to rescue him. He's got a broken leg, mind, so he'll be out of action for a while.'

She paused and then offered, 'Tilly's young man seems nice. I know the children at the Christmas party were all thrilled with the presents he gave them when he played Father Christmas.'

'He is nice,' Olive felt obliged to confirm truthfully. 'And generous. It was lovely of him to think of doing that for the children.' Her maternal anxiety couldn't be abated, however, and before she could stop herself she was saying anxiously, 'Tilly is so young, though, and there's a war on. Even if there wasn't, he's American; ultimately he will go back there. It's his home, after all.'

Audrey Windle gave Olive a sympathetic look. Then, in an effort to distract her, she gestured towards a WVS mobile canteen, which was parked close by and manned by three very busy WVS workers.

'Do you think we should offer to give them a hand? They look very busy.'

'Yes. I was just going to ask you the same thing.' Olive knew hard work was always a good antidote to worry. She'd still be able to keep an eye on Tilly from the mobile canteen, and it went against the grain with Olive not to offer to help fellow members of the Women's Voluntary Service if she thought she could be useful.

'Want some help? I should say we do,' the woman behind the counter told Olive and Audrey fervently. 'It's the firemen I feel the most sorry for. Parched, they are, after the fires they've had to put out.'

Olive nodded, quickly getting to work alongside Audrey. It was a small enough thing to do, set against what the fire and rescue services were doing – the providing of cups of hot tea – but everyone who worked in the WVS knew how much that homely brew meant to both the bombed-out and frightened, and those who were desperately trying to protect and save them.

'Ta.' One of the firemen took the cup of tea Olive had just poured for him, his helmet pushed back to reveal his soot-smeared face.

After draining the tea almost in one gulp he told her grimly, 'He's good at planning, Hitler is, you've got to give him that. Coming in at night when the Thames's tide was at low ebb and then knocking out one of the main pumping stations first so that there wouldn't be enough water pressure for our hoses. Lost a hell of a lot of buildings we could have saved, that did, never mind the poor souls that was in them that's now under them. We've had to send one of our lads home. Found a couple of kids in one of the buildings – both of them gonners – same age as his own kids. He wouldn't have it that we couldn't do anything for them. Had to be dragged off in the end . . .'

'Those men are saints,' Audrey breathed fervently to Olive once the firemen had gone.

'Most of them are, but sadly there are some bad apples. Sergeant Dawson told me that they've had to investigate cases of fire and rescue workers – and men in the Home Guard – helping themselves to things from damaged buildings.'

'Yes, I'd heard that as well,' the vicar's wife said sadly. Then, changing the subject: 'It's such good news, though, isn't it, about Sergeant and Mrs Dawson giving that young boy Barney a home?'

'Yes it is,' Olive agreed warmly.

Barney was a bit of a tearaway, and worse – at least according to Olive's complaining neighbour, Nancy. After the death of his mother and grandmother Barney had been roaming the streets and constantly escaping from official care because he was afraid that when his father got leave from the army, he wouldn't be able to find him. His parents had been separated, and Olive had been able to tell from the start that Sergeant Dawson, who lived at number 1 Article Row, had a bit of a soft spot for the boy.

When Barney had run away from the second children's home that had taken him in and had been found begging in the streets with a group of older boys, at Sergeant Dawson's suggestion and with the agreement of the local authorities it had been arranged that Barney would move in with the Dawsons until such time as Barney's father was able to take charge of his son once again.

'I just hope that Mrs Dawson will be able to cope,' Audrey continued with some anxiety. 'I wouldn't say that to anyone else, Olive, and especially not Nancy, knowing how unkind she can be.'

'You needn't worry that I'll say anything to anyone else,' Olive assured her, 'but it's no secret to those who lived in Article Row when the Dawsons' son was alive that it hit Mrs Dawson particularly hard when they lost him.'

'The vicar and I came here after their little boy's death, but Mrs Dawson was so much of a recluse I remember that I didn't even realise that Sergeant Dawson was married at first.'

'It's going on for ten years now since they lost him. So sad . . . He was always very poorly, and Mrs Dawson devoted every minute to him. But I'm sure that Sergeant Dawson wouldn't have offered Barney a home if he felt it would upset his wife in any way.'

'You're right,' Audrey agreed. 'I hope it works out well for them all. Sergeant Dawson is such a good sort – look at the way he taught you and Anne to drive so that we could take up Mr Lord's offer of his son's van for WVS use.'

Olive nodded vaguely. She was listening to Audrey but her attention was really on Tilly and the rest of 'her girls,' as she had come to think of her lodgers.

Sally, in her nurse's cape, no doubt thinking of her young man, George, a doctor working under the plastic surgeon Mr Archibald MacIndoe in a hospital in East

Grinstead, where they did their best to repair those men who had been burned in the course of duty. Agnes, the orphan who had come to lodge at number 13, now newly engaged to Ted Jackson, who, like her, worked on the London Underground; she was still at the stage of gazing dreamily at her pretty little engagement ring. And then of course Dulcie, from Stepney in the East End, with her brash bold cockney ways and chippy exterior, which, as Olive knew, concealed an inner vulnerability. They had all three come to be extra daughters to her over the months they had lodged with her. It seemed odd to think now that she had viewed the thought of taking in lodgers as an unwelcome necessity. Now she wouldn't have wanted to be without her girls for anything, and the house would seem empty without them.

Another straggling line of firemen was snaking across the water hoses and dangerous mounds of rubble that had once been buildings, towards the WVS mobile canteen, their needs commanding her attention.

'Just look at all this mess,' Dulcie complained, picking her way with distaste over the grimy rubble, so that she could join Sally as she went to meet Tilly and Drew.

As always Dulcie was dressed up to the nines, looking more as though she was going out on a date than coming to make a silent tribute to the strength of St Paul's and the city, Sally thought ruefully. Dulcie was a game soul, and loyal to those who mattered to her, though you might not think that from looking at her.

'You're better watch that ankle of yours in those shoes on all this rubble,' Sally warned, glancing down at the ankle Dulcie had broken at the beginning of the Blitz in

September. 'If I were you I'd wear a pair of shoes with lower heels than those, Dulcie.'

'Well, you aren't me, are you?' Dulcie retorted in typical fashion. 'You'd never catch me wearing them ugly black things you've got to wear,' she added disparagingly, looking down at Sally's sturdy shoes.

'Try telling me that when you've been walking miles up and down hospital corridors and wards,' Sally responded. She worked as a theatre sister at St Bartholomew's Hospital.

'And besides,' Dulcie continued, 'for all I knew Wilder could have turned up with Drew and the last thing I want is for him to see me not looking my best. I just hope this doesn't mean that we won't be able to go to the Hammersmith Palais's New Year's Eve dance,' she added, as she and Sally met up with Tilly and Drew. Not even her scowl or her sharp tone of voice could hide the fact that Dulcie was a stunningly beautiful young woman, with her blond curls and her perfect English rose complexion. She had the figure to go with her face as well, and Tilly wasn't surprised that the young American pilot Drew had introduced to Dulcie should be so keen on her.

'I'm sure that nothing will prevent Wilder from getting up to London to take you to the dance, Dulcie,' Drew assured her.

'It's all very well you saying that, but there's been talk of leave being cancelled, and there not being any trains running.'

'If that's the case then he will just have to fly here in a fighter plane,' Drew teased Dulcie, who pulled a face at him.

19

Wilder, the young American she was dating, was a member of the American Eagles, the fighter pilot unit that was attached to the RAF. These brave young American pilots, ignoring the fact that their country had not joined the war and was insisting on remaining neutral, had nevertheless come over to Britain and offered their services to the RAF. Their 'uniform', such as it was, consisted of well-worn 'pants' to fly by the seat of, a swagger, fiercely chewed gum, and well-worn heavy-duty flying jackets. Needless to say they attracted girls like honey attracted bees.

'I know one thing that does mean,' Dulcie grumbled, 'and that's that they'll be making even more fuss at Selfridges about having us up on the roof doing fire-watching duties because of this lot, especially Miss Cotton, since she's the one always going on about it.'

Every business in the city was supposed to provide fire-watchers from their staff to make sure that any falling incendiaries were extinguished before the flames could take hold. So far Dulcie, who worked in the cosmetics department of the luxury store on Oxford Street, had managed to wriggle out of doing any fire-watching herself by claiming that her broken ankle was still too weak for her to risk clambering about on the roof. Though it was not, of course, too weak for her to go dancing on it. Of course not!

'We ought to be getting back now that the light's starting to go,' Olive told Audrey Windle with an anxious look towards the girls. 'I'd hate for us to be caught out in the open if Hitler decides to come back again tonight.'

'You're right,' her friend agreed. 'We've got WVS tonight and I thought we'd go through those bags of second-hand clothes Sergeant Dawson brought in to the church hall on Saturday. I feel guilty about taking them. They must belong to someone . . . even if . . .'

Even if their owner was no longer alive to wear them, Olive knew that Audrey meant. They had an arrangement with a local laundry that had offered to launder the clothes they brought in for a very modest amount paid for out of the funds they raised, as and when they could, which at least meant they handed out clean and fresh clothes to those in need.

It was growing darker by the minute, only thankfully small fires now illuminating the nightmare scene of destruction surrounding them as Olive gathered together her small brood.

'It's all right if Drew comes back with us for supper, isn't it, Mum?' Tilly asked, tucking her arm through Olive's.

'Yes, of course,' Olive agreed, earning her arm a small squeeze before Tilly dropped back, no doubt finding a much more romantic place to tuck her arm with Drew, Olive guessed. She might be thirty-seven but that didn't mean that she couldn't remember what it was like to be young and in love, which was why she was so concerned for her daughter. She knew the intoxication that came with true love. Sometimes even now she'd wake up in the early hours, vulnerable with sleep, aching inside for the warmth of loving male arms to turn to, and a loving husband to love her back.

They all had their torches but it made sense for them to use only one of them, to save their batteries. Olive and Audrey led the way, coming to an abrupt halt when they nearly walked into a wooden barrier blocking off a side

21

road, a notice pinned to it warning, 'No Access – Unexploded Bomb'. Olive played her torch carefully to either side. On one building, its windows bombed out, the holes gaping blackly like rotting teeth in a dusty red-brick mouth, they all saw someone had chalked, 'London can take it.' Fiercely Olive blinked away her emotion.

Down the next street they passed a group of men still searching quietly in the filthy soot and dust-coated rubble of what had once been a row of buildings but that was now a line of jagged roofless outlines against the darkening sky.

Olive started to walk more quickly, hissing to the girls to 'keep up', not wanting to raise her voice in case the sound disturbed the men listening so carefully at those still mounds of rubble, just in case there might be someone inside them still alive.

'Ugh. Look, I've got soot and grease on my gloves,' Dulcie complained once they were all standing together in the safety and warmth of number 13's hallway. Holding up her hands, she displayed for everyone else's inspection the pretty gloves that had been a Christmas present from Olive, who had knitted a pair for each of the girls from wool she had unravelled from old jumpers and the like, handed over to the WVS for reuse. The money she'd paid for the items and the work she had to do, not just in the knitting but also in unpicking and then washing the wool in the first place, was rewarded every time she saw her girls go out with their hands warmly wrapped in their gloves.

'Give them to me. It will wash out with a bit of Dreft,' she assured Dulcie, in the general bustle of coats, scarves and hats being removed and hung on the hall coat stand, prior to everyone hurrying into the warmth of the cosy family kitchen at the back of the house.

Olive's kitchen, with its duck-egg-blue and cream colour scheme, gave her a thrill of pride every time she walked into it. Her late father-in-law had bought the kitchen units for her, having had them copied by someone he knew after Olive had seen and fallen in love with them at a furniture exhibition the year before he had died.

Number 13 had been Olive's in-laws' home and she had inherited it from them. It had been her and Tilly's home all Tilly's life, and Olive loved it dearly.

Tonight, with thoughts of the destruction they had all just seen, she was more conscious than ever of how precious her home was to her. They had been lucky so far that no bombs had fallen near Article Row. The previous night's air raid was the closest the falling bombs had come so far. Now, looking round, Olive felt a pang of something approaching guilt because her home was standing when so many weren't; that those she loved and cared about where safe when so many weren't, she acknowledged.

It was Sally, with her practical nurse's manner, who was putting the kettle on and lighting the gas, whilst Tilly got out the mugs, handing them to Drew, the two of them exchanging tender smiles as their fingers touched.

'Come on, you two lovebirds,' Dulcie, whose sharp eyes never missed a thing, teased them. 'I'm gasping for a brew after being out in all that dust and smoke. I dare say there's all sorts in them cinders we were breathing in,' she added darkly.

'What you mean?' Agnes squeaked. When Dulcie gave her a meaningful look she demanded, turning slightly green, 'You mean bodies and things?'

'Well, what do you think happens when people get burned to death? There's bound to be summat left,' Dulcie insisted.

'That's enough of that kind of talk, thank you, Dulcie,' Olive warned her lodger, then sent Agnes to get the milk from the larder.

Hurrying back into the warmth, Agnes reflected on how lucky she was. Abandoned as a baby outside a local orphanage, she'd been terrified at seventeen when the matron had told her that she'd found her a job on the underground and a room to rent. She'd dreaded having to leave the only home she'd ever known. But now number 13 was her home, and the other girls her best friends, especially Tilly, whose bedroom she shared. And it wasn't just the other girls who'd changed her life. She'd met Ted, a young underground train driver, at work, and she loved him with all her heart, even if the two of them couldn't even think of getting married for years. Ted had a widowed mother and two young sisters to support, so they wouldn't be able to marry until Ted's sisters were grown up and settled. Ted was, after all, the sole bread-winner in their small household. Agnes understood and respected that. In fact, she admired her Ted more than ever for wanting to do his duty by his family.

But . . .

But Ted's mother did not want her to marry Ted. Agnes was sure of it, even though Ted told her that she was being silly.

Agnes gave a small sad sigh. She had longed all her

life to be part of a proper family, but Olive, her landlady, showed her far more warmth and kindness than Ted's mother. The reason for that was that Agnes had been left on the orphanage doorstep with nothing to indicate anything about her parentage, or who or what her family had been. Ted had explained to her that his mother's own mother had grown up in poverty with the threat of the poorhouse always hanging over her. Because of that, respectability – the kind of respectability that came not just from being able to pay one's way in life but, just as important, from knowing who one's antecedents were – was very important to Ted's mother. She had strong views about bad blood being passed on to her grand-children. These were views that Ted did not share. Agnes knew that Ted loved her and sometimes she thought that she was being very greedy indeed to want Ted's mother to love her as well, but Mrs Jackson's animosity was a hurt she could not put aside.

The tea brewed, they all settled down around the table, the lack of chairs for everyone allowing Tilly to perch on Drew's knee, determinedly ignoring the look Olive was giving her as she did so.

'Do you think it's true what that fireman told us, about the Germans deliberately planning things so that the firebombs would land at the lowest point of the tide, so that the fire engines couldn't get a proper water supply?' Tilly asked Drew.

'I guess so. Wouldn't you say so, Ted?'

'It certainly looks like it,' Ted agreed. 'And it worked as well.'

'It definitely has,' Sally joined in grimly. She'd been on duty when they'd started bringing in the first of the casualties. Two firemen had died in one of the ambulances before they'd even got them to Barts. She'd thought briefly of George, her young man, whilst they'd worked as swiftly as they could in the hospital's operating theatre, moved down in the basement for the duration – not because she knew he'd be concerned about her but because they knew all about treating badly burned patients at East Grinstead. They dealt with the young airmen who had survived their burning planes, as well as other disfigured patients.

It wasn't just burns the patients being brought into Barts had suffered, though. Some had lost limbs, some had been badly crushed, and there'd been dreadful tales of the fate met by some of the dead: flesh and fabric melted together, and blown off bodies by the force of the bombs, terrible, terrible things that you just did not want to think about but that you couldn't help but think about later, trying to sleep.

Sally had come to London originally because she had needed desperately to escape from her home in Liverpool. As a young nurse in training in Liverpool she had befriended another young nurse, Morag. Following the deaths of their parents in a boating accident Morag and her older brother, Callum, had moved to Liverpool when Callum had secured a job as a teacher in the city. Right from the very start Sally had been attracted to tall, dark-haired and good-looking Callum. However, it had been Callum's good nature, his concern for his sister, his care for his pupils and his gratitude to her own parents for the friendship they had extended towards the siblings that had turned Sally's semi-infatuation into something much stronger.

When Callum had hinted that he had equally strong feelings for her and that they had a future together, Sally felt she was the happiest girl in the whole world. But then her mother had become fatally ill with cancer. Sally had been devastated. Morag had insisted on helping Sally to nurse her mother, sharing the duty of care with her, just, so Sally had naïvely thought, as though she too were a daughter of the family. Sally had also believed that Morag's care for her father had simply been the care of a loving daughter. But then her eyes had been brutally opened when, after her mother's death, she had found Morag and her father in an embrace that had shown her quite clearly the true nature of their relationship.

Worse was to follow. Sally's father and Morag were to marry, and Callum, far from condemning his sister, had taken Morag's side, accusing Sally of being unfair to both her father and his sister.

Sally had left Liverpool in the grip of almost unbearable anger and misery. Work, the kindness of Olive, her landlady, the friendship of Tilly and her fellow lodgers, and most of all the love she now shared with another and far more worthy young man, had done a great deal to make her feel once more that life was worth living. But there was still a hard kernel of anger and pain inside her because of what Morag had done. The death of her mother, followed within months by her father's remarriage to the girl Sally had thought of as her best friend had been something she could never accept.

Sally looked at the mince pie she had just put on her plate and pushed it away. Now her father and Morag had a baby, Callum had told her, when he had found out where she was and come here, to number 13, in an attempt to persuade her to 'make up' with his sister. Sally, of course, had refused. How little he had known her, and of her love for her mother, to dare to ask that of her. How unworthy he had been of her mother's kindness, and the love she herself had once believed she felt for him. Not that any of them cared about what she felt. Not one little bit. They had proved that . . .

Sally's throat closed up. She could well imagine the happy Christmas they would all have had. Her father, putting up for his new daughter the same Christmas lights he had once put up for her. No doubt Callum would be there too, if he was on leave from the navy. Traitors all of them – yes, even her father – to her and, even worse, to the kindness and love her mother had shown them. They didn't deserve a single second of her thoughts. She had a new life now. A happy life, with a job she loved, working as a theatre nurse at Barts Hospital, and a new love in George Laidlaw, the young New Zealander from Christchurch who had come to London to train as a doctor and who was now working in Sussex.

She shouldn't – mustn't – think about the past any more. She had locked the door on it and left it behind. George knew nothing about her past. It hadn't been necessary for her to tell him when they had first met, and by the time she had realised that George had assumed that both her parents were dead, Sally had felt that there was no point in resurrecting the past and all the pain that it contained. She hadn't fallen in love with George overnight. Their love had grown at a quieter deeper pace. Dear George. He loved her so much. She was safe with him. He would always put her first. And she loved him too. The past was best left where it was – in Liverpool.

Thinking of George reminded Sally that she had promised to go down to the hospital in the new year once she had some decent leave that would allow the two of them to have a few days together. Her appetite returning, Sally picked up the mince pie she had pushed away earlier and tucked in to it, unaware that Olive had noted her distress and was relieved now to see that it had passed.

Life brought enough problems and upset for young hearts, especially young female hearts, to worry about, without their having to carry the added burden of the war and Hitler's bombs, she thought protectively.

Still seated on Drew's knee, even though she could tell from the looks her mother was sending her that Olive wasn't entirely happy about their public intimacy, Tilly gave him a tender, loving look. She was in no mood to comply with her mother's unspoken wishes. Her close brush with death hadn't just left her feeling more shaken and vulnerable than she wanted to admit, she had been brought face to face with the possibility of her own death. In those few seconds she had grown from a girl to a woman. And now as that woman she was filled with a fierce hunger to live every single moment of her life to its fullest capacity with the man she loved. Drew had saved her. Drew had kept her safe and made her feel safe. Tonight, instead of saying good night to him she wanted to be with him. Tonight she wanted to lie in his arms and be close to him, to share with him everything that there was to share.

The girl she had been such a very short time ago would instinctively have retreated from that kind of intimacy, shying away from it, and a little afraid of it. The woman her near miss with death had created had no such fears.

Instead she wanted to embrace that intimacy, whilst they both still could.

'Quick, switch the wireless on, someone, otherwise we're going to miss the six o'clock news,' Olive instructed, as she filled the kettle for a fresh pot of tea. They'd eaten at five o'clock after their return from St Paul's and, like everyone in the land, Olive wouldn't have wanted to miss the regular early evening news bulletin from the BBC, even if that meant she'd be all in a rush afterwards to get washed and changed for her WVS meeting.

It was Dulcie who responded to her request. Dulcie had proved surprisingly adept at tuning in the wireless, even though she complained that if she wasn't careful the mesh on the front, close to the tuning dial, scratched her nail polish.

Olive loved her wireless. She often listened to it when she was alone in the kitchen after the girls had gone to work, humming along to popular songs as she did her housework, listening carefully when Elsie and Doris Waters were in charge of the popular *Kitchen Front* programme with its tips for housewives anxious to make their rations stretch as far as they could. Both Olive and Audrey Windle agreed that they hated missing Mr J.B. Priestley's *Postscript* broadcasts. Nancy, being Nancy, said that listening to music made housewives lazy and that she wouldn't have a wireless in her house at all if it hadn't been for her husband insisting.

The kettle was boiling. Tilly and Agnes had got the teacups.

'You sit down here, Mrs Robbins, then you can hear

the news properly. Tilly and I will sort out the tea,' offered Drew.

He really was everything that any mother could want in a prospective son-in-law – should she be wanting to see her daughter married – but the problem was that Olive did not want to see Tilly married, not for a long time yet.

Right now, though, Olive wanted to concentrate on listening to the news.

Accompanied by various 'shushings' and, 'It was you wot spoke, not me,' from the girls, the newsreader, Alvar Lidell tonight, began his broadcast in a very hushed tone as he reassured the country that, despite Hitler's attempts to destroy the spirit of Londoners, the city was standing firm, and with it St Paul's. Olive suspected that this wasn't the only home in which a small cheer went up at this announcement. There was also an announcement confirming the news that a full corps of Canadians would be stationed in Britain.

'So many people from the Commonwealth coming to help – Australians, New Zealanders, Indians, and Canadians – it's wonderful, isn't it?' Olive murmured, 'especially when many of them have never even been to this country before.'

'What's not wonderful is the way in which America is holding back,' said Drew grimly.

'That's not your fault,' Tilly assured him loyally. 'You've been sending articles back to Chicago, that tell what it is really like here, Drew.'

There was also a brief mention of the Greeks' offensive against the Italians in Albania, plus an even more care-fully worded announcement about the ongoing situation in the Middle East, before the news bulletin came to an end.

War! No wonder they all crowded round the wireless to listen to the news. Those dry, dusty facts translated for so many of them into events affecting the lives of loved ones both at home and abroad, Olive thought sombrely as she went upstairs to wash and change into her smart WVS uniform ahead of her meeting.

TWO

'Who on earth can that be knocking on the front door at this time of night?' Olive complained, as she was hanging up her coat in the hallway. She had only just got in from her WVS meeting and was looking forward to what she hoped would be an uninterrupted night's sleep in her own bed without any air-raid sirens going off. She'd made the air-raid shelter, at the bottom of the garden, as comfortable as possible but there was nowhere like your own bed, even though Olive made sure that the shelter beds had immaculately washed and ironed linen and cosy blankets.

'Don't worry, I'll go,' she called into the kitchen where the girls were making cocoa and toast, the smell of this homely but appetising fare making her empty stomach rumble.

Automatically she switched off the hall light as she reached the front door to make sure that the house didn't contravene the blackout regulations.

The sight of a man in army uniform standing on the doorstep, his face shadowed by his cap, had her asking uncertainly who he was, recognition only dawning when the visitor announced cheerfully, 'It's me, Rick, Dulcie's brother, Mrs Robbins. I've come to see Dulcie.'

'Rick!' Dulcie exclaimed excitedly from the dark hallway, obviously having recognised her elder brother's voice, rushing past Olive to throw herself into his arms. 'I know you said you'd got leave and you'd come and see me, but I thought that you wouldn't be able to get here, with London being out of bounds to servicemen on leave because of the bombing.'

'Where there's a will, there's a way,' her brother told her, tapping the side of his nose in a knowing way. 'I'd have been up in London before now, but Mum was a bit pulled down so I stayed on there longer than I'd planned.'

'Dulcie, let Rick get inside so that we can shut the door and put the light on,' Olive protested.

It was Rick himself who took charge in a nicely masculine way, smiling at her and then bundling his sister inside before calmly closing the door, at the same time managing politely to remove his cap.

The conversation in the hall could be heard through the open kitchen door, and Tilly felt her stomach muscles tense. She'd had a huge crush on Rick when she'd first met him. He'd made it clear, though, that he wasn't interested in her, and he'd hurt her by doing so.

But things were different now. She'd been a girl then; she was a woman now, and more importantly, since then she'd met and fallen in love with Drew. But she'd never said anything to Drew about Rick or her silly crush on him.

Drew. She pressed closer into the curve of his arm,

34

whilst the five of them, Drew and herself, and Agnes and Ted and Sally, looked towards the hall door.

Once he was in the kitchen and the introductions had been made Rick allowed himself a second look at Tilly. She'd been a pretty girl and now she was an even prettier young woman, and one who'd got herself a steady bloke, by the look of things. Pity that; he'd been looking forward to seeing her and dancing with her on New Year's Eve. In fact, he recognised, he'd thought rather a lot about Tilly recently, imagining and anticipating that pretty giveaway blush of hers when she saw him. Only she wasn't blushing and she wasn't interested in him at all. Rick was an easygoing good-natured young man with a philosophical outlook on life. There were plenty of other pretty girls. But Tilly had been that little bit special, even if his sister had warned him off her, telling him that she didn't want him flirting with the daughter of her landlady, who was a very protective mother.

Once again Sally went to fill the kettle. Now it was Dulcie's turn to perch on a male knee as she sat close to her brother.

'Desert was it, mate?' Ted asked with a nod in the direction of Rick's well-tanned face.

'North Africa,' Rick confirmed, adopting the same brisk economical way of speaking.

'Sidi Barrani?' Drew guessed, removing his cigarettes from his pocket to offer them around.

Rick nodded as he lit one and inhaled the smoke deep into his lungs, the kitchen light illuminating the angles of his battle-hardened desert-tanned profile before he blew it out again.

'Which reminds me,' he told Dulcie, 'I met up with a

friend of yours in the desert – that Italian guy from Liverpool. Good chap. It can't have been easy for him, seeing as it was the Italians we were fighting, but he never hesitated for a minute. He's on leave as well. He's gone home to see his parents in Liverpool.'

Dulcie tossed her head. It was a pity that Wilder hadn't been here to listen to Rick's comment. She'd have to get her brother to repeat it in front of him. The good-looking Italian she'd flirted with at the Hammersmith Palais in an attempt to make some of the other Selfridges girls jealous didn't mean anything to her, but it wouldn't have done Wilder any harm to hear that another attractive man was keen on her.

Olive, who had been watching Tilly closely, knowing how she had once felt about Rick, wasn't as relieved as she once would have been to see how uninterested in him Tilly was. Olive wasn't at all happy about the way Tilly had been behaving tonight. She had sensed a new, almost reckless determination in her strong-willed daughter, and she was relieved that Tilly lived at home under her own watchful maternal eye.

'How are your parents, Rick?' Olive asked politely 'Have they settled down all right in Kent?'

After the death of Dulcie's younger sister, Edith, Dulcie and Rick's parents had moved to Kent to get away from the bombs.

'I suppose Mum is still going on about Edith, is she?' Dulcie asked before Rick could answer Olive. 'She always was Mum's favourite. I expect she thinks she's up there in heaven caterwauling along with the angels now.'

'*Dulcie*,' Olive protested, but Dulcie simply tossed her head.

'Well, it's true. She was Mum's favourite and that is what she will think.'

Everyone at number 13 knew about the rivalry that had existed between Dulcie and Edith when they had both been living at home before the war. Edith *had* been their mother's favourite and favoured child, a fact about which Dulcie had vigorously complained for as long as they had all known her. Initially Olive had believed that Dulcie must be exaggerating. It seemed impossible to her, as the parent of a much-loved only child, that any mother could favour one child to the extent that Dulcie had claimed. However, after Dulcie had damaged her ankle during an air raid, Olive had visited Dulcie's mother to alert her to the fact that Dulcie was in hospital. She had discovered then that Dulcie's mother did indeed favour her younger daughter above her elder, and the compassion that Olive now felt for Dulcie, despite her often brash manner, dated from that visit. Not, of course, that she would ever hurt Dulcie's keen pride by letting her know that. Hence her chiding comment.

Dulcie ignored Olive's gentle rebuke. She wouldn't want anyone else to know it for the world, but deep down inside her there was still a small, scratchy, sore place that hurt every time she thought about the way her mother had favoured – and loved – Edith more than she had done her.

Edith had been their mother's pride and joy right from the minute she had been born, and that pride and joy had only grown once Edith had developed a singing voice that, according to the agent who'd taken her under his wing, would give her a career that would rival that of Vera Lynn.

Their mother had been devastated when Edith hadn't returned home from a singing engagement when the Blitz had been at its worst. Her body, like so many others, had never been recovered, and they had been told by local officials that they must assume that Edith had been killed. The horribleness of there being no body and every-thing that implied – there were the most awful stories about absolutely nothing being left of people apart from what looked like a patch of sticky toffee on the ground – meant that their mother had been unable to bear to continue to live in London. Edith had been everything to her, whilst she . . .

Seeing his sister's expression and guessing what she was thinking, Rick swiftly changed the subject.

'John's home on leave as well,' referring to the son of the builder for whom their father worked. 'I left him down in Kent with his mum and dad. He said to give you his best.'

Making a speedy recovery, Dulcie preened herself. John had always been sweet on her, right from their shared schooldays.

'Dad's settled in Kent really well. John's dad and uncle have got a nice little business going down there and Dad reckons they did the right thing moving out of London. You should go down and see them if you get the chance.'

'What, and have Mum going on about how much better than me Edith was?' Dulcie scoffed. 'No, thanks. You are coming to the New Year's Eve dance, aren't you?' she demanded.

'Of course I am. There's no way I'm going to miss out on the chance to dance with all those pretty girls,' Rick laughed.

'Deserve a medal, you lot do, for showing them what's what in the desert,' Ted chipped in, giving Rick an approving look. 'Read about it in the papers, I did,' he continued in his quiet way.

'We had the RAF to give us a hand,' Rick told him. 'Mind you, for once I think I'd rather have been up in the air than down on the ground. Gets everywhere, that sand does, and I mean everywhere,' he emphasised feelingly, causing the other two young men to respond with broad man-to-man grins whilst the girls affected not to understand.

Then, just as Olive was beginning to feel concerned that the conversation might be venturing in a direction best conducted in male-only company, Rick said, 'I saw a bit of what the German bombs have done to London on my way from the station, and if there's anyone deserves a medal from anyone then it's them what have had to cope with being blitzed. Compared with what I've seen, marching through sand and firing off a few rounds at the enemy is child's play.'

Rick was really a very pleasant young man, and a very thoughtful one, Olive admitted, when he tipped Dulcie firmly off his knee and announced, 'You'll all be wanting to get some sleep. Is it still all right for me to kip down at Ian Simpson's, do you know, Mrs Robbins?'

'It sure is,' Drew answered him for Olive, explaining, 'I lodge there and Ian told me that you were welcome to stay.'

Cocoa mugs were quickly drained, everyone standing up, the girls going to help the young men retrieve their coats and hats, Tilly pulling a small private face to Drew as she whispered, 'It's a pity Rick had to arrive now and not during the daytime tomorrow.'

Drew knew what she meant. Rick's arrival and the fact that he too was staying at Ian Simpson's meant that Drew and Tilly wouldn't be able to say a long lingering good night in the discreet darkness of the blacked-out street.

'We've got tomorrow night,' he reminded her, 'and since it's New Year's Eve I bet there'll be plenty of slow numbers being played at the Hammersmith Palais.'

Tilly nodded, her heart thumping in excited anticipation of the dance and the chance for her and Drew to be close.

Stifling a yawn, Sally helped Olive clear away the empty mugs. She'd offered to work New Year's Eve since she couldn't be with George, who was on duty. It was disappointing, of course, not to be able to welcome in the New Year with him but there'd be other dances and hopefully other New Years. She gave a small shiver despite the warmth of the kitchen. It didn't do to risk tempting fate by looking too far ahead or making too many plans during wartime.

It was funny the changes the last months of the year had brought to them all, Tilly thought a little later, lying snugly in her bed whilst Agnes slept peacefully in the bed next to hers. Last New Year's Eve they had all been heart- and fancy-free, except for Agnes, and they had tended to stick together when they went out dancing. Tomorrow's New Year's Eve, though, it would only be her and Dulcie going out together with their partners. It was a pity – Tilly had enjoyed it when they all went out together. It had been fun. But that was what happened when you met someone special, she acknowledged. You wanted to be with them every minute you could. She felt sorry for Sally, who couldn't see George. New Year's Eve, even more than Christmas, was a time when people in love wanted to be together, to make all those sweet special promises to one another.

Falling in love might have changed the amount of time they spent together but it hadn't and couldn't change the closeness of their friendship. The four of them were still close friends, of course, and they always would be. Tilly knew that they'd all drop everything like a shot if one of the others needed them.

As she had done every single night since he'd first put it round her neck, Tilly reached for Drew's ring, holding it tight as she whispered a prayer for him, to join all the other prayers she said every night for those she loved, and for their country.

THREE

'You look lovely, beautiful, and I'm the luckiest guy in the world.'

Tilly's face flushed a pretty pink as she listened to Drew's obviously heartfelt compliment. He'd been waiting for her when she'd come downstairs in the plum-coloured silk velvet dress her mother had had made for her in the early months of the war. With its nipped-in waist and bias-cut full skirt it emphasised Tilly's slender figure, the colour of the rich velvet complimenting the dark hair and pale Celtic skin she'd inherited from her mother. Her dancing shoes might be well-worn now, but thanks to Drew she was wearing a pair of brand-new silk stockings – given to her not directly by Drew himself, but passed tactfully to her mother to give her, along with a pair for each of the other girls, to be wrapped up as extra Christmas presents. She was wearing another of Drew's Christmas gifts to her, too: a gorgeous shimmering silver-grey silk shawl, which she'd draped round her shoulders, to wear underneath her best coat with its velvet collar and cuffs.

At Drew's own appearance Tilly's breath caught in her

throat. He looked so smart in his dark lounge suit and crisp white shirt worn with the dark maroon tie with the tiny gold fleck that she'd given him for Christmas. The tie had been a lucky find, having been handed over to her mother's WVS group along with other men's clothes. It had caught Tilly's eye as they sorted through the clothes and its Gieves & Hawkes label had had Dulcie announcing knowledgeably that it must have been very expensive when new. Tilly had been honest with Drew, explaining to him that even if she had the money for an expensive new tie she doubted that she would be able to buy one because of the ongoing shortages. Drew, to her delight, had said that he loved the tie, and tonight he was wearing it to prove that statement.

Wilder, Dulcie's date, was wearing his habitual leather flying jacket over a white shirt and a pair of black trousers, whilst Dulcie's brother, Rick, who was going with them, was in his army uniform. Rick's good looks meant that no girl was likely to spend too much time looking at his clothes, Tilly admitted, but to her relief she had discovered with his return that Rick and his good looks no longer had any effect on her whatsoever.

Only now could she admit to herself that a tiny corner of her had been worried that Rick might remember her crush and perhaps comment on it in a teasing way. Thankfully he had done nothing of the kind, and the only thing to spoil her happiness was the niggling feeling of guilt because she hadn't told Drew about that silly girlish crush.

Within minutes of the young men arriving at number 13, all five young people were piling into the taxi picked up by Wilder on his journey from the station to Article

Row, having asked the cabby to wait with the promise of a good tip if he did, and were being waved off from the darkened hallway by Olive.

As they were engaged, and knowing how little privacy they had, Olive had given Ted and Agnes permission to spend a couple of hours together in her front room before they went to join in whatever traditional celebrations still might be allowed to take place in Trafalgar Square. Olive herself had accepted an invitation from the Windles to see the New Year in at the vicarage, which was within easy walking distance. Prior to getting to know Audrey, Olive had never had a really close friend. Orphaned and then married young, she had been far too busy, especially whilst she had been nursing first her husband and then later both her in-laws. Their friendship might only have come about because of the war and the fact that they were members of the same WVS unit, but it was genuine and Olive found Audrey a wonderfully soothing antidote to her neighbour Nancy's acerbic and often spiteful attitude to their shared neighbours.

This evening's get-together might not be going to be a party as such, but since it was New Year's Eve Olive had decided to wear her own silk velvet dress. The rich amber fabric had been a present to her from Tilly and Agnes, and she treasured the dress as much for that as for its lovely material and elegant style. At thirty-seven, Olive was nearly as slim as her daughter, so that its boat-shaped neckline and three-quarter sleeves, along with its neatly fitting bodice and gentle A-line skirt, suited her perfectly.

She might not have spent all afternoon washing and then drying her hair, like Tilly, Dulcie and Agnes, but her natural waves meant that her weekly home shampoo and set always left her hair framing her face in a pretty natural style.

Olive knew that there was no need for her to warn Ted about the standard of behaviour she expected from the young couple left alone in the house in her front room. Ted was simply not the sort of young man to behave in anything other than the most respectable and responsible manner. And Agnes, bless her, being the timid girl that she was, was hardly likely to encourage him to break any rules.

Going upstairs to her bedroom to check her appearance and get her best coat before setting out to walk up to the top of Article Row and then across to the vicarage, Olive had a strong suspicion that she might not have been able to say the same thing about her own daughter. Tilly had always been passionately intense about everything she did and passionately proud of everyone and everything she loved. That was her nature. Drew was a well-brought-up young man – Olive could see that – but a passionate young woman in love for the first time, combined with the urgency that war brought, was not a combination that could allow any protective mother to do anything other than react with some concern.

Still, Olive thought, ten minutes later as she said good night to Ted and Agnes, and let herself out into the dark street, at least it was Drew and not Wilder who was Tilly's beau. Try as she might, Olive couldn't quite take to the other young American. She was prepared to accept and understand that a young man from another country, who had come to Britain expressly to offer his help in its fight against Hitler, might be justified in feeling proud of himself but whilst Wilder's arrogance and the comments he sometimes made about others might boost him in his own eyes, in Olive's they did him no favours at all.

Dulcie, though, seemed pleased that he had shown an interest in her. Whether she was pleased because she liked Wilder himself or because she liked the excitement of going out with a young American with plenty of money in his pockets, Olive didn't know. Whilst there were plenty of young men in uniforms from other countries to be seen on the streets of London, Americans were a much rarer sight. There was quite a lot of openly expressed ill feeling in some quarters about the fact that America was remaining aloof from the war, and no doubt in Dulcie's eyes that made Wilder and his ilk, who had volunteered to put their lives at risk, and who behaved as though they were something very special because of that, all the more potently dangerous, and challenging to a young woman. Drew might be American but Olive didn't think she had ever met a more modest and considerate young man.

The night air was yellowy grey with what now seemed like an ever-present pall of smoke from the burned buildings. It felt gritty in the lungs and left behind an unpleasant taste. The occasional car and taxi moved slowly along the road that ran past the church and the vicarage, their dimmed lights just about picking out the white paint on the edge of the pavement, which had been put there because of the high number of road accidents in the early days of the blackout. A bus rumbled past the end of the road. The church hall and, beyond it, the church itself loomed up out of the darkness. Olive's walking pace quickened as the cold air bit into her lungs.

Normally she would have walked to the vicarage with

Nancy, her next-door neighbour, and her husband, but they had gone down to Nancy's daughter's in-laws in the country to spend Christmas and the New Year with them. Olive knew that Nancy wasn't the most popular inhabitant of Article Row, especially with the younger generation, as she was one of those people who seemed to delight in finding fault with others, but they had been neighbours for a long time.

Olive had always got on reasonably well with her, although this last year she had found herself having to bite down on her tongue a bit over some of the things Nancy had said, especially about Sergeant Dawson. Olive liked Sergeant Dawson. He was a kind man – a good man – and Nancy had gone far too far when she had tried to suggest that he might be showing too much of an interest in women without a man to protect them. Nancy had been referring to her when she had said that, warning her, Olive knew, and ever since then she had felt uncomfortable about being in the sergeant's company on her own. Not because she felt there was any truth in Nancy's aspersions – she didn't – no, it was because she suspected that Nancy might be peering round her lace curtains to see if her suspicions were being confirmed.

Poor Sergeant Dawson. They hadn't had an easy life, he and Mrs Dawson, with losing their son when he had been a young boy, and then Mrs Dawson turning into a recluse because of it.

The vicarage was in front of her now. Olive opened the gate and walked up the path to the front door. The vicarage, the church and the church hall had all been built by the same wealthy merchant who had built Article Row.

Audrey opened the door to Olive's knock, greeting her warmly, and then taking Olive's coat, hat and scarf from her after Olive had tucked her gloves in the pockets.

'Oh, Olive, I do love that dress. The colour is perfect on you,' she complimented Olive with the genuine admiration of a true and good friend.

Olive smiled her thanks and tried not to shiver in the draught that was coming into the square hallway from under the badly fitting doors. A vicar's stipend was only modest, Audrey Windle had given Olive to understand, and had not stretched to such luxuries as new doors and window frames, even before the war when such things had been readily available.

'Come into the sitting room,' Audrey invited, opening a door into the large, shabbily furnished room.

Two well-worn leather sofas and two armchairs that didn't match either each other or the sofas were pulled up close to a sullen-looking fire in the large fireplace. The Afghan and tartan rugs on the chairs and the sofas showed how the occupants of the house normally tried to keep warm. Dark red velvet curtains, which had obviously come from somewhere else originally because you could see where the original hems had been let down, were drawn over the blacked-out windows. The only piece of really good furniture in the room was the baby grand piano, which was Audrey's pride and joy.

The vicar, a quiet, kindly man, who always seemed to have a bit of a cold, was standing talking with his curate, whilst several fellow members of Audrey's WVA group, along with their husbands, were clustered as close to the fire as good manners would allow.

War brought people together in so many new ways,

forging friendships that would never have been possible before the war, Olive acknowledged. Now they had a common goal – to stay strong for their country and the brave men fighting for it.

'Thank you for those sandwiches and the mince pies you brought down earlier, Olive, and for helping me set up the buffet in the dining room,' Audrey said, adding, 'Oh, and did I tell you that I had a letter from Mrs Long? She often mentioned how grateful she was for everything we did for her after she lost her husband.'

The Longs had lived at the last but one house on Article Row, number 49. Their son, Christopher, had at one stage attended the local St John Ambulance brigade with Tilly. As a conscientious objector Christopher had not joined any of the armed services. Initially he had been in a reserved occupation, with the Civil Service, but then he had been obliged to join the bomb disposal service, something that, according to Tilly, he hadn't wanted to do one little bit. She was so lucky, Olive reflected. Some poor families went through such dreadful things. It was true that she had been widowed young but she had had her baby to keep her going. After she had been widowed Mrs Long had left London to return to her home town in the South of England.

'Have you seen what the Luftwaffe did the other night?' Anne Morrison asked Olive after the vicar had poured her a class of elderberry wine.

'Yes. We all went down to have a look at St Paul's,' Olive replied.

The sitting room door opened again, bringing a fresh draught of cold damp air against Olive's legs as she stood with her back to it.

'Oh, it's Sergeant Dawson. No Mrs Dawson, though,' Anne informed Olive with a small sigh. 'Poor woman. One does feel sorry for her.'

'Yes,' Olive agreed without turning round. Drat Nancy for going and making her feel so self-conscious when she had no need to feel that way. Those who said that Nancy was a bit of a troublemaker certainly had a point.

'Good evening, ladies.'

'Good evening, Sergeant Dawson,' Anne acknowledged the policeman's greeting happily. 'I was just saying to Olive here how very lucky we were to have you teach us both to drive. My husband said so at the time although I know there were those – no names mentioned but she's a neighbour of yours, Olive – who were inclined to disapprove of females learning to drive, despite the fact that they have benefited from us doing so.'

Anne was a large, solidly built, jovial woman, and when she laughed, as she was doing now, her whole body seemed to shake with good-natured mirth.

'All the credit doesn't lie with me,' Sergeant Dawson responded with his own smile, tactfully avoiding her reference to Nancy, much to Olive's relief. 'I had two very able pupils.'

'Oh, excuse me, will you, please,' Anne stopped him. 'Only I've just seen Vera Stands and I need to have a word with her about the church flower rota.' With another smile she strode off, leaving Olive on her own with the sergeant and no ready excuse to take her own leave. She was about to ask politely if the Dawsons had had a good Christmas and then just in time she remembered that the sergeant had once told her that Christmas was naturally a very difficult time for them both, but especially for his wife, because of the loss of their son.

Instead, she asked him, 'Is it definitely all official now, I mean about you and Mrs Dawson taking Barney in?'

'Yes. He had to spend Christmas in a children's home outside the city, much to his disgust, but he'll be coming to us in time for the new school term. Mrs Dawson's been getting his room ready for him. She's had me giving it a coat of distemper to freshen it up a bit.' A rueful look crossed the sergeant's face. 'I just hope that she isn't going to spoil him too much.'

Olive could tell from both his expression and the sound of his voice how much the sergeant was looking forward to Barney's arrival.

'Oh, and there's something I ought to tell you,' he continued. 'It's about Reg Baxter and that vacancy there was going to be at the ARP station, the one that I thought you should put your name forward for?'

Olive nodded. She'd felt both surprised and a bit over-whelmed when Sergeant Dawson had suggested that she volunteer to fill a vacancy at their local ARP unit, but the sergeant had insisted that she would be an ideal candidate.

'It seems that Reg Baxter has decided not to retire and move after all,' the sergeant told her, 'and the other vacancy, the one that Mrs Morrison had applied for, that's gone to a chap from Court Street.'

Olive was surprised to discover how unflatteringly she was thinking of the men who had turned down the opportunity to have someone as capable as her fellow WVS member join them. Before the war such a thought wouldn't have crossed her mind. The war, though, had shown her just how capable and resourceful her own sex was, and how proud she was of what women were doing to help with the war effort.

That neither she nor Mrs Morrison had been offered the membership of the local ARP unit wasn't Sergeant Dawson's fault, however, and Olive could see from his expression that he felt slightly uncomfortable about the news he had had to give her.

Even so, she couldn't resist saying with a small smile, 'Sergeant Dawson, the ARP unit doesn't know what it will be missing in not taking on Mrs Morrison. She's a first-class organiser, and she makes the best hotpot I've ever tasted. She regularly brings one round for our WVS suppers.'

'Archie, please, Olive. We agreed when I was teaching you to drive that we had known one another long enough to be on first-name terms. Hearing you address me as "Sergeant Dawson" makes me feel that you think of me as someone of your late in-laws' generation.'

'Oh, no, I would never think that.' Was she blushing? Her face certainly felt hot, and no wonder after such a silly gauche remark, far more suitable to someone Tilly's age than her own. Of course she didn't think of Sergeant D— Archie . . . as someone of her late in-laws' age. How could she when it was perfectly obvious that he wasn't? His dark hair might be greying slightly at the temples now, whilst fine lines fanned out around his eyes when he smiled, but he was still tall and lean, with a very manly bearing and . . .

And nothing, Olive stopped herself firmly, allowing herself to say only, 'Somehow I don't think that Nancy would think it proper for me to call you Archie. You know how she is about such things.'

'Yes, I know how she is,' he agreed, 'but in private, when we are talking to one another, then surely it can be Olive and Archie?'

She ought to say 'no' but that would be rude. He didn't know, after all, about that silly awareness of him she had developed – or those secret, dangerous, unwanted and unacceptable thoughts of envy she sometimes had for the obvious contentment of the marriage he and his wife shared.

'Very well,' she agreed.

Nestled in Drew's arms, her head tucked into his shoulder, as they moved slowly together on the dance floor, Tilly gave a small sigh as the final strains of 'A Nightingale Sang in Berkeley Square' died away. The song had been one of the hits of the year and now, on New Year's Eve, as the dancers and those sitting out broke into applause, and the band stood to take their break, she told Drew, 'It's such a lovely song that it always brings a lump to my throat. But it's hard to imagine *any* kind of bird singing in any of London's squares right now, thanks to the Blitz.'

'It's a song of hope for the future, for better times ahead,' Drew reminded her, his arm round her as the lights came up over the darkened dance floor and they started to make their way towards their table – Dulcie's favourite table, which she had bagged the minute they had arrived.

'Dulcie's brother seems a nice guy,' Drew commented. 'He was really friendly last night back at Ian's when I was asking him about the desert campaign. Of course, there was stuff he couldn't tell me but he gave me a real good idea of what it's been like for them out there. I've noticed that you don't say much to him, though. Don't you like him?'

Tilly felt a pang of guilt, her straightforward nature making it impossible not to be honest with Drew when she loved him so much.

'It isn't that. I mean, there's nothing wrong with Rick, it's just, well, I had a bit of a crush on him for a little while, when I first met him.' She pulled a small face. 'So silly, and I'm ashamed of myself now. I'd grown out of it even before I met you, but I was just a girl then. I wanted to tell you but I didn't want you to think—'

'What I think is that he's the one who is keen on you, not the other way around,' Drew astonished her by saying.

'Rick, keen on me? Oh, no.' Tilly shook her head vehemently. 'No, he wasn't in the least bit interested in me.'

Hearing the honesty in Tilly's voice made Drew smile. She was the best girl any guy could want. He didn't for a single minute doubt her, but he knew his own sex and he'd seen the looks Rick had been giving Tilly when he thought that no one was watching him.

'Take it from me,' Drew corrected her, 'he's interested, but no way is he going to get a look-in.'

'No way at all,' Tilly agreed, stopping at the end of the dance floor to kiss Drew's cheek. 'You're the only man I want, Drew.' She paused to tuck her arm through his as they headed for their table, then asked him, 'Have you told your family yet – about us, I mean? Mum had a lovely letter from your mother with her Christmas card but it didn't say anything about you and me, but then if you have written to them they probably wouldn't have got your letter before they sent the Christmas Card.'

'I've told them that I've met a very special girl,' Drew answered her, turning his head as he did so, so that she couldn't see his expression. He changed the subject to warn her, 'Dulcie's heading our way with Wilder, and I know he isn't your favourite person.'

'I don't like the way he treats Dulcie,' Tilly admitted. 'I know she seems worldly-wise on the outside but I'm afraid that Wilder might hurt her. You said that you don't think she's the only girl he's seeing, but I don't think she knows that.'

Drew nodded, feeling guiltily relieved that she had taken his lead on the subject. It wasn't that he wanted to deceive Tilly – there was nothing he wanted more than to be completely honest with her – but it just wasn't possible. Not at the moment, not yet. Just as it wasn't possible for him to be totally honest with his family about his feelings for Tilly. If he wasn't being totally honest with Tilly then it was because he loved her and wanted to protect her, that was all.

'Not long until midnight now,' Dulcie announced, coming to sit down next to Tilly as Drew pulled up a chair for her.

'So don't you go and disappear with some fast piece,' Dulcie warned her brother. 'I don't want the only member of my family I've seen over Christmas disappearing with some girl just as it strikes midnight.'

'If anyone's likely to disappear to have an illicit bit of how's your father with some girl he's just met, it's that fly boy of Dulcie's, not me,' Rick muttered in an aside to Drew whilst Dulcie was talking to Wilder. When Rick realised that Tilly had overheard him, he apologised. She shook her head in response to his, 'Sorry . . .' She was more concerned about the fact that Rick's opinion of Wilder matched her own than she was about his sturdy male language. She was very fond of Dulcie and would hate to see her hurt.

'Do you think there'll be many there?' Agnes asked Ted as they hurried arm in arm through the cold night air in the direction of Trafalgar Square, to share in the traditional way of bringing in the New Year.

'I should think so,' Ted assured her. 'Londoners aren't going to let something like a few German bombs stop them from celebrating.'

At Barts Sally looked at the watch she wore pinned to the front of her uniform apron, as she emerged from the operating theatre for her break. Ten minutes to go. She and George had promised that they'd think of one another the moment midnight started to chime. For someone who prided herself on being so matter-of-fact she was surprised how emotional she felt that they weren't seeing out the old year and welcoming in the new one together.

Setting off in the direction of the stairs, she thought that she might as well go to the canteen, where she could at least welcome in the New Year amongst the other staff who were on their breaks.

She almost made it, would have made it, if she hadn't been stopped in her tracks by the totally unexpected sound of George's voice calling out breathlessly from behind her.

'Sally.'

She spun round to stare at him in disbelief, then she was running towards him, ignoring the rule that nurses never ran unless there was an emergency. After all, there *was* an emergency of sorts, the emergency of reaching the man she loved and wanted to spend the rest of her life with, before the clocks struck midnight.

Her, 'What are you doing here?' was muffled against his lips as he kissed her and then kissed her again, lifting her off her feet to hold her tight, his face cold from the air outside, but his body warm beneath his overcoat as she unfastened the buttons and burrowed close to him.

'I wanted to see in the New Year with the girl I love,' he answered her question.

'You got leave?'

'Not exactly, but I'm off duty until tomorrow evening, so I thought I'd risk coming up to London. I'll have to go back on the first available train, though,' he warned her.

'You came all the way to London, because . . .'

'Because I wanted to kiss my girl and wish her a Happy New Year,' he finished for her.

For a minute Sally just looked at him, and then her voice trembled slightly as she whispered, 'Oh, George.'

'It's midnight,' he whispered back. 'Happy New Year, my darling girl, and may it be just the first of a lifetime of Happy New Years for us.'

'Oh, George, don't say that,' Sally begged him. 'Don't tempt fate by talking about the future. Just kiss me instead.'

'Oh, Ted.' Tears filled Agnes's eyes as she turned towards her fiancé amongst the crowd of people who had braved the threat of Hitler's bombers to come out to celebrate the arrival of the New Year around the fountains in Trafalgar Square. Unlike before the war, there were no lights to illuminate the scene, only starlight shining fitfully through the still heavy pall of smoke, but from what Agnes could see, the couples who turned to one another didn't seem to mind the lack of light – quite the opposite.

People were reaching out for one another's hands, the sound of 'Auld Lang Syne' growing louder and stronger. As she looked at Ted, Agnes was sure that the diamond in her ring sparkled even more brightly than usual. She was so lucky, and so happy too, even if sometimes she did wish that Ted's mother would be a bit more friendly. Ted had told Agnes not to worry about his mother's lack of warmth towards her, stating in his calm good-natured way that eventually she'd come round. Never having known the love of her own mother, she had dearly hoped that Ted's mother would take to her. Maybe one day she would, Agnes told herself hopefully, as she snuggled closer to Ted.

'I love you,' Drew mouthed to Tilly, knowing that it would be impossible for her to hear his voice in the cacophony of cheers, whoops and 'Happy New Years' that had filled the dancehall as midnight struck. Now they were standing up for 'Auld Lang Syne', the dance floor packed, people covered in streamers and the balloons that had been let down from the net above them.

'I love you too,' Tilly mouthed back to him. Everyone was laughing and hugging, Rick looking very happy with the pretty little redhead on his arm, and Dulcie glowing from all the male attention she was getting from single servicemen eager to get their share of the kisses being exchanged to bring in the New Year.

'Where's Wilder? He's missing all the fun,' Tilly asked Dulcie, cupping her hand to the other girl's ear so that she could hear her, her other hand holding tightly onto Drew's.

'Gone to the gents',' Dulcie yelled back.

Truth to tell, she wasn't as concerned about Wilder missing the countdown to midnight as she might other- wise have been, thanks to the admiring attentions of a young naval officer who, Dulcie had to admit, looked far more handsome in his immaculate uniform than Wilder did in the worn leather jacket that he had insisted on keeping on, despite the heat in the packed the dancehall.

In fact, if anything, the young naval officer, with his open delight in her company, was far better company than Wilder, who had been offhand all evening, complaining that London's way of welcoming in the New Year was a poor drab thing compared with New York's.

'Well, New York isn't being bombed by the Germans, is it?' Dulcie had snapped at him at one point in the evening, turning her back on him to sit with her arms folded dismissively across her chest. That was when the young naval officer – Mike – had seen her and had given her a look of bashful hope.

When the band had played a ladies excuse me, and Wilder had announced that he didn't want to dance, she'd gone over and asked Mike to dance instead, encour- aging him to come over to join their table, where she'd introduced him to the others, telling Wilder prettily that she'd felt it was her duty to take pity on 'one of our brave servicemen, who hasn't got a dance partner'.

Wilder had responded with a grunt, and the unkind comment that Britain's armed forces might be brave but they weren't strong enough to defeat Hitler, and then he'd got up and walked off.

That had been half an hour ago.

Well, if Wilder thought that she was the sort of girl who got all anxious and upset about that kind of behaviour, he was going to find out that he was wrong, Dulcie decided, getting up to go and grab hold of her brother's hand.

'Come and dance with me, Rick . . .'

Later, from the dizzyingly blissful delight of Drew's arms as they swayed romantically together beneath the dimmed lights to an intimately slow dance number, Tilly murmured to him, 'I think that Dulcie and Wilder have had a bit of a tiff.'

'Mmm,' Drew murmured back. 'Have I told you that your hair smells of honey and roses, and that your lips taste of paradise?'

Tilly closed her eyes and melted into him.

They had been so close tonight, mentally, emotionally and physically. Being held this close to him, being able to feel all of him against all of her was dangerously exciting. There was an ache low down in her body that made her want to press even closer to him, an awareness within her that the kisses they shared, no matter how sweet they were, could not alone satisfy the need that ached inside her.

Tilly knew what married intimacy entailed but she had

never imagined until she had met Drew that she would hunger for that intimacy so strongly and passionately before marriage.

They stayed on the floor until the notes of the last waltz of the evening had died away, returning to their table to find Rick and Dulcie waiting there for them but no sign of Wilder. He appeared a couple of minutes later, removing his handkerchief as he did so, Tilly's heart hammering as the lights came up and she saw on it the telltale marks of bright orange lipstick. Bright orange when Dulcie was wearing deep pink.

Anxious for her friend, Tilly deliberately leaned across to block Dulcie's view of Wilder, asking Rick with forced nonchalance, 'When did you say your leave finished, Rick?'

He too leaned forward, and the look in his eyes suggested to Tilly that he too had seen those lipstick marks as he folded his arms on the table, forcing Wilder to sit back.

'Tomorrow.'

Tilly nodded, glad of his sensitivity to Dulcie's feelings.

It was later, after the taxi had dropped the four of them off at the top of Article Row – Wilder remaining in the taxi, having turned down Drew's suggestion that he stay the night at Ian Simpson's, insisting that he needed to get back to his base – that Tilly told Drew what had happened as they hung back behind Dulcie and Rick.

'That's one of the things I love about you,' Tilly told him, cuddling up to him. 'The fact that you're so honest, Drew. I know you'd never deceive me about anything.'

Drew swallowed hard, conscious that there was

something he hadn't been honest about with Tilly, and it was a very big something, a something that grew harder for him to bear with every fresh kiss they exchanged and every promise of shared love they made. What would happen when he did tell her? Would he lose her? He wouldn't be able to bear that. He loved her so much, with her brave bright spirit, her fierce loyalty to those who mattered to her, her compassion for others, and her passionate nature.

Tilly didn't object when Drew suddenly turned to her in the middle of the dark street, took her in his arms and kiss her fiercely. Why should she, when she loved it when he kissed her like that? The only thing was that it was a bit out of character for him to do so in such a public place. But then it was New Year.

Lying awake in bed waiting for Tilly and Dulcie to come in – Ted had brought Agnes home shortly after Olive had returned to number 13 herself, and Sally wouldn't be off duty until the morning – Olive reflected on her own evening out. She was a sociable person by nature and naturally sympathetic to others, which often meant that people brought their troubles to her knowing they could confide in her and trust her not to repeat what they had told her to others. Normally Olive enjoyed and valued that role, but the trouble, as she was now discovering, was that there was no one for her to turn to when she herself needed to confide.

The evening had been very pleasant, a few hours of relief from the constant anxiety of the war, even if the recent bombing had been a major topic of conversation. And an incident had happened that had left her feeling wretched and guilty.

It had been about half-past eleven when Sergeant Dawson – Archie – had announced that he was taking his leave of them so that he could call round at the ARP post to wish his colleagues there all the best for the New Year and still make it home in time to welcome in 1941 with his wife.

Obviously he'd shaken hands with all those close to him, and naturally Olive had held out her hand to shake his; not to have done so would have been unthinkably rude. But then instead of shaking it he had simply held her hand between his own and . . .

Olive closed her eyes against the sharp knife of emotion that turned inside her, as she remembered the feelings that had swept her, the memories and the longing she had had no right to feel. How could she have allowed that to happen? How could she have felt, standing there with Sergeant Dawson clasping her hand in the warmth of his own, that shocking agonising need for the warmth of a man's arms around her, combined with that awful surge of jealousy against those women who were lucky to have what she did not: the presence of loving husbands in their lives and in their beds.

Even now, remembering how she had felt, Olive could feel the small beads of sweat breaking out on her forehead. She was thirty-seven years old. She had been a widow for nearly eighteen years. Never once during those years had she felt the way she had felt tonight, watching Sergeant Dawson walk away from her, then turning to look at her friends with their husbands. Marriage could be hard work. All women knew that, once they were married. Decent respectable women – the kind of woman she had always believed herself to be – did not lie in their beds at night with their bodies aching because they were on their own.

What she had felt meant nothing, Olive assured herself. It was just because it was New Year. Because of the war. It certainly wasn't Sergeant Dawson's fault. He had simply been kind, she knew that. Her heart thudded anew, and then thankfully she heard the front door open, Tilly and Dulcie's voices reaching her from the hallway. She was a mother and a landlady, she had responsibilities and duties, and instead of dwelling on certain things she would be far better off ignoring them – and making sure she didn't experience them again.

Dulcie wasn't the only person to be concerned about the Home Secretary, Mr Herbert Morrison's, January announcement that he intended to make it compulsory for London's residents and businesses to form their own fire-watching group from amongst their inhabitants and employees, as Olive discovered when she attended one of her twice-weekly WVS meetings at the vicarage. Audrey Windle told them that she felt they should extend the length of their normal meeting to make time to discuss 'Mr Morrison's request for people to form fire-watching groups.'

'Well, as to that,' Nancy sniffed, immediately bridling, 'I hope that you aren't going to suggest that any of us take up such dangerous work, Mrs Windle. That's men's work, that is, and besides, what are our ARP wardens being paid for if it isn't to sort out that kind of thing?'

'Well, yes, of course,' the vicar's wife agreed quickly in a placatory tone, 'but the thing is that, as Mr Morrison has said, and as we all saw with the dreadful bombing raid on the 29th of December, with the best will in the world neither our Home Guard nor the fire brigade can be on hand everywhere they are needed. No one's suggesting that anyone should put themselves in danger. It's simply a matter of making sure that those of us who feel that we do want to be involved can be as safely as possible.'

'Well, I don't want to be,' Nancy informed the vicar's wife flatly. 'Like I said, it isn't women's work. We're all doing enough as it is, if you ask me.'

'I don't know, Nancy,' Olive felt obliged to speak up, as much in defence of poor Audrey Windle, who was looking rather desperate, as anything else. 'We've been very luck in Article Row so far, but we've all seen and heard about the damage that those incendiary bombs can do if they aren't spotted and dealt with quickly. The Government must think that it is safe for women to deal with them because they've sent out those leaflets to every household telling people what to do, and it's normally women who are home most of the time, not men.'

Nancy was giving her an extremely baleful look but Olive wasn't going to back down. As she'd been speaking she'd realised that although she hadn't given it much thought before, she did actually believe that it was important for householders to do everything they could to protect their homes from the incendiary bombs being dropped by the Germans. Unlike other bombs, the incendiaries were not designed to explode and kill people, but rather to cause serious fires. The initially long, large bombs each contained many small incendiaries. As it fell it opened, showering the ground with these smaller incendiaries, which burst into flames as they landed.

If discovered quickly, it was a relatively simple matter to dowse the flames, either with a stirrup pump, which used water, or by raking the burning matter into sand and smothering the flames with it. But the effectiveness of these courses of action depended on the incendiaries being spotted and dealt with quickly, and it was to this end that the Government had announced to the country via the BBC news that they must form themselves into fire-watching groups.

Giving Olive a grateful look Audrey Windle pressed on hopefully, 'We've all read the leaflets. They explain very clearly how we set about organising local fire-watch teams and make out a rota for fire-watching.'

'I've heard that you have to go up on the roof and stay there all night when it's your turn,' one of the other woman broke in. A large person, her ample chins shook with anxiety as she continued, 'I couldn't do that.'

'No, of course not, Mrs Bell,' the vicar's wife agreed, 'but as Sergeant Dawson explained to me, in many cases husbands and wives are working together, so that, for instance, the husband will be the one to do the active watching but then he will call down to his wife, who will be perhaps waiting at an open bedroom window – with the lights out, of course – to tell her where the bombs have fallen. Then she will get ready the stirrup pump, which the Government is making available to households, and together they'll go out and tackle the incendiaries with the help of their neighbours, who they will alert about the bombs.'

'It's taking advantage of our good nature, that's what it is,' Nancy sniffed, folding her arms in front of her bosom in a way that said that she wanted no truck whatsoever with Mr Morrison's scheme.

Olive's assessment of her neighbour's frame of mind was confirmed when Nancy turned to her and said, 'There's no one to do it in Article Row anyway, is there? Mr Whittaker at number 50 is too old; you couldn't expect the Misses Barker at number 12 to get involved, nor Mrs Edwards at number 5, since her husband's already working as an auxiliary fireman.'

'There's Mr Ryder at number 18,' Olive pointed out. 'I'm sure he'd want to be involved, he being retired from the Civil Service.'

'Mr Ryder? With that bad leg of his?' Nancy shook her head, adding triumphantly, 'And it's not as if you could do anything, is it, with you being a household full of women.'

'Why should us being female stop us from getting involved?' Nancy's attitude reminded Olive of how she had felt when she and Mrs Morrison had been rejected by the ARP – and they had been rejected she felt sure, no matter how tactful Sergeant Dawson had tried to be.

Mrs Morrison clapped her hands and said approvingly, 'Oh, well done, Olive. I'm certainly going to have a word with Mr Morrison and see if we can't get something set up.'

Audrey Windle was smiling at her with relief, whilst Nancy was giving her a very angry look indeed.

'I hope you aren't thinking of setting yourself up in charge of some kind of fire-watch, Olive,' Nancy told her grimly. 'Because if you are I'm afraid that me and my Arthur will definitely have a view.'

What was Nancy trying to say? That she wasn't up

to the job of organising a small team of neighbours to keep a watch for falling incendiaries and to deal with them when they did fall? Olive very much resented Nancy's attitude, and instead of putting her off the idea it actually made her feel very determined to carry it through.

'Well, if Arthur wants to join in he'll be very welcome,' was all Olive allowed herself to say.

'Arthur? He's far too busy at it is, and I'm not having him going and risking getting a cold in this bad weather with that chest of his.'

'I'm sure that Ian Simpson will want to be involved, and Drew, of course,' Olive continued, ignoring Nancy's mean-spiritedness.

'Well, yes, your Tilly would love that,' Nancy agreed cattily. 'Every time I see her these days she's linked up to that American. In my days girls waited until they'd got an engagement ring on their finger before being so familiar with a young man.'

'You and me are the same age, Nancy,' Mrs Morrison cut in and then laughed, saying, 'and I remember me and my hubby walking down the Strand with our arms wrapped around one another on his first leave home from the front and we'd only been walking out a few weeks before he joined up. We weren't the only ones, either. That's what happens during wartime.'

Mrs Morrison had definitely taken the wind out of Nancy's sails, Olive could see, but knowing her neighbour as she did, Olive suspected that sooner or later Nancy would find a way of getting her own back. Olive didn't know why she was finding it so difficult to get along with her neighbour these days. They'd always managed to rub along well enough before. But that had been when she had merely been a daughter-in-law in her in-laws' home. Since number 13 had become hers, Nancy had been noticeably more critical of her. Olive tried to be charitable and to put Nancy's almost constant carping about her young lodgers and Tilly down to the natural reaction of a mother parted by the war from her own daughter and her grandchildren, but there was no doubt that Nancy could be hard work.

'I'm so glad you've decided to organise a fire-watching team for Article Row, Olive,' Audrey told her later as they said their good nights.

Olive had deliberately held back on the pretext of wanting to ask the vicar's wife more about Government's provision of stirrup pumps so that she wouldn't have to walk home with Nancy, who had gone off in a very bad mood indeed.

'Nancy isn't very happy about it,' Olive felt bound to admit.

'I'm afraid Nancy makes it her job not to be happy about a great many things,' Audrey sighed ruefully. 'Now, I'm going to ask the vicar to have another word with the warden to arrange for someone to come along and give everyone who's interested a proper demonstration of a stirrup pump. Everyone who signs up for fire-watch duties will be given a hard hat as well as the stirrup pump, and every local council has been asked to provide supplies of sand for people to use. You might want to think about having some moved to Article Row so that your team can access it easily if need be.'

'Yes, we could put it in one of the gardens. I'd say mine, but Nancy is bound to think I'm giving myself preferential treatment if I do that. Maybe Mr King will let us put it in the back gardens of one of his houses, since they're unoccupied at the moment,' said Olive.

Mr King was a local landlord who owned several now empty properties at the other end of Article Row from Olive.

'That's a good idea,' Audrey approved.

'We've got a couple of rakes in the garden shed. My father-in-law used to be a keen gardener and Agnes's fiancé, Ted, came over and cleaned and sharpened everything in he autumn for Sally. She's very kindly taken charge of the garden and its veggies for us.'

A little later, making her solitary way home, Olive discovered that although initially she had worried about what she might be getting herself into, now she actually felt rather proud of herself for making that decision. For all that Nancy had been so unpleasant about it, surely it was far better to get involved and do something to protect the homes of which they were all so proud rather than risk an incendiary starting a fire that no one spotted until it was too late, and it had taken hold, possibly threatening the whole Row.

FOUR

'I expect that you and your young man have got something special planned for the evening of Valentine's Day on Friday – that's if Hitler doesn't come calling with more bombs,' Clara Smith, the girl who worked with Tilly in the Lady Almoner's office at Barts Hospital, asked as they sat side by side in front of their typewriters, shivering in the room's icy February chill. The two girls were working through yet another batch of new patients' details for their files, and trying to keep warm with extra layers of clothing because the radiator in their office had been turned off to conserve precious fuel.

Tilly loved her job and felt very proud of the fact that her head mistress had recommended her for the post. She'd worked hard not to let her or the Lady Almoner down, even though the war had brought an increase to her workload that had felt daunting at times.

'Drew is taking me out for dinner,' Tilly answered. 'I don't know where, though. Drew says that it's going to be a surprise.'

Being taken out to dinner sounded awfully grown up

and sophisticated, not like going to the pictures or even going dancing at the Hammersmith Palais. Her mother wasn't very keen on them going out alone, just the two of them, Tilly knew.

'Ooh, a surprise, is it? Well, I wouldn't be surprised if his surprise includes an engagement ring, it being Valentine's,' Clara informed her with the wisdom of a girl who already had an engagement ring on her finger.

Tilly felt her heart turn over. There was nothing she wanted more than to have Drew's ring on her finger – a wedding ring, though, not just an engagement ring.

'Mum thinks I'm too young to get engaged,' she felt obliged to tell Clara. She didn't want the other girl secretly thinking when she didn't have an engagement ring to wear after Valentine's Day that Drew didn't love her enough to give her one. 'She says that she doesn't want me rushing into anything just because we're at war.'

'That's typical of the older generation,' Clara criticised roundly. 'They don't understand. It's because of the war that people want to get engaged and married, in case anything happens, and it's too late.'

'Well, Mum got married just a few years after the last war,' Tilly felt obliged to defend her mother, 'and she was eighteen herself then, but by the time she was twenty she'd been widowed and she'd got me to look after.'

'That was then,' Clara told Tilly. 'Things are different now. If you ask me I'd rather be married to my fiancé and have something special to remember him by than have him die without ever doing, well, you know what, if you know what I mean.'

Tilly did indeed know what Clara meant. Her face might have grown hot because of what Clara had said but it was no hotter than her body grew at night when she was alone in bed thinking about Drew's kisses and how they made her feel.

It was an open secret, if you listened properly to what some of the bolder girls had to say in the canteen at lunchtime, that there were plenty of girls who weren't prepared to deny their young men their physical love when they were going off to war, even if they didn't have a wedding ring on their finger.

'Our boys are being so brave and risking their lives for us, us being brave and taking a risk to make them happy is the least we can do. Leastways that's what I think,' one of the more outspoken girls had announced when this very subject had come under discussion one lunchtime.

In one sense the war had brought Drew to her, but the thought of it taking him from her made Tilly's blood chill as ice cold in her veins as though she had been standing outside without her coat in the cold February wind. Suddenly she couldn't wait for her working day to finish and for the reassurance of finding Drew waiting outside the hospital's main entrance to walk her home, as he sometimes did if he could snatch enough time away from his work as a reporter. Not that Drew was one to shirk his duty to his work – far from it, he often worked long into the evening, reporting on bombing incidents, talking to the dispossessed, taking photographs. As often as her mother would let her, Tilly went with him when he worked in the evening, gathering material not just for his articles but also for the book he planned to write about Fleet Street when the war was over.

She was lucky to have Drew here in London, Tilly

knew. So many sweethearts were separated because of the war; so many brave men in uniform. Take the Royal Navy and the Merchant Navy, for instance, manning the all-important convoys that risked not just the dangerous winter seas to bring much-needed supplies back to Britain, but Hitler's U-boats, as well. Then there was the army fighting to hold back Rommel's men in the desert, and the RAF doing everything they could to stop Hitler's Luftwaffe from bombing Britain.

No wonder the whole country read their newspapers so keenly and gathered so anxiously around their wirelesses to catch the BBC news broadcasts. Tilly's heart swelled with fresh pride as she acknowledged just how important her wonderful Drew's role was in keeping the country informed.

'Wait up, Olive.'

Olive pulled her coat more firmly around herself as she stood in the icy February wind waiting for Nancy to catch up with her. Like her, Nancy was carrying a shopping bag.

'If you're going to the grocer's you'd better watch out,' she complained, her voice shrill with discontent. 'He told me he hadn't got a jar of meat paste in the shop last Thursday, but on Tuesday Mrs Mortimer from Parlance Street told me that he'd had a new order of it in. You mark my words, he's stockpiling things, keeping them back until the price goes up.'

'I'm sure that's not true, Nancy,' Olive responded. 'He'd probably sold out, that's all. And as for shopkeepers profiteering by keeping tinned goods back, there's a new law been brought in to put a stop to that.'

'It's all very well for you to say that. How's this new law going to be imposed, that's what I want to know? And that's another thing: I don't know how Sergeant Dawson can do his job properly, taking as much time off as he has since they've had that rough boy living with them.'

'Sergeant Dawson is simply using up some leave that was owing to him so that he and Mrs Dawson can get Barney properly settled in.'

'Oh, he told you that, did he? And when might that have been?'

'No, Sergeant Dawson didn't tell me that. Mrs Windle did.' Thank heavens Nancy didn't know just how relieved she was to be able to tell her that and put her in her place, Olive thought guiltily.

'That's all very well,' Nancy responded, bridling angrily, 'but like I've said to you before, Olive, a woman in your shoes – widowed and on her own – can't be too careful where her good reputation is concerned. You've only got to think about that widow from the other side of Farringdon Street. She'd got men calling all hours of the day and night, her and her daughter. Said she was interviewing lodgers.' Nancy gave a disparaging sniff. 'And that reminds me, I was telling my daughter about your Tilly taking up with that American over Christmas and she said that she could never fancy getting involved with a foreigner herself, and especially not an American, on account of them remaining neutral.'

'Drew's a lovely young man. The kind of young man any mother would be pleased to have making friends with her daughter,' Olive informed Nancy, putting aside her own maternal concerns about the relationship, before adding briskly, 'Excuse me, Nancy, but I've just remembered that I promised I'd call in at the vicarage to see Audrey Windle, and I don't want to miss the lunchtime news on the wireless, so I'd better let you go and get on with your shopping on your own.'

Without giving her neighbour the opportunity to object Olive set off across the road, her cheeks pink with angry colour. It was one thing for Nancy to criticise her but she wasn't having her criticising Tilly.

Audrey wasn't in, but at least calling at the vicarage had given Olive the chance to escape from Nancy. She started to cross the road again and then stopped as she saw Mrs Dawson coming out of the front door to number 1. Knowing how reluctant Sergeant Dawson's wife was to talk to anyone, Olive hesitated, not wanting to ignore her but not wanting either to make her feel uncomfortable. But then to her surprise, instead of walking away, as Olive had expected, Mrs Dawson crossed the road and came over to her.

'I'm just going out to see if I can get a tin of Spam,' she announced chattily. 'Barney loves it fried with a bit of potato. It's his favourite dinner.'

'He's settled in well then, and it's all working out all right?' Olive asked once she had overcome the shock of Mrs Dawson's unfamiliar talkativeness.

'Oh, yes. He's ever so bright. Had me in tucks the other night, he did, imitating them from that *ITMA* programme on the wireless.'

'It will be good to hear a child's voice in Article Row again,' Olive smiled. 'It's been so quiet with the Simpson children evacuated.'

'Yes, it has, although my Archie says that quite a lot of them that was evacuated into the country to live with other families have been brought back by their mothers because they missed them so much.'

'Yes, we've seen that through the WVS as well,' Olive agreed, 'although of course the Simpson children are with their mother, and she is with her parents. That makes a big difference.'

'I'd better be on my way,' Mrs Dawson said. 'Archie forgot his sandwiches this morning so I'm going to call by the station and drop them off for him. I've told him that I'm not going to be able to run round after him now that I've got Barney to think about. He's got to come first now. Oh, I can't tell you the difference it makes having Barney living with us. I think that Archie assumed that it would be him and Barney that would pal up, but it's me and Barney that have really hit it off. Of course, Archie says that's just because I let Barney wind me round his little finger, but if a boy that's gone through what he has doesn't deserve a bit of spoiling then I don't know who does.'

Olive nodded, but privately Mrs Dawson's words had made her feel rather sorry for Archie Dawson. She must not be critical, though, she warned herself. The Dawsons – and especially Mrs Dawson – had had such a lot to bear, first with their son's illness and then his death. Olive had worried a bit, when she'd first learned that the Dawsons were taking Barney in, that Mrs Dawson's vulnerable emotional state might mean that she couldn't cope with a healthy young boy in the house after the tragedy of her own son, but she'd obviously been wrong. Having Barney around had given Mrs Dawson a new lease of life, and she was pleased for her as well as for Barney himself, Olive reflected, as she headed for the shops.

'Watch out, you'll end up breaking that mug if you slam it down any harder,' Sally told Dulcie, wincing. 'What's wrong with you, anyway?' she asked. 'You look as though you've lost a shilling and only found a penny. You've not had another row with Wilder, have you?'

It was common knowledge at number 13 that Dulcie's relationship with Wilder was somewhat tempestuous.

'Well, I dare say you wouldn't be feeling too pleased yourself if your George had told you that he couldn't get leave after promising to take you out somewhere special on Valentine's Day.'

'Well, Wilder *is* in uniform, Dulcie,' Sally felt obliged to point out.

Dulcie's scowl told her that her comment was not well received. 'That's as maybe, but he was able to get time off easily enough when he wanted to go to watch some silly boxing match last week. Of course, I know he wanted to take me somewhere special,' she added hastily, ''cos he thinks a lot of me, Wilder does.'

Sally nodded. The truth was that she didn't think that Wilder thought very much of anyone other than himself, but she knew that beneath her sharp exterior Dulcie had an unexpected vulnerability, so she kept her thoughts to herself.

'A fine thing it's going to be, me having to say that I had to stay in on Valentine's Day when everyone else at work is talking about where they went,' Dulcie continued.

Sally looked at her. 'Well, if you're at a loose end you could always come to Sussex with me for the weekend,' she told her. 'They're having a dance at the hospital on Saturday for those patients who are well enough to attend. George was saying only the last time I spoke to him that they're short of girls to partner the men. There's two single beds in the room where I'm staying. I'm sure Mrs Hodges, the landlady, won't mind you using the spare bed.'

'What? Me go to some hospital to dance with sick men?' Dulcie demanded scornfully. 'I'd have to be hard up before I'd want to do something like that.'

Repressing her instinctive urge to let Dulcie see what she really thought of her callousness, Sally mentally counted to ten, and then told her firmly, 'Well, it's up to you, of course, Dulcie. I'd be the last person to suggest that you sacrifice having a good time to benefit anyone else, but those poor boys have been through an awful lot – and lost an awful lot – for our sakes, you know. They are always so grateful to have visitors. They'd be especially grateful to have the opportunity to dance with a girl as pretty as you. Of course, if you're thinking that Wilder might not approve . . .' she added craftily.

'Huh, it's not up to him to approve of what I decide to do. I'm perfectly capable of making up my own mind about that, thank you very much.' Privately after what Sally had said, Dulcie was thinking that it might not be a bad idea to be able to tell Wilder truthfully that she had gone to a dance without him and been asked to dance by scores of smitten young men. That would teach him not to use his leave to go to boxing matches instead of taking her out.

'All right then,' she told Sally grudgingly. 'I'll go but if Wilder finds out that he can get leave after all, I'll have to change my mind,' she warned.

'That's fine,' Sally agreed. Whilst George had told her how keen the hospital was to get girls to attend the Saturday night dance they were giving for their patients, she suspected that Dulcie wasn't exactly the kind of girl he had had in mind. She hardly had the milk of human kindness flowing through her veins. As Sally had seen for herself on her first visit to the hospital the previous month, some of the men were terribly badly disfigured from the injuries they had suffered, so much so in some cases that their own relatives refused to visit them. It was too late now, though, for her to regret having made her impulsive suggestion.

On Valentine's Day Tilly was up early, wishing that the morning wasn't so dark and that she could watch for the postman's arrival from her bedroom window.

However, when she went downstairs, she discovered that she had had her own personal postal delivery because there was a card lying on the hall floor with her name on it but without a postage stamp, showing that Drew must have posted his card to her on his way to work. Smiling happily, Tilly hugged the card to her.

On her own way downstairs, Olive watched her. It didn't seem so very long ago that she had been the one to secretly send her daughter a Valentine's card. Now

Tilly had no need of such maternal care, because she had Drew. Olive could remember how she herself had felt on receiving that precious first Valentine's card from Tilly's father: the excitement; the longing; the shared stolen kisses. What was that ache in her heart? What was wrong with her? She was thirty-seven and not a girl any more.

No, she wasn't a girl but she was a mother, she reminded herself as she followed Tilly into the kitchen, thinking sadly as she did so that these days she and Tilly were hardly ever alone together. Was Tilly avoiding being alone with her because she knew that her mother was concerned about the growing intensity of her relationship with Drew?

'From Drew?' Olive asked, nodding her head in the direction of the card Tilly was still clutching to her chest as she followed her into the kitchen.

'Yes,' Tilly acknowledged happily. She wasn't going to open her card until she was on her own. Reading Drew's first Valentine's card to her was something very special and very private.

Olive started to fill the kettle and then stopped, turning round to put it down and look at her daughter.

'Tilly, I hope you haven't forgotten what I said to you about you being so young and—'

'I'm old enough to know how I feel about Drew, Mum,' Tilly stopped her mother immediately. This wasn't a conversation she wanted to have – not today on Valentine's Day, when all she wanted to think about was Drew and their love for one another.

Olive could feel her heart thumping.

'You're eighteen, Tilly, that's all, and there's a war on.'

'Exactly,' Tilly shot back. 'I'm eighteen and there's a war on. Boys my age are joining up to fight and die for this country, Mum, just like my dad did. If Drew was one of them I—'

She broke off as the kitchen door opened and Agnes came in, her face pink as she clutched a white envelope. 'The postman's just been,' she beamed, breathless with an innocent happiness that for Olive contrasted painfully sharply with Tilly's hostility towards her.

Now wasn't the time to talk rationally to her daughter, Olive recognised.

Later, when the girls had all left for their respective jobs, as she put away the washed and dried breakfast things and then set about sweeping the kitchen floor as she listened to more of Elsie and Doris Waters' *Home Hints* on the wireless, Olive reflected that all she wanted to do was protect her daughter, and it hurt her that Tilly couldn't see that. It was a pity that she had agreed to be on WVS mobile canteen duty tonight to fill in for a colleague from another branch of their organisation, before her regular WVS meeting, Olive reflected. Now she would have preferred to remain here at home so that she could mend things with Tilly before she went out for the evening. The last thing she wanted was her passionate and sometimes headstrong young daughter going out in a rebellious mood, and with discord between them. Despite what Tilly seemed to want to believe, Olive could remember perfectly well how it felt to be young and in love on Valentine's Day.

It had, after all, been on the evening of Valentine's Day that Tilly's father, Jim, had proposed to her.

Without realising she had done so, Olive stopped

sweeping, her gaze clouding with memories as she clasped the handle of her brush.

There had been no special meal out for her and Jim the night he had proposed. He'd arrived home on leave unexpectedly, and she'd found him waiting patiently in the rain for her outside the small clothing company where she'd been taken on as a machinist. He'd had a bit of a cough even then, she remembered. They'd been walking out together for just over a year. She'd met him through one of the other girls at the factory whose brother he'd been on leave with. She'd liked him right from the start. Tall, and handsome, and with the kindest eyes and smile she'd ever seen, he'd made her feel so safe with him and so proud to be his girl, even if his parents, especially his mother, had thought that he could do better for himself and hadn't really approved of her, left orphaned as a teenager and with no family of her own to support her. It had brought her so much joy to see him standing outside the factory, smoking a Woodbine as he waited for her, the collar of his army greatcoat turned up against the drizzle, that she had felt as though the sun had come out. He'd brought her a Valentine's card that he bought for her in Paris. She still had it upstairs, along with the letters he had written her. As if in a dream, Olive leaned her sweeping brush against the table and headed for the stairs.

Upstairs in her bedroom she kneeled down on the floor to pull Jim's battered suitcase from underneath her bed. Since Olive kept a spotless house there wasn't so much as a speck of dust on the case, the familiar lock clicking open beneath her fingers. Fingers that trembled slightly as though she were still that young girl he had courted with so much love and tenderness. She couldn't remember the last time she had done this, Olive acknowledged as she opened the case.

Inside it was Jim's greatcoat and the medal he had received for his bravery in the field. 'Everyone gets them, if they live long enough,' he had told her. There had been so much pain in his eyes on that leave home – his last before the end of the war. She'd found out later from his nightmares that he'd been the only member of his platoon to survive when the trench they were in had come under attack, and that he'd stayed with two of his dying fellow soldiers until the end rather than make his own escape. That had been Jim all over, always thinking of others before himself. It had been the gas from those attacks that had damaged his lungs, which had ultimately led to his death. The man who had come home to her after the war had been a shadow of the young man with whom she had fallen in love, but today it wasn't that sick dying Jim she wanted to remember. Today she wanted to remember the handsome young soldier who had brought her a Valentine's card from Paris, and with it a special bottle of scent.

Very carefully Olive folded back Jim's greatcoat, smoothing the front of the fabric, much as she had smoothed Jim's poor damaged chest in those last awful months and weeks of his life.

Beneath the coat, carefully wrapped in tissue paper and tied in blue satin ribbon, were the letters he had written to her and the cards he had sent her.

That special Valentine's card, though, wasn't with the others. Instead it was in the box in which she had received it – a lovely silver-coloured box with a red satin heart on the front of it and the words 'To my Sweetheart' written on it.

Was it her imagination or did even the box still smell of foreign places and war? For a moment tears blurred Olive's eyes as she opened the box to reveal the card inside it. On top of a delicate cream lace underlay, hand-painted pink and blue flowers on their green stems twined all round the red satin heart decorated with tiny seed pearls at the centre of the card. Inside there was a small verse: 'Here is my love, from a heart that's true. A true blue heart that beats just for you.'

Jim had told her that there was a shop in Paris that sold cards made especially for the British servicemen to send home to their girls. Olive's hand shook, a tear rolling down her face. Quickly she brushed it away, her desire to protect her precious memento overcoming her emotions.

What was she doing up here behaving like this? She was far too old for this kind of silliness. And too old to sometimes miss and long for the comfort of a protective loving pair of male arms to hold her, for that special something that a loving couple shared?

Yes. She really didn't know what was getting into her these days, Olive berated herself, as she replaced the card in its box and put it back in the case, closing it and pushing it back under the bed.

'I thought you said that it was a good train service to this East Grinstead place and that it didn't take long. Not much, it doesn't. We've been on this train for three hours now,' Dulcie complained to Sally as she glowered from the February landscape beyond the dirty train window to her companion who was seated opposite her in the full compartment.

'It is – normally,' Sally responded. The train crash in which she had been involved on her way back from Liverpool before Christmas had left her feeling a bit on edge when she had to travel by train, but she was determined that no one else was going to know that. Not when she had survived that crash almost without a scratch whilst others had lost their lives.

Even without the anxiety of the train journey she was regretting having invited Dulcie to come along with her. The other girl had done nothing but complain from the moment she had agreed to come. Even as late as this morning Sally had been hoping that Wilder would get in touch with Dulcie to say that he had got leave after all. Dulcie might be the one who was complaining volubly that he hadn't, but privately she wished every bit as strongly as Dulcie that the opposite was the case, Sally reflected grimly. She must have been crazy to have actually felt slightly sorry for Dulcie because Wilder had let her down. George had certainly thought so when she had told him during yesterday's telephone call that she was bringing Dulcie with her.

'I can't see her doing much to cheer up our chaps,' George had protested.

'She can be fun, and she is very pretty,' Sally had defended her decision and her fellow lodger, but in her heart she knew that George was probably right, especially if Dulcie continued in the mood she was in right now.

They were sharing their carriage with a pale, thin young woman with an anxious expression, who was dressed in what were obviously good quality although rather dull-looking clothes and who was sitting primly in her seat with a shopping basket on her knee covered with a white cloth that now had several smoke smuts on it from the open window. The window had been opened by a young boy travelling with his mother, who was having to give more attention to her baby than her infant son. An older respectable-looking couple, occupying the remaining seats, exchanged speaking looks at the little boy's boisterous behaviour.

'Oh, you're going to East Grinstead as well, are you?' the young mother asked, looking relieved. 'Going to the hospital, are you?' she asked hopefully. 'Only this is my first time. My Lance got took there after his plane was shot down. Got burned, he did, according to what I've been told, but they say that he's going to be all right. First time I've been able to visit him, this is, what with the kiddies.'

Sally's sympathy was immediately aroused. Having seen the patients at the hospital, she knew the terrible injuries most of them had suffered. At the hospital they received the very best, not just of medical care but, thanks to Mr Archibald MacIndoe's innovative method of treating his patients, of emotional and psychological care as well. For the families at home, though, there was very little support, and even her one brief visit had been enough to show Sally how badly affected many of the relatives were by the injuries suffered by their loved ones.

'This is your first visit to your husband then?' she double-checked.

'Yes. Yes. Brought the kiddies with me 'cos I ain't got

no one to keep an eye on them. Besides, Lance hasn't even seen the baby yet.'

Dulcie gave Sally a cross look. Why she was getting involved with this badly dressed woman with her runny-nosed children Dulcie did not know. She stuck her own nose up in the air to signal that she wasn't going to follow suit. And as for that dim-looking girl seated opposite her, with her basket on her knee, she smelled of mothballs and looked like she was wearing something more suited to her grandmother, Dulcie thought unkindly.

'We're going to the hospital as well,' the man joined the conversation.

'Our son's a patient there,' added his wife. Her hand trembled as it rested on his arm, Sally saw.

'Mr MacIndoe is very pleased with his progress so far. He's having skin grafts. It's a long process and Bryan gets impatient.'

'That's a good sign that he must be starting to heal,' Sally offered gently, before explaining, 'I'm a nurse. My . . . my boyfriend is a doctor at the hospital.'

She didn't normally disclose that kind of information – the minute you said you were in the medical profession people always wanted to discuss symptoms and operations with you – but on this occasion she knew that she would feel uncomfortable listening to harrowing tales of awful injuries from people who might assume that she was 'one of them' when she wasn't.

'Yes. We're going down there to a dance,' Dulcie chipped in, suddenly realising that she was being excluded from the conversation. Dulcie did not like being excluded from anything.

88

'It's for the patients,' Sally felt bound to explain hastily when she saw the pained look on the older couple's faces. 'As you know, Mr MacIndoe believes that it is very important to get his patients as involved with normal everyday life as he can, even whilst they are still having treatment.'

'Yes,' the girl with the basket unexpectedly spoke up, her cut-glass accent making Dulcie bridle slightly. 'They've begun to call East Grinstead "the town that doesn't look away".'

'You're visiting someone yourself?' the young mother asked.

'Yes. My . . . my brother.'

'Well, since we're all travelling to the same place,' Sally said with a smile, 'perhaps we should introduce ourselves. I'm Sally, and this is Dulcie,' she announced promptly, extending her hand to each of the others in turn.

'Pleased to meet you, I'm sure,' the young mother replied. 'I'm Joyce, and that's William over there, and this here is Pauline.'

'Edna and Harold Chambers,' the male half of the elderly couple introduced them.

'Persephone Stanton,' the other girl included herself, in her very upper-class accent.

A faint wash of pink brightened her pale face when Dulcie demanded, 'Persephone? What kind of a name is that?'

'It's Greek,' she explained. 'Daddy is a Greek scholar.'

Thankfully, before Dulcie could put her foot in it again, Joyce called out wearily to her little boy, 'William, don't keep on touching them windows. I keep telling you they're dirty.'

'But I like touching them,' the little boy protested, 'and there's nothing else to do.'

Opening her bag, Sally delved into it for the pencil and notepad she always carried with her, tearing out a sheet of paper and handing it to the boy with the pencil and a smile as she suggested, 'Why don't you count how many houses you can see from the window, William?' her kindness earning her a grateful look from Joyce, who told her in a confiding undertone, 'He's such a handful at the moment. He's only at school in the mornings, see, on account of his proper school being bombed. Running wild all over the place, he is, with a gang of older boys. I've warned him that he'll get himself into trouble and then where will we be? Of course I can't say anything to his dad, not wanting to worry him.'

'Haven't you got any family who could help?' Sally asked her sympathetically.

'Not really. I'm from the north but I've moved down to London 'cos it's easier to get to the hospital but I don't really know anyone there yet.'

'A boy that age needs a man around to teach him his manners,' Harold Chambers announced firmly. 'Need a bit of strong handling, young boys do.'

Seeing the stubborn look crossing the little boy's face and the anxious guilt on his mother's, Sally stepped in hastily, asking the first thing that came into her head in an effort to change the direction of the conversation.

'How old is your little girl?'

'Pauline. She's nine months. Born in May, she was.'

May. The same time as her half-sister. Pain spiked through Sally, catching her off guard. Normally she refused even to think about her half-sister, even to acknowledge within her own thoughts that she existed. Nine months old. That meant that she would have had nine months of love from Sally's own father that she had had no right to have at all.

Sally shivered and turned towards the window.

'So where are we going then?' Tilly asked Drew, as they left the house arm in arm.

'I'm not telling you until we get there. It's a surprise,' Drew insisted. 'Oh, damn!' he exclaimed ruefully. 'I've gone and left part of your surprise on the kitchen table at Ian's. We'll have to call in there and get it.'

Tilly nodded.

'I'd better check on the fire whilst we're here,' Drew added as he unlocked the front door to let them both into the house. 'Ian's gone down to his in-laws for the weekend, so I'm in charge of keeping in the fire.'

'You mean you've got the house to yourself?' Tilly asked as she followed him into hall.

Ian employed a cleaner to keep the place tidy but it lacked the well-polished special look that her own home had, that touch that came from a home having a woman in charge who loved it, she recognised. When she and Drew had their own home she would keep it every bit as spick and span as her mother kept number 13. Their own home . . . The thought of having the right to share a house with Drew as his wife brought the now familiar surge of giddy excitement and anticipation mixed with urgency.

'Yes,' Drew confirmed, 'and that being the case, we had better not stay here for very long. I'll bet that Nancy is keeping a watch out. You know what she's like, and your mom will have something to say if she thinks I'm breaking the rules.'

Tilly pulled a face. 'Nancy's so nosy. Anyway, we've got a perfectly legitimate reason for being here.'

'You mean these,' Drew asked her, reaching for the carefully wrapped box of chocolates he'd left on the kitchen table.

'No, I mean this,' Tilly told him, sliding her arms round him and raising her face to his for a kiss.

'That is not a perfectly legitimate reason,' Drew told her several minutes later, his voice thick with emotion as he finally stopped kissing her.

'Don't talk,' Tilly whispered to him, placing her fingers against his lips. 'Just kiss me again instead, Drew.'

'Tilly . . .' he began to protest, but Tilly silenced him in the most effective way she could, kissing him again with passionate intensity.

The only thing that Drew had told her about their special Valentine's evening out had been that she should wear the lovely dress she had worn on New Year's Eve, which Tilly knew must mean that he was taking her out dancing. Now, as she pressed herself closer to him, the rich plum-coloured silk velvet shimmered in the hall light as their bodies moved closer together and Tilly wound her arms tightly around Drew's neck.

'I want to stay here – with you – just the two of us . . . together,' she told him fiercely.

Drew shook his head. 'You know we can't do that.'

'I thought you loved me,' Tilly protested.

'I do,' Drew assured her, 'but you know what I promised your mom, Tilly. What *we* both promised her. Don't look like that,' he coaxed her, adding firmly, 'Wait here. I've got something special to show you.'

As he released her and turned away to start to climb the stairs, Tilly made to follow him but Drew shook his head and told her firmly 'No, Tilly. You must wait down here. Otherwise, I'm not going to show you.'

He meant it, Tilly could tell.

Reluctantly she stood in the hallway and watched as he bounded up the stairs two at a time. She heard a door open and then close. Drew's bedroom door. Her heart turned over and then started to race. She looked at the stairs. If she followed him up to that room; if she kissed him as she had done before, then . . .

Then it wouldn't be fair to Drew, she warned herself. Because he had promised her mother, and she loved him too much to want to make him break that promise, knowing how badly he would feel about it if he did.

The bedroom door opened and then closed again, and then Drew was coming downstairs toward her carrying a sheaf of typed papers.

'I've started writing the book,' he told her, shaking his head when she reached out to take the pages from him. 'No, I'm not going to let you read it – not yet.'

'When did you start? You never said anything.'

'The night we went to see St Paul's.'

Silently they looked at one another and Tilly knew that he too was remembering how close she had come to losing her life.

She stretched out her hand towards him and Drew took it, wrapping his large hand around her small one, making her feel safe and protected, and loved just as he had done then.

'I wasn't going to say anything yet, because I'm not sure . . . well, I don't know how you'll feel about it, but it just feels so right, even though it's not exactly what I planned.' He looked away and then back at her. 'It's about us, Tilly, about you and me and our war as well as the people of London's war – the brave ordinary people of London – and I'm writing it so that we'll never forget. I never want to forget what our war has been like, just as I know that I shall never be able to forget that moment when I thought that I might lose you.'

'You're writing about us . . . about me? I'm going to be in a book? But I'm not important enough to be in a book.'

'Yes, you are, Tilly. You are the most important person in the world to me.'

'When can I read it?'

'Not yet. Not until it's finished.'

Tilly's heart swelled with loving pride. She just knew that Drew's book was going to be wonderful.

'I'm going to take this back upstairs and then you and I are going to go out and enjoy our Valentine's evening,' Drew told her.

'However lovely my treat is, Drew, it can't make me any happier than you've already made me,' Tilly told him.

When he came downstairs again, though, Tilly remembered that she had something else to tell him – a message from her mother.

'Mum's decided that she's going to go ahead and set up this fire-watching team for Article Row. She wants to ask you and Ian to join the team.'

'I can't speak for Ian. I'll tell him, though, of course,

and needless to say I want to join. I think it's really commendable of your mother to take this on, Tilly, but then she's that kinda person, always wanting to help out where she can.'

'I dare say she'll rope in all of us at number 13. I can't see Dulcie being keen, though. She's already creating about having to do fire-watch duty at Selfridges. Oh, but you'll never guess. The Misses Barker from number 12 got to hear about Mum's plans – from Nancy, I suppose – and they've both said that they want to be involved.' Tilly laughed. 'That was definitely one in the eye for Nancy, although given their age I can't image that Mum's going to want them climbing on roofs or leaning out of attic windows so that they can spot falling incendiaries. They must both be in their sixties.'

Drew laughed too, but said, 'No, but they will be able to help clear away any of the incendiaries that have fallen in the area. It will be team work that will keep Article Row safe, Tilly. Come on, we'd better make a move otherwise we'll be late.'

'Just one more kiss before we go?' Tilly pleaded.

Not that she needed to plead very hard. She could see that from the look in Drew's eyes.

Their train was predictably late in arriving at East Grinstead station. As George was meeting them at the station, Sally and Dulcie said their goodbyes to the others, who were all lodging within walking distance. As they queued to hand over their tickets to the waiting ticket inspector, Sally suspected that the majority of the passengers exiting the station had travelled to the small town to visit relatives at the hospital. With several young women amongst them, it looked as though there would be a reasonable number of partners for the men at Saturday night's dance, which gave her all the more reason to regret that she had ever invited Dulcie to join her.

That feeling increased when they were still waiting for George fifteen minutes later, and Dulcie had complained about his tardiness for every one of those fifteen minutes. It didn't help that it had started to rain, a fine miserable freezing drizzle that was slowly soaking through Sally's knitted gloves.

'If you was to ask me I'd say the best thing we could do is get on the first train back to London,' Dulcie informed her in a sharp voice. 'I don't know why I ever let you talk me into coming here.'

A car was coming towards them, its headlights dimmed for the blackout. It pulled to a halt right in front of them. It was a very smart and expensive-looking car indeed, Sally recognised. When the driver's door opened and George climbed out she could hardly believe it, simply standing staring at him in disbelief until he opened the passenger door and called out, 'Come on and get inside before you get even wetter.'

This was more like it, Dulcie decided, having immediately settled herself in the comfortable front passenger seat and pulled the smart tartan car rug she had found there across her lap, leaving George to deal with her weekend case, and Sally with no alternative other than to climb into the back of the car. Sally's boyfriend must be doing well if he could afford a car like this.

Only, as George explained once he was back in the driver's seat and indicating to pull back out into the road, the car actually did not belong to him, but to his boss, the famous pioneering surgeon.

'Mr MacIndoe said I could borrow his car to pick you up when he realised that our last op of the day had run over, and that meant I'd had to leave you both standing in the rain. He sends his apologies, by the way. Oh, and if you don't mind I just want to drive back to the hospital before I drop you off and see that you're settled in, just to check that my patient is comfortable. He was still pretty much out for the count when I left him.'

Before Dulcie could voice what Sally knew would be objections, she assured George quickly, 'Of course we don't mind. It's a treat to be chauffeured in such a lovely car, isn't it, Dulcie?'

'So where's this dance being held then?' Dulcie demanded, not vouchsafing an answer.

'At the hospital. We have a room there that we can use and it will be more comfortable for the men. Although the townspeople here are marvellous about not making the men feel self-conscious about their injuries, some of the patients are pretty reluctant to leave the hospital. That's why Mr MacIndoe is so keen to have these social events. He believes that it's as important to get the men back into living normal lives as it is to deal with their physical injuries. The mental and emotional trauma they suffer is every bit as bad as the physical stuff, although, of course, some of them handle it better than others. Those with families – wives and girlfriends who rally round – do the best, although we do get some who hate what has happened to them so much that they refuse to see them. We have to remember that most of these men are RAF – young, strong, good-looking men who had the world at their feet before they were injured. Men that other men envied, men who girls always looked twice at in their smart uniforms and because they are heroes, instead of because of the severity of their injuries. Now, here we are . . .' George told them as he swung the car into the road that led to the hospital, its bulk outlined as a dark shape against the slightly lighter sky by the thin moonlight escaping through the clouds.

'I shouldn't be too long,' George told them as he brought the car to a halt. 'I'll have a word and see if I can get you each a cup of tea whilst you wait for me.'

'Would it possible for me to go with you, George?' Sally asked. 'Just out of professional curiosity. That's if Ward Sister will allow it.'

Sally knew from George and her previous visit that the nursing care provided to Mr MacIndoe's patients was rather different from the ordered routine of Barts Hospital. Mr MacIndoe had a rule that the nurses smile at their patients at all times and, indeed, that they actually teased them and flirted with them a little, to help boost the men's confidence.

'Sister won't mind – she's an old Barts nurse,' George assured her, as he got out of the car, opening the rear door for Sally first and then going round to help Dulcie out of the front passenger seat.

The minute they entered the hospital Dulcie wrinkled her nose against the fiercely pungent smell of clean linoleum and disinfectant.

'I'll leave you here in reception,' George told her. 'I'll ask someone to bring you a cup of tea. We won't be very long.'

* * *

Ten minutes later, growing increasingly bad-tempered, Dulcie wasn't best pleased, having stopped a nurse who was going off duty to ask her where her cup of tea was, when the other girl said she didn't know and then added, 'Your stocking seam's gone and run all over your leg.'

A quick look over her shoulder showed Dulcie that the nurse was right and that her carefully applied eyebrow pencil 'stocking seam' had run with the rain.

'Where's the nearest toilet then?' she demanded.

'Down the corridor, turn left, then right and it's halfway down that corridor on your left.'

She was gone in a swirl of her cloak before Dulcie could say anything more. Showing off, Dulcie thought crossly. Not that she'd got any reason to do so, not with those thick ankles of hers.

Down the corridor. Well, that was easy enough. 'Turn left, and then right, and it's halfway down the corridor on your left.'

The other girl might have said just how long the corridors were, Dulcie thought indignantly when she finally found the ladies', and was able to inspect the damage to her 'seams' by standing on the lavatory lid with the door open so that she could see the back of her legs in the slightly spotted mirror above the washbasin.

Ten minutes later, her seams fully restored to their original smartness, and her handkerchief rather the worse for wear, having been used as both a flannel and a towel, Dulcie set off back to the reception area.

Down the corridor and then turn into the other corridor and then . . . Had she come this way? Dulcie wasn't sure, and the corridor she was in now seemed to go on for miles.

It never came easily to Dulcie to admit that she was wrong – about anything – but even she was beginning to feel that she was going to have to turn round and retrace her steps when, to her relief, up ahead of her she saw a pair of double doors. Hurrying towards them, she pulled them open and then came to an abrupt halt.

She was in a ward. It was filled with men – men sitting or lying in bed, men seated in chairs, men leaning against walls and talking to other men, men in uniform, men in pyjamas, men talking, men smoking, and men simply lying silently in their beds swathed in bandages. Tall men, short men, men with dark hair and men with fair hair. But men who all had one thing in common – the severity of their injuries.

Other young women might have turned away, unable to bear the evidence of what war could do to the human body, but Dulcie wasn't like that. She lacked that delicate female sensitivity and imagination that made most of her sex so aware of the pain of others. On the other hand, she wasn't the sort to shrink from such things either. It simply wasn't in her nature. She had grown up in the poverty of the East End. In that world there had been adults who had rickets as children and as a result had weak and twisted limbs, men who had lost limbs during the Great War, a little boy three houses down from where Dulcie had lived had suffered horrendous burns when he had pulled a pan of boiling soup over onto himself.

Now, instead of turning away from the sight of young men with badly burned faces and missing limbs, she simply stared curiously at them.

One of the men who had been standing closest to the door, smoking a cigarette, put it out and called out, 'Hey, boys, look. We've got a stunner of a pretty girl come to visit.'

Immediately all the men who were able to do so turned towards her.

'Who are you looking for?' the young man who had spoken up asked her.

'No one,' Dulcie replied. 'I got lost on my way to reception.'

Confident by nature and toughened by her upbringing, Dulcie felt no self-consciousness at being the only young woman amongst so many young men. Their obvious interest in her she took as no more than her due. Flirtatious comments and tributes to her prettiness were something she took in her stride, preening herself like a queen amongst her courtiers as she accepted them, whilst privately thinking that it was just as well that she had reapplied those rainwater-damaged 'stocking seams'.

'Well, reception's loss is our gain,' one of the men told her appreciatively.

This was Dulcie's favourite milieu – being at the centre of male attention – and whilst it was true that these men bore the scars of their injuries very openly, they had enough confidence and enough youthful verve despite their bandages for her to decide that tomorrow's dance might be good fun after all. And it would just serve Wilder right if she did have fun after the way he had let her down. In Dulcie's opinion he should have made much more of an effort to see her tonight.

'Going to the dance tomorrow?' asked one of the young men, who had limped over to her. He was rolling a cigarette with one hand, the stump of his other, missing arm heavily bandaged, like almost all of the left-hand side of his face.

'I might be,' Dulcie responded coquettishly.

'There's no way that Mr MacIndoe is going to let you go dancing tomorrow night,' one of the other men warned. 'You've got surgery on Monday.'

'All the more reason to have a good time on Saturday,' the young man responded.

The doors at the other end of the ward opened to admit a pretty young nurse, accompanied by George and Sally.

'Dulcie, what are doing in here?' Sally asked.

'You were gone so long I thought I'd have a look round,' Dulcie fibbed. She wasn't going to make herself look daft by admitting she'd got herself lost.

Sally gave the ward sister an apologetic look. It was typical of Dulcie that she'd managed to find her way into the ward that contained in the main those men who were reaching the final stages of their treatment and rehabilitation before being discharged, and who were therefore far more likely to react as high-spirited young men in her presence than very sick patients.

Since George had come into the ward with the ward sister only to check up on another of his patients, Sally pointed to the doors through which she and George had just come, and told Dulcie, 'We're going back this way.'

George had finished checking up on his patient and was waiting for them to join him. As they did so, Dulcie glanced casually at the man George had been examining and then stopped, moving closer to exclaim in astonishment, 'David!'

It was David James-Thompson, the dashing barrister who had married Dulcie's arch-enemy from Selfridges – the posh daughter of one of Selfridges directors.

How Dulcie had enjoyed flirting with David and encouraging him to pay attention to her as a means of getting at the snooty Lydia, who had made it so plain that she looked down on her. David had wanted to take things further than the mild flirtation Dulcie had instigated, but Dulcie had refused. If she'd been the type to allow herself to fall in love, which she wasn't, then falling in love with a man like David – a man who would one day inherit a title and whose mother had chosen his wife for him – could only lead to heartache. But even though she knew that she had made the right decision, standing here looking at him was making her heart thud in a most un-Dulcie-like way – something that Wilder had never been able to achieve.

David's handsome face was exactly the same, even if the amusement and the confidence had gone from the familiar hazel eyes. It was very rare for anything or anyone to wrong-foot Dulcie or catch her off guard. But right now something had.

David wasn't looking at her. He had turned his head right away from her so that he didn't have to look at her, turning his body away from her too, and that was when Dulcie recognised from the movement of the bedclothes that David no longer had much of a body; that in fact beneath the bedclothes where the outline of his legs should have been there was nothing. David has lost his legs. And most of one of his arms, she realised as she looked properly at him. She had been so surprised to see him, so taken off guard by the sight of his familiar handsome face that initially she hadn't looked beyond that face.

Sally's hand on her arm was drawing her away, George coming to stand on the other side of her, both of them almost walking her out of the ward so that she was through the doors and in the corridor beyond it before she could think to object.

David watched her go. Seeing Dulcie had affected him in a way that he had truly believed was no longer possible. Not sexually – that was impossible, thanks to his injuries from the Messerschmidt bullets, which had ripped apart his lower legs and his groin as well as damaging his arm. No, seeing Dulcie had brought back to life, if only briefly, his war-numbed emotions. Seeing Dulcie had reminded him of a past that in its way had been every bit as bleak as the only future he could now look towards.

He had been very young when he had recognised that his mother didn't even like him, never mind love him, absorbing that knowledge as a truth without any need for it to be put into words, as young children do. Later, using his legal brain to try to rationalise his mother's attitude to him, he had decided that initially her antipathy toward him sprang from the loss of her own elder brother toward the end of the Great War. His mother had worshipped her elder sibling; she talked about him all the time. Her private sitting room had been filled with silver-framed photographs of him where it had been bare of photographs of both David and his father. David had never been allowed to touch those precious photographs, his small chubby baby hands smacked hard whenever he tried to reach for them when his mother was holding them.

David could still vividly remember his mother's excitement on her brother's rare visits, even though he had been very young at the time. No one had been allowed to interrupt them. His mother had wanted her precious brother to herself. Apart from these rare glimpses, David's visual memories of his uncle came from his mother's photographs. These had shown a thin and delicate man, as befitted the poet he had been. A poet who, according to David's mother, had made the ultimate sacrifice for his country.

Perhaps things might have been different for David if he had taken after his mother's side of the family and physically resembled his dead uncle, but he did not. David had the strong muscles and the height of his father's family, and that had been another reason for his mother to reject him. His father's family were good country stock but not anywhere near as blue-blooded as his mother's family, with its earldom at the top of their family tree. At the top of the family tree and far out of the reach of his mother's branch of the family until the Great War had scythed through its younger branches, resulting in the deaths of the three male cousins, their deaths putting his mother's brother, Eddie, in direct line to inherit the earldom on the death of the then current earl.

He had been a child still when his uncle had been sent home from the trenches, suffering from the gas poisoning that had killed him. A child with scarlet fever, whose mother had therefore been banned from going to nurse her sick brother, the sick brother who had died, whilst he . . . the naughty child, whose illness had meant she was unable to see her brother, to nurse him, maybe to save him, was then the cause of the whole family losing the earldom and the status and riches that went with it. His mother had never forgiven him for that, and David knew that she never would.

His marriage to Lydia had been the price his mother had demanded from him as mere interest on the debt she believed he owed her. Lydia would ultimately inherit a very good fortune indeed and Lydia's family, with their connection to trade through the great-grandparents from whom that fortune came, had been keen to cement their progress up the social ladder by marrying their daughter to a young man who would ultimately inherit from his own great uncle and then his father the title of Sir David and the pretty Oxfordshire manor that went with it. Not that his mother, forced to accept his father's proposal when the Great War had left so many young women of her generation without prospective husbands, thought very much of his father's family title. A mere baronetcy could after all hardly compare with an earldom; good stout hearty beefy English county blood could not match the purity of blue blood that for centuries had never been mixed with anything other than more blue blood.

How his mother had railed against the fact that, as the last of her family, she could not claim the earldom and all that went with it, always concluding her furious tirades with the cruel words that David could never have been good enough to wear the family ermine.

'How I came to produce a child like you I shall never know,' she was fond of declaiming.

If fate had been unkind to her it had been equally unkind to him in giving him a mother who had no love for him. His father, a decent, good man in his way, had quickly been cowed by his far more domineering wife,

106

and David had learned from him that it was easier to give in to his mother than to stand up to her. He had often wondered if Lydia realised that, for all her fussing over her, his mother secretly despised her. Lydia would certainly never have been considered good enough for his mother's precious brother or the earldom.

Perhaps it was that early rejection by his mother that had made him the man he was, and that had fostered in him that streak of earthiness and enjoyment of the company of rich robustness of ordinary people. People like Dulcie. David didn't know and he cared even less. In fact, he didn't care about anything right now other than the pain where his lower legs should have been. No, he didn't care, but he still couldn't help watching Dulcie walk away from him, until she had disappeared through the door at the other end of the ward.

'You know the group captain, do you, Dulcie?' George asked once they were out of the ward.

'Yes, I do, not that you'd know it from the way he went and showed me up by ignoring me,' Dulcie responded with a small angry sniff. 'Of course, it will be on her account, that stuck-up wife of his. Always was jealous of me, she was, and I dare say he won't want any of his pals telling her that he's been talking to me when she comes to visit him.'

'That won't happen, Dulcie,' George informed her. 'Neither David's wife nor his parents visit him. They're ashamed of him, you see, because of his injuries, and that will be why he didn't acknowledge you. He'd be afraid that you would reject him like they did.'

Dulcie could hear the disapproval of Lydia and of

David's parents in George's voice, and immediately played up to it.

'Not visit their own son? Well, they ought to be ashamed of themselves, him being like he is. Mind you, I never liked the sound of that mother of his, and as for Lydia, the only reason she married him was because one day he'll have a title.'

George seemed to be considering something, but even Dulcie, who made a point of never allowing anything to catch her off guard, was surprised when he asked her, 'Dulcie, how would you feel about visiting David tomorrow afternoon at visiting time?'

'What, after him ignoring me today?'

'We desperately need to get him properly on the road to recovery and that's not going to happen until he feels that people accept him as he is, and that they still care about him despite his injuries.'

Listening to her fiancé as they walked towards the hospital exit, Sally tried to send him a warning look. She didn't think that Dulcie was the right person to ask to show compassion to a man in David's condition.

But George was giving her a small shake of his head as he continued, 'Of course, I realise that it would take a really special girl to do that for David, Dulcie. Not many girls would feel comfortable talking to a young man as badly injured as David is – a young man who right now is feeling very sorry for himself and very angry indeed because of the way his wife and mother have turned their backs on him. It would take a very unselfish and kind young woman indeed, a young woman who is the complete opposite from his wife.'

Sally grimaced to herself. She knew what George was

doing and why. He was using on Dulcie the psychological skills he was being taught at the hospital for helping his patients, but Sally still wasn't sure that was a good idea.

Listening to George, Dulcie, oblivious to what George was doing, bridled with delight at the thought of doing something that would make her look better than Lydia. How she'd enjoy telling them back at Selfridges that she'd had to step in and help David because his wife had turned her back on him. That would show everyone who was the better woman. And it would show David as well. He might have been sweet on her but he had still gone and married Lydia. Not that she, Dulcie, had wanted him to marry her, but she wouldn't have minded having him ask her.

Ever practically minded, though, she asked George, 'What if he doesn't want to talk to me? There'd be no point in me visiting him then, would there? And I'd look a real charlie sitting there with him refusing to even look at me.'

'I think he'll want to talk to you, Dulcie. He watched you leaving the ward. I turned round to have a look. It was probably a shock for him to see you. And I expect he was worried about what you'd think. After all, I dare say the last time you saw him he was standing on his feet and uninjured. Now he's lost both his lower legs and an arm, and there were other injuries . . . to his groin.'

A flutter of something unfamiliar gripped Dulcie's belly. David had been such a tall, broad-shouldered, male man, as proud of being a handsome man as she was of being a pretty girl.

'Well, his face is all right,' was all she allowed herself

to say, 'and you can't see that he's not got any legs whilst he's in bed, can you? Mind you, I can't say that I'm surprised about that wife of his – she never did have much about her. And I dare say there won't be an heir then now either, by the sound of it.'

'No, Dulcie, there won't,' George confirmed sadly. 'It's a lot to ask of any young woman, Dulcie, I know that, and I wouldn't blame you one little bit if you felt that you aren't up to it.'

'Who says I'm not up to it? I'm not like that stuck-up wife of his. Like I said, there's nothing wrong with his face.' She paused and then asked anxiously, 'He can still talk, can't he? I mean, what's happened to him hasn't . . .?'

'Yes, he can talk, Dulcie,' George confirmed.

'All right, I'll do it then,' she agreed.

They were outside the hospital now, the thin fitful moonlight glistening on the wet road as George opened the car doors for them and then got into the driving seat.

'Nancy's just arrived,' Mrs Morrison told Olive in a rueful whisper as the two WVS ladies queued up for their mid-meeting cup of tea in the church hall.

'She said she'd be late this evening,' Olive replied. 'Her husband's on fire-watching duty this week and she wanted to wait for him to come in before she came out.'

'I've never known anyone make her own virtue so much of a stick to beat others with,' said Mrs Morrison pithily. 'I know she's your next-door neighbour, Olive, and I don't like speaking ill of anyone but—'

'She doesn't mean any harm,' Olive felt bound to defend her neighbour, even though privately she agreed with what Mrs Morrison was saying. 'It's just her way.'

'You are a very charitable person, Olive,' Mrs Morrison smiled.

Olive didn't feel particularly charitable ten minutes later, though, when Nancy, having got her own cup of tea and several sizeable pieces of the broken biscuits that Mrs Dunne, the grocer's wife, brought to the meetings, settled herself in the empty chair next to Olive and began importantly, 'I don't like to be the one to tell tales, Olive, but I think you should know that after you'd gone out this evening, I saw your Tilly leaving the house with that American.'

'It's Valentine's Day, Nancy. Drew is taking Tilly out somewhere special,' Olive automatically defended the young couple. But her defence only increased Nancy's smug air of superiority.

'Well, that may have been what he told you and your Tilly, for all I know, but what I saw with my own eyes was the pair of them straight heading back to the Simpsons' and going in there together,' Nancy told her with obvious relish.

Olive felt her heart sink. 'I dare say Drew had probably forgotten something,' was all she dared to allow herself to say. She could feel the maternal bands of anxiety and apprehension tightening round her heart, but the last thing she wanted, knowing her neighbour as she did, was for Nancy to see how she felt.

Nancy, though, was not to be put off. 'I don't think so, Olive,' she insisted. 'I don't think they'd forgotten anything at all. In there for ever such a long time, they were. I was looking out of my front window waiting for my hubby to get home, on account of me wanting to get down here and being worried that he'd be delayed fire-watching,' she excused her nosiness, 'and I'd say it was a good hour before they left.'

Olive could feel the smile she had forced for Nancy's benefit tightening on her face as she struggled not to betray what she was really feeling.

'You know what your trouble is, Olive? You're far too soft with Tilly. She's bound to get herself talked about, carrying on like she is. I'd never have let my daughter get away with that kind of behaviour, but then she's not that sort of girl.'

This was Nancy's payback for the words they had exchanged recently about fire-watching, Olive knew, and she could well understand why Nancy looked so pleased with herself.

Olive's cup of tea had gone cold. Right now she'd give anything for the strengthening cheer of a good cup of hot strong tea in the privacy of her own kitchen, where she could come to terms with what Nancy had just told her, but she had a duty to give this evening to the WVS, and a duty to protect Tilly from their neighbour's spiteful curiosity, Olive reminded herself as she forced what she hoped was a calm smile.

'I expect Tilly and Drew got talking about his writing and forgot the time,' she said lightly.

Nancy raised one straggly greying eyebrow and exclaimed loftily, 'Well, you might want to believe that, Olive, but if I was in your shoes I'd have something to say to your Tilly about getting herself a bad reputation. But then, of course, I always kept a close eye on my own daughter. It's all very well folk volunteering for all sorts

112

and having folk make a fuss of them because of it, but in my opinion it's putting your own family first that matters most.'

With that Nancy ate her broken biscuits with every evidence of enjoyment, before announcing that she was going to have to leave the meeting early, 'because I want to make sure that my Arthur gets a decent supper.'

More like because she wanted to stand in her darkened front room with the black out blind lifted so that she could watch for any comings and goings on the Row, especially if those comings and goings were Tilly's, Olive thought miserably.

FIVE

The house in which Dulcie and Sally were staying wasn't very far from the town centre. Sally had stayed there on her first visit to see George, and she knew that the rooms were clean and the landlady, Mrs Hodges, welcoming. The discovery that Persephone, the upper-class girl from the train, was also staying at the same lodgings had Dulcie pulling a face to Sally as the landlady ushered them into her warm cheerful kitchen with its scrubbed wooden table and welcoming Aga. After Mrs Hodges, who was on her way out to a WI meeting, had announced that she'd left them some cold supper in the larder, Sally turned to George and suggested that they go to the local chip shop and bring back some chips.

'That's if you fancy some, Dulcie?'

'I fancy them more than I do a cold supper,' Dulcie acknowledged.

'What about you, Persephone?' Sally asked.

The other girl immediately coloured up and looked embarrassed as she told them, 'Daddy doesn't approve of things like fish and chips.'

'Poor girl,' Sally told George ruefully once they were

alone together, walking arm in arm the short distance to the chip shop on the high street. 'I feel a bit guilty leaving her with Dulcie. Dulcie will make mincemeat of her. Which reminds me, do you think it was wise to encourage Dulcie to visit David?'

'I don't know, but I'm hoping so,' George admitted. 'As I said earlier, physically he's not mending as well as he should be, and Mr MacIndoe feels that is because he's been rejected, not just by his wife but his parents as well. But I know I'm taking a risk in encouraging Dulcie to visit him.'

'A big risk. Surely he needs someone who will be a real and regular support to him? Dulcie isn't like that, George. Oh, I know that right now she's all fired up with enthusiasm but that enthusiasm is more about her scoring over David's wife than generated by any real desire to help David himself, and when it fades—'

'I know, I know . . . but we've been getting pretty desperate. Mr MacIndoe thinks that we could lose him if we can't find a way to give him a reason to fight for life. He hates losing patients.'

Sally squeezed George's arm understandingly.

In the kitchen of their lodgings, Dulcie eyed Persephone. As far as Dulcie was concerned she was a very poor specimen of a girl: too thin, wearing old-fashioned clothes, and with that posh accent that reminded her of Lydia. Not that Persephone had any of Lydia's high-handed manner about her. Dulcie certainly wouldn't have tolerated it if she had.

'So it's your brother you're going to see tomorrow then, is it?' Dulcie asked her.

'Yes.'

'I'm going to be visiting a patient as well,' Dulcie told her. 'Asked to specially, I've bin, on account of me already knowing him and him needing someone who's got the gumption to visit him, not like that wife of his. I always knew that she wasn't up to much.' Dulcie tossed her blond hair. She was enjoying have a justifiable reason to criticise Lydia openly. 'Turned her back on him now, she has.'

Persephone made a small sound of distress and said in a shocked voice, 'Oh, poor boy, how awful for him, and how good you are to visit him.'

'Yes, I am,' Dulcie agreed. 'But then that's me all over, putting myself out for others. Always been like that, I have. Where's Sally with them chips? Canoodling with that fiancé of hers, I expect. You'd think she put a bit of speed on. I'm starving . . . That's the trouble with some folk. They are just naturally selfish and don't ever think of others. So what's up with him, then, your brother? Got burned, has he? There was plenty on that ward I was just on that had, and plenty with no arms or legs either. And George was saying as how they are the ones that have been operated on and are getting better. If that's true then I'd hate to see them as haven't had anything done yet,' Dulcie told the other girl with the kind of relish that rather belied her words. 'An 'orrible state, some of them must be in, if you ask me. 'Ere, what's wrong with you?' she asked when Persephone lifted a hanky to her eyes to wipe away her tears.

'I'm sorry. I was just thinking about my brother.'

'Well, you'd better not go crying all over him when you go to see him tomorrow. According to George, this

Mr MacIndoe, who's in charge, doesn't like it when relatives make a fuss. He says it upsets his patients. He's even got the hospital to take on pretty nurses and told them to smile at the patients, 'cos he reckons it's good for them to see a cheerful, pretty girl. I wouldn't be surprised, if he was to see me talking with David when I see him tomorrow, if doesn't ask me to smile at the other men there, with me being so pretty meself.'

Having queued up for and got their chips, Sally and George set off back for Sally's lodgings at a smart pace, linked up closely together, George carrying the chips beneath his coat to make sure that they didn't get cold, Sally having refused, saying they would make her clothes smell. Although George also lodged in the town, Sally had quite understood when his landlady had told her very politely that she didn't allow unmarried couples, even engaged couples, to sleep beneath her roof. George wasn't the sort to push for the kind of favours and intimacies that went with marriage, which in Sally's view made the sweet sensuality and passion of their shared kisses and the very evident control George had to force on himself to stop him from wanting to take things further, all the more tenderly special. Without even pausing for a single kiss they rushed back.

Not that Dulcie was in the least bit grateful for their sacrifice.

'What kept you? I'm starving,' she complained the minute they arrived.

'There was a queue,' Sally told her, as they all sat down at the kitchen table and began to unwrap their newspaper parcels.

Persephone had said that she wasn't hungry but now Sally insisted on coaxing her to share her own fish and chips.

'Here, take a chip,' she offered, holding out the parcel to her.

It was obvious from the uncertain way in which Persephone carefully removed a chip that she wasn't used to eating with her fingers, Sally guessed. Taking pity on her, she put down her food and got up to get a plate and a knife and fork.

When Persephone tried to refuse, she told her firmly, 'I'm a nurse. You didn't eat anything on the train, and you need to keep your strength up. I realise that you might not feel like eating, but you must.'

'Mummy and Daddy are both so upset about Roddy's accident that we've just got out of the habit of . . . well, with rationing and everything, and then Cook leaving because her married daughter's had a baby . . .'

Listening in, Dulcie raised her eyebrows at Sally behind Persephone's back but Sally firmly ignored her. She felt sorry for the young girl, who looked so worn down and apprehensive.

Of course, once they had all finished their supper, had had a cup of tea and then cleaned up it was time for George to leave. Sally naturally accompanied him to the door and outside into the darkness of the blackout where, beneath the bare branches of the climbing rose that covered the small porch, they were able to exchange a few precious kisses.

'Come and sit in the car with me for a few minutes,' George begged Sally, taking hold of her hand.

Uncertainly she looked back towards the closed door to the house. 'I shouldn't really,' she began.

'Please, Sally. We may not get another chance to be properly alone together, and there's something I want to say.'

Silently Sally nodded her head.

As George led her towards the car she could almost feel the air of determination that surrounded him, and a responsive tremble of emotion made her own insides feel all fluttery in a way that she considered to be most unlike her normal self.

Mr MacIndoe's car smelled of good leather and wood, and it was certainly warmer and rather more private than the shelter provided by her landlady's front door, Sally had to admit. Not that she suspected for a single moment that George had anything improper in mind. George, bless him, simply wasn't like that. One of the things she liked most about George was his reliability and his decency. Decency in a person meant a lot when you'd experienced a lack of it in someone of whom you'd thought better.

Inside the car, she shook her head when George offered her the warm plaid car rug, but she didn't turn away when George moved as close to her as the car seats would allow, her knee touching his, her flesh warmed by the comfort of that contact with him.

George reached for her hands and Sally let him hold them.

'There isn't room for me to go down on one knee to you here,' he began ruefully. 'Sally, you know how much you mean to me, how much I love you and want you to be mine. At Christmas you didn't want us to become

119

formally engaged because you didn't want to steal Agnes and Ted's thunder, but today is Valentine's Day, even if this isn't the kind of setting I'd have chosen for my proposal, so please will you agree to be my wife now, Sally? I promise you that I will be the best husband I can be. I love you so very much.'

His voice broke over those last words, the simple heartfelt emotion making Sally's eyes fill with the sting of tender tears.

'George, darling, yes, of course I will,' she answered.

His kiss betrayed how much her answer meant to him, her own senses responding both to the moment and to George himself with an answering passion that told her how right her answer was, and how right they would be together.

'I've got the ring.' George told her gruffly once he had stopped kissing her. 'It arrived last week. Ma's sent a letter for you as well, but if you don't care for it, then . . .'

The ring to which George was referring was his grandmother's ring, which she had left to him for his bride-to-be. He had told her about it when he had first asked her to marry him, just as he had also told her all about his family in New Zealand – his doctor father, and his mother, who had been a nurse, and how they would welcome her into the family as his wife.

'I shall love it,' Sally told him truthfully. Wasn't this what life should be all about? The gift of love, and respect for that love passed down through the generations, signifying the importance of family? Wasn't that what she had once felt she had had in her own family and what she felt so bitterly devastated about losing? When they married, George's family would become her family, and the children she and George would have would be children of that family, and that mattered very much indeed to Sally.

'Here's Ma's letter,' George told her, reaching into his inside pocket to pass her a bulky envelope with her name written on it, and then diving into that same pocket again to remove a small dark green leather box.

A small tender kiss, and then he was opening the box and reaching for her ring finger.

How different this occasion was from the one she had imagined the day she had looked into another young man's eyes and believed she had fallen in love. It was time to put the pain and betrayal of the past behind her for ever now, Sally knew. She owed it to George and their future together to do so. Morag, Callum and her father weren't worth a single one of her tears and never had been. She looked down at the ring George was sliding onto her finger and knew that the tears that were filming her eyes were not for the past, but instead were tears of happiness.

The ring, with its oblong emerald stone flanked by two small diamonds, was beautiful, and all the more so, Sally truly felt, because of the way the gold ring was worn and thin from its previous use, surely representing the love with which it had originally been given and worn.

'If you don't care for it . . . ?' George was saying.

But Sally shook her head and told him truthfully, 'I love it.'

It fitted her perfectly, and her first thought when she looked down and saw it on her own ring finger was how much her mother would have loved this moment and all that it represented.

Her, 'Oh George,' was soft with love and the emotions inside her heart that Sally rarely allowed other to see.

There was just time for another tender kiss, not so much an ardent kiss of longing and uncertainty this time but rather one of contentment and mutual commitment, and then Sally was opening her letter from George's mother. It was hard to read it properly in the dim light from George's torch, but she could look at the photographs that had fallen out of the envelope.

One photograph was of a chubby baby – easily recognisable as George himself, as he had George's curly hair – held in the arms of his parents: George's father, so like him that Sally would have recognised him anywhere; his mother standing calmly facing the camera in such a way that Sally knew immediately that they would get on and respect one another. The others were of George as he was growing up: a bungalow with a long low veranda in the background and a dog sitting at George's feet. Happy photographs of a happy childhood with loving parents. The same kind of childhood she herself had had.

George's mother's letter was friendly and welcoming, taking their relationship a step further on from the letters she and Sally had already exchanged, making it plain that she was happy to welcome Sally as her son's future wife. A nurse herself before her marriage to George's father, she was, she wrote, looking forward to meeting Sally once the war was over. There was nothing in the letter to suggest that George's parents expected their son and Sally to make their future lives in New Zealand, but Sally already knew that that would be what they and George himself would want. Without a family of her own to tie her to England any more she knew that she would not want to stand in George's way, even if right now the thought of that new life felt just a little bit alarming.

'I'm sorry that this evening hasn't been as romantic as you deserve,' George told her.

'Not romantic? Being proposed to here, in this very expensive car, and given this beautiful ring, never mind being kissed so very, very well?' Sally teased him gently.

'You know what I mean,' George protested. 'I would have liked to have come up to London and taken you out somewhere swish where we could have drunk champagne and danced.'

'George, I felt far more at home seeing the work being done here at the hospital than I would have done in some expensive nightclub,' Sally assured him. 'And we will get to dance together tomorrow evening, even if there isn't any champagne.'

George smiled lovingly at her. 'I knew the minute I met you that you were the girl for me,' he told her, 'and I was right. I do wish, though, that I could have made tonight a bit more special, taken you somewhere we could have been on our own.'

'It will be spring soon, and then summer,' she told him softly. 'Maybe we'll be able to arrange to have a few days away together.'

'Yes,' George agreed, his voice thickening and then cracking slightly, his arm tightening around her.

They both knew what was being said, what was being offered and promised. There was no need for either of them to spell it out in actual words. She wasn't a girl, Sally told herself. She was a modern young woman living in a country at war. They had already agreed that they wouldn't marry until the war was over, and no one knew when that would be.

They looked at one another in the heavy intimate silence they themselves had created with their unspoken feelings.

In the room she was sharing with Sally, whilst Sally was still outside with George, Dulcie undressed quickly with her dressing gown draped round her shoulders to keep out the cold of the chilly bedroom, deciding as she did so, that she was looking forward to seeing David again. George's comments about David's parents and his wife had aroused her curiosity. She liked the thought of hearing how badly Lydia had behaved and thus being able to criticise her with justification. The thought that talking about Lydia might be painful for David simply didn't occur to her. The thought of David's injuries didn't put her off, either. He still had his handsome face, after all, and even if he hadn't, Dulcie wouldn't have shrunk from him. Her sense of self-preservation protected her from concerning herself about the emotional pain of others. She had decided very young that it was up to her to protect her own emotions because no one else was going to do that for her, especially not her mother. So she had simply cut herself off from thinking about things that were hurtful. She just wasn't the sort to look beneath the surface of things in order to find out how another person felt.

In Olive's front room, Ted and Agnes were sitting on the sofa together holding hands, having just finished listening to a romantic play on the wireless that had made Agnes cry. Ted had mopped up her tears, gently reminding her that it was only a play. It was lovely being with Ted, Agnes thought. He always made her feel so safe and happy, and so proud now that she was wearing his engagement ring. Being engaged made her feel like she'd got her own special place in life, a proper place, not just Agnes the orphan, but Ted's fiancée and wife-to-be.

Agnes smiled at Ted. It was Valentine's Day evening and she and Ted were together, and later on, after he had had his cocoa and before he left, when she walked with him to the door to say good night to him, Ted would take her in his arms and kiss her and she would kiss him back. Just thinking about kissing Ted and being kissed by him gave Agnes a lovely squidgy happy and excited feeling in her tummy. They wouldn't kiss here in Olive's front room, of course; that would not be proper. There was no need for that thought to be put into words. It was understood between them and, like so much of their relationship, did not need to be talked about. It was just the way things were, and accepted by them both.

'You've been out there ages,' Dulcie complained when Sally eventually came in to the bedroom, 'and now you've gone and woken me up switching on that lamp. What are you doing?' she demanded, when Sally sat down on her bed and spread the photographs from the letter George had given her on the bedspread, and began to reread George's mother's letter. Her mouth dimpled into a warm smile as she recognised again the warmth of George's mother's welcome into their family.

125

'Looking at these photos,' she answered Dulcie without taking her gaze off the letter.

About to turn her back and try to get back to sleep, Dulcie suddenly noticed Sally's ring.

'You're engaged?' she demanded

'Yes,' Sally confirmed. 'George asked me before Christmas but he wanted to wait until his mother had sent him his grandmother's ring before we made it official.'

'Well, for myself I'd rather have me own ring and not an old one that someone else has worn,' Dulcie sniffed, 'but if you're happy with it then I suppose it doesn't matter.'

'I'm very happy with it,' Sally assured her, lifting her gaze from George's mother's letter to look down at her left hand. Her ring was special to her because it was special to George. She knew how much it meant to him to give her his grandmother's ring, and how much he loved her.

So now Sally and Agnes were both engaged, Dulcie thought when Sally had eventually turned off the bedside lamp. And anyone could see that Tilly was head over heels with Drew. Who would ever have thought that the three of them would be spoken for before her? Not that she couldn't have been spoken for if she'd wanted to be. There was John, who had always had a soft spot for her, and Wilder, of course. Dulcie didn't want to settle down with anyone at the moment, but by rights Wilder ought to have recognised that a girl like her needed to be treated a bit special, like. He could have proposed just so that she could have told the others that he had, even though she'd have turned him down. He was going to have to pull his socks up a bit if he wanted to keep her, Dulcie decided. Mind, if she were ever to wear an engagement ring it would have to be a lot better than Agnes's, and Sally's. She'd want diamonds, three of them all together like she'd seen on the ring fingers of the rich women who came into Selfridges to shop. Women like Lydia . . .

Tilly had had the most wonderful evening. She had felt a little bit out of her depth at first when she had realised that Drew had brought her to the Savoy for their evening out, but Drew had soon seen to it that she recovered her confidence, telling her that she looked far far prettier than any other woman there, and that he far preferred the sparkle in her eyes to the glitter of the expensive jewellery other women were wearing.

In no time at all they had been ensconced in their very private table in the restaurant, chosen by Drew so that they could watch what was going on all around them whilst remaining relatively private themselves, and within half an hour of their being seated, Tilly was thoroughly enjoying herself as she and Drew playfully fought to see who could recognise and identify the most VIPs.

There was nothing she and Drew enjoyed more than people-watching, Tilly thought happily as they sat together at their little table, and if the meal they were being served – a rather thin soup followed by a fish dish followed by the promise of a 'truly romantic' pudding, was probably rather a long way from the Savoy's famed pre-war standards, Tilly was far too much in love and far too happy to care.

In between courses they got up to dance, joining other diners on the floor, Tilly feeling so very proud to be with Drew, whom she believed was the kindest and the very best man there, making her quite the luckiest girl.

In between talking about themselves and the wonder of their love for one another they talked about Drew's book and about the war.

'Are you still planning to write about the gangs that go around looting after the bombs have fallen?' Tilly asked him as she sipped her wine and felt very grown up and sophisticated.

'Oh, yes,' Drew confirmed. 'I've found out that some of the looters are so well organised that they don't even wait until the all clear sound. Instead they follow the emergency services and are even breaking windows themselves under cover of the falling bombs in order to get into shops and homes.'

'That's terrible,' Tilly told him, both shocked and angered.

'The trouble is that most of these looters are so quick and so good at using emergencies that it's next to impossible to catch them red-handed, and so they get away with it. There are even stories of looters actually removing not just watches and jewellery but also clothing from the bodies of the dead.'

Tilly shuddered, and Drew reached across the table to hold her hand.

'I'm sorry, I shouldn't have told you that.'

'Of course you should,' Tilly defended him. 'And I'm glad that you did. I want you to share your work with me, Drew. I don't want to be protected from what's happening. I just wish that you could find some way to actually catch these people in the act and then unmask them in your articles. They should be punished for doing anything so dreadful.'

She sounded so passionately indignant, but looked so enchantingly pretty, that Drew immediately wanted to kiss her. He loved her so much, his brave strong-hearted Tilly.

Happily the musicians had struck up for a slow waltz and they were still waiting for their 'romantic pudding' so he was able to suggest that they get up to dance.

It was wonderful being held tightly in Drew's arms whilst they swayed slowly together, the top of her head resting against Drew's jaw, Tilly thought dreamily as the lights dimmed and the warmth of Drew's hand on her back brought her even closer to him so that they could steal a lingering kiss, after which Tilly decided that a visit to the ladies' room to repair her lipstick might be a good idea before she returned to the full light of their table.

When she pushed open the door to the powder room, another girl was already seated at one of the satin-covered stools, in front of the individual dressing tables, looking into the mirror in front of her, only it wasn't her lipstick she was gazing at, but the very pretty diamond ring sparkling on her ring finger.

Seeing Tilly looking at it, she told her in obvious excitement, 'My boy has just given it to me. I'm so thrilled. He's in the RAF and I had wondered . . . well, I'd hoped, but he hadn't said so much as a word, other than to promise me that he wanted to make tonight very special for both of us.'

The powder room was empty apart from the two of them, with no cloakroom staff in attendance to overhear them. But even so, Tilly was surprised when the other girl – a pretty strawberry blonde wearing a deep pink satin dress – confided, her cheeks flushing almost the same colour as her frock, 'I'm just so glad now that I agreed to spend the night here in London . . . with him, so that we can really be together. My parents think I'm staying at an all-girls' hostel, but Rory has booked us a room here.'

When Tilly's eyes rounded the other girl asked fiercely, 'You don't approve?'

'It isn't that,' Tilly assured her. 'I was just thinking how brave you are.'

'Rory is the one who is brave,' the other girl told her softly. 'He's flown fifty missions now. Every time he flies I wonder if this will be the night he doesn't come back. Now, if that should happen, then at least I will have had tonight. It's the least we can do for them, isn't it?' She paused, reapplying her lipstick carefully. 'Give them what we can of ourselves to cherish and to fight and live for, don't you think?'

She was standing up before Tilly could do anything more than nod, and then watch her enviously as she left the powder room.

'You're very quiet,' Drew commented several minutes after she had rejoined him.

Tilly quickly told him about the girl in the powder room.

'I wish so much that was us, Drew,' she told him passionately.

'What? You wish that I was a fly boy?' Drew teased her, deliberately choosing to misunderstand her. Tilly, though, knew him far too well to fall for his ploy.

'You know I don't mean that. And you know too what I do mean.' She broke off when they were served with what looked like a very small pink heart-shaped blancmange with a fanfare that it didn't really deserve.

'Yes, I do know what you mean,' Drew agreed once their waiter had withdrawn from earshot. 'I understand too why you're saying it.' He reached for her hand as he had done earlier in the evening, holding it firmly within his own. 'I feel privileged and honoured to have your love, Tilly, and to know that you'd do that for me.'

'For us,' Tilly insisted fiercely. 'For both of us, Drew. I want—'

A small shake of his head, accompanied by a gentle squeeze of her hand, had her pausing for breath and allowing him to say into that silence, 'There is nothing I want more than for us to be together properly, Tilly, but I have a responsibility to you, and I have given an assurance to your mother. I wouldn't be able to look myself in the eye if I dishonoured that responsibility and that assurance. I don't want . . .' Drew paused, his conscience stabbing him as he told her truthfully, 'I don't want our love to be blighted or sullied by lies and deceit. It and you are worthy of better than that.' It was the truth, Drew assured himself, even if for now there were other deceits that he couldn't own up to. For Tilly's own sake. He would have willingly told her everything if he didn't know that doing so would threaten their love. One day he would tell her, of course. One day, but not yet.

'Oh, Drew . . .' Oblivious to what Drew was thinking, Tilly was overwhelmed by a flood of pride and love for him. He was so honest and decent, so trustworthy.

'Come on,' Drew coaxed her. 'We'd better eat this

131

so-called romantic pudding. They'll be playing the last waltz of the evening soon, and we don't want to miss it.'

It was nearly two o'clock when their taxi pulled up outside number 13. Tilly had had a delightful ride back, snuggled up in the back of the cab in Drew's arms. Not that he had done anything more than simply hold her, but being held safely in Drew's arms was a perfect way to end what had been a very special evening, Tilly acknowledged, as Drew paid off the taxi and they hurried to the front door.

In number 13's kitchen, Olive heard Tilly's key in the front door and stood up. Agnes had gone up to bed nearly an hour ago, but Olive hadn't felt able to follow her up to her own bed. Not with the weight of so much anxiety hanging over her.

'Mum, you shouldn't have waited up for us,' Tilly protested when she opened the kitchen door and saw Olive seated at the kitchen table.

'I'm sorry if we kept you up late, Mrs Robbins,' Drew apologised, adding, 'I won't stay and keep you up even longer.'

'Oh, Drew, we were going to have a cup of cocoa together,' Tilly reminded him.

But Drew shook his head, telling her gently, 'I think it's late enough,' before adding a polite, 'good night, Mrs Robbins.'

'Good night, Drew,' Olive said politely back.

Whatever doubts she might have about Tilly's behaviour, she couldn't fault Drew's good manners – or his trustworthiness. A young man as deeply in love as Drew so obviously was with Tilly might find that his desire to be trustworthy could be all too easily overwhelmed by her passionate rebelliousness. Olive felt the now-familiar ache of anxiety and despair tighten around her heart.

Of course Tilly had to see Drew to the door and of course once there it was several minutes before she came back, her lipstick having rather obviously been quickly reapplied in the hallway before she re-entered the kitchen.

'Poor Drew. I promised him a cup of cocoa and now—'

'Tilly, before we go to bed there's something I need to talk to you about,' Olive interrupted her.

It couldn't be put off any longer. She'd had all evening to think about what she must say, and a very long evening it had been as well, sitting here in the kitchen, on her own for the last hour, wondering about the true nature of that stolen hour Tilly had spent at the Simpsons' with Drew and what it might have led to.

Tilly stifled a yawn. 'If it's the fire-watching here on Article Row—' she began

'No it isn't,' Olive stopped her. 'It's about you going back to the Simpsons' tonight with Drew and the pair of you staying alone there for over an hour.'

Olive watched with a sinking heart as the colour came and went in Tilly's face before guilt gave way to a very definite look of defiance. Only now could she admit how much she had been hoping against hope that her daughter would be able to tell her that Nancy had been mistaken. Instead, Tilly was confirming all Olive's own secret fears and doubts by demanding instead, 'Who told you about that? Oh, I know. Nancy, of course.'

'So it's true then?' Olive asked, unable to conceal her distress. 'Instead of going out, as you had told me you were doing, you and Drew went back to the Simpsons'?

You have let me down, Tilly, and not only that, you deceived me as well. I know how you feel about Drew—'

'No, you don't,' Tilly stopped her mother bitterly. 'If you did you'd let us get married. That's what I want, it's what we both want, it's all I want. You had what you wanted, Mum. You married Dad. You had your time together, and you had me, but you won't let me and Drew have our love, and that's not fair.' Angrily Tilly began to turn away from her mother, and then stopped.

'And as for me deceiving you, I wasn't and I didn't. We only went back to the Simpsons' because Drew had forgotten the chocolates he'd bought me. We went to collect them, that's all. We started talking, about . . . about Drew's work, and we forgot about the time, so yes, we probably were in the Simpsons' for an hour, but we weren't doing anything wrong. Drew gave you his word about that,' Tilly reminded her mother proudly, 'and as he keeps telling me, nothing is going to make him break it.'

Tilly was shaking inside but she didn't want to let Olive see how let down and upset her mother's attitude made her feel.

As for Olive, instinctively she knew that Tilly was telling her the truth. She made a small conciliatory movement towards her daughter, but Tilly stepped back rejecting it and rejecting her.

She should never have listened to Nancy and let her get under her skin, Olive berated herself. She had let the other woman's unkind words play on her own secret anxieties and now this was the result. Tilly had become angry with her and even more protective about Drew and their relationship.

Olive felt so tired and alone. If Jim had lived, things would have been so different. He'd have been able to speak to Tilly as a father. But he wasn't. Tilly didn't have a father, and she, Olive, didn't have a husband.

Olive knew that she couldn't let Tilly go without at least attempting to sort things out between them. She took a deep breath. It was so important that she find a way of getting her headstrong daughter to understand how cruel and hard life could be to those who broke society's rules. And the truth was that Olive was beginning to suspect that Tilly – her Tilly, whom she had shielded and protected from babyhood – was headstrong enough to do exactly that, because she felt so strongly about Drew and her love for him. How could she find the words to discuss so difficult a subject? Olive wasn't like Tilly. She didn't have and never had had Tilly's fiercely passionate nature. She had loved Jim. She had enjoyed the tenderness of their lovemaking. But there had never ever been a time when they had been courting when she had been tempted to break those rules that said what a girl could and should and could not and should not allow a young man.

'Tilly, I'm sorry you feel that I don't understand.'

'You don't,' Tilly told her fiercely. 'You keep saying that you do, but you don't. You can't. This is *our* war, Mum, not yours. It's my generation of young men and young women who will suffer the most from this war. You forget that. We are the ones whose sweethearts could be lost, whose lives will be empty. We've seen what happened to your generation. We've seen all those women whose men never came back. We've grown up watching them live alone. Do you really blame us for wanting to have what we can whilst we can? That's what you don't and won't understand. You had Dad in your life, Mum. You and he were married, you had me, but you want to deny me those things because you're afraid for me. You had some happiness but you can't see that I want mine too, even if it is short-lived. In fact, that only makes me want it all the more, just in case I do lose it. Just in case I do lose Drew.'

Tilly was trembling, shaking with the intensity of her emotions, Olive could see, and she herself felt as though she were drowning in the darkness of her own pain. Tilly spoke so passionately about what she needed now, and so lightly about enduring future loss. She had no idea, no awareness of how swiftly and permanently the pain of that loss could make it feel as though the happiness that had gone before it had never been. All she wanted to do was protect her daughter, but Tilly was behaving as though she, Olive, was trying to hurt her, by denying her her chance of happiness.

Without giving her the opportunity to respond, Tilly had gone, the sound of her heels on the stairs making what seemed to Olive to be an angrily rejecting noise that deliberately distanced her from her mother.

Olive closed her eyes. To squeeze back her tears? As a young mother, a young widow, she hadn't allowed herself to feel sorry for herself, and she certainly wasn't going to do so now.

With quiet resolve she began the familiar task of leaving the kitchen ready for the morning. One day, please God, Tilly would have children of her own and then perhaps she would understand how she felt right now, Olive tried to comfort herself.

In their shared bedroom Agnes was already asleep. With the room so familiar to her, Tilly didn't need to disturb Agnes by switching on the light in order to get ready for bed. Despite the shortages that rationing was forcing on everyone, the bedroom was as cosy as Olive could make it, with warm rag rugs beside both beds and a square of carpet that covered most of the floor and protected the girls' feet from the cold linoleum. No winter night went by without Olive ensuring that every bed had its hot-water bottle, and automatically, as she burrowed beneath the warmth of the bedclothes, Tilly placed her feet on the blissful warmth of her own.

As always, though, the last thing she did before settling down for the night was to reach for Drew's ring, where it swung from her neck on its chain. Holding Drew's ring wasn't, of course, as wonderful as holding Drew himself would have been, and Tilly blamed her mother for that. Why wouldn't she understand that in trying to protect her from being hurt if she should lose Drew, her mother was in reality denying her the chance to have what she could have of him and their love? Arguing with her mother wasn't going to bring her round, though, Tilly knew. She would have to find another way to convince her.

SIX

'. . . And she's only been to see you that once and never come again, never mind that she's your wife? Well, I call that proper disgraceful, I really do. Mind you, I can't say that I'm surprised, her being the sort that she is.' Dulcie was rather enjoying herself. After all, it was far warmer here in the hospital that it had been this morning, dragged out by Sally to 'explore', in the cold drizzle, East Grinstead's high street with, in Dulcie's eyes at least, its boring old black and white timbered buildings and its shops with nothing on sale that could ever have compared to Selfridges at its height. Plus she'd received plenty of appreciative male attention from the other patients since she'd been shown into the ward half an hour ago, and now she was getting to dig some of the dirt on her old enemy, Lydia, into the bargain. And she'd got out of helping to get ready the large empty room that was being used for tonight's dance because she'd promised to sit here with David and bring him out of himself a bit.

'She isn't my wife any more.'

David's grim words – his first proper words to her

since she had sat down at his bedside – stopped Dulcie mid-flow as she stared at him in astonishment.

'Well, she might not be acting like she is, but legally—' she began.

'We're getting a divorce. After all, there isn't much point in a husband who can't perform his marital duties. Not when, like Lydia, you've got husband number two lined up, who can.'

Another girl might have recoiled from or been embarrassed by this reference to the extent of David's injuries, but Dulcie didn't possess that kind of sensitivity.

'I suppose the chap she's going to marry is the one I saw her with in London, when my young man took me out for dinner. Booked in as Mr and Mrs, as bold as brass, they were. I must say, though, that I'm surprised that Lydia's prepared to show herself up by letting you divorce her.'

'She isn't,' David told her. 'She's divorcing me – for adultery.'

Dulcie's eyes rounded. 'But I thought you said you couldn't . . .' she began.

He hadn't been at all pleased when he'd been told that Dulcie was coming to visit him. Seeing her yesterday had been a shock, reminding him far too painfully of a life he no longer had, the person he no longer was. He'd planned to ignore her in the hope that she would go away. He'd forgotten that Dulcie simply wasn't the kind of girl you could ignore, and now, to his astonishment, he discovered that there was something grimly cathartic about talking to her.

'It doesn't have to be real adultery, Dulcie,' he explained wryly. 'The solicitor just finds someone – a woman – who for a sum of money agrees to say that she and I spent the night together at an hotel after Lydia and I were married but before I ended up here.'

'You mean you're letting her get away with turning her back on you so that she can marry someone else?'

'It's the done thing when one is a gentleman.'

'Well, I don't know why you'd want to be a gentleman when Lydia certainly isn't a lady,' Dulcie told him roundly, giving him a reproving look when he started to laugh. Dulcie didn't like people laughing at her.

Someone else, overhearing the sound of David's laughter, was very pleased by it.

Mr Archibald MacIndoe, the surgeon, accompanied by George, had just entered the ward to take a look at his patients and talk with them. He turned to the younger man and said to him approvingly, 'Good work getting that young woman to spend some time with the group captain, Laidlaw. She's obviously raising his spirits, and that's just what we need to see.'

As George said to Sally later, when he joined her in the room that Sally and some of the duty nurses and other staff were decorating for the evening's dance, 'I have to admit that, like you, I wasn't sure if I'd done the right thing getting Dulcie to visit David.'

'You were obviously a better judge of the situation than me,' Sally told him generously, as he handed her a cup of tea.

The room hummed with everyone's chatter as they worked, pinning up decorations and inflating balloons, so that George had to move closer to her and raise his voice slightly as he responded.

140

'David certainly looked as though he was enjoying Dulcie's company when I took a quick peek into the ward ten minutes ago. He was actually joking with one of the other men and warning him off attempting to get Dulcie's attention.'

Sally smiled at him, her smile widening as he gave her an appreciative look.

'That's just the spirit we need to see in him,' George continued. 'He's recovered very well from the amputations and the skin grafts, and technically there's no reason why ultimately he shouldn't go home. He'll always be wheelchair-bound, of course, but with both his wife and his parents turning their backs on him . . .'

'He feels safer here?' Sally guessed. 'Poor boy. Come on,' she said after she'd finished her tea, 'if you've got some time to spare, you can hold the ladders for me whilst I put up this bunting the local WI has loaned us for the party. Apparently it was made for the celebrations after the end of the last war, so I've been warned that it's getting a bit fragile.'

'It's much the same era, then, as the gramophone we were also offered,' George grinned, 'and the records. Luckily one of the patients is a bit of a swing music fan and he's volunteered his own gramophone and records, provided his favourite nurse rewards him with a kiss, apparently.'

'No patient would ever get away with that at Barts,' Sally laughed.

'No, and neither would any other hospital I know of have barrels of beer on the wards for the patients, but then this is not like any other hospital, and our patients are not like most other patients. They are young, otherwise healthy and fit young men with all that that means, with the kind of injuries that no one should ever have to face. As Mr MacIndoe says, whatever it takes to get them to want to work towards the most normal kind of life they can have has to be undertaken. Mending their bodies as best we can on its own isn't enough.'

Archibald MacIndoe wasn't Dulcie's only champion. Ward Sister, making one of her inspections of her territory, noted the hubbub of activity and laughter coming from the end of the ward where was the group captain whose lack of interest in his own ultimate recovery had been causing her some concern. Speedily she made her way to David's bed and even more speedily assessed the situation.

A young woman who could look not just comfortable but actually preen herself at the attention she was receiving from a group of young men with the kind of injuries her patients had, and bring a smile to the faces of those young men who were able to smile, was someone who should be encouraged to repeat her visits, as far as Sister was concerned.

If Dulcie herself wasn't aware of the huge compliment she had been paid when she was actually offered a cup of tea by Sister herself, then others on the ward certainly were and duly took note.

Not that Dulcie was anyone's fool. She wasn't. She'd seen the looks one of the pretty nurses had been giving David, and she'd seen too the respect with which he was treated by the other men. With or without his legs, having a man like David as one's admirer could only add to a girl's status, especially now that Lydia wasn't going to be on the scene.

'Of course I'm going to the dance,' Dulcie responded to one young pilot's question.

'Good, the group captain can go with you,' Sister informed Dulcie, arriving at David's bed just in time to hear Dulcie's announcement, and quickly forestalling David's attempt to refuse by suggesting, 'I'm sure that your friend won't mind pushing your chair, will you, dear? We can get a couple of the other patients to help you if it's too heavy.'

'You don't have to go to the dance with me, you know. Lydia certainly wouldn't have wanted to,' David told Dulcie once Sister had gone, and he had asked the other men to 'push off so that I can have Dulcie to myself for a few minutes'.

'Well, I'm not Lydia, am I?' Dulcie retorted. 'You don't want to let her get away with what she's done, you know, David. Walking out on you and then getting you to give her a divorce when she's the one that's done wrong.'

'I can't blame her, Dulcie. She and I never pretended to be in love with one another, after all, and she's not like you, you know.'

'And what's that supposed to mean?' Dulcie demanded.

'It means,' David told her, 'that you are the kind of girl that a man just can't help being tempted to fall in love with.'

Dulcie gave a contented sigh. The compliments David was paying her were no more than her due. Of course, it was a pity that David had lost his legs and wouldn't be able to dance with her like he had done at the Hammersmith Palais that night he had joined her there, but the truth was that she had enjoyed herself far more here today, basking in the admiration of a group of young men whom she knew would not make real advances to her because she was David's friend and they admired and respected him, than she did when she went out with Wilder. David was far more relaxing than Wilder, with his sometimes uncertain temper, his unreliability, his constant attempts to persuade her into a more sexual relationship with him than she wanted. That didn't mean, though, that she intended to traipse all the way down to East Grinstead regularly. It was nearly thirty miles from London, after all, and in the country, which had no appeal whatsoever for Dulcie. She wasn't like Sally, who had announced over breakfast this morning that she couldn't wait for the weather to warm up so that she could go for long walks in the nearby countryside.

Although Mr MacIndoe allowed open visiting, knowing how difficult it often was for some families to come down and see their loved ones, hospital routine still had to be followed, and it was time for David to have a rest and for the nurses to attend to their patients' needs.

Dulcie swept out of the ward as regally as any queen enjoying the adulation of her admirers, feeling very pleased with herself indeed.

She was still feeling pleased with herself over an hour later as she regaled Sally with how well received her visit had been, over an early tea of sardines on toast in their landlady's kitchen.

'And Sister specially asked me to push David's chair to the dance tonight on account of him only agreeing to go because of me. Of course, he was always pretty keen on me.'

Feeling that Dulcie had enjoyed enough admiration for one day, Sally turned to Persephone, who had returned to the house ahead of them, asking her gently, 'How are you feeling? I hope you don't mind, but George was explaining to me about your brother's condition and how both your parents are too upset by it to be able to come and visit him. You've been a wonderful sister to him, Persephone, and it can't be easy for you. I know from nursing patients who've suffered mental damage from the war that they are the very hardest to treat.'

Persephone jumped and looked flustered. The poor girl obviously wasn't used to anyone paying her attention or showing her any concern, Sally thought sympathetically.

'Poor Roddy,' she responded unsteadily. 'He was to have been a professor, you know. Daddy was very cross with him when he enlisted.'

'Mental damage? Dulcie asked. 'What's up with him, then?'

Sally exhaled silently. Really, Dulcie could be dreadfully thoughtless at times.

'Persephone's brother was badly burned when he tried to rescue his men. It's left him mentally scarred, Dulcie. All the men suffer inwardly, as well as outwardly, because of what they've been through, but for some men that inward suffering is very bad indeed.'

'It was Dunkirk,' Persephone told them both simply. 'They were captured when they were heading for the coast. They tried to escape, and my brother was shot and left for dead. The others were locked in a barn and then it was set on fire.'

She was sitting bolt upright, the hands she had folded

neatly in her lap shaking terribly. Sally reached out and covered them with one of her own.

'Sometimes he thinks he's still there. He doesn't understand that he's safe now here in England. He lost his sight so he can't see anyone. He . . . sometimes he can be violent. He thinks he's protecting his men. Then other times he just screams. I think he'd be better if he could come home and have familiar things around him, but Daddy just can't bear the thought of it. He was so very clever, you see. Brilliant, everyone said, and now . . .'

Tears rolled down her face, causing Sally's heart to tighten with angry grief.

There was a good turnout for the dance, with both the nurses and the townspeople there to make sure that the men had as good a time as it was possible for them to have.

Dulcie might have pushed David's chair into the room where the dance was being held, but naturally she left it to his friends to secure the table of her choice for their party, right slap bang where everyone could see them.

The bunting, despite its age, still managed to put on a brave show, Sally thought, rather like the men themselves, who despite their various injuries were all spruced up and clean-shaven.

Sally, who had lent a hand herself, along with the nurses on duty, to ensure that those men who were not able to help themselves did get a shave, knew how much it meant to these proud young men to feel that they were accepted.

Some of the nurses were already getting their patients up to dance to the swing music records, and Sally quickly joined in, asking a young man who was undergoing some particularly painful facial reconstruction surgery, and to whom George had introduced her earlier in the day, if he would dance with her.

Just wait until she told Wilder about this dance, Dulcie thought happily. She'd certainly make sure that he knew that she hadn't been sitting around on her own all weekend because he hadn't been able to get leave. She'd tell him about David too, of course, and she might even just drop into the conversation the fact that one day David would be a sir. Wilder liked to think that because he was American and had money, that meant that she was lucky to be going out with him. Dulcie hadn't said anything before, but now that David was back in her life it wouldn't do any harm to let Wilder know about him.

The young owner of the gramophone had a good selection of records, including 'Whispering Grass' and 'A Nightingale Sang in Berkeley Square', and Sally, held tightly in George's arms when they finally managed to snatch a dance together, certainly didn't mind the fact that the latter was being played for the third time.

The sight of the stones in her engagement ring catching the light brought a soft smile to her lips and had her moving discreetly closer to George.

'Happy?' he asked her.

'Very. It was so kind of your mother to write to me as she did, George, welcoming me to your family so warmly.'

'She'd have done that anyway, but I know that having lost her own parents just after she and Dad were married, she's especially aware of your own loss in that regard.'

For once Sally was glad that George was slightly clumsy on his feet as she missed a step and he apologised as though it had been his fault.

She had never intended actually to deceive George when she had told him that she had no family. That was, after all, what she felt and believed – and very passionately, as well. She had denied her father because she had felt that his betrayal meant that he wasn't her father any more. Her words, though, were now having unintended consequences. George, and now his family, believed that both her parents were dead, and that wasn't the truth. George's mother had written the kindest of letters to her in which she had sympathised with her because of that loss. The reality, of course, was that her father was not only very much alive, but that he had remarried after her mother's death and that she, Sally, had a half-sister who would be one year old in May.

Sally hated deceit of any kind. It was because of deceit that she had cut herself off from her father. But how could she explain the real situation to George now? She couldn't. They had initially exchanged family histories as colleagues and virtual strangers. There'd been no need for her to go into detail and she certainly hadn't wanted to reveal the extent of her own hurt. It had been too raw and she had had no idea then that they would end up loving one another.

And then there was the issue of how George's mother might judge her – a young woman she had only heard about from the son who had fallen in love with her, and who she was having to trust would love him as any mother would want their child to be loved – if Sally were

148

to attempt to explain her history now, and her reasons for behaving as she had.

Logical and reasonable though her thinking was, nothing could make her feel comfortable about the situation, Sally knew. She loved George. She didn't want there to be any secrets between them. But even now, Sally also knew that she did not want to talk about what had happened, even to George. The reality for her was that though her father was alive, to her he was no longer her father. She still believed that it would be a betrayal of everything she felt for her mother if she were to accept even within herself that she had a father and a half-sister. She was the only person now to keep loyal to her mother.

One day, she hoped, she would be a mother herself, and when she was . . . When she was, would she be able to understand and accept a daughter-in-law who had deceived her own son?

George's teasing, 'Are you all right? Only you are looking very fierce' had her smiling. Surely it was true that she did not have a family any more, even if that was by her own choice? She had cut herself off from her past. Her father belonged to that past.

SEVEN

'Morning, Mrs Robbins.'

'Morning, Barney,' Olive responded with a warm smile pushing back the stray lock of hair that was being tousled by the boisterous March wind.

She'd seen Sergeant Dawson and Barney heading for Article Row as she turned out of it. She was on her way to meet up with Audrey Windle and some of the other members of their WVS group. They were going to help out at one of the refuge centres organised by the Government to provide assistance for people made homeless by the bombing.

She hadn't planned to stop. Nancy's warnings to her about her widowed status, and her own shameful thoughts – and feelings – about Sergeant Dawson had made her feel self-conscious about anyone, including Sergeant Dawson himself, thinking the wrong thing, but since Barney was virtually standing in front of her she had no choice.

No amount of washing and ironing of his clothes on the part of Mrs Dawson had managed to tidy him up completely, Olive thought ruefully. The collar of his shirt, in contrast with the immaculate neatness of Sergeant Dawson's shirt, was slightly crooked at one side, one sleeve of his Fair Isle pullover baggy and stretched, whilst his knees, below his grey short trousers, were distinctly grubby.

'I was wondering,' he said, eyeing her determinedly, 'if you would mind if I was to go into your garden to see if there's any shrapnel there?'

Olive smiled again. Collecting shrapnel had become something of a hobby and a contest between young boys in the aftermath of the bombing.

'Of course not, Barney. In fact, I'm sure that Sally would be very pleased if you were to remove any shrapnel that might be there from our veggie bed.'

Barney's answering brisk nod of his head was so very much in the manner of Sergeant Dawson, and so obviously copied from him, that it really touched Olive's heart.

'You go and tell Mrs Dawson that we're on our way, will you, Barney?' the sergeant instructed. 'I want to have a few words with Mrs Robbins.'

'He's settled in really well,' Olive commented when Barney nodded his head again and set off for number 1.

'Yes, he has. It hasn't all been plain sailing, though. We've had Nancy round every week since he came to us, and sometimes more than once a week, with some complaint or another. Her latest is that she found him in her garden. Told me that she thought he was looking to see what he could steal.' The sergeant's voice was grim with protective indignation. 'I told her that he would only have been looking for shrapnel. Of course, he should have asked her first, but he's a boy who hasn't had anyone in his life to show him how things should be done until now. The truth is that he pretty much ran wild and did as he pleased. I keep telling Mrs Dawson that we're going to have to be a bit stricter with him, help him to understand that rules are there for a reason, but the minute my back's turned she's ignoring what we've agreed.'

'I expect she just wants him to be happy,' Olive responded. After all, wasn't that what all parents wanted – for their children to be happy? Happy and safe. It might be nearly a month since Valentine's Day but things were still not back to normal between her and Tilly. Not really. Tilly hadn't said anything but there was a distance between them that hurt, and so far Tilly had rebuffed all her attempts to bridge it.

A sudden gust of March wind caught at Olive's headscarf, whipping it away before she could grab hold of it. Sergeant Dawson, though, was faster, snatching it up as the wind whirled it around and handing it back to her.

'I couldn't find my Kirbigrips this morning,' Olive told him, as she thanked him and took her scarf from him. 'You can't buy them any more because of the war.'

Their hands touched briefly, Olive immediately pulling her own hand back.

Archie Dawson's hands were those of a man who worked hard with them: good strong hands. A true man's hands, Olive recognised. The kind of hands that belonged to a man who would do all those things about the home that a woman couldn't always do for herself, no matter how practically-minded and determined to be independent she might be. The kind of hands that belonged to a man who would always try to keep those he loved safe. Her Jim's hands had gone so frail and thin in the last weeks of his life. His sickness had taken all the strength from them so that he hadn't even been able to hold a cup to his lips. Olive had had to do that for him.

'Why I wanted to have a word with you was to tell you that we've got the stirrup pumps at last. The best thing would be for me to bring one round, show you how it works and then leave it with you, seeing as you're the one who's going to be in charge of our local fire-watching group,' he told her.

'Oh, yes . . .'

Of course Archie Dawson's only reason for talking to her was to do with something official. And that was exactly what she herself wanted. What she wanted and the way things must be.

'I could come round tomorrow evening after I come off duty, if that suits?'

'Yes, yes,' Olive agreed.

'It's very good what you've done sorting out a fire-watching group for Article Row, Olive.'

His unexpected praise pierced her guard. Before she could stop herself she heard herself telling him, 'Nancy doesn't think so. In fact, she disapproves. She told me that she didn't think that Jim's parents would have approved.'

'That's nonsense. For one thing, knowing how Jim's ma felt about her house, I can't see her not welcoming someone making an effort to make sure that Article Row is kept safe.' He paused and then said, 'Jim would have been proud of you, Olive.'

'Would he?' She wasn't sure. Sometimes now Jim seemed so far away from her that she found it hard to think what he would have felt had he been here now.

'Of course he would. You've been a wonderful mother to your Tilly and— What is it?' he asked when Olive made a small distressed sound and shook her head.

'Nothing,' she fibbed. 'I mustn't keep you any longer. Mrs Dawson will be wondering where you are.'

'I doubt it. She complains that I've kept under her feet now that she's got Barney to look after.'

'Oh dear.' Her immediate stab of sympathy took Olive's thought away from her own worries. 'Is she finding Barney a bit too much?'

'No, she dotes on him. I'm the one who she's finding a bit too much. She says that I'm too hard on the lad – you know, about having a set bedtime and that kind of thing.'

'All children need rules,' Olive agreed.

'I think so, but Mrs Dawson doesn't agree with me. In fact, I'm in the doghouse right now for telling her that being so soft on Barney won't do him any good in the long run. She's afraid, you see, that he won't want to stay, and she's taken to him that much that she can't bear the thought of him going.'

'I'm sure things will work out,' Olive offered.

The sergeant gave her another rueful look but made no comment other than to say, 'I'll see you tomorrow evening. About seven?'

Holding on to her headscarf, Olive nodded before they went their separate ways.

EIGHT

'Drew, please let me come with you when you meet up with this man who's promised to talk to you about this gang of looters he's involved with,' Tilly coaxed as she snuggled up next to Drew in the fuggy beer-and-cigarette-scented warmth of their favourite Fleet Street pub, Ye Olde Cheshire Cheese.

'Tilly, you know I can't. It might not be safe. Your mother would never forgive me if anything happened to you, and I'd never forgive myself.'

'What about if something happened to you? I'm tired of having to do what my mother says all the time, Drew. I hate being eighteen. Why can't I be twenty or, even better, twenty-one, and then I could please myself what I do? You said that I could be involved in finding out more about these looting gangs,' she reminded him.

'And you can, but not tomorrow afternoon, Tilly. Look, I'll make it up to you, I promise. We're going dancing at the Café de Paris in the West End tomorrow night, remember, with Dulcie and Wilder.'

The newly refurbished nightclub had recently reopened and was very popular with the smart set. Dulcie had insisted on Wilder taking her there to make up for not being able to take her out on Valentine's Day. The famous 'Snakehips' Johnson was to be the band leader for the evening. Once she would have been thrilled at the thought of such a treat, Tilly acknowledged, but not now.

'Dancing? Who cares about that? I want to be with you when you talk to this looter, Drew. We're a pair, you said. I want to share what you're doing. I don't want to be pushed to one side and kept safe.'

'You don't want to go dancing? Is this the Tilly who told me that she wanted to go to the Hammersmith Palais so much that she fibbed to her mother?' Drew teased.

Tilly wasn't so easily placated, though. 'I was just a silly girl then. I've grown up now . . . since I met you. I just want to be with you, Drew,' she repeated. 'I want to share in what you're doing.'

'Sweetheart, don't look at me like that,' Drew protested, reaching for her hand. 'You know what I've promised your mother.'

'I know that no matter what we promise her, she prefers to believe Nancy than me,' Tilly objected angrily. 'She's proved that. She might say that she accepts that Nancy was wrong and that she's sorry she doubted me. I think she wants to doubt me so that she's got an excuse not to let us get married now, like I want to do. She just doesn't understand. She doesn't *want* to understand.'

Drew pulled her closer. He knew how upset Tilly still was about the quarrel she had had with her mother over their Valentine's Day call at the Simpsons'. He blamed himself for Nancy's mischief-making and had said so to Tilly's mother, who had readily accepted his explanation and even apologised to him for doubting them, but that hadn't been enough for Tilly. Unusually for her she had refused to forgive her mother. Drew had tried gently to persuade her to think again. He knew how much she loved her mother and how much this misunderstanding between them must secretly be hurting her, but Tilly had proved unexpectedly determined not to relent. The reason for that, as Drew knew, was Tilly's longing for them to be able to marry – and soon. It was a longing he shared, but he didn't want to make the situation even worse by encouraging Tilly to continue her hostility towards her mother. Drew admired and liked Olive, and in the end he knew that what hurt Olive would hurt Tilly as well, even though right now she would refuse to accept that.

'Sometimes I think that you're more on my mother's side than mine,' Tilly complained. 'It makes me wonder if you really do want to marry me, Drew, or—'

'Of course I want to marry you. Of *course* I do. You must never think otherwise, Tilly. The only way I could ever stop wanting you to be my wife would be if you told me yourself that you didn't want that. You must never ever doubt how I feel about you, Tilly. Please promise me that you won't.'

Tilly's anger and distress melted away as she heard the genuine emotion in his voice.

'Very well,' she agreed, 'but you've got to admit that you do always seem to agree with Mum.'

'I'm not really taking your mother's side, Tilly, I just don't want—'

'Would you be as willing to understand if it was your mother who was doubting you and refusing to accept that you're old enough to know your own mind?' Tilly interrupted him.

The bleak, almost haunted look that suddenly shad-owed his eyes suspended her voice, leaving her more concerned about Drew than she was about herself.

'Drew, what is it?'

'Nothing.'

'There must have been something to make you look like that,' Tilly persisted.

Drew was still holding her hand, and now he began to play with her fingers, stroking them gently, a habit he had when he was thinking deeply about something.

'Tilly, I don't—' he began.

Tightening her fingers comfortingly round his, Tilly interrupted to tell him lovingly, 'You don't want there to be upset between me and Mum, I know that, Drew, and so does she.' Tilly's voice sharpened, her focus so much on her own grievances that she failed to see the shadow in Drew's eyes darkening still further before he banished it to listen to her. 'That's why she keeps asking you to give her your word about what we can and can't do. And that's not fair, it really isn't. I've tried to explain to her how I feel. There are so many women who are alone now because they lost someone during the last war. I see it when I'm typing up records at the hospital of patients' names and details, I've seen it on Article Row with the Misses Barker, and I see it with Mum as well. Now we're in the middle of another war and if we were to lose one another, Drew, if I were to be the one to have to live on without you, then I know how much I'd need the comfort of my memories of you and our love. Mum's denying me the opportunity to be happy now and to make those memories because she thinks that us being together properly would make it harder for me. I don't understand how she can say that. She had her own special time with Dad and she had me because of that.' Tilly gripped Drew's hand tightly, her voice blurred with anguish. 'What she's saying to me now makes me wonder if she would have preferred not to have had me, Drew.'

'Tilly, you must never think that,' Drew protested, anxious to comfort and reassure her. 'Your mother loves you dearly, anyone can see that.'

'Yes, she does, but does she secretly wish that she hadn't had to love me? Does she secretly think that her life would have been easier without me? If she hadn't married Dad, if she hadn't had me, then perhaps she might have met and married someone else . . .'

'Tilly, your mother would never think anything like that.'

'How do you know? How do any of us know what someone else really thinks? We can only know what they tell us, can't we?'

Tilly couldn't possibly know how guilty those words made Drew feel or how much they cut into his conscience. He should have told her the truth right from the start. If he had . . . If he had then she wouldn't be with him like this now. If he had she would have rejected any advances he had made to her, he knew. He mustn't think about that now, though. He must concentrate on re-assuring Tilly that her mother truly loved he.

'Your mother has always told you that she loves you,' he reminded her gently. 'You've said that yourself.'

'She's said the words, Drew, and I've always believed them, but now with her being the way she is over us, I can't help questioning—'

'Why don't you talk to her? Why don't you tell her what you've told me?'

'What's the point? She'll only tell me what she wants me to hear. She wouldn't want to hurt me, I know that. So she'll say that I'm wrong, but how can I know that? How can any of us know what another person really feels?' Tilly moved even closer towards Drew, seeking the comfort of his nearness.

Putting his arm around her as she nestled against him, her head on his shoulder, Drew closed his eyes briefly against the terrible weight of his conscience. He had been so close to telling Tilly everything, so very close. And if he had, would she now be putting him in the same category as her mother, as someone who – she felt she couldn't trust to be honest with her? If only he'd told her right from the start. But he hadn't known then that this – they – would happen, and by the time he had known it had been too late to tell her the truth because he had been afraid that the tenderness of their burgeoning new love wouldn't be able to bear the strain of what he had to say and that she would reject him. Now they must both pay the price of his cowardice – he himself because of the wretched misery he had to live with because he hadn't told her, and Tilly because his deceit placed in jeopardy her complete trust and belief in him.

'Come on,' he told her. 'We'd better start heading back to Article Row. I'm getting hungry and your mom makes a terrific fish pie.'

Recognising that Drew was trying to lighten her mood, Tilly smiled. It was after all true that her mother was a wonderful homemaker and cook, somehow managing to make their rations stretch to genuinely tasty meals. Drew's insistence on 'helping out' because he was eating so many of his meals at number 13 benefited them all, of course, especially when it came to the boxes of food that came for him from his home in America. Tilly's mother had tried to refuse this largesse but Drew had simply told her that if she did then it would be wasted because it was far too much for him alone. So her mother had accepted the food but had insisted on donating some of it to the WVS for distribution to those who were homeless.

Friday's traditional fish pie, though, came from everyone's rations, even if it was likely to be supplemented by tinned tomatoes from Drew's mother's gifts.

The people who eventually assembled at number 13 ready for Sergeant Dawson's stirrup pump demonstration did not include every member of Olive's group. Sally was working nights, for one thing, and had left for the hospital, and Ian Simpson and several other neighbours had all been called up for fire-watching duties by their employers. Dulcie, meanwhile, had retired to her bedroom, having flatly refused to get involved, saying that she planned to varnish her nails ready for her evening out at the Ritz. However, there were enough people there to fill Olive's kitchen and spill out into her hallway.

All of them were, of course, familiar with the sight and the function of a stirrup pump. The devices had been around from the beginning of the war, after all, but since this was the first time they were going to be given the equipment in an official capacity as recognised fire-watchers, rather than individual householders, a mood of determination and responsibility was very much in evidence amongst the older members of the group, especially the Misses Barker, who had been telling Drew how they had wanted to volunteer to drive ambulances during the last war but how their parents had refused to let them.

'I expect that was because they wanted to protect you,' Olive offered, overhearing the conversation and giving Tilly a meaningful look.

There wasn't time for Tilly to retaliate, because a knock on the door had her mother going to admit Sergeant Dawson and one of the young messengers employed by their local ARP unit, who had wheeled round the wheelbarrow from which he and the sergeant removed a Redhill container, a long-handled scoop, a hoe, a galvanised metal bucket and the stirrup pump itself, carrying them into the kitchen, where they carefully put them down in the middle of the circle formed by the would-be fire-watchers.

'Ideally every household should have its own pump, but we've been issued with only enough to provide each street with a couple at the moment,' Sergeant Dawson informed them before accepting Olive's offer of a cup of tea.

'Olive's given us chocolate as well,' Miss Mary Barkers told Sergeant Dawson happily.

'It's from Drew really. His mother sends it to him from America,' Olive put in quickly. Nancy wasn't here but she'd become so aware of her neighbour's tendency to find fault that automatically she felt defensive.

'After we gave young Barney his English lesson the other day he asked us if he could have a look in our

162

tool shed to see if there are any spare wheels in there. Of course, we had to tell him that there aren't.'

The two Misses Barker were retired teachers, and at Sergeant and Mrs Dawson's request were giving Barney extra lessons to make up for the time he had had off school before they had taken him in.

'He's hoping to build himself a bit of a go-cart with some boys he's got friendly with at school,' Sergeant Dawson told them. 'They've got some ideas of making their own fire truck. Some of the older boys started making them and following the fire engines, and now the younger ones want to do the same. Barney says that he wants to make an Article Row fire truck.'

'Oh, how brave of him!' Jane Barker applauded, asking her sister, 'Might there be something in the shed amongst Father's things that he could use, Mary?'

'Aren't you worried that Barney could get hurt?' Olive asked the sergeant.

'There's no harm in him making his fire truck, but when it comes to him using it you can be sure that I shall be keeping a very watchful eye on him,' he assured her.

Olive busied herself pouring the sergeant and the messenger boy cups of tea. After handing the messenger boy his cup she hesitated. If Tilly hadn't been so deeply engrossed in her conversation with Drew she could have asked her to give the sergeant his tea, but as it was she had no alternative but to take a deep breath and then offer him the cup and saucer.

'Thanks, Olive.'

When a man had large hands, as Archie Dawson did, it was unavoidable that that hand should touch her own when he took the cup and saucer from her. That might be completely natural, but her own reaction to that brief contact was neither natural nor acceptable in a widow of her age where a married man was concerned, Olive mentally chastised herself.

'I've heard that in some streets they're setting up a collection so that they can buy their own extra pumps,' Eric Charlton, one of the tenants who rented number 48, one of Mr King's properties, announced. A short mousy-looking man with a thin moustache, who worked at the Ministry of Agriculture and who had turned his back garden into a model of a 'grow your own' plot, his comment earned him the immediate disapproval of Mr Whittaker from number 50.

'Ruddy government,' he said angrily, 'making us pay for what they should provide us with. It's bad enough having to form our own fire-watching team without being expected to pay for equipment as well.' Scowling he glowered at poor Mr Charlton, who huddled closer to his rotund wife, as Len Whittaker gave vent to his feelings.

Anxiously Olive listened to him. His anger did not bode well for the unity of their small group.

As though he had guessed what she was thinking, Archie Dawson leaned towards her and told her in a comforting undertone, 'Don't worry about Mr Whittaker leaving, Olive. I reckon he's just taken the huff because you'll be having the stirrup pump at this end of the Row. After all, it isn't as though he couldn't afford to buy himself one. He's reckoned to be pretty comfortably off.'

'You wouldn't think so from the state of his house,'

Olive whispered back, equally discreetly, as she stepped back slightly from him and tried not to blush when she saw the slightly questioning look he was giving her. She had to stop being so silly. Archie Dawson was a neighbour, after all, and a very good one. He had done nothing wrong. 'I've started taking him down a plated-up Sunday dinner since the Longs left, and number 50 is so threadbare inside you'd think that he didn't have two pennies to rub together,' she told him, determined to behave normally. 'Poor Mr Charlton was only telling Sally the other day that he's worried that the seeds from the weeds in Mr Whittaker's garden are going to blow over and take root in his plot. He has to wage a constant war against them.'

'A bit like us, then, with these,' the sergeant told Olive with another smile, gesturing towards the waiting equipment before turning back to the assembled volunteers and telling them, 'I know that most of you will be aware of how incendiary bombs work, but since we've had the Germans dropping this new and more dangerous version of them on us I thought that to start off I'd just run through with you exactly what they are. German planes drop a large bomb casing loaded with small sticks – bomblets – of incendiaries. This casing is designed to open at altitude, scattering the bomblets in order to cover a larger area. Originally the purpose of these was to light up targets for the following planes to drop much heavier bombs on, but since they've realised how much damage these incendiaries can inflict on people and their homes, the Germans have taken to dropping even more of them, and they've modified them to make them even more dangerous.

165

'An explosive charge inside them ignites the incendiary material, which is usually magnesium. This causes a fire, which can extend six to eight feet around the bomb, showering anyone who tries to get close to it with burning pieces of metal. Magnesium can't be put out by throwing water on it, although of course the fires caused by the sparks can be dowsed in water. It is because of these sparks that we have to have buckets of sand in which to dowse the incendiaries, and why we need to act with speed before they can explode properly.

'The actual incendiaries, as many of you will have already seen, are bomblets weighing about two pounds, contained in a relatively narrow cylinder. At one end of this cylinder there is a set of sharp fins, which enable the incendiary to penetrate surfaces such as roof tiles and the wooden beams beneath them. It is very, very dangerous for anyone to try to pick up one of these incendiaries without taking the precautions I am going to outline to you in a minute. I must stress how dangerous these newer incendiaries are. They are at their most deadly when they are nearly burned out because that's when their flames reach the explosive, which is located under the fin. It is therefore the fin and just above it that is the most lethal part of these devices.'

'Well, I'd heard that the best way to tackle an incendiary, if it hasn't got fastened into anything, is to grab hold of it, smash it down hard on something to separate it from the fin,' Eric Charlton said.

'I have heard of firemen doing that,' the sergeant agreed, 'and I've also heard of firemen who have lost a hand, or more, through doing it. Here on Article Row we aren't looking for heroes, especially dead ones.'

Olive noted with gratitude the collective sucked-in breaths of his listeners. How wise he was to give them all a stark warning of the danger of trying to be too gung-ho.

'Now,' Sergeant Dawson continued, 'when it comes to those incendiaries that can be dealt with, this is how to do that.' Turning towards Olive he asked her, 'If I could trouble you for a bucketful of water, Ol— Mrs Robbins?' before turning back to his audience.

'If you aren't already doing so just make sure that you fill what you can with cold water at night, just in case, especially baths, because should a local water main be hit then your stirrup pump isn't going to work.

'Hitler's incendiary bombs are designed to penetrate any roofs on which they land, via their sharp fins. Then once they're safely inside, they'll explode, showering whatever room they're in with burning magnesium sparks that will quickly start fires. Our task as fire-watchers is to make sure that that doesn't happen, and that's why every time there's an air-raid warning the first thing you do is make sure that those who are supposed to be watching for falling incendiaries do so. That's why you need a team of watchers, in pairs say, one every five or six houses. It's the same principle as that old warning that a stitch in time saves nine. Spotting where the incendiaries fall means that with luck your team can get to them and put them out before they get the opportunity to do any damage. And that's where your Redhill container and your long-handled shovel and hoe come in.

'Say, for instance, one of you saw an incendiary fall, the closest watcher would send his or her partner round to the house concerned with their equipment. The long handle of the hoe and the shovel mean that it's possible for whoever is using them to keep well away from the bomb itself whilst they scoop some sand out of the container to put on the bomb to put the fire out. The sand and the bomb can then be hoed up and placed in the container itself to be doubly sure it is out.

'As an alternative, or if a fire has already taken hold, what you must do is carefully open the door onto the room with the fire, making sure that you keep the door between you and the fire, and then aim the water from the pump either at the ceiling to fall on the fires, or at the fire itself.

'Keeping your sand in a wheelbarrow can be a good idea. Then you've got it readily transportable.'

'Well, I certainly won't be filling my wheelbarrow with sand,' Mr Charlton protested. 'I need my barrow for my gardening. And there's no point in saying we buy more. They can't be had.'

'I'm sure we'll be able to manage between us,' Olive assured him. It was so kind of Sergeant Dawson to put himself out like this, especially when some people were being so unenthusiastic.

'If you wish, on Sunday after church I'll be available to give a practical demonstration of what I mean whilst it's still light,' the sergeant offered generously.

'It all sounds very complicated and dangerous. If you ask me I'd say it would be better for us to let the professionals deal with any fires, instead of trying to do it ourselves,' said Mrs Charlton apprehensively.

'Nonsense,' Miss Jane Barker spoke up firmly, 'although, Olive my dear, if I can make one suggestion it would be that you pair up those of us who aren't as agile as we once were for fire-watching duty with a younger person who is steadier and swifter on their feet. I do believe too that we can manage our garden without our wheelbarrow, if that will help.'

Drew smiled as he listened to her. He felt so proud to be accepted by these brave and stalwart people that he had come to admire so much. When he wrote his articles for his newspaper back at home he tried to convey something of the simple unselfconscious, shrugged aside as 'nothing special' bravery, of the ordinary people of London, but so often he felt that he was not doing them justice. The truth was, he suspected, that you had to be here to understand and appreciate the true nature of a Londoner's determination to save their city.

It was gone ten o'clock before everyone had gone, the Misses Barker and, rather surprisingly, Mr Whittaker, lingering until well after the sergeant had excused himself to return to his duties.

'Of course, the fact that Mr Whittaker is still here has nothing to do with Mum's offer of supper,' Tilly said ruefully to Agnes, as she mashed up a tin of American corned beef with some cold boiled potatoes, whilst Agnes diced some onions, ready to make the mix into corned beef hash, for Olive to fry for supper.

'I feel sorry for him,' Agnes told her as Tilly wrinkled her nose, grateful that Agnes had volunteered to slice the onions, knowing that Tilly was going out dancing the following night and wouldn't want any lingering smell on her hands. 'He must be so lonely living on his own, especially now that the Longs have gone and their house is empty.'

'You're a softie, do you know that?' Tilly teased her. 'He's such a crosspatch and so mean.'

'He used to give money to the orphanage,' Agnes told her. 'We all used to be frightened of him because when we walked past his house he would come out into the garden and glare at us. Matron always said that we shouldn't judge him because only God knows what is truly in a person's heart.'

'Is that mash ready, girls?' Olive demanded, hurrying in from the front room where she'd settled her 'team'. 'Put the kettle on again, will you, Tilly? They'll have to eat their supper in here. I'm not having my front room smelling of fried meat and potato and onions, even if it is a blessing to be able to have onions again after last year's shortage. Sally's done us all proud with those she's grown.'

'Please change your mind and take me with you tomorrow, Drew,' Tilly begged a little later when everyone else had left and she was saying a final good night to Drew in the protective darkness outside the front door.

'You know I can't,' said Drew.

'That means that I'm going to have to do something far more dangerous than sit with you whilst you listen to someone telling you about the looters,' Tilly sighed.

'What do you mean?' Drew demanded, alarmed.

'I mean that now I'm going to have to go round the markets whilst Dulcie looks for a new dress to wear tomorrow night.'

Drew relaxed. 'Oh, yes, that sounds very dangerous indeed,' he agreed, mock solemnly.

'It will be,' Tilly assured him. 'You don't know what

Dulcie can be like when she's got her mind fixed on something. From the minute she persuaded Wilder to go to the Café de Paris she's been going on about getting herself what she calls "a really posh frock like ladies and that wear", and knowing Dulcie, that will mean going round every second-hand stall in London until she finds what she wants.'

'Mmm, sounds a terrible way to spend a Saturday afternoon,' Drew agreed, bending his head to kiss her.

'Afternoon *and* morning,' Tilly told him, holding him off for a few seconds before wrapping her arms around his neck and responding to his kiss with an appreciative, 'Mmm. Drew, that is so nice.'

NINE

'Well, what was wrong with that pretty crêpe de Chine we saw on that first stall we looked at, Dulcie, the grey one with the cream lace collar?'

'That thing? It looked like something a schoolteacher would wear. No, I want something much better than that. I want the sort of thing a proper lady with a title would wear, Tilly. After all, it *is* the Café de Paris that Wilder's taking me to.'

Tilly sighed. She wanted to urge Dulcie to be careful about making too much of an effort on Wilder's behalf. She didn't want her friend to end up being hurt, although she knew that if she said as much to Dulcie herself she would tell her scornfully that nothing could hurt her.

'What's going on over there?' Dulcie demanded.

'Where?' Tilly asked her. It was a raw cold March day with spring still too far away for anyone to feel that winter was ever going to end. Huddled into her coat, her knitted hat pulled right down over the tips of her ears to keep them warm, Tilly would have given anything to be with Drew instead of here.

'That stall we was looking at a little while back, the one that had next to nothing on it and them women hanging around looking shifty. You know, the ones that I said looked like they were some sort of Soho men's club cabaret dancers – or worse. The canvas has been let down like she's about to close the stall but them women are still there. Summat's going on there and I want to know what it is.'

Without waiting to see if Tilly was with her, Dulcie immediately plunged into the crowd, leaving Tilly to follow her as she set off at a fast walk between the market stalls. Sliding on the greasy cobbles, Tilly almost had to run to catch up with her.

''Ere, I'm closed. You can't come barging in here. So take yourself off,' the stall holder was protesting to Dulcie by the time Tilly caught up with her and managed to wriggle her way around the canvas as Dulcie herself had done.

'Closed, is it?' Dulcie demanded, eyeing the tumble of clothes spilling out of the half-open scruffy and worn-looking suitcase that was now lying on the otherwise bare boards of the stall. 'So what's them then?'

'It's private orders, that's what it is,' one of the three girls they had seen at the stall earlier told Dulcie, eyeing her angrily. There wasn't any hesitation or shrinking back in the other young women now, Tilly noted. Quite the opposite. Their manner reminded Tilly of alley cats ready to fight over a piece of discarded fish. Enclosed in this small space with them, Tilly couldn't help staring a little at their garish stage makeup. They were all wearing bright blue eye shadow, rouge staining their cheeks and their lips covered in deep red lipstick, whilst

173

their carefully curled hair was beginning to uncurl in the cold damp air.

It wasn't in Tilly's nature to judge others unkindly. The girls looked thin and tired, and she felt both curious about them and the life they must live, as well as slightly sorry for them.

Soho cabaret dancers, Dulcie had labelled them, and in such a way that it had been obvious that she didn't think very much of them at all. Tilly wasn't so naïve as not to know that the services provided by many of the girls who worked in Soho's clubs went far beyond merely dancing for customers.

Now, close up to them, Tilly could see where their eye shadow had run into the tired creases around their eyes. They smelled of cigarettes, mingled with cheap scent and sweat, and it was an effort for Tilly not wrinkle up her nose a little in distaste.

Dulcie, on the other hand, wasn't paying much attention to the girls she had been so scathing about earlier. Instead she was confronting the stall holder.

'*Private* order? More like looted – stolen – from somewhere *to order*, if you was to ask me. There's a law against that, you know.'

'You just be careful what you're saying, missie,' the stall holder warned Dulcie angrily. 'Genuine second-hand, these things are, and round here we have a few laws of our own about what 'appens to people who go round accusing other people of fings they ain't done.'

Feeling concerned for Dulcie's safety, Tilly touched her arm and warned, 'Dulcie, I think . . .'

But Dulcie shook her hand off and, without even looking at her, told the stall holder, 'I'm from the East

End meself, so I ain't going to be saying nuffink to no one.'

Amazed to hear Dulcie speaking in such an unfamiliar and strong East End accent, Tilly looked at her friend but Dulcie wasn't taking any notice.

'Oh, come on, Marge, ignore her. Let's have a look see what your 'Arry's brought us,' one of the showgirls was demanding, reaching towards the case as she spoke to pull out the contents.

Dulcie had been right when she had suggested that the clothes were looted, Tilly suspected, as half a dozen beautiful gowns spilled out onto the boards. She could see quite plainly on one of them a label that said 'Norman Hartnell', whom everyone knew was one of the Queen's favourite couturiers. If Drew had been here he would have wanted to know by what means the dresses had got here and where they were from, Tilly knew.

The girls, including Dulcie, were already diving in and picking up the dresses, the gloves off quite literally as the young women examined the merchandise.

'See this one,' one of them announced triumphantly grabbing the dress with the Norman Hartnell label. 'I swear on me ma's life that I saw one of them debs wearing one just like it when my friend took me to the Ritz. 'Ere, that's mine,' she objected angrily when Dulcie made a sudden swift movement and dragged the gown from her possession.

'Not now it isn't,' Dulcie informed her emphatically and with obvious satisfaction, bundling the dress up and thrusting it into Tilly's hands. 'Ere, you take this, Tilly, and then we'll go and meet up with our Ricky.

Him and his mates will have come out of the boxing club by now.'

Blinking a little at this piece of fiction, Tilly clutched the dress and stayed silent.

'She's not going anywhere with that Norman Hartnell. It's mine,' the girl who had originally picked up the dress yelled furiously at Dulcie, trying to make a grab for it and failing as Dulcie placed herself determinedly in front of Tilly.

Dulcie turned to the angry-looking stall holder, telling her, 'I'll give you a fiver for it.'

'That's my frock and she isn't having it,' the showgirl was insisting.

'Stop that screeching, will you, Eliza?' the stall holder demanded. 'You'll have the whole of ruddy Scotland Yard down on us if you keep on like that. And as for you,' she confronted Dulcie, 'Ten guineas, that frock is. Like it says on the label it's a Norman Hartnell, and if you can't pay then Eliza here will, won't you?'

'Ten guineas. You told us that we could have the stuff for five guineas apiece, with Dot here finding out from her gentleman friend when the house would be empty—'

An angry shove in the ribs from one of the girls, who seemed to be their leader, had Eliza glowering at her and nursing her side.

'A fiver, and I won't even say a word to no one about . . . anything . . .' Dulcie announced smugly.

'No, it's mine . . .'

'Oh, for Gawd's sake, Eliza, put a sock in it, will yer? Marge is right, that racket you're creating will have the Old Bill sniffing round here and no mistake. Give it to her, Marge,' Dot instructed, pushing aside the others to come and stand in front of Dulcie and Tilly, her hands on her hips as she surveyed them both, but her attention focused primarily on Dulcie.

'Give us your fiver then,' she demanded, holding out a hand, the bright red nail varnish she was wearing chipped and the nails underneath it slightly grimy.

As Dulcie did so, she added grimly, 'You might have got away with it this time, but I've got a good memory for faces, so don't come round here trying them kind of tricks again 'cos it won't work, and you'll end up the worse for it, I can promise you that. There's friends of mine that won't take too kindly to what you've done, and that yeller head of yours won't so look if you was to be accidentally tarred and feavvered, like.'

Tilly couldn't stop herself from giving an audible indrawn breath of shock, but Dulcie didn't look in the least bit concerned, as she handed over her money.

Taking it from her, the stall holder told her, 'Now buzz off, the pair of you, and remember, don't come back.'

'Well, if that wasn't a piece of luck. Not that it was just luck, of course. You've got to keep your eyes open and your wits about you if you want to get bargains like that,' Dulcie announced happily, as she linked her arm through Tilly's and guided her away from the market.

'But, Dulcie, you don't even know if the dress will fit you,' Tilly felt bound to point out.

''Course it will fit me,' Dulcie told her, coming to a standstill and pulling Tilly round to face her. 'It's bound to.'

'How can you know that?' Tilly asked

Dulcie heaved an exaggerated sigh. 'Them girls was

the same size as me and them frocks had been pinched to order for them, so it's bound to fit me, see?'

'If the dresses were stolen.' Tilly began as they set off walking again, her conscience pricking her, 'then—'

For a second time Dulcie stopped dead in the street and whirled her round.

'Now you listen to me, Tilly. What went on by that stall is between you and me and the gatepost and it isn't going to get told to anyone else, understand? As far as anyone else is concerned, we saw the frock on a stall and we was told that it was second-hand. You aren't to go saying anything to anyone about looting or anything like that. Besides, what would happen if you was to report it? Nothing, that's what, except that someone else would end up with my dress, and I'm not having that.'

There was nothing she could say that would persuade Dulcie to change her mind, Tilly knew, just as she knew how shocked and disapproving her mother would be if she were to learn the truth about the dress.

There was one person she intended to exclude from Dulcie's ban on her mentioning what had happened, though, and that was Drew.

'Come on, there's a shop down here where they rent out fur jackets, and I want to see what they've got.'

Tilly looked at her watch. It was one o'clock. Drew would be meeting his contact any minute now. She would far rather be with him than going looking at fur jackets with Dulcie, and she suspected that if he had seen what had happened this morning even Drew would have agreed that she would be safer with him than with Dulcie.

'I'm going to Fleet Street to see Drew,' she told Dulcie, feeling very grown up and independent. 'I'll meet you back home.'

'All right,' Dulcie agreed, adding unexpectedly, 'Here, you take this and put it in your handbag,' thrusting the dress at Tilly. 'Just in case anyone decides to try and take it back,' she explained when Tilly looked surprised.

Immediately Tilly's surprise turned to concern.

'You don't think they will, do you?'

'You never know with people like that,' Dulcie told her. 'And just be careful with it,' she warned.

'It will be dreadfully creased up,' Tilly protested.

'That's all right, your ma will know how to press out the creases,' Dulcie assured her.

They parted on the corner of the street, Dulcie to go in search of a fur jacket, and Tilly heading for Fleet Street, her heart already lifting at the thought of being with Drew. He would remonstrate with her, of course, but he wouldn't send her away. Tilly smiled happily to herself.

Half an hour later she pushed open the door to their favourite Fleet Street pub, Ye Olde Cheshire Cheese, and breathed in the now familiar smell of beer and cigarettes, pausing for a moment to let her ears adjust to the level of noise in the busy public house. Then she headed straight for the room where she and Drew normally sat.

A couple of the regulars at the bar, newsmen to whom Drew had introduced her, nodded in her direction. Tilly smiled back but didn't stop, her heart lifting as she stood up on her tiptoes to look past the busy bar along which drinkers were crowded three and four deep.

She could see Drew. He was seated at their favourite table, alone. Tilly frowned, feeling both disappointed that she was going to miss out on such an exciting interview and pleased that she would now have Drew all to herself.

He hadn't seen her so she sneaked up behind him, placing her hands over his eyes as she mimicked the voice Dulcie had used earlier with the stall holder to demand teasingly, 'Guess who?'

Immediately, Drew stiffened and reached up to remove her hands, as soon as he touched them, exclaiming, 'Tilly, you wretch, you scared me half to death.'

He had recognised her simply from touching her hands? Tilly felt thrilled to know this as he pulled up a chair for her.

'What are you doing here anyway? You promised me . . .'

'I know but I had my fingers crossed behind my back,' she told him. 'I'm obviously too late, though. What did he say, Drew? What did he tell you? Was it—'

'He didn't show up,' Drew stopped her. 'I guess he was either handing me a line or someone frightened him off.'

He looked so disappointed that Tilly immediately tried to cheer him up, announcing, 'Well, wait until I tell you what happened when I was out with Dulcie this morning . . .'

After she had finished explaining about the stall holder, the showgirls and the dresses she asked, 'Do you think it's true that the dresses were stolen to order, Drew?'

'It certainly sounds like it.'

Tilly moved closer to him. She would far rather

spend her afternoon here with him than shopping with Dulcie.

'Oh, Sergeant Dawson.' Self-consciously aware of how flustered she sounded, Olive stepped back into the hallway. What an idiot she was, behaving like this. It wasn't Archie Dawson's fault. It was just her being silly. She needed to start behaving like the respectable widow she was. After all, she had known Archie Dawson for going on for twenty years – twenty years during which she had looked upon him only as a kind neighbour and a good husband. Nothing had changed. Except that she herself was perhaps approaching what was often referred to as 'a funny age'. She'd heard of gossipy tales of respectable women suddenly shocking people by going off the rails – they all had. Such tales were the meat and veg of gossip to people like Nancy, and she certainly wasn't going to be the subject of one of them. The mere thought was enough to have her getting a firm grip on herself.

'Archie,' the sergeant reminded Olive, before following her into the house. 'And I just thought I'd pop round and make sure that you are happy about using that stirrup pump.'

'That's really kind of you.' Olive was determined to put her thoughts into actions as she showed him into the kitchen, adding, 'I've just put the kettle on, if you've got time for a cup of tea?' The sooner she got back to normal and treated Archie Dawson as she had always done, the better.

'Oh, I've always got time for a brew,' the sergeant assured her.

Olive snatched a quick look at him. To her relief there

was certainly nothing in his manner toward her that even hinted that she might have given him the wrong impression – about anything.

Feeling heartened, Olive told him, 'I've just been trying to work out who ought to be paired up with whom.' She pulled a small face as she waved her hand in the direction of the piece of paper and pencil on the table.

'Would you like me to give you a hand with it?'

For a moment she hesitated, a refusal trembling on her lips, but then she reminded herself of her vow to behave normally.

'That would be very kind of you,' she told him truthfully, adding, 'I've made a list of all those who've volunteered to take part. And Agnes, bless her, has actually asked if she could be with the Misses Barker. I was going to put Tilly with them but I dare say if I did she'd start complaining that she wants to be with Drew.'

Olive didn't realise how much the tone of her voice had given her away until Sergeant Dawson said gently, 'Something's upsetting you, Olive, I can tell. If you'd like to get it off your chest then I can promise you that it won't go any further.'

Olive was glad to have the excuse to turn her back on the sergeant as she felt tears stinging her eyes.

'That's very kind of you,' she answered, hoping that he wouldn't detect the small quiver in her voice that she was fighting so hard to control. 'But I'm sure you're far too busy to have the time to listen to my problems. Mrs Dawson—'

'Mrs Dawson has taken Barney out with her to buy him some new clothes. She said it would be easier if just the two of them went.'

Was that a note of sadness she could hear in his voice? How lucky Mrs Dawson was to have a husband who wanted to share in such a task with her. Was he perhaps feeling excluded because of the close bond Mrs Dawson had formed with Barney, just as she was feeling excluded because of the close bond Tilly had formed with Drew?

'Barney's grown a good two inches since he came to us. He's a smashing lad,' Archie Dawson continued proudly.

'He's a very lucky boy to have you and Mrs Dawson to take him in,' Olive told him.

The sergeant shook his head. 'No, we're the ones who are that. Best thing we ever did was take him in. Mrs Dawson—' He stopped and shook his head. 'I don't need to tell you the difference it's made to her, Olive. She was only saying the other day how kind you've been, always making a point of stopping and speaking with her when she's out. Not like some. Nancy was round at our house again this morning complaining about Barney. That is one thing about the lad: he doesn't seem to understand that he needs to keep to the rules when it comes to things like going to school. I'm having to keep a bit of an eye on him in that regard, but don't let on to Nancy that I told you that. Now,' he continued firmly, 'let's have that cup of tea and you can tell me what's troubling you.'

'Oh, I couldn't,' Olive protested.

'I can promise you that whatever you tell me will not go outside these four walls,' the sergeant assured her.

Weakly Olive took a deep breath. It would be such a relief to confide in the sergeant and to get a man's point

183

of view, and in the end it was surprisingly easy to sit companionably across the table from him as she tried to explain to him her concerns for Tilly.

'She behaves as though I am her enemy instead of a mother who loves her and wants to protect her. She says that I don't understand, and that I want to deny her the pleas— the comfort of being married to Drew,' Olive corrected herself, flushing a little as she tried not to feel self-conscious about accidentally bringing up the pleasure that could come from a happy marriage. She didn't want the sergeant to think that she was being too 'forward' or, even worse, drawing his attention to the lack of that pleasure in her life as a widow. Once such thoughts would never have occurred to her, but now, thanks to Nancy, she was acutely aware of them.

'I'm worried that she might do something that she might later regret.'

'Tilly's not the sort to do that,' the sergeant reassured her, 'and that young man of hers certainly isn't the sort to encourage anything like that.'

'No, he isn't. I like Drew but he is American and . . . well, I know it's selfish of me but . . .'

'You don't want to think of your Tilly going off to live in America. That isn't selfish. That's only natural. If your Jim was still alive he'd soon have young Tilly sorted out.'

'Yes, I've been thinking that myself,' Olive agreed. 'Tilly is just at that age where she needs a father's wise words. She's such a good daughter, and we've always been so close, but now . . .'

Olive's voice trembled and then so did her body when,

unexpectedly, the sergeant reached across the table and placed his hand over hers.

It was just the kind gesture of a good neighbour, of course, and the sergeant would be horrified if he knew about that sudden shameful pounding of her heart. It was only because she was so worked up over Tilly, of course. Nothing more than that.

'Where is Tilly now?'

'She's out shopping with Dulcie. Drew and Wilder are taking the girls to the Café de Paris this evening – Wilder's treat to Dulcie to make up for not taking her out on Valentine's Day.'

'Wilder? Now there's a young man I wouldn't want to see walking out with my daughter if I had one,' the sergeant told Olive forthrightly.

'No, I must admit that I can't really take to him myself. Oh goodness, is that time?' Olive looked at her watch and then pushed back her chair to stand up. 'I've taken up far too much of your time. What must you think of me?'

The sergeant had stood up too and now, as she turned towards the kitchen door, to her bemusement he came up to her and placed a hand on her shoulder, turning her to face him. Then reaching for both her hands he held them in his own and told her gently, 'What I think of you, Olive, is that Jim was a lucky man to have been married to you, and I know he felt the same way. I can remember how proud he was of you and Tilly. Said he'd got the best girls in the whole world.'

'His mother certainly didn't think that. She never really wanted him to marry me, and then when his parents had to take us in she soon let me know that she wasn't happy about that. Jim's parents did stand by me, though, when Jim died. Without them I don't know what would have happened to me and Tilly. That's what Tilly doesn't understand.'

'You can't blame her too much for that, Olive. Tilly knows how much you love her and that you'll always support her. Be honest, if she was to find herself in the same situation you were in, there'd be no question about you taking Tilly and your grandchild in, would there?'

'Of course not.'

The sergeant smiled. 'Perhaps part of the reason Tilly can't understand your fears for her is because she can't ever imagine being in the situation you were in. She knows that she will always have you to turn to and I can't imagine you ever wanting that to be any other way. It must have been very frightening for you: you had a very sick husband who was dying, a young baby, no parents or family of your own to turn to. You must have very felt alone.'

'I did,' Olive admitted. And she still sometimes felt very alone now, but of course she couldn't say that.

'I've taken up enough of your time,' she said instead.

But the sergeant merely smiled again and told her firmly, 'Let's have a look at that list of yours, and then I'll run through the stirrup pump again. You've got your sand delivered now, have you?'

'Yes. It came this morning. Mr King's happy for us to have the sand at the Longs' old house, especially with four of his houses being empty at the moment. Every household is going to have a bucket of sand that they'll keep filled from the stockpile at number 49.

186

Drew, bless him, has organised the wheelbarrows to collect the empty buckets and then deliver them to all the houses. We couldn't expect the likes of the Misses Barker to carry heavy buckets of sand around. I do like Drew, and if Tilly was older and there wasn't a war on, and if . . .'

'He wasn't American,' Archie Dawson teased her gently.

'Am I being selfish and unfair?' Olive asked him anxiously.

'No,' the sergeant told her firmly, 'you're being a mother, and you're a damned fine one too, Olive.'

TEN

'Oh, Dulcie, you look ever so glamorous, just like a film star,' Agnes gasped, awestruck as Dulcie twirled round the kitchen to show off her new dress. 'It's ever such a lovely frock.'

'Of course it is,' Dulcie agreed. 'It's Norman Hartnell. And it's not a frock, it's a *gown*.'

It was a beautiful dress, Olive acknowledged, as she watched the light catching on the thousands of tiny crystals sewn onto the midnight-blue silk, just a few sprinkled here and there on the bodice, growing in number the further down the skirt they were. It wasn't just the fabric that made the dress so outstandingly glamorous, though. There was also the cut – on the bias – and, Olive thought privately, made for a girl who had been slightly more slender than Dulcie on the bust and the hip, so that its fit on Dulcie was such that any susceptible young male would be stopped in his tracks, Olive suspected. Not that it was in any way vulgar. That would have been impossible for such a dress. No, the overall effect was, as Agnes had so rightly announced, one of film-star glamour.

To have found such a dress on a market stall amongst what Dulcie had described as a tangle of rubbishy stuff had indeed been wonderful. Dulcie had told her that 'having got the good eye that I have for quality,' she had quickly realised that the frock was exactly that, even before she had seen the label.

Tilly, who had returned home slightly later than Dulcie, explaining that she had decided 'on impulse' to meet up with Drew – avoiding Olive's gaze whilst doing so – hadn't had much to say about their shopping trip other than that Dulcie had been very lucky to have acquired the dress.

Buying and wearing second-hand clothes was a fact of life of the war, but Olive had to admit to herself that there were many, many times whilst she was sorting through the clothes that were brought in to them at the WVS that her heart ached for the possible fate of the original owners. One couldn't give in to sentiment, though.

'You do look lovely, Dulcie,' she agreed. It was, after all, the truth.

'Just wait until you see the little fur bolero I've got on loan that I'm going to wear with it,' Dulcie boasted. 'I shouldn't wonder if them society photographers, that are bound to be at the Café de Paris seeing as that's where all the rich posh folk go, don't want to take a picture of me tonight. What's Tilly doing?' she demanded. 'Wilder and Drew will be here soon. I just hope that Wilder remembers what I told him about him having to wear something smart, and not that leather flying jacket of his.'

'Didn't you say that Wilder was going to get changed

189

at Ian's?' Olive reminded her. 'If so I'm sure that Drew will make sure that he's properly dressed, Dulcie.'

'Drew will make sure who is properly dressed?' demanded Tilly, coming into the kitchen in her own evening dress. Looking at her daughter, Olive's heart ached with both love for her and anxiety. The silk velvet, bought on a trip to one of London's markets just after the beginning of the war, if anything looked even better on Tilly now that she was little bit older than it had done when it had first been made. The damson colour of the fabric suited Tilly's Celtic colouring to perfection, her slender neck rising from the boat-shaped neckline as elegantly as any swan's. Love had brought a new confidence to her daughter, Olive recognised. Tilly held herself just that little bit taller, her skin glowed with the happiness that was revealed in the shine in her eyes and the smile that lifted the corners of her mouth.

If Dulcie looked eye-catchingly glamorous, then Tilly looked truly beautiful.

Sally, coming into the kitchen on the heels of Tilly, did a small double take as she saw Dulcie.

'I hope you aren't thinking of appearing in that down at the hospital,' she teased Dulcie. 'You'll cause a riot if you do.'

Preening herself afresh, Dulcie told her, 'Well, I suppose I might wear it if there was to be a dance – just to show David, him going to be a sir one day and knowing what quality is.'

Sally exchanged looks with Olive. Dulcie had no awareness of irony, nor much of a sense of humour other than for her own jokes.

'I'd better go,' Sally told Olive, 'otherwise I'll be late

on duty. You'd think by now that I'd be used to working nights, but somehow you never do get used to it.'

Within minutes of Sally leaving, a knock on the front door heralded the arrival of Drew and Wilder, with a taxi waiting to transport them all to the West End and the Café de Paris.

They were setting out early at Dulcie's insistence, because despite the fact that Wilder had booked a table she wanted to make sure that she liked its position whilst there was still time to opt for another.

'I don't want to be given some table stuck away in a corner like we was when you took me to the Ritz that time,' she informed Wilder now, as he complained that no one went to a nightclub so early in the evening.

Despite all her reservations about Tilly's relationship with Drew, Olive knew that no mother's heart could fail to be secretly lifted by the fact that her own daughter's escort looked so very comfortably at home in a dinner suit that fitted him perfectly, whilst Wilder, who always looked so determinedly raffish and bad-boyish in his beloved leather jacket, actually looked far less attractive in a dinner suit in which he was plainly not at ease.

Naturally the men had brought corsages for the girls, but whilst Tilly's orchid was a perfect colour for her dress, the glaringly bright yellow of Dulcie's brought a pursed-lipped look of disapproval in Wilder's direction and an irritated, 'What made you choose that colour?'

Wilder's equally irritated, 'You're blonde so I thought it would go with your hair,' didn't do anything to mend matters.

Olive recognised that for all that she herself often felt irritated by Dulcie, and even critical of her, just as though she was Dulcie's mother and not merely her landlady, the sight of someone else betraying that irritation brought an immediate surge of protective emotion towards Dulcie and an increase in her growing dislike for what she often considered to be the less than gentlemanly way in which Wilder treated her.

As she hugged both girls before they left she whispered discreetly to Dulcie, 'You could always "forget" about your corsage and leave it in the cloakroom by mistake. To be honest, Dulcie, the diamanté on your dress mean that neither it nor you need any added enhancement.'

Dulcie had been right about the fur bolero, Olive acknowledged, as she waved the quartet off. It suited the style of her gown perfectly. It was, though, once again the sight of Tilly's shining happiness that lingered in her mind after they had gone, and she and Agnes had settled down together to a quiet evening of listening to the wireless and knitting squares of unravelled wool to make blankets for those in need.

'Doesn't Dulcie look lovely in her new dress?' Tilly asked Wilder loyally as their taxi rumbled toward their destination. He hadn't yet paid Dulcie any compliments on her appearance. The Cafe de Paris was housed in the basement of a five-storey building, and, recently refurbished, it was claimed by its owner to be safer from bombs than any other nightclub in the whole of London.

In response, Wilder gave a grunt and announced, 'If you were to ask me I'd say that we could have had a better night at somewhere where the real action is.'

'But the Cafe de Paris is *the* place to go,' Tilly protested.

'Yes it is,' Dulcie agreed. 'David was saying the last time I saw him that all the upper-class set go there.'

If Dulcie had hoped to provoke Wilder into some jealous comment about David, she would be disappointed, Tilly recognised, when instead Wilder simply shook his head, and told her, 'Who gives a damn about the upper class and where they like to go? Give me somewhere that's got a decent game of poker going or a roulette table over that any day.'

They'd reached their destination, Drew paying off the cabby. Coventry Street, where the Café de Paris was, was just off Piccadilly Circus, and it hurt Tilly to see everywhere looking so dull and dark under the blackout. It was so sad to see one's much-loved city reduced to such grimness, Tilly thought, as she tucked her arm through Drew's.

As they headed for the nightclub she noticed that, unlike her and Drew, Wilder and Dulcie were walking at least two feet apart.

Once they were inside the building they had to go down a long steep staircase to the nightclub itself, where they were greeted by an elegantly coiffured redhead with the longest red nails Tilly had ever seen, who took their names, ignoring Tilly and Dulcie – although not Dulcie's dress, Tilly noted – to flash a warm smile at both Wilder and Drew, but especially at Drew, Tilly saw indignantly.

In the cloakroom they both had to part with a sixpence to hand in their coats, the levy of such a charge causing Dulcie to start objecting that she thought she might prefer to keep her own fur on, 'seeing as this place is really a cellar and my Norman Hartnell is sleeveless. Everyone knows that cellars are cold and damp.'

Despite this statement being delivered in an accent as close as Dulcie could manage to the accents of Selfridges' more well-to-do customers, the cloakroom attendant was patently unimpressed, giving a silent sniff that somehow conveyed her opinion that young women who were ready to argue about parting with a sixpence were not in a position to criticise somewhere like the Café de Paris, even if they were wearing a Norman Hartnell.

'Who does she think she is, acting all high and mighty with us?' Dulcie complained to Tilly as they left the cloakroom, in a wave of the expensive scent she had sprayed liberally on a piece of precious cotton wool after nipping into Selfridges before returning to number 13, and which she was now wearing tucked into her bra.

'I dare say she could tell that we aren't upper class,' said Tilly comfortably. Not being thought of as out of the top drawer didn't worry her at all. She was perfectly happy as she was.

Predictably, given the time, they were the first to arrive. Having been shown to a table which, as Dulcie had requested, was slap-bang at the front of the very small dance floor, Dulcie still tried to argue for one right opposite it. That table, she was informed, was already booked by someone else and no, it didn't make any difference that they had arrived first.

'Well, I suppose it will have to do,' Dulcie conceded.

Drinks were ordered and the menu studied, Wilder announcing grimly, 'It doesn't matter what we order, it will still be the same crap.' He looked at Drew. 'Wouldn't you just give anything for a proper American steak?'

Tilly could tell from Drew's expression that he hadn't liked either Wilder's language or his comment, but before he could say anything it was Dulcie who reminded Wilder fiercely, 'We'll have none of that sort of language, thank you. And I'll thank you to remember too that we're on rations here in this country because we're fighting the Germans.'

The room was beginning to fill up now, with elegantly gowned women and their male escorts, many of whom were in uniform, drifting in to find their tables.

The nightclub was very small – Tilly didn't want to think disappointingly small, out of loyalty to her city – the air heavy with cigarette smoke and expensive scent. The red and gold décor was certainly very rich-looking, and she felt a small tingle of anticipation in her tummy when the master of ceremonies came down one of the pair of stairs that led up to a small balcony area, to announce the imminent arrival of the the West Indian Orchestra led by the fabled Ken 'Snakehips' Johnson.

Immediately the waiting diners began to clap, a group of three couples who had arrived late momentarily blocking Tilly's party's own view of the space where the orchestra was assembling. One of the women – a brunette with hard eyes, on the arm of a much-medalled naval officer – hesitated just as she was about to walk in front of them. Later, Tilly wondered if it had been fate that had made Dulcie look up at the woman; some inbuilt female instinct. Whatever it had been, the look on Dulcie's face was enough to have Tilly reaching for her arm when she stood up and announced sharply, 'Well, look who it isn't! Mrs David James-Thompson, but not, it seems, escorted by the gentleman I saw her booking into the Ritz with for the night, not so very long ago, never mind her own husband.'

There was a pause that Tilly truly thought could quite rightly be described as ghastly. The nightclub was only small, and Dulcie had a voice that carried quite a long way when she chose to make it do so.

'Dulcie . . .' she begged, but Dulcie shrugged off her attempt to tug her back down into her seat.

An angry tide of red was spreading over the brunette's pale, heavily *maquillée* face, the hard-looking eyes hardening even more. The two couples she and her escort were with were giving Tilly's party coldly dismissive looks.

Dulcie, though, didn't care. From the minute she had recognised David's wife, Lydia, Dulcie had been filled with righteous indignation on David's behalf, not to mention the chance to have a go at her old enemy and put her in her place.

'Oh, I say,' the young naval officer was protesting, tugging at his tie as he did so, plainly feeling uncomfortable in the way that men did when faced with warring women.

'Told you about the husband she's dumped because of the wounds he got defending his country, has she?' Dulcie asked him, whilst Tilly looked helplessly at Drew.

This time the young officer's 'Oh, I say' was decidedly muted, whilst the two other couples exchanged looks that suggested they had not known.

'Lydia, sweetie, surely you don't actually know this person?' one of the other women asked.

'Know her? Certainly not,' Lydia told them. 'She's just a little shop girl from Selfridges. A frightful type – dreadfully common.'

Tilly held her breath. To call Dulcie common was like waving a red rag at a bull. 'Drew,' she pleaded, but it was too late.

Dulcie pushed back her chair and walked to the front of the table, raising her voice to make herself heard above the sound of the orchestra tuning up.

'Common, is it? And me wearing a Norman Hartnell frock. You don't get one of them for being common.'

'Goodness, yes, it is a Hartnell. I remember seeing Honoria Fanshawe wearing the same model the other week,' one of the two women with Lydia acknowledged.

'Well, we all know the only way that a girl like you could possibly end up wearing Hartnell. Your . . . friend . . . is obviously very generous in return for your favours,' Lydia told Dulcie with a coldly contemptuous look.

'What? You dare to say that to me when I saw you, as bold as brass, booking into the Ritz with that old chap who most definitely was not your husband.'

'Why, you . . .' There was no mistaking Lydia's fury. She stepped towards Dulcie, who was looking more as though she was thoroughly enjoying the confrontation than feeling shocked or upset by it.

'Poor David,' Dulcie continued, very much getting into her stride. 'No wonder he says that he's well rid of you. According to him you never was much of a wife in that department.'

'Charles, I think you'd better call the manager,' the older of the two women with Lydia announced acidly. 'I can't imagine how these people have been allowed in here.'

'Oh, that's rich,' Dulcie told her, in full flight now, 'trying to get us thrown out. She's the one who ought to be shown the door.' She nodded in Lydia's direction. 'You be warned,' she told the apprehensive-looking naval officer, 'don't you go losing your legs, like her husband did, or she'll drop you as well.'

'Charles, call the manager.'

'I think that's enough, Dulcie,' Drew said quietly. 'We all know how loyal you are to David, but this isn't really the place—'

'How dare you speak to me like that, you . . . you nobody. I'll have you thrown out of this place,' Lydia hissed at Dulcie, before turning on her heel and stalking off to the table that Dulcie had wanted to move to, leaving her openly fuming.

'Do you think she can get us thrown out?' Tilly asked Drew uncomfortably. Now that Lydia and her party had gone, Tilly could see that everyone in the room was looking in their direction.

'I don't know,' Drew admitted, 'but perhaps it might be a good idea if we left anyway.'

Wilder, who had been steadily supplementing the whiskies he had ordered with his own whisky from a flask he had concealed in his jacket pocket, and was now quite obviously the worse for drink, suddenly stood up unsteadily, to announce, 'I've had enough of this place. Never wanted to come here anyway. Wanna play poker instead,' before heading for the stairs at an unsteady walk, leaving the others with no option than to follow.

Predictably, Dulcie was not pleased. 'It will make me look like I'm letting her win,' she protested, as she and Tilly collected their coats.

Outside the club they had to walk to Piccadilly Circus to find a cab, but as Drew was escorting both girls into it Wilder suddenly announced, 'Not coming with you. Going somewhere else.'

'Wilder,' Drew protested, but Dulcie poked her head

out of the still open cab door and said crossly, 'Oh, let him go, Drew.'

'It's not that late. We could still go to the Hammersmith Palais, if you like?' Tilly suggested to Dulcie. She couldn't help but feel a little bit sorry for her, all dressed up as she was, and Wilder deserting her.

'What? Go to the Palais in me Norman Hartnell? No, thanks,' Dulcie refused.

'Where to, mate?' the cabby asked Drew impatiently.

The unexpected and shrill rising sound of the air-raid warning shocked them all into silence for a few seconds whilst they looked at one another.

'Where's the nearest shelter?' Drew began, but Tilly shook her head.

'No. Let's go home. Mum will be worrying, and we aren't that far away.'

Nodding, Drew told the driver, 'Article Row, please.'

They were almost home when they heard the ominous drone of the German planes followed by the first of the bombs starting to fall, the magnesium flares as they exploded lighting up the night sky.

'Whose idea was it not to head for the closest shelter?' Dulcie began to complain. 'We'd have been safer if we'd stayed where we was.'

Under cover of the darkness inside the taxi Tilly reached for Drew's hand. The incendiaries were falling thick and fast around them, fire engines racing past them with their bells ringing.

'That's your lot. I'm not going any further,' the cabby told them when a fresh explosion of incendiaries lit up the sky.

'Come on,' Drew urged the two girls, 'we'll have to make a run for it.'

'Run in these shoes, and with me bad ankle?' Dulcie protested, but she still hitched up her skirt and grabbed Tilly's arm as she followed her out of the cab.

At number 13 Olive and Agnes's quiet evening had also been disrupted by the air-raid warning. With the fire-watching group not officially in action, and after so many bomb-free weeks, the sound of the alarm caught them off guard.

They looked at one another for a few precious seconds before Olive announced, 'Agnes, you go down to the shelter. I'm going to go on fire-watching duties. It will give me a chance to see if it will work.'

'If you're doing that then I'm coming with you,' Agnes insisted stalwartly. Inside she felt nervous, but she wasn't going to let Olive go out on her own, not after everything her landlady had done for her.

At least Tilly would be safe at the Café de Paris, Olive reasoned as she clamped on one of a pair of hard hats she'd been given by Sergeant Dawson and offered the other to Agnes, before they pulled on their coats.

Outside, the incendiaries were already falling. Jane Barker, coming to her front door, looked relieved when she saw that Olive was already outside.

'We were just wondering if we should come on duty, even though nothing official has been arranged yet,' she told Olive. 'We've equipped ourselves with a rake and a spade, just in case.'

Not really wanting her elderly neighbours to put themselves at risk, Olive suggested, 'Why don't you go back inside and fill the bath with water as Sergeant Dawson instructed us? That way, if an incendiary should fall through your roof, you'll be able to dowse it and put out any fire.'

'Good idea, Olive,' she beamed. 'We can open the trap-door to the loft as well, just to be on the safe side.'

Olive took hold of the handles of the wheelbarrow filled with sand, now parked usefully and as out of sight as possible in the front garden, although of course Nancy had already complained about the untidiness of the sand-filled wheelbarrows standing in so many of the Row's small front gardens.

She was just pushing it through the gate, Agnes carrying the spade and the hoe, when she saw Tilly, Drew and Dulcie come running down the Row.

Relief at knowing her daughter and lodger would be here at Article Row under her protective watch was mixed with surprise that they had come home so early.

'Wilder didn't want to stay at the club so we've ended up coming home,' Tilly told her. No need to mention to her mother the altercation between Dulcie and Lydia. 'We knew once the bombs had started to fall that you'd be worrying, even though the Café de Paris is so safe.'

This was more like her old thoughtful loving girl, Olive acknowledged, as she gave her daughter's hand a grateful squeeze.

'You'd better go and get changed out of those clothes, all of you, and then you can help me keep an eye out for any incendiaries falling here,' Olive told them.

'What, spend the evening out here? No, thank you,' Dulcie retorted huffily. She was still in a bad mood at the disruption of her much-anticipated night out.

You'd never have got David behaving like Wilder, she told herself bitterly upstairs in her room, reluctantly removing her lovely new dress. David would have been proud to show her off wearing a Norman Hartnell dress. He'd have bought her the right kind of corsage. He would have treated her like a lady. He would have . . . Inside her head Dulcie had an image of David coming to the Hammersmith Palais and dancing with her there. He had been ever such a good dancer. So tall and handsome and so . . . so gentlemanly, even if he had tried it on a bit, and him an engaged and soon-to-be married man. She could forgive him that. After all, he'd backed off when she'd said no, she wasn't the sort to get involved with a married chap. Backed off and disappeared from her life. But that hadn't mattered. There were plenty of men who wanted to date her and she wasn't ready for marriage, tying herself down to a man who'd want her at his beck and call just like her mother had been at her father's beck and call. And then there would be the kids, too many of them too quickly after one another. No, she wasn't ready for that, and she doubted that she would ever be, Dulcie admitted, as she hesitated between going into a full sulk, putting on her night clothes, going back downstairs and listening to the wireless with a cup of cocoa, or going out and joining the others.

Sociable by nature, never one to miss out on whatever was going on, as much as she disliked the idea of mucking in and helping out, Dulcie knew she did not want to stay in on her own. And besides, wouldn't she be far more help to Olive than that dopey Agnes, who always stood about waiting to be told what to do instead of working it out for herself? If Agnes saw an incendiary land two feet in front of her she'd have to ask someone else whether or not to put it out, Dulcie thought scornfully, as she pulled on her oldest clothes, and then tied her hair up in a scarf.

Outside in the street it looked rather like Bonfire Night, the incendiaries, as they burst into flames, like thousands of sparklers throwing off their fierce white light.

Initially it looked as though Article Row was going to be lucky. Up above them in the night sky the flare from the falling magnesium incendiaries was so bright that they could easily see the bombers looking for fresh targets.

'They'll be after the docks, not us,' said Mr Edwards, who, like so many of the other neighbours, had come out to see what was going on.

But just as he spoke a sudden shower of bombs descended at the bottom of the row, falling from the basket that contained them.

'Quick, one's gone through the roof of one of Mr King's houses,' Olive warned. 'Come on, Agnes, we'll go and deal with it.'

'No, me and Mr Edwards can do it,' Drew began, but Olive shook her head. She was already on the move, telling both Agnes and Dulcie briskly, 'You come with me, girls. Tilly, you stay with Drew.' As she hurried towards the house she recognised that she had another reason to thank Sergeant Dawson for his forethought, since he had suggested to Mr King that he gave her a spare set of keys for just this kind of emergency.

Leaving the wheelbarrow outside, but instructing Agnes to carry in the bucketful of water and Dulcie the bucket of sand, Olive, paused in the hallway before hoisting the hose onto her shoulder as Sergeant Dawson had shown her, grabbing the hoe and the shovel in her other hand and hurrying up the stairs with Dulcie and Agnes at her heels. Mr King's houses, which were all let out, weren't anything like as well cared for inside as her own home. The war had meant fewer tenants but Olive actually welcomed the dank musty smell that came from the unused and unheated building, hoping the damp would make it less easy for the fire to take hold.

The smoke coming from beneath one of the bedroom doors warned her that her hopes were misplaced, though.

'Keep back,' she warned the two girls, as she opened the door, 'and pull your scarves up round your faces. We don't want to be breathing in smoke.'

Dulcie, never willing to take orders from anyone, started to complain that her lipstick would come off on her scarf if she did that, but her protest ended in a coughing fit from the smoke escaping from the room.

''Ere, we can't go in there. It's too dangerous,' she coughed, forgetting to use her 'refined' Selfridges voice in the panic of the moment when she saw how quickly the fire had taken hold.

If the sight of the bedroom carpet well and truly on fire had momentarily filled Olive herself with shock, the sound of the fear in Dulcie's voice and the realisation that she was responsible for the safety not just of the house but, far more importantly, of the two girls with her, was enough to have Olive stiffening her spine and deciding that no German incendiary bomb was going to get the better of her.

Aiming the nozzle of the hose at the fire and then pulling the door almost closed as they had been instructed, Olive called back to Agnes, 'Start pumping.'

After what seemed like a lifetime the satisfying hiss of the water hitting the flames brought her a wave of relief. This was no time for complacency, though.

'Get ready with that sand,' she warned Dulcie. 'As soon as we've got this fire under control we need to take up the bomb and put it in the sand bucket.'

Outside in the street, Drew was wishing that Ian Simpson wasn't at work and that he had a few more young men to help him. Not that Tilly wasn't a good helper – she was – but Drew didn't want her to be in danger, and it *was* dangerous out here, he recognised, even if the residents were reacting to the falling bombs with what he now knew to be typical British resilience.

'Look, that's another lot falling,' Tilly gasped pulling the tin hat one of the Misses Barker had handed her further down over her head.

'Come on,' she urged Drew, as a fresh basket of incendiaries fell from the sky down at the far end of the road.

'Tilly, wait,' Drew protested, but it was too late, she was already pushing the barrow down the street at some speed.

Up above them two incendiaries landed on the roof of number 46, close to the end of the Row, both of them easily piercing the roof slates.

As they hurried over, the front door of the house opened and the Polish refugee family who were living there came running out.

And then the most horrific thing happened – so awful that it sucked the breath from Tilly's lungs and almost stopped her heart. As the Polish father ran out into the street to attract their attention, one of the falling incendiaries hit him, its fin piercing his back.

For a handful of seconds no one moved, not even the man who had been hit. Everyone was silent. Then that silence was broken, first by the man's agonised scream and then by the shocked cries of grief of his family.

People were coughing in the smoke billowing out of the incendiaries as they hit the ground.

Automatically Tilly started to run towards the injured man, who had fallen to his knees on the cobbled road, although without any idea of what she might usefully do.

'Tilly, keep back,' Drew yelled frantically.

The man's screams of pain filled the street, blotting out even the sound of the bombers, his family rushing towards him, as Drew cursed and warned them to stand back. It was obvious to him that nothing could be done for the man, who had collapsed and was now lying face down in the street.

At the sound of Drew's voice Tilly froze. The shock of what she was witnessing kept her rooted to the spot, her body cold with sick horror, even whilst she could feel a hot sweat of nausea rising up inside her. And yet when Drew ordered her to start pumping water, somehow she managed to do so.

The poor man was still screaming, whilst Drew trained the hose, even whilst he knew that it was just a waste of time. The man's family tried to go to him. Afraid for them, Drew urged them to stand back, lifting the nozzle of the hose to spray water at the children, making them cry even harder as they clung to their white-faced mother.

Other neighbours were rallying round, throwing sand on the other incendiaries that were still burning on the cobbled road. The man groaned and tried to move, and then screamed again. There was nothing he or anyone else could do, Drew knew that, but it was impossible for him to ignore that scream of terror and plea for help from another human being. Dropping the hose Drew went to the dying man, fighting his way through the smoke of the other incendiaries burning round him, and ignoring Tilly's pleas for him not to put himself in danger.

Terrified for Drew's safety, still in shock from the horror of what had happened to the man who lay dying in the street, Tilly, who all her life has been so optimistic and always looked on the bright side, was suddenly filled with a conviction that Drew was going to suffer the same fate as the dying man.

She cried out to him not to go, but all he did was shout over his shoulder to her, 'Keep pumping, Tilly,' as he frantically hosed down the dreadful blackening scorched thing in the middle of the road that had been a human being. The smell that reached him reminded him so sickeningly of the roast pork served at his parents' summer barbecues that he knew he would never be able to think of those sun-filled summer events without thinking too of this awful human tragedy that was happening in front of him. He dodged the still falling incendiaries, trying to get as close to the dying man as he possibly could, knowing that nothing he or anyone else could do would save him, but unable to endure the thought of simply leaving him where he was in his terrible mortal agony.

Upstairs in number 38, Olive had put out the fire and was on her way back down the stairs behind Dulcie, having handed her the hose whilst relieving her of the bucket with its still smoking, sand-covered incendiary.

Outside on the Row, Olive quickly realised that the

fire they had just put out wasn't the only one. The smoke from the fires started by the bombs was so thick that it was impossible to see more than a few feet ahead. Through it, neighbours came rushing up to her, begging her to come and put out their own fires. Mrs Edwards told her that her husband had gone down to the ARP unit to see if they could get a fire engine, and added in a dark whisper, 'Of course, he'll ask them to send an ambulance as well but it's obvious there won't be any point. Poor Tilly.'

'What?' Olive stopped her, letting the bucket of sand clatter to the pavement. 'What's happened to Tilly?'

'Well, she saw the whole thing, didn't she? She and that young of man of hers were standing right there when the incendiary hit that poor man, so my hubby said.'

Olive didn't wait to hear any more, pushing her way through the crowd now gathered in the street but keeping as far away as they could from the falling incendiaries. She could see Tilly now, standing stock-still by her wheelbarrow, her face turned away from Olive as she looked to where Drew was spraying water on something on the ground that was burning and smoking.

Then, as Olive watched, an incendiary fell between where Tilly was standing and where Drew was hosing down the dreadful-looking 'thing' on the cobbles. As the incendiary hit the cobbles it exploded, sending up a wall of white fire between Tilly and Drew. Someone screamed a terrified horrible primeval howl of sound so raw that it was impossible to tell if came from a female or a male throat.

Through the anguished agonised yells of warning and despair, all Olive could hear was her daughter's voice

208

crying out Drew's name as she released her barrow and almost threw herself towards the fire that separated her from him.

Later Olive didn't know where she got the strength somehow to force her way through the crowd just in time to drag Tilly back.

'No. No,' Tilly protested, trying to fight free, as through the flames they could both see Drew's face contorted with pain, his clothes on fire.

All around them people were leaping into action, shovelling sand on the burning incendiaries, playing hoses on the fires, but not even the screech of a fire engine could drown out the agony of pain Olive could hear in her daughter's voice as she cried out, distraught, for the man she loved and she tried to fight free of her mother to get to him.

'Don't look, don't look, Tilly,' Olive begged her as she struggled to hold her, whilst the most terrible screams of agony split the night air.

ELEVEN

In the Café de Paris, believing they were safe, and completely oblivious to the bombs being dropped overhead, the rich and well-connected *jeunesse dorée* danced and flirted. Until that was, one of the falling bombs somehow found the ventilation shaft to the club.

Over thirty-six people were killed outright, including 'Snakehips' Johnson, whose head was blown off his body.

By the time some of the dead, the dying and the injured reached Bart's Hospital, where Sally was on night duty, as acting sister, those working to rescue them had such tales of chaos and horror to tell that even they, bomb-hardened though they were, were weeping.

When Sally joined other nurses helping get the wounded into the hospital, one ambulance driver, tears pouring down his face, told her over and over again about seeing a young man carefully restoring the ripped-off arms and legs to his girlfriend's torso whilst her head remained several feet away.

'And then there was the ruddy looters,' he told Sally bitterly, 'down there like carrion crows, they was, ripping off rings and necklaces and the like. There was even bodies with their finger cut off so that they could get their rings.'

Her heart thumping, Sally looked frantically through the injured being brought in, all too aware that Dulcie and Tilly had been planning to go to the Café de Paris. When she couldn't see either them or the two young men she still couldn't feel relieved. Barts wasn't the only hospital in London, after all, and from the stories they were being told the carnage was such that it would be some time before a full tally of those killed and injured could be made.

Sally was a trained nurse, though. Her duty here now at Barts was to the injured.

She needed to be at her post in the operating theatre scrubbing up for what she knew would be a long night of operations. The night sky was filled with the sound of enemy planes, dropping bombs and the fierce defensive of the ack-ack guns, but Sally pushed those sounds to the back of her mind to concentrate on her work and her patients.

At number 13 a brisk knock on the front door had Olive looking anxiously from Tilly's white, set face as she lay unmoving in her bed.

Since they had brought her back to the house her daughter had neither spoken nor moved of her own volition, initially remaining seated in the kitchen chair into which Olive had guided her, staring in front of herself unseeingly, her body occasionally breaking out into shudders that racked it from head to toe, until Olive, aided by a willing Agnes and a grumbling Dulcie, had managed to get her upstairs and then undressed enough to get her into bed. Normally so fastidious, for once Olive had had more important things on her mind than the smell of smoke on Tilly's clothes and the unpleasant odour filling her clean bedroom.

Now, as she sat next to Tilly's bed on the bentwood chair from which she had removed Tilly's silk velvet evening dress, carefully hanging it in the wardrobe, she reached for her daughter's hand and held it in her own. It felt so cold and lifeless, just as Tilly's face looked equally drained of blood and life, almost as though Tilly was wanting to give up on life.

Olive shuddered herself, her hold on Tilly's hand tightening as she heard someone knocking on the front door and then Dulcie calling up, 'It's Sergeant Dawson.'

'I'll sit with Tilly whilst you go down,' Agnes offered, coming into the room.

Olive hesitated and then nodded, a delicate pink flush of colour staining her face as she made her way downstairs. It wasn't because it was Archie Dawson that she was going down to see him, it was because he was their local police officer. There were probably things he would want to know, reports he would need to write.

They were on their own in the shadowy darkness of the hallway.

'Olive, I've just heard the news. How is Tilly?' She was taking a step closer to him before she knew what she was doing. 'Olive.' The emotion in his voice when he repeated her name and then reached for both her hands was almost too much for her. Tears threatened her composure, as she gave in to her need for the comforting warmth of his hands around her own. It meant nothing that it shouldn't have meant. He was simply comforting her, the kind gesture of one neighbour to another, nothing more than that. Nothing at all. And yet . . . For a moment her composure failed her.

'Oh, Archie,' she said, with such aching intensity that he drew her closer.

'Olive . . .'

She could feel the warmth of his breath against her ear. Upstairs a floorboard creaked, the sound making them spring back from one another. 'Tilly is dreadfully shocked,' Olive answered him, struggling to appear calm and in control, and to keep her voice even and level against the thud of her racing heartbeat. It was Tilly who mattered, not her, Tilly he had come to ask her about. Tilly, who was lying upstairs in such a dreadful state, and no wonder after what she had witnessed.

'When Tilly saw what was happening to Drew I really thought that she was going to throw herself into the flames after him.' Olive's voice broke afresh. 'I only just managed to hold her back. I don't know what would have happened if the others hadn't been able to extinguish the fire and the bomb and save him. That poor man from number 46 couldn't be saved, though. I didn't see what happened but Tilly did, according to what Drew told me. He was more concerned about her having witnessed that than he was about himself. Such a dreadful terrible thing to have been pierced by the fin of the incendiary and then have it burn into him.'

Sergeant Dawson's grip on her hands tightened sympathetically.

213

'I had no idea what had happened until Drew told me,' Olive continued shakily. 'Tilly won't talk about it. She won't say anything. She's just lying upstairs in her bed without moving. The only time she's spoken was when I told her that Drew was all right. She just looked at me and said, "You're lying. I know he's dead. I saw him burning, just like that other man." That's all she said. Then she turned away from me and wouldn't even look at me.'

'Shell shock,' said the sergeant matter-of-factly. 'I've seen it happen to the most battle-hardened men. She'll be all right, Olive. Just give her time. How is young Drew?'

'Well, he's burned, of course, but thankfully nothing like as badly as we all feared. The ambulance men took him to hospital. Mr Edwards went with him and he's sent a message to say that he's been told that Drew will be sent home as soon as his burns have been dressed. Tilly wanted to go with him, of course, but she was in such an overwrought emotional state that the ambulance men wouldn't let her. Thank goodness.

'The Polish family can't praise him enough for what he did trying to save that poor man. Drew has sent a message via Mrs Edwards that as soon as he's able to do so he's going to come round and see Tilly. I don't think she'll be able to accept that he's alive until she's seen him for herself. I just wish she'd say something. It's so unlike her to be like this. I feel almost as though it's not my Tilly who's lying there.'

Catching back her emotions, Olive forced herself to be calm, as she told the sergeant ruefully, 'Dulcie says that none of this would have happened if they'd stayed safely at the Café de Paris.'

When Archie Dawson shook his head Olive looked at him enquiringly.

'As for that, I've heard that there's been a bomb hit it and that there's over thirty been killed and many more injured.'

'Oh, no!' Olive protested.

'I'm afraid so,' the sergeant told her. 'And Buckingham Palace has been hit as well.'

'The King and Queen?' Olive asked apprehensively.

'Both safe, and the princesses, thank the Lord.'

'I suppose you'll want to talk to us all about what happened here earlier. For the records and everything?'

'At some stage, but not right now. That's not what I've come round for now. I heard from one of the other men about what happened, and bearing in mind what you'd told me about Tilly in confidence, I just wanted to make sure that you were all right.'

He had come round because of her? He had been concerned for her? Olive felt a welling up of emotion inside her that brought a new ache to her throat.

He was being neighbourly, that was all, doing his duty as an ARP warden and their police officer, and if that hadn't been the case, if there had been something more personal about his visit, then she naturally would have rejected that something more personal and not felt moved by it.

With that in mind Olive stepped further back from him as she told him politely, 'Well, thank you for calling round, Sergeant. Your kindness is much appreciated. I'm sure that Tilly will want to thank you herself once she's back to normal.'

Only she wasn't sure just when her precious daughter would be back to normal, Olive was forced to admit over an hour later when the doctor had also called to see Tilly and had given Olive 'something to help her sleep', repeating what Sergeant Dawson had said about Tilly being in shock.

Olive only hoped that he was right. Tonight she would sleep in Agnes's bed so that she could be close to her daughter, leaving Agnes to sleep in hers. Once Drew was released from hospital, she and Sally could and would nurse him between them. That surely would prove to Tilly that she wasn't in any way against her young man, and Tilly herself, once she was back to normal, would, Olive hoped, recognise now just why her mother had been so anxious to protect her.

She'd been right about it being a long night, and they weren't through it yet, Sally thought wearily, as she went to leave the now empty basement theatre to go for her break. She'd stayed behind after the operation had finished, dismissing her juniors to go for their breaks ahead of her, but remaining herself just to check that everything in the operating theatre had been left as it should be. Something was nagging at her and keeping her here. The smell of blood still hung on the air, despite the scrubbing the operating theatre had been given after each operation. The injuries from the Café de Paris bomb had been truly dreadful: pretty young girls who would never dance again because they had lost one or both legs;

handsome young uniformed men who would not now be able to take part in the war because of their injuries. And they were the lucky ones. At least they were still alive.

As far as Sally was able to tell, neither Tilly, Dulcie nor their escorts had been amongst the injured or the dead.

No, there wasn't anything she hadn't done, she decided, as she left the operating theatre and headed for the stairs.

She took a short cut across the foyer to reach the nurse's dining room for her break. The sounds of planes, dulled and softened in the underground theatre, were much louder up here. She winced as one in particular sounded as though it were coming in right overhead. The proximity of the plane, though, was forgotten as she came to an abrupt halt. Now she knew why she hadn't felt able to leave the theatre. The surgeon who had performed the last op had, for some reason, left his notes there. She'd seen them and meant to pick them up for him but she'd forgotten. She'd have to go back for them.

She'd just turned round to go back when the familiar sound of a New Zealand accent reached her through the bustle and busyness of the foyer. A young man was talking to the porters who had just wheeled him in. He was wearing an air force uniform, badly smeared and darkened with blood, so much so, in fact, that his flight lieutenant's insignia was barely discernible.

'Where do you want us to take the Aussie?' one of the porters was asking a hovering sister.

Seeing the look on the young man's at being so wrongly labelled, Sally went over to the trolley. 'He isn't from Australia, he's from New Zealand,' she told the porters.

An appreciative smile from the young man had Sally smiling back. He was one of George's countrymen, after all, a man from the country she herself would probably be calling home one day.

'That was quick of you,' he complimented her,

'My fiancé is from New Zealand,' Sally told him, whilst professionally checking him visually. There was a tourniquet on his arm, which she also checked.

'I'm all right,' he told her tersely. 'It's those other poor sods . . . sorry, but . . .' A large muscular forearm was lifted to his eyes. 'It was supposed to be so safe down there, so everyone said.'

'You mean the Café de Paris?' Sally guessed.

He nodded. 'I've seen men – pals – shot down, I've seen men injured, I've seen bombs dropping before, but I've never seen anything as bad as what I saw tonight. Young girls – pretty girls in pretty dresses – covered in blood with . . .' His voice broke.

Sally patted his arm gently. After all, she'd seen the same victims.

'Were you there on your own?' she asked him.

'There were three of us. The other two of them got it in the blast. They were on the dance floor. I wasn't. That saved my life. Funny, isn't it, how things work out? If I hadn't asked a girl to dance with me who turned me down, I'd be dead too, because she is.'

He started to cry, dry heaving sobs that tore at his throat. Sally patted him again. She needed to get back to the theatre for those notes.

She was on her way down the corridor when she was stopped.

'Sorry, Sister,' the man on the temporary barricade told

her. 'Bomb's just dropped on one of the theatres. Luckily it was empty so no one's been hurt. It hasn't gone off, but no one's allowed down there until the UXB lot have come and checked it out.'

'Which theatre?' Sally asked.

When he told her, she had to lean back against the wall to steady herself. The theatre into which the bomb had fallen had been the one she had been heading for. If she hadn't stopped to comfort a young man because he had a New Zealand accent she could have been there when it landed.

'You alright, Sister?' the man asked.

'Yes . . .' she told him. 'Yes. I'm fine.'

And it was the truth. She was. Because of a man from New Zealand. Because she had had the good sense to put her past behind her and allow herself to love George.

'Oh, Drew. It's true. You're alive; you're safe.'

Hurling herself into her boyfriend's arms as he came in through the front door of number 13, Tilly clung fiercely to him whilst she sobbed out her relief against his shoulder. She didn't care who saw them, or what her mother said. She didn't care about anything except that Drew was here.

She'd been upstairs in her room, trying to summon the willpower to get ready for Sunday morning church, whilst inwardly grieving for the Drew she had convinced herself she'd lost, even though her mother had assured her he was safe and well, when she'd heard the door. She'd left it for her mother to answer but then, unbelievably, she'd heard Drew's voice, and she'd rushed downstairs and into his arms. Now she couldn't stop touching him, patting his face and his arms and chest just to reassure herself that he was whole and not like that poor, poor man whose image she couldn't get out of her mind.

'Oh, Drew, Drew . . . I wanted to go in the ambulance with you but they wouldn't let me.'

'I should think not,' he teased her gently. 'You're far too pretty to be allowed anywhere near a male ward.'

He was glad that she hadn't been allowed to accompany him – not for his sake but for hers. There had been victims of the night's bombings on the ward including some from the Café de Paris: men with their bodies hideously and cruelly damaged; men crying for the girls and the limbs and the lives they had lost. He had spoken to some of them, torn between his gut instinct as a reporter to capture the raw intensity of the moment, and a natural sensitivity against treading on such horribly tender ground.

'I want to talk,' one of the men had told him. 'I want to talk about it and about her, because that's all that's left of her now – my memories of her.'

Just remembering that now was enough to have Drew wrapping his arms around Tilly in a fiercely protective and possessive hug. He loved her so much. She was everything to him.

'I'm sorry you've been so upset,' he whispered to her as he wiped the tears from her damp cheeks.

'It wasn't your fault. You were just being brave and trying to help that poor man. I'm such a coward.'

His finger against her lips silenced her. 'No, you aren't. You are my Tilly, and—'

'Hold me, Drew. Hold me and kiss me,' Tilly begged him. 'Just hold me.'

Three hours later, standing outside their church, Drew's arm around her, she felt so proud that the miraculously, and thankfully only mild, burns he had suffered were badges of honour that brought members of the congregation over to praise him.

'Tilly, are you sure you are well enough to go to work today?' Olive asked anxiously on Monday morning as she watched her still pale, but resolute daughter heading for the front door.

'Yes, of course, Mum. Don't fuss,' Tilly told her, her face breaking into a loving smile as she saw Drew coming down the front garden path towards her. They had arranged the previous day that he would walk her to work this morning, and the joy that filled her at the sight of him illuminated her face.

Smiling at Olive, Drew handed her a copy of the *Daily Express*.

'Hot off the presses,' he told her. 'My landlord brought it back with him when he came in off his night shift.'

A brief glance was all Olive needed to show her that the front page was devoted to the dreadful bombing of the weekend, this a far cry from the cheering news she had read in the previous week when the British destroyer *HMS Vanoc* had accepted the surrender of a German U-boat – U-boat number 99 – the captain of which had been a top U-boat ace in terms of Allied tonnage his vessel had sunk. Hard on the heels of that victory had come the further good news that the *Vanoc* had sunk U-boat number 100. The glow of pride everyone felt in those victories might not have faded, but the weekend's bombing had subdued people's spirits, Olive acknowledged as she closed the front door and made her way to the kitchen.

The morning wireless news had finished. Anne Shelton's lovely voice was filling the kitchen. Soon it would be time for Doris and Elsie Waters' tips and advice for housewives, but before she could listen to that, Olive needed to get the breakfast things cleared away.

Agnes came hurrying into the kitchen to drink her now cold cup of tea, one eye on the clock as she berated herself for oversleeping.

'I'm sure they'll understand down at the station, Agnes, after the weekend we've had,' Olive tried to reassure her. 'After all, normally there's no one more punctual than you, and if you tell them that you were kind enough to swap beds with me so that I could be in Tilly's room over the weekend, I'm sure they'll understand.'

'I hope so,' Agnes breathed anxiously, racing into the hall to collect her coat and cap. She was very proud of her smart London Transport uniform, just as she was proud of working in the ticket office. The dull grey worsted uniform piped in blue, which had been too big for her when she had first started work at Chancery Lane ticket office, now fitted her very neatly indeed. This was in part due to her having grown a couple of inches and filled out, and partly due to the fact that Olive had seen to it tactfully that Agnes got her uniform properly altered to fit her.

'There'll be a lot to do today as well, clearing up after people had used the station as a shelter from the bombs. Dead against that, Mr Smith is,' Agnes told Olive, referring to the office manager, who had scared her so much when she had first started work but with whom she now got on a lot better. As Ted had told her at the start, there was a kind side to Mr Smith once you got to know him.

'Tilly said something this morning about you all meeting up after work today to have tea at Lyons Corner House in Leicester Square,' Olive commented.

'Yes,' Agnes confirmed, 'we arranged it last week 'cos we haven't had tea together, just the four of us, for ages. Mind you, if Tilly doesn't feel up to it I know we'll all understand. I don't know how she coped the way she did with what happened on Saturday night, I really don't.'

Agnes gave a shudder, and then she was gone, the door closing after her.

'Are you sure you're well enough to go to work?' Drew asked solicitously as they walked down Article Row together. He intended to go into the newspaper office later, after he had seen Tilly safely to her own job and had made sure that she was all right. The memory of the way in which she had been ready to run into those flames for him would never leave him, he knew. If she had been hurt; if he had lost her . . . His hand tightened around hers as he held it deep inside the pocket of his raincoat.

'The four of us – Dulcie, Sally, Agnes and me – are all meeting up for tea at Lyons Corner House in Leicester Square after work,' Tilly told Drew as they walked together. 'It was Agnes's idea. She said last week that we hardly get together, just the four of us, any more and that she wanted to hear all about the Café de Paris. She

223

did say yesterday after church that she'd understand if I didn't want to go after what happened, but I said that I would. I would feel really mean if I backed out. I don't really want to go, though, Drew. I don't really want to go anywhere without you at the moment.'

'I know,' Drew told her softly. 'I feel the same way about you. I feel I can't bear to let you out of my sight, but then I remind myself of how lucky we are to be living so close to one another, and free to see one another when so many other couples . . .'

Now it was Tilly's turn to whisper a passionate, 'I know,' to him as she gripped his hand tightly.

'I won't be far away this evening, and I'll walk you all back to number 13 when you've finished your tea.'

'Oh, Drew, you are so wonderful. I don't deserve you.'

'No. You mustn't say that. I am the one who doesn't deserve you.'

There was an intensity in his voice and the look he gave her that made Tilly's heart tremble with love.

Apart from those houses that had been damaged by the falling incendiary bombs, Article Row was more or less back to normal. The March softening of the weather was causing buds to burst on the hedges if you peered closely enough through air still thick with the smoke of the previous night's bombs, but Olive, normally so attuned to the changes in nature, wasn't in the mood to notice these signs of spring as she made her way down Article Row. She had promised to go and meet the workmen Mr King was sending to repair the door that had been damaged at number 49, the Longs' old house, on Saturday night. She felt it was the least she could do after he had so generously allowed them to store the sand for the incendiaries in the back garden there. She also wanted to call in on Mr Whittaker, just to check that he was all right and take him a bit of lunch. He might be grumpy and not generally liked, but Olive's tender heart recognised that he was an old man who, under his cross exterior, was probably very frightened by what was happening.

As she approached number 46, Olive averted her gaze. The discolouration on the cobbles was all that remained now to show where that poor man had died. Archie Dawson had been quick to get in the team of workmen to clear up all the signs of what had happened after the body had been removed. The family that had lived there were gone. They had moved out on Sunday. Olive had, of course, gone round to see if there was anything she could do to help. The poor wife had been so distressed, and no wonder, lapsing into her own language and wringing her hands as she wept for her lost husband.

A man, accompanied by two boys in their early teens, with a handcart, was holding the door to number 49, and wrenching it from side to side, more as though he was making the situation worse rather than improving it, Olive thought worriedly. Seeing her watching them the man released the door, leaving it yawning on its hinges so that Olive could see into the dusty hallway. He gave her a smile.

'Nice day, missus.'

'Yes,' Olive felt bound to agree. 'If you've come to mend the door—' she began, intending to point out to them that she had the keys.

But before she could do so the man said, 'Oh, don't

you worry, missus. We'll have it fixed in no time. Doing this all the time, we are. Won't take us two ticks. We'll just put a new lock on it for now, to make sure that no one can break in, like. We don't want that happening in a nice place like this, do we, lads?'

The two boys grinned and then laughed.

'That wouldn't do at all. Not somewhere decent like this.'

The man was obviously trying to be friendly but Olive couldn't take to him. It wasn't just that his manner was unpleasantly ingratiating, there was also the feeling that he was making fun of her. Mocking her. Not taking her seriously.

'Mr King, the owner of the house—' she began firmly, but once again the man interrupted her.

'Oh, yes, we know Mr King. Sent us round here to sort this out, he did. You don't need to worry yourself about anything, missus. You can leave everything to us.'

He was turning away from her, not wanting to have her hanging around interrupting their work, Olive suspected, but just as she was about to walk on to Mr Whittaker's she saw Barney coming down the hallway of the house towards the still open front door. When he saw her the boy stopped dead, flashing her an uncertain look.

'Hello, Barney,' Olive smiled. 'No school today?'

'No, they aren't having any lessons today on account of the bombs,' Barney told her.

Olive knew that many of the schools did have to close after heavy bombing raids. 'I suppose you've come to see what's going on, have you?' he asked him with a friendly smile.

'He's helping us out, aren't you, Barney lad,' the workman told her.

Olive smiled again, then continued on her way to the end house to see Mr Whittaker. Privately she didn't think she'd have wanted Barney hanging around with them if he were her child. Apart from anything else, the two boys with the man were much older than Barney. Barney himself had obviously been embarrassed and uncomfortable, and Olive wondered if he actually was genuinely off school or if he had simply decided to take the day off. Whatever the case, it wasn't her business and it wasn't her place to say anything to the Dawsons either, she decided, all too conscious of how Nancy and her interest in what Barney was doing was viewed by Mrs Dawson in particular. Yet she was concerned about Barney, and she knew instinctively that no matter how soft-hearted Mrs Dawson might be with the boy, Archie Dawson would not approve of him hanging around with the kind of people Olive had seen.

Having pegged out her washing before taking Mr Whittaker's dinner down to him – even though she knew that later in the day she would be bringing it back in still damp and smelling of smoke, and then trying to get it aired in the kitchen – Olive was on her way back from the bread shop where she'd had to queue for well over half an hour before she'd been able to buy a couple of loaves.

Walking briskly to ward off the cold, and refusing to look at the gaping empty spaces where, before the weekend, buildings had been, Olive paused briefly outside the vicarage. She could have done with a chat over a cup of tea with Audrey Windle – there was something about

Audrey's kind, calm manner that was wonderfully comforting – but she knew that her friend would be busy with her own household and parish duties.

The ring of a bicycle bell behind her as she turned into Article Row had her turning round, to find Archie Dawson peddling swiftly towards her.

'You didn't see anything of Barney this morning did you, Olive?' he asked, so brisk and obviously concerned that she didn't have time to feel self-conscious.

'As a matter of fact I did,' she told him as he brought his cycle to a halt and placed one foot on the pavement. 'I saw him at lunchtime when I took Mr Whittaker his dinner. He was with two older boys and a man who looked like their father and who was doing some repair work on number 49.'

Archie Dawson sighed heavily and adopted a worried frown.

'Is everything all right?'

'Tall and thickset, with sandy hair and a shifty look about them, were they, these lads?' he asked.

'Well, yes,' Olive was forced to admit. Adding, 'I did think that they seemed much older than Barney for them to be proper friends.'

'They're part of a gang he used to run around with before he came to us. Only took him up because he was small enough to get through scullery windows for them.'

Olive's shocked look had Archie Dawson reaching out to pat her on her arm.

'It's all right. Luckily Barney told me what they wanted from him before they could get him into trouble. He's a good lad, Barney is, but you know what kids are like:

always looking for an older kid to look up to and, boys being boys, they always seem to pick the ones that have got a bit of a swagger and that about them. The Farleys certainly have that. Full of it, they are, and a thoroughly bad lot to boot, the whole lot of them. They've got a reputation for being quick on the scene when a house gets bombed, picking over whatever there is to be picked over and helping themselves. The two lads you saw with Barney have an older brother who's in prison at the moment and half a dozen cousins who probably should be, or have been at some time. And their father and his brothers are just as bad. It's the old man, their grand-father, who runs the family. A real sharp card, he is, and not above doing a bit of blackmail if he thinks it will get him what he wants. Well known to us down at the station, all of them. Barney might be from a rough family but they weren't thieves. What were they doing on Article Row, I'd like to know?'

'Well, they said that they were working for Mr King, and that they'd come to repair the damage done by Saturday night's bombs.'

'That could be true. They're slippery characters, and they run a bit of a salvage and general maintenance business that seems to be legitimate, but if you were to ask me I'd say it was just a cover for their real business of thieving. Proving that, though, is another matter. I've warned Barney about keeping away from them and I've explained why to him, because you can be sure that it won't be one of them that ends up in trouble when there's someone else they can put the blame on. Not that I think that Barney would deliberately do anything wrong, but he misses his dad. Talks about him all the time. Poor little tyke.' Archie craned his neck and peered down the road through the smoke. 'There's no sign of anyone outside number 49, but I'd better get down there and check. Thanks, Olive.'

As she watched him cycle off, Olive hoped that he would be able to save Barney from the influence of the boys she'd seen him with earlier.

'Goodness, this place is busy,' Sally pronounced as the four girls squeezed round their table in the packed Corner House teashop.

'I expect everyone's thinking like we are that they want to get back home early in case there's an air raid,' Agnes offered, giving Tilly an anxious look as she asked her, 'Are you sure you're all right?'

'I'm fine,' Tilly assured her. And she was, because sitting discreetly several tables away was Drew, who had met her from work and escorted her here, and who would be walking them all home afterwards.

'Well, if you was to ask me I'd say that coming here was a daft idea, Agnes,' Dulcie put in her two penny-worth, 'especially when we could all have gone home to number 13 and had a proper decent tea there that would have cost us nothing.'

'Agnes was right to suggest that we had a get-together, Dulcie,' Sally stuck up for the other girl. 'We've all become so busy in our own lives that we hardly get time to talk together any more, even though we live under the same roof.'

'Talk? What is there to talk about? You make it sound as though we're ruddy politicians or summat, Sally. Me, I'd rather spend me free time doing something that's

230

more fun than yacking. And where's that nippy we gave our order?'

'Nippy' was the name given to the neatly dressed waitresses who worked in the Lyons Corner House teashops, women trained to deliver the most speedy service there was to be had. Lyons teashops were, after all, patronised by the working public of the country, people who wanted a decent meal served in double-quick time so that they could get back to the important business of serving their country. Of course, it was also patronised by plenty of people – friends, families, couples – who came in for one of its famous pots of tea and perhaps a piece of toast or, if they were lucky, a teacake, to be lingered over whilst they shared their special time together.

In one corner a pianist was playing a cheerful polka although there was no room for anyone to dance. Dulcie tapped her foot in time to it until she spied something that had her half standing up in outrage.

'Just look at that. I knew it,' she declared to the other girls. 'That ruddy nippy who took our order is serving them two Free French men in uniform before us even though we gave our order first. 'Ere, you . . .' she called out loudly.

Agnes cringed back in her seat whilst Sally gave a firm tug on Dulcie's arm.

'What is it?' an older waitress demanded, suddenly appearing at their table.

'That nippy,' Dulcie began, but Sally shushed her and spoke over her to say calmly, 'We seem to have been waiting a long time for our order.'

'Well, what did you order?' the waitress demanded.

'Three of us ordered egg on toast and one of us ordered sardines.'

'Well, that's it then,' the waitress sniffed. 'It's the sardines. Run out of them, we have.'

'But I've just seen our nippy taking two plates of them to those soldiers,' Dulcie began angrily.

'Well, that will be on account of them having come in earlier to order them. Regular customers, they'll be. So now, miss, if you'd like to choose something else from the menu . . . ?'

'I'll have the eggs, like everyone else,' Dulcie told her, her glower deepening when one of the French soldiers, who had obviously overheard the row, raised his teacup to her and gave her a wicked smile.

'Bloody French,' Dulcie swore. 'Just look at them. You'd never think that they'd given in to Hitler, would you, the way they strut around London?'

'Not all of them, Dulcie,' Tilly protested.

There were plenty of men in uniform in the teashop: navy, RAF, army, Polish airmen who had joined the RAF, as well as the Free French and a good smattering of uniforms from the Dominions, especially Canada. Tilly tried to distract Dulcie from her anger by pointing this out.

'Well, yes, there's plenty that are standing by us, even them as don't have to, like Wilder and the American Eagles.'

Tilly smiled and nodded, relieved when the waitress arrived with their tea and eggs on toast.

From his corner table tucked back against the wall, Drew was well placed to keep an eye on Tilly, even if she did have her back to him and even if the other girls were mostly out of view. He had heard the row, though, and he had smiled to himself. Trust Dulcie to say things as she saw them. He glanced down at his newspaper, the *Evening Standard*, which was carrying yet more grainy photographs of the appalling desolation inflicted by the weekend's bombs. Inside the paper were heart-rendingly graphic interviews with survivors of the Café de Paris bomb, but no more heart-rending and graphic than the interviews he himself had conducted. He had telegraphed some of them back to Chigaco for his father's paper, but had received a curt wire back telling him that the American people did not want to read about such unpleasant things over their breakfasts and that in future Drew was to stick to heart-warming stories about the Brits in desperate need of the food parcels they were receiving from generous Americans to keep them from starving, and how grateful they were to America for that. If necessary he could send in articles about the incredible bravery of young American fly boys, but his father had warned him that his paper's stance on the war was that it did not have and could not have anything to do with encouraging them. Too many good American lives had been sacrificed in the Great War for that.

Thinking of his father's wire now, Drew swallowed back the acid taste of his own angry bile. He and his father thought so differently about so many things. There was no real closeness between them, no real father-and-son relationship. He looked again at Tilly. She was lucky to have the mother she had, and Drew was determined never to do anything that would damage that relationship or give Tilly cause to do anything impetuous that she might regret later on in her life. Love wasn't just about the couple who loved, it was about the past and the future – and the family they would create together.

He looked again at Tilly. The tension he had seen in her shoulders when he had first sat down had gone and he heard her laugh. A smile curled his own mouth. This get-together with the other girls would do her good.

'Oh, Dulcie, do stop it,' Tilly protested. 'You're making me laugh so much that my tummy hurts.'

All of them were in fact laughing at Dulcie's clever imitation of a customer, who had come in to protest that her box of face powder had 'leaked' because the cardboard was of inferior quality and that because of that she wanted Selfridges to replace it with a new one.

'The things they try on! Honestly, you'd have to see it to believe it. One of the other girls was telling me that they had one woman in with six pairs of nylons, all of them laddered, complaining that she'd bought them in '39, and that now when she'd come to open the packets she'd found that they were all faulty. Rose, the salesgirl, told me that she recognised right off that they were American nylons, her having worked on the nylons counter for going on for ten years – and cheap ones at that – the kind that some of the merchant seamen bring back and that get sold on the market. Just imagine the cheek of the woman coming into Selfridges and trying to claim they was ours.' A toss of Dulcie's head accompanied her words.

They had all eaten every scrap of their eggs on toast, and their spotted dick, with its somewhat watery custard, as well as emptied two full pots of tea, and now it was time for them to leave; Sally for the hospital, where she was on night duty, and the other three for number 13,

234

Tilly deliberately slowing her walking pace so that she and Drew could trail slightly behind Agnes and Dulcie, so that she could have him to herself.

'You look a lot more like my Tilly now than you did this morning,' Drew told her.

'I still can't forget what happened on Saturday,' Tilly admitted, smiling up at him as she added, 'but somehow you can't not laugh when Dulcie starts telling one of her tales.'

TWELVE

'And now they're saying that women over the age of twenty who aren't married will have to register for munitions work before long, and that once you do you can be sent anywhere, and that you have to go. It was on the news, and then Drew brought us the papers to show us that it was in there as well. He reckons that after a while they'll make it that more women have to do it by adding in more ages. Not that Sally or Tilly or Agnes will have to do it on account of them all being in protected jobs. Well, I don't care what anyone in the Government says, I'm not leaving London. I'm just not,' Dulcie told David determinedly.

It was Easter weekend and she'd arrived at the hospital half an hour ago, having travelled down from London early Saturday morning, and now, as she made herself comfortable on the chair at David's bedside, she was eager to air her grievances about the proposed new law to be brought in by the Minister of Labour, Mr Ernest Bevin, which called for all young women between the ages of twenty and thirty to register for essential wartime work in munitions.

'It was bad enough having to do that ruddy fire-watching, without this,' Dulcie continued. 'I was talking to one girl and she's got a sister who's in munitions, and she says that it turns your skin yellow working with all that stuff, and that you have to wear a scarf round your head. Mind you, the money's good. Not that I'm going to let anyone tell me what to do, and I'm certainly not going to let anyone send me away from London.'

'Well, in that case, Dulcie, I suggest that you find out where your nearest munitions factory is and then go round there and have a word with someone on the quiet to make sure you can get in there before you have to register. That way you'll be able to choose where you work rather than waiting to be sent somewhere,' David responded.

'I suppose you're right,' Dulcie agreed. 'There's a place at Woolwich I could try. 'Cos if they was to send me out of London then I probably wouldn't be able to come and see you. And if you was to ask me then I'd say that me coming to see you is just as much doing my bit as working in some munitions factory. Because like Sister was saying to me when I arrived, she doesn't know how you'd go on now without having my visits to look forward to. Bin a tonic for you, I have.'

'Yes, you have,' David agreed gravely, after he had recovered from the small spluttering sound he'd had to choke back behind his hand.

That was the thing about a man like David, who was a proper gentleman: he knew how to treat a girl right. Not like Wilder, who she hadn't seen hair nor hide of for over a week, although he had sent her a brief scribbled note telling her that the RAF had said that the Eagle Squadron, manned by American volunteer pilots, was now officially operational.

Not that a scribbled letter was anything much. You'd have thought after the way he'd just gone off and left them, and then all those bombs falling, that he'd have come up to London to see how she was. Not that Dulcie was going to tell David that she felt that Wilder was neglecting her. She didn't want David to think that Wilder was anything other than totally besotted with her.

'Yes, I'll do as you suggest and take meself along to Woolwich and have a word with them there,' she told him instead. 'I dare say they'll be only too pleased to have someone like me offering to work for them.'

'I'm sure they will,' David agreed, somehow managing to keep his expression deadpan.

Against all the odds he was discovering that he was actually looking forward to Dulcie's visits and enjoying her company. There was something about Dulcie that always lifted his spirits without him being able to say what exactly it was. It certainly wasn't her interest in him or her concern for his health.

David smiled to himself. He reckoned he must be the only patient in the entire hospital whose visitor did not, upon arrival, ask how he was but instead started to talk about herself. That, though, was one of the things that made him look forward to Dulcie's visits. With Dulcie there was no false emotion, no faked sympathy, no embarrassment or discomfort. His injuries might simply not have existed, because Dulcie was far too wrapped up in herself to be concerned with them. It meant that with Dulcie he could be himself. His real self, not the injured, helpless, dependent, pitiful David that Lydia and his mother saw when they looked at him, but the David who still existed inside his damaged body. In short, Dulcie treated him as though there was nothing wrong with him at all. Not out of compassion or because she was deliberately avoiding a difficult subject but because, being Dulcie, she was totally oblivious to everything and anything that did not concern her directly. Other people, other men in his position, might have found her selfish and self-centred, David knew, but he much preferred what others would have called selfishness in her to the sickly patronising concern of those who were fortunate enough to be sound in body and mind. Acknowledging that reminded him of something he still had to tell her, once he could break into her monologue about her own life.

In order to get Dulcie's attention David had already learned that one needed to focus with determination on one's target, and once one had spotted a potential gap in the conversation one had to take aim with all guns blazing. 'My mother came to see me last week,' he broke into Dulcie's diatribe against Mr Ernest Bevin, and his Ministry for Labour.

'I thought you said she never came to see you?' Dulcie challenged him. It wasn't in her makeup to question why she should feel so antagonistic towards the idea of a mother visiting her son. If she had done she would have told herself that her anger was on David's behalf because his mother had previously ignored him, and had nothing whatsoever to do with her own relationship with her mother or the fact that she felt let down by it.

'She doesn't normally, but she had something to tell me that she thought I ought to know,' David responded.

'And what was that?'

'She wanted to tell me about Lydia being at the Café de Paris the other weekend.'

Dulcie digested this statement warily. Lydia had obviously told David's mother about seeing her and the row they had had because she had wanted it reported back to David. Instinctively Dulcie reacted just as she had done as a child when Edith had gone running to tell their mother about something Dulcie had done that would get her into trouble.

Leaping to defend herself, she said sharply, 'Well, of course Lydia would tell your mother about her seeing me there and what happened. Not that it was much of a row or anything, us having words, but—'

'You were at the Café de Paris the night it was bombed?' David stopped her. He was surprised at the intensity of the surge of relief he felt that she had obviously escaped from the bombing and was safe. Not that he was going to dwell on that feeling. What was the point? Dulcie might be willing to come and see him. She might even give the impression of enjoying her visits to him, but David wasn't a fool. He wasn't the man she had flirted with any more, and Dulcie certainly didn't have any female interest in him as the man he now was.

'Yes, Wilder took me to make up for not taking me out on Valentine's Day. Not that we stayed long, and that was just as well, seeing what happened there. Horrible, it was. Sally said they had that many coming in injured from it they could barely cope. And I don't know how Lydia could have the brass face to complain to anyone about me. She wasn't even with that chap I saw her with at the Ritz. She was with some young officer, and—'

'She's dead, Dulcie. She was killed. Lydia's dead. She was one of those who got it with the bomb. That's why my mother came to see me. She came to tell me that Lydia is dead.'

For once in her life Dulcie was truly lost for words. Stumbling uncertainly she told him, 'Well, that must have been a shock for you, and no mistake. Must have upset you as well, her being your wife and everything—'

'Not really,' David stopped her. 'To tell you the truth, I didn't feel a damn thing. Shocking of me to say that, I know,' he continued when Dulcie simply sat and stared at him, 'but it's the truth. Now I have shocked you.' He pulled a face, his voice bitter. 'But then of course I dare say it is far more shocking that a young woman like Lydia should be killed whilst she was out enjoying herself than a man like me should lose his legs. After all, I was only doing my duty and serving my country. I dare say there are even those who'd think I deserve what happened to me.'

'Don't be daft.' Dulcie tried to stop him, grabbing hold of her scattered thoughts, and well aware what Sister would have to say if she thought that one of her patients had been upset, but David ignored her.

'If I hadn't joined but stayed at home instead, in a

safe job, then Lydia would be alive now,' he continued, 'at least that's what my mother seems to think.'

'Sounds like your ma is a bit like mine,' Dulcie told him stalwartly. 'Always thought more of our Edith than me, our mother did, and since she was reported missing and presumed dead, all Ma has ever done is go on about how much she misses her.'

'Do *you* miss her?' David asked her. 'Your sister, I mean.'

'No I don't,' Dulcie responded truthfully and emphatically. 'Not one little bit. Of course I wouldn't have wanted her to die – but I don't miss her. Her and me never got on. Always our mum's favourite, she was, and didn't she know it. Mean and spiteful, I always thought her, running to our mum to tell tales and get her sympathy. Spoiled her rotten, Mum did, putting her up on the kitchen table when she was little and getting her to sing for the neighbours. Never said one word to her, Mum didn't later, when Edith started borrowing my good clothes without a by-your-leave. Shared a bedroom, we did. That's why I got meself a room at number 13, 'cos I was sick of Edith parading around in my things. Rick, our brother, wot's out fighting that Rommel in the desert was the only one who understood how I felt. If Mum hadn't encouraged her to think she could be a singer she might even be alive now because it was on account of her going to sing in public that she got killed the night the place was bombed. Not that they ever found her body. Mum's never bin the same since that happened. She might have thought the world of Edith but I never did. I'm sorry she's gone, for Mum's sake, but not for me own,' Dulcie announced defiantly.

'I feel the same way about Lydia,' David told her. He looked at her and then admitted, 'You are the only person I can say that to, Dulcie. I've had doctors and nurses in here telling me how sorry they are about Lydia ever since my mother came to break the news. It's getting on my nerves having to pretend that I care, but I don't. I can't, and to be honest I don't even want to care.'

'Well, why should you?' Dulcie responded pragmatically. 'After all, she went and let you down, didn't she? Carrying on with that chap I saw her with at the Ritz, and then acting like she was something special and looking down her nose at me at the Café de Paris, never mind that I was wearing me Norman Hartnell gown and her with some other chap in tow, and it plain to see what was going on between them. Mind you, I give her as good as I got,' she added with some relish. 'Told her in no uncertain terms, I did, what I thought of her and the way she'd treated you.'

'Was that what the row was about?' David asked.

'Yes. Well, me and her never did get on,' Dulcie felt bound to acknowledge.

'Which was why you flirted with me when I saw you in Selfridges, was it?' David teased her.

Bridling slightly, Dulcie shook her head. 'I never flirted with you. I'm not the sort to do that, and I won't have you saying that I was. You were the one that bought me that vanity case.'

'You know what I think, Dulcie?'

'What?' Dulcie asked warily.

'I think that you and I are two of a kind.'

'Well, as to that I'm as good as that Lydia was any

day of the week, no matter what your ma might like to think,' Dulcie was quick to claim. She didn't really understand what David was getting at, but knowing that he was prepared to talk to her the way he had about Lydia certainly made her feel justified that she had challenged the other girl at the Café de Paris.

THIRTEEN

'There, that's a barrowful of sand ready for the Misses Barker,' Drew smiled at Tilly as he tipped the final shovelful of sand from the stockpile in the garden of number 49 into the waiting wheelbarrow.

The Easter sunshine slanted across his face, his look of male pleasure in a physical job well done making Tilly smile and filling her heart with so much tenderness that she released the handles of the barrow she had been about to wheel out through the back garden gate and then along the path to the Misses Barkers'. Instead, she went to put her arms around him. The jumper he was wearing smelled dangerously of soap and just a hint of fresh male sweat. Dangerously, because being this close to him always brought home to Tilly all that she was missing because her mother refused to allow them to marry.

Smiling down at her, Drew picked out of her curls the pink blossom that had come from the gnarled apple tree in the middle of the neglected garden.

'I took the paper into work so that everyone could

read that piece you wrote about the looters,' she told him proudly. 'It was so good, Drew.'

'Not as good as it could have been if I'd been able to speak directly to some of those involved.'

Tilly smiled understandingly. She knew how disappointed he'd been that he hadn't been able to make contact with any of the looters.

'Well, you know what Sergeant Dawson said after he'd read your article. He said that even the police are having trouble infiltrating the looting gangs.

'When are you going to let me read your book?' Tilly wheedled, changing the subject as she leaned against him. She already knew the answer, but nevertheless she regularly attempted to persuade Drew to change his mind and let her read the book he was writing.

'Not until it's finished,' Drew answered as she had known that he would.

'But if it's about the war and all of us, then . . .' she began, and then stopped, her face clouding over.

Olive, who had come down initially to make sure that Mr Whittaker was all right, and who had then decided that she may as well pop into number 49 to see how Tilly and Drew were getting on, paused with the back door half open as she witnessed their intimacy.

'Don't look like that, Tilly,' she heard Drew say. 'I hate it when you look unhappy.'

Olive swallowed painfully. Drew wasn't the only one who felt like that.

'I can't help it,' Tilly told him, both of them oblivious to the fact that they weren't alone and that their conversation could easily be overheard. 'I really can't, Drew. We don't know when the war will end or what's going to happen, who is going to win, whether we'll still be alive when it's over.' Her voice broke and Drew tightened his hold on her.

The awful sight she had witnessed the night the incendiaries had fallen on Article Row still tormented Tilly, he knew, even though she didn't like talking about the effect it had had on her. He hated seeing her so distressed and knowing that there was so little he could do to comfort her.

'I hate living the way we are,' Tilly continued passionately. 'I hate feeling that we're wasting time now, marking time until the war is over, just to please my mother. We're alive now; we don't know if we'll even be alive tomorrow. I want to live now – with you – as your wife. My mother claims she's protecting me, but protecting me from what? Being happy? Is that what she really wants? We might only have today, Drew. I can't bear knowing that, and knowing that my mother is stopping me from being with you.'

'Oh, Tilly.'

'It isn't fair, Drew. It really isn't. Mum hasn't said a word about the fact that Sally and George have gone away together for Easter, and yet she won't even let us get engaged. I felt so envious of Sally this morning, going away with her George, just the two of them, with no one to spy on them or tell them what to do.'

'Sally is older than you,' Drew felt honour-bound to point out, 'and her situation is very different from yours. She doesn't have a mother to worry and be anxious for her.'

Drew had wanted his comment to remind Tilly of how much more fortunate than Sally she was to have her mother but, to his dismay, instead Tilly lifted her head from his shoulder to look up into his face and tell him bitterly, 'Lucky her. I wish I had her freedom.'

Behind the half-open door Olive felt the pain knot her stomach and send her heart into a shocked race of maternal hurt. Releasing the door, she walked blindly towards the hallway, opening the front door to stumble out into the April sunshine, Tilly's cruel words still ringing in her head.

Out in the garden, Drew gave Tilly a small admonishing shake. 'You don't mean that,' he challenged her.

'No,' Tilly agreed. 'I don't. I just wish that she'd understand.'

'As no doubt your mother wishes you would understand her,' Drew told her gently.

'I've had enough, Drew,' Tilly told him. 'When I saw Sally coming downstairs this morning with her case, she looked so happy, and so . . . so expectant . . .' was the only way Tilly felt able to describe Sally's look of glowing anticipation and joy. 'I want to look like that for you. I want . . .'

She didn't need to say or try to explain any more. Drew was taking her back in his arms, the wheelbarrow and its contents forgotten as he kissed her and Tilly kissed him back.

'I know how impatient you are for us to get married, Tilly,' Drew told her as he released her, 'and I feel the same, but perhaps we do need to be a bit more patient with your mom and give her more time to get used to the idea.'

'You say that, but I'm frightened, Drew. I'm so afraid that something will happen to part us. It makes me feel that I have to do everything I can to make sure that we're together now.' Overhead, clouds covered the sun and Tilly shivered. 'It hurts me so much that Mum can't – won't – understand that. Sometimes I even think that maybe she wants us to part. I know that's silly but I just feel so afraid and . . . and so alone sometimes, Drew. Ever since that night . . .'

'Oh, my poor darling girl,' Drew tried to comfort her. 'I promise you that whilst I have breath in my body I will never let anything or anyone come between us or keep us apart. I mean that, Tilly. You have my word on that. You are my girl. You are the only girl for me. Nothing can change that. I want you to tell me that you believe me when I say that, and that you will stop worrying.'

'I believe you, Drew,' said Tilly sombrely.

'Promise me?' Drew insisted. 'Promise me that you know that I will never ever stop loving you, Tilly?'

'I promise,' Tilly told him. She could feel the love and the truth in his promise to her. But not even Drew's assurance could banish the fear that had taken root inside her heart. What if it was something else that parted them? Something that did have the power to separate them for ever? Death had that power. Tilly closed her eyes against the panic and fear exploding inside her. She must not burden Drew with the awfulness of her dread, or worry him about the truly horrible and increasingly intense nightmares in which she could see him burning to death behind the wall of fire that separated them. She was too ashamed of her own weakness and fear to tell him that the main reason she was so angry with her mother for keeping them apart was because she had become convinced that she was going to lose him and that he would be killed. She had always thought of herself as a strong person, but she'd been wrong. She wasn't strong, she was cowardly and weak, and that was something she hated knowing about herself, never mind admitting to anyone else, especially when everyone else was being so brave.

'Come on. Let's deliver this barrowload of sand to the Misses Barker before lunchtime,' Drew told her, reaching for the barrow. Tilly nodded. She felt so ashamed of her cowardice and her fear, so unable to discuss it with anyone because of that shame, and so very alone with those feelings.

Olive had almost reached number 13 when she saw Barney coming towards her accompanied by two older boys. He gave them an anxious look, as though somehow he felt he needed to seek their approval, before responding to her 'hello'.

'Up to no good they are, you mark my words,' Nancy, who was standing at her front gate, her arms folded, announced as soon as Olive came within earshot.

The last thing she wanted right now was to have to stand and listen to one of Nancy's complaints, Olive thought miserably, but knowing Nancy as she did, she recognised that there was no escape and that Nancy fully intended to have her say.

Olive had to admit that she herself didn't much like the look of the two youths with Barney. She had recognised them as the two boys who had been helping out the man repairing the door to number 49, but she didn't want to encourage Nancy to complain about Barney so she kept her thoughts to herself, saying instead, 'Barney's a nice boy, Nancy.'

'With the background he's got? How can you say that? The Dawsons shouldn't be allowed to foist him off on decent folk like they have.'

'I've got to get in,' Olive excused herself. 'Drew and Tilly will be coming in for their lunch any minute.'

'I'm surprised that you're letting your Tilly spend so much time alone with her young man, Olive. It's asking for trouble, if you ask me.'

'Well, I'm not asking you, Nancy, and now if you'll excuse me . . .'

Olive could feel her ears burning with a mixture of anger and guilt as she turned her back on her open-mouthed neighbour and hurried inside. If she'd stayed and had to listen to more of Nancy's criticisms and complaints, Olive felt that she wouldn't have been able to trust herself not to snap fiercely at her, especially when she criticised Tilly.

Tilly . . . Olive's hands trembled as she removed her coat and went to fill the kettle.

What she had heard Tilly saying had shocked and hurt her, but surely it also confirmed that she was right to think that Tilly wasn't mature enough yet for marriage. Putting the kettle down without turning on the gas, Olive found herself staring at the wall. All she was trying to do was protect Tilly, as any loving mother would. She was right to do that, wasn't she?

'Oh, this is lovely. Heavenly, in fact.'

George smiled at Sally as they walked arm in arm together through the pretty woodland glade with its spring carpet of bluebells, a fresh green canopy of unfurling leaves overhead, the sunlight dappling light and shadow through the branches.

They'd arrived in the small Berkshire village just over an hour ago and, having booked into the White Hart, the pub-cum-hotel where they were staying, they'd come out to explore their surroundings.

It had been Sally who had suggested that they try to get away over Easter since, after Good Friday, they were both off for the rest of the Easter holiday. It was Sally too who had chosen their destination and booked their rooms after another sister at Barts had recommended the place to her. Two rooms, booked in their real names, not the subterfuge adopted by some young couples who chose to share a room under an assumed married name. Two rooms, each with its own bed, but tonight Sally fully intended that they would be using only one of those rooms and sharing its bed.

Thinking of that now, she asked George, 'Did you get you-know-what?'

Was he really blushing slightly? If so, that only made Sally love him all the more.

'Yes,' he confirmed, 'but I'm not sure that we should be doing this, Sally. Do you really think that it's wise?' he questioned, the huskiness in his voice betraying to her what he really thought.

'We'll have to make sure that we *are* wise – and careful,' Sally told him firmly.

'The trouble is,' George admitted, turning her towards him, 'I can't trust myself to be as wise and as careful as I should be when I'm with you like this, Sally.'

Heady words, and they were going to her head, Sally

admitted. What other reason could there be for her smiling up at him and telling him in a voice that was as tremulous as his had been husky, 'Sometimes I don't want you to be.'

The spring breeze ruffled the skirt of Sally's dress, with its dark blue and purple floral design against its cream background, teasing the hem and flattening the fabric against her legs. Sally, though, locked in George's arms, was oblivious to the breeze.

'So are you and Ted going to the pictures as usual this evening?' Tilly asked Agnes, who had come to join her and Drew after delivering a parcel of Olive's Easter baking to Mr Whittaker at number 50.

'Yes. We were going to go upriver this afternoon for a bit of a treat and take Ted's sisters and mum with us, but his mum was worried that it would be too expensive, so Ted's gone round there instead.'

'Here's Barney,' Drew announced as the gate into the garden of number 49 slowly opened and the Dawsons' foster son crept in.

'Hi, Barney. Come to give us hand, have you?' Drew called out to him.

'You've given him a shock, Drew,' Tilly said as Barney froze and stared at them. 'I don't think he realised we were here.'

The gate opened again and two older boys came in, both of them coming to an abrupt halt as they saw Drew, Tilly and Agnes.

'Any shrapnel in here, mate?' the older of the two boys called out to Drew. 'That's what we're looking for, init, Barney?'

'They must be the two boys that Mum was talking about over lunch, the ones that she said she didn't much care for,' Tilly told Drew quietly so that the boys couldn't hear her. 'She thinks they're too old for Barney, and so does Sergeant Dawson.'

'Too old and probably a bit too knowing,' Drew agreed, before calling to them, 'Well, you're welcome to have a look round, whilst we're in here filling these barrows.'

'Go on, Barney mate, you have a good scout around,' the older boy instructed, as he himself came towards them. He produced half a cigarette from his trouser pocket and lit it, drawing the smoke in to his lungs and holding the cigarette between his thumb and his first finger with practised ease.

'Heard about the ghost that's bin seen here, have you?' he asked, adding before they could say anything, 'Don't believe it meself but Barney swears he saw summat and so does our Stan. That's me brother what's with him. Reckon they saw summat outside what disappeared into the house through the front door, even though it was shut. There's bin noises heard too, sort of bangings and shiftings, like. My old man's with the heavy-lifting repair lot and he reckons that there's plenty of people say that some of them that's died are still hanging around, like they was still alive. That Mr Long died here. And there's the ghost of a woman been seen down near Whitechapel crying out that she can't find her baby.'

At Tilly's side Agnes gave a small moan.

'It's all right, Agnes,' Drew reassured her, giving the

boy a cool warning look. 'There's no such thing as ghosts.'

'You can say that, mister, but Barney over there reckons he's definitely seen summat. You ask him. Come on, you two,' he called out to Barney and the other youth, stubbing out his cigarette. 'There's a bomb site over on Hamble Road I've heard about where there was four houses flattened. I reckon we'll find summat there.'

'Poor Barney did look scared,' Tilly told Drew after the boys had gone. 'He kept on looking up at the windows the whole time he was here.'

'Oh, don't, Tilly,' Agnes begged her, looking nervously in the direction of the upstairs windows herself.

'If Barney was scared it was probably because he'd been fed ridiculous stories of something that doesn't exist,' Drew told them both firmly, watching Tilly tense when the sound of a fighter plane was heard in the sky overhead.

'It's all right, it's one of ours,' Drew reassured her, knowing instantly why she had tensed. Tilly might not talk very much about what had happened the night Article Row had been bombed but that didn't mean that Drew didn't know how much it had affected her.

'I knew that,' Tilly insisted.

Sitting in the vicarage's pretty garden, drinking tea out of the delicate china cups that Audrey Windle had once told Olive had been a wedding present from her husband's great-aunt, Olive and Audrey also heard the Spitfire overhead, and looked up.

'They're saying that it's very likely that the Luftwaffe

will bomb us again, now that the war seems to be going in their favour and not ours,' Audrey told Olive, adding, 'My nephew is rejoining his squadron next week. He's delighted, but naturally my sister is very anxious for him. He tells her not to worry, of course. These young ones have such courage and faith. I envy them that.'

'They don't know what we know. This is their first war. It's our second,' Olive pointed out sombrely.

'You'll go ahead and drive for the mobile canteen service then, will you, Olive?' Audrey asked her, changing the subject. 'Only I could see how pleased Mrs Finch was when she learned that you could drive.'

'Yes. I'll be happy to do it, if they want me to,' Olive confirmed.

It had been flattering to know how keen the mobile canteen arm of the WVS were to put her on their list of available drivers.

'I'm so glad that Mrs Dawson has decided to join our WVS group,' Audrey continued. 'She's a changed person since they took Barney in. A true example of charitable kindness being its own reward.'

'. . . And the boy with Barney told us that he thinks that there's a ghost at number 49,' Agnes informed Olive breathlessly as the four of them sat down for a cup of tea later in the afternoon.

'All nonsense, of course, and I told them so,' Drew chipped in.

'But that boy said that Barney had heard strange noises coming from the house,' Agnes reminded him.

'I'm sure if Barney tells Sergeant Dawson that he thinks that number 49 has a ghost, he'll say exactly what you've said, Drew,' Olive responded. What she couldn't say, though, was that she suspected that Archie Dawson would be extremely concerned to know that Barney was still hanging around with the Farley brothers.

'Mrs Vincent says that she knows a couple of villagers who'll let us borrow their bikes tomorrow, and that we should go and have a look at the ruins of the castle on the outskirts of the village,' Sally informed George, as she rejoined him in the cosy bar after speaking with the landlady.

When the spring light had faded into darkness, the landlord had lit the log fire in the pub's large inglenook fireplace, and Sally and George had eaten their evening meal basking in its warm glow.

'I recommend the chicken pie and no questions asked about where the chicken came from,' the landlord had winked at them when they had asked what was on the menu. And as Sally had said once she had tasted it, the pie had almost been as good as Olive's cooking, as had the rhubarb flummery that had followed it.

Out here in the countryside it was almost possible to forget that there was a war, or at least it had been until a group of young men in RAf uniform had arrived in a couple of sports cars.

'I can't help contrasting them with your patients,' Sally told George when the airmen had left and the sound of their cars' engines had faded.

'I know, I was just thinking the same thing. Fancy a stroll to walk off dinner before we go up?' he asked with a studied casualness that made her smile tenderly at him and gently touch his knee beneath the table.

'Aren't I the one who should be feeling apprehensive and trying to put things off?' she teased him.

A few minutes later, when they were strolling along the village street, her hand tucked through his arm, George admitted, 'I don't want to disappoint you.'

'You won't,' Sally assured him lovingly. 'You couldn't. Come on, let's go back.'

Sally had elected to go to George's room rather than have him come to hers. She felt he would be more comfortable that way because it would make it clear to him that she wanted what was going to happen as much as he did, and that he wasn't compelling her in any way. Sally smiled to herself at the thought of George, dear George, who was so gentle and kind compelling her to do anything.

Their bedrooms were next to one another and virtually identical, tucked up in the eaves of the centuries-old White Hart, with its slate roof and tiny windows with deep stone ledges. The landlady had already covered the windows with the blackout curtains, and after her bath in a bathroom that smelled pleasantly of George's cologne Sally dressed herself in the pretty pale blue chemise and matching French knickers set bought on impulse in the days when she had believed she would be wearing them for a very different man, and so nearly thrown away in furious misery when she had been packing to leave home. It had been the thought of her mother grieving over such a waste that held her back then, just as it was her memories of her mother that were pushing her forward now. Other young women might find it odd and even hard to understand that she should think of her mother at a time like this and feel that she would approve of what she was doing, but Sally knew that her mother would have loved George and would have understood perfectly why, in their world of death and destruction, Sally wanted to create this small brief oasis of special commitment for them both. They couldn't marry. It would be frowned upon with George at the stage he was with his career, and even more so by her own matron. But they could do this. *She* could do this, Sally felt. She could give them both this special time, this special memory to sustain them until the was was over.

Pulling on her dressing gown, she made her way along the bare boards of a corridor that creaked with every step she took until she was outside George's bedroom door. Knocking briefly she didn't wait for an answer, simply lifting the old-fashioned wrought-iron latch and stepping inside.

George, like her, was wearing a dressing gown – his being a smart paisley – beneath which she could see the trousers of a pair of handsome-looking burgundy silk pyjama bottoms. He was pacing the wooden bedroom floor, smoking a cigarette.

When he saw her the tips of his ears went red.

'The bed looks comfy,' Sally told him, deliberately teasing him as his ears burned even more.

'Sally, are you sure you want to do this?' he asked her anxiously. 'Because if you don't—'

'Shush. And yes, I do,' Sally told him tenderly, going to him and placing her fingertips against his mouth.

Taking her hand in his, George said, 'I just hope you won't be disappointed. I haven't . . .' He paused, looking uncomfortable.

'Neither have I.'

'I don't want to disappoint you,' he repeated.

'You won't,' Sally reassured him as she had done earlier before shrugging off her dressing gown and putting her arms round his neck. 'Or at least you won't if you kiss me very soon, darling George.'

With something between a groan and a self-deprecatory laugh, George gathered her in his arms, his heart thudding heavily into hers.

Later, much later, after they had shared the uncertainty of that first exploratory time, and then come together again with newly discovered confidence and joy, Sally lay in George's arms, her head pillowed against his shoulder, her hand resting on his bare chest, her voice soft with love as she whispered to him, 'See, I was right, wasn't I? I knew it would be wonderful. I knew *you* would be wonderful, George.'

'You are the one who is wonderful,' he responded emotionally.

FOURTEEN

'Of course, when I told them that I was working for Selfridges but that I'd felt it me duty to go into munitions on account of me having a brother who was out fighting in the desert, they offered me a job straight away. Well, it stands to reason that they would, doesn't it?'

'But aren't you just a little bit worried that you won't like it, Dulcie? I mean, you've been working with them lovely cosmetics and everything at Selfridges, and one of the women who works with me has said as how her niece is working in munitions and that she doesn't care for it at all. It's turned her skin yellow, and she says that you have to wear horrible clothes. She says too that there's some girls there who are really rough types.' Agnes gave a small shudder.

Listening to them, Olive suppressed a small sigh. Agnes was a dear, and wouldn't knowingly hurt anyone, but there was no getting away from the fact she could be naïve at times.

'Well, of course I won't be mixing with that sort. And I dare say I'll be promoted in no time at all, me being a cut above them. That's what David says, anyway,' Dulcie informed Agnes, giving her an angry look. 'As for the clothes, you have to wear them to protect yourself, 'cos you're dealing with dangerous chemicals. That's what Mr Finch, who's the foreman, told me. Anyway, I don't see how you can say that about working in munitions when you're working on the underground in that awful uniform.'

'I think what you're doing is very brave, Dulcie,' Tilly chipped in.

'You're right, it is. But of course I felt it was my duty, didn't I, when Mr Bevin said about our boys needing more munitions and that. You only have to listen to the news to know that they're having a hard time out in the desert where our Rick is.'

Sally suppressed a small smile as she listened. The reality was, of course, that if Dulcie hadn't volunteered she would have been called up for munitions work anyway eventually, and that her decision to find herself a job at a local munitions factory meant that she'd avoided the risk of being sent to a strange town where she knew no one. Now at least she could continue to lodge at number 13. Not that Sally blamed her for wanting to do that. Number 13 had become home to all three lodgers.

Having looked at her watch, Sally finished her cup of tea and stood up. 'I'd better go otherwise I'll be late for my night shift.'

Olive watched her as she hurried to the door.

When Sally had returned from Berkshire on Easter Monday there had been such an obvious glow of happiness and contentment about her that Olive had guessed immediately what had happened. Not that she would have said so to Sally, if Sally herself hadn't introduced the subject when they had been alone in the kitchen together doing the washing up.

'I suppose you've guessed what happened whilst we were away,' she said quietly. 'It was my idea, and what I wanted. We can't marry yet, and sometimes I feel that George doesn't realise how special he is to me and how much I love him. I wanted him to know how I really feel. I wanted us to have something to hold on to. I dreamed of my mother afterwards. She was smiling and happy for me. I know she would have loved George.'

Olive could still feel the sharp echo of the pang of envy she had felt witnessing Sally's obvious joy. And if she had been aware of that air of completeness and fulfilment that surrounded her, then how much more aware of it must Tilly be?

Just one brief look at her daughter's face now as Tilly watched Sally hurry out of the room told Olive that she was right to fear that Tilly was aware of the change in Sally and the reason for it.

Sally was so lucky, Tilly thought enviously. There had been no one to stop her being with George as Tilly so desperately wanted to be with Drew. And, of course, George, unlike her own Drew, would not have told her that her mother was only trying to protect her by refusing to acknowledge that she was adult enough to make her own decisions.

Tilly thought of the girl she had overheard in the ladies' at the pub in Fleet Street when she and Drew had gone there for a drink on Saturday night – a girl who had looked as though she was more or less her own age, and wearing a new shiny wedding ring – who had been boasting to her friend that she had forced her parents' hands by telling them that there was every risk that their grandchild would be born out of wedlock if they didn't let her marry her sweetheart, and quickly.

If Drew had been a different type of man she might have been able to persuade him to do the same, but then if he had been the type to agree to something like that, then he wouldn't have been her Drew, Tilly was forced to admit, as she turned to Dulcie, in an attempt to give her thoughts a new direction.

'So what is it that you have to wear then, Dulcie?' she asked.

Dulcie pulled a face. 'Well, when you get there, you have to sign on and then you have to go into this room and get changed out of your own clothes, on account of you not being allowed to wear anything with metal in it in case it causes a spark and you blow the whole place up, what with all them detonators and that around.'

Listening to Dulcie, Tilly's hand went straight to the neckline of her floral blouse, beneath which she was wearing Drew's ring on its chain. She didn't think she'd be willing to take any kind of work that meant she couldn't have it close to her.

'Then we have to work a month on days and a month on nights, and we don't get to finish until Saturday afternoon. Mind you, we do get a hot meal whilst we're there, and they have the wireless going, not that you can hear much of it with all them machines. The place stinks, an' all, with all them explosives and that, and you can't go to the air-raid shelter until the foreman says that you can even though the air-raid warning has gone. One of the girls I got talking to told me that it's horrible when there's a bombing raid and you're working nights, 'cos you know that it's the munitions factories they're after. She says they built the factories down along the Thames so that there's plenty of water to put out the fires if they do get bombed.'

'Oh, Dulcie, I think you are ever so brave volunteering to work there,' Agnes exclaimed admiringly, making up for her earlier faux pas.

Watching Dulcie acknowledge Agnes's praise very much as though she considered it to be no less than her due, Olive felt that now wasn't the time to spoil things by reminding Agnes that Dulcie had had no alternative, given her age and the new law the Minister for Labour had proposed. It did, though, make her think about how she'd be feeling if it was Tilly who was obliged to go and work in munitions. There was no getting away from the fact that not only was the work itself dangerous, but also that the munitions factories along the Thames were, as Dulcie had rightly said, a known target for the Luftwaffe's bombs. Of course, Tilly wasn't old enough yet to get caught up in the Government decree that young women who were not either married with children or involved in reserved occupations had to go into munitions. Plus the fact that she was working at Barts meant that she was in a reserved occupation. Not that that meant that Tilly was safe from Hitler's bombs – none of them was.

'Come on, Drew,' Tilly announced, getting to her feet. 'We're on fire-watch duties tonight.'

The awfulness of what had happened might have filled her with a constant fear for Drew's safety and a dread that she might lose him, but she certainly wasn't going to let it stop her from doing her duty. Her fear was for losing Drew, not for anything that might happen to herself.

'Of course I won't be able to do any fire-watching now that I'm going into munitions,' Dulcie announced determinedly. 'Not with me working nights every other month, and then needing to make sure that I get me sleep so that I can concentrate on what I'm doing. Very important work it is, filling shells and that.'

Olive managed to refrain from pointing out that Sally's work as a nurse was also very important and involved working nights but that Sally still managed to do her fire-watching as well. Knowing Dulcie as she did, she realised there would be little point.

'You didn't have to do this tonight, you know,' Drew told Tilly once they were outside and he had checked the thankfully empty sky. 'I'm sure that your mother would have got someone to stand in for you.'

'I don't want her to do that,' Tilly replied. 'I'm not going to let what happened turn me into a coward who can't play her part in doing her duty, Drew, and anyway, it's you I'm scared for, not myself. I know what you being a reporter means. Every time there's a bombing raid you'll be off wanting to be there to get your story, putting yourself in danger.'

'Yes, it is my job,' Drew agreed gently, 'and like you, Tilly, I feel that I want to do whatever I can to defeat Hitler and everything that he stands for. That's why I

266

came here: so that I could report back to people at home in America exactly what's happening, so that they can understand and so that hopefully we'll join in your fight against Hitler. If I can't do that job properly then how can I face your boys in uniform, knowing how much more they are doing?'

'What you're doing is important, Drew. I know that. I'm just so afraid for you . . . for us.'

'I know,' Drew comforted her, reaching for her hand and squeezing it reassuringly. It hurt him to see her bright optimistic trusting confidence stripped from her by the shocking reality of war.

They were halfway down the road when they heard the first rising wail of the air-raid warning, both of them stopping to look at one another and then up at the sky.

'You go back,' Drew urged Tilly. 'I'll come with you and then ask Mr Edwards to take your place and be on fire-watch with me.'

'No . . .'

'Tilly . . .'

'No. I want to be with you, Drew, whatever happens, and besides, I'm not running away from doing my duty. What kind of person would I be if I did? I might be afraid of losing you but I'm not afraid for myself.'

'You won't lose me, Tilly. And nothing's going to happen to me. I'm extra specially lucky, you see.'

'What makes you think that?' Tilly demanded, raising her voice so that he would be able to hear her above the banshee scream of the siren as it fought with the ominous thrum of the engines of the incoming enemy planes.

'I don't think it, I know it,' Drew told her promptly.

'I must be lucky, Tilly, because you love me. I couldn't be any luckier than that.'

When Olive heard the air-raid siren her first anxious thoughts were for Tilly, although she urged Agnes and Dulcie to head immediately for the Anderson shelter at the bottom of the garden, quickly starting to gather up everything they would need, and putting on the kettle to make a Thermos of hot tea.

'You fill the Thermos for me, will you, Agnes?' she instructed, going to the hall to collect her coat and headscarf. 'I'm going to go and change places with Tilly.'

Outside, the darkness was already being probed by the bright beam of the searchlights, the dull thunder of the batteries accompanied by the trace of the rounds they were firing into the sky. Olive didn't pay them any attention, though, as she ran down the road towards Drew and Tilly.

'Tilly, you go back and get in the Anderson,' she instructed when she reached them. 'I'll do the fire-watch with Drew.'

'No, Mum, I'm staying here,' Tilly told her. When Olive opened her mouth to protest Tilly forestalled her, saying, 'When you asked us all to join your fire-watch group you didn't say anything about me being treated like a child and sent out of danger every time we had an air raid. I'm not a child and I'm not going to be stopped from doing what I should. Other girls my age and younger are doing their bit and I'm going to do mine. If you were me you'd be the same.'

What Tilly was saying was true, Olive knew. As much as she wanted to beg her to seek the comparative safety of the Anderson shelter in their garden, another part of her felt desperately proud of her daughter for insisting on staying, and she recognised that there was no point in trying to argue with her.

'Go on, Mum, you go back,' Tilly was urging her.

'Don't worry, Mrs Robbins, I'll take care of her,' Drew assured her.

'Very well,' Olive agreed, but she couldn't stop herself from turning round to look back down the road once she had reached her own front gate. Tilly and Drew weren't watching her, though. They were walking close together, Tilly pushing the barrow whilst Drew carried the stirrup pump and the rake. Once it would have been her side that Tilly would have wanted to be close to.

On their own now, Drew looked up at the sky. 'I've just checked my watch, they're coming in every minute.'

'And heading for Chelsea, by the look of it,' Tilly responded to Drew's comment, gasping as he suddenly grabbed hold of her and yelled, 'Down, Tilly, down!', pushing her to the ground as he spoke, just as one of the bombers came in so low above them that Tilly thought at first it would hit the houses. Mercifully, it seemed that on this occasion Article Row wasn't the bombers' target. Instead, as she had already said, it seemed to be Chelsea that was getting the worst of the Luftwaffe's attack, the sky in that direction so red that Tilly felt as though the whole of that part of London must be on fire.

*　　*　　*

In the Anderson shelter Olive was counting not just the hours but the minutes and the seconds as wave after wave of bombers came over, her heart in her mouth with anxiety for Tilly.

'I hope that munitions factory where I'm going to be working doesn't get hit,' said Dulcie crossly. 'That's all I need, for the ruddy factory to go up in flames and me having to find meself another job after the trouble I've gone to, and handing in me notice at Selfridges. Ever so sorry to see me go, they were, as well. But it's like I told them, I have to do me duty.'

Olive winced as yet another loud explosion momentarily drowned out Dulcie's voice, and Agnes jumped visibly.

It was dawn before it was over; the longest air raid of the war so far, as Sergeant Dawson told them when he called round on his way down the Row to check that everyone was all right, after the all clear had sounded.

'There's over a thousand been killed, so I've heard, and more than two thousand injured. There's whole streets gone, and hardly a London borough that's not been hit. There's still fires on Gray's Inn Road, and on Oxford Street . . .'

'Selfridges?' Dulcie asked.

'Yes, that got hit, but not badly.'

Sally confirmed what Sergeant Dawson had already told them when she came back from her night shift.

'One of the ARP men amongst the injured said that Hitler sent so many bombers over in revenge for us bombing the centre of Berlin last week. I don't know if that's true but I do know that we've never had so many injured people in.'

Sally looked exhausted, Olive thought, and no wonder.

'One of our doctors told me that Piccadilly is inches deep in broken glass, and that hardly a building has been left undamaged, and that there are fires everywhere from the bombs and from damaged gas mains.'

'Hitler might think he's breaking our spirit but we won't let him,' said Tilly fiercely. 'He can destroy London's buildings but he will never break its spirit.'

Three days later, after an attack that was even heavier than the one the city had suffered on the Wednesday, it seemed to Olive, as she drove one of the WVS mobile canteens into one of the city's worst hit areas, that Tilly had been right. Despite the damage to the city and its buildings, and the terrible loss of life and injuries suffered by its people, far from being cowed by the onslaught, Londoners were even more determined to withstand everything that Hitler could throw at them.

The raid, which had started at 9.15 on the Saturday night, continued relentlessly until 4.15 on the Sunday morning. This time the Luftwaffe had concentrated its attack on the Thames, from Tower Bridge downstream to the docks in the east.

At church on Sunday people spoke sombrely of what had happened, and those who had been lost, whilst Olive watched Tilly anxiously. Her daughter might be going to work and fulfilling her fire-watching duties with the kind of determined courage that would make any mother proud, but she wasn't eating properly, picking at her food, looking strained and on edge unless Drew was with her.

Oblivious to her mother's watchful concern, Tilly smiled up at Drew when he came round for lunch after church. 'That was a really good piece you wrote about Wednesday's bombing.'

'And you, of course, aren't at all prejudiced in my favour,' Drew laughed.

'Certainly not. You are a wonderful writer, Drew. You make things come so alive. The stories you wrote about those people you interviewed . . . they made me feel so proud to be your girl. You wait, they'll be giving you your own byline soon.'

'Sometimes I feel I should be doing more than just writing about the war.'

'What kind of more?' Tilly asked him, alarmed.

'Well, there's Wilder in uniform . . .'

'But he's a pilot; you're a reporter. Drew, promise me that you won't do anything silly like volunteering.'

She was getting agitated and upset, and Drew was immediately remorseful.

'No, of course I won't.'

'Promise me,' Tilly begged him.

'I give you my word, Tilly. As an American I couldn't go into a British uniform anyway, although that wasn't actually what I meant. I was wondering if I could volunteer in some other way. Join the ARP, perhaps. Just do something.'

'You're doing your bit writing about the war, especially the pieces you send back to America,' Tilly assured him. She didn't understand what was happening to her sometimes. She'd always thought of herself as a plucky type of girl but since she'd fallen in love with Drew – since that night when she had thought she had lost him – she'd begun to feel as though she hadn't known herself at all, she was so afraid of losing him. Was this how her mother had felt when her father had been ill? Had she, too, been this afraid?

FIFTEEN

'It's so awful that St Andrew's has gone,' Tilly said, holding out her teacup as Olive lifted the pot to offer refills. The whole household, apart from Sally, who was still at work, sat eating their evening meal and mourning the destruction of the famous Holborn church. 'Drew took photographs of it only in January.'

'Yes. Mrs Windle is very upset about its loss. It was the largest Wren church in London after St Paul's, and we're lucky we still have that standing. She told me that if it wasn't for the St Paul's fire-watching team being on hand, so many incendiaries fell on it during the last bombing raid that it would have burned down. We've lost Gray's Inn Great Hall, as well, and all the books in it. Over thirty thousand, Mrs Morrison said.' Olive couldn't help giving a small shiver. With so many bombs falling in Holborn it was a miracle that Article Row had been spared.

Not that Nancy saw it that way. She had come round earlier in the day to complain to Olive that the washing she had hung out to dry on Monday had been covered in ash and smuts. 'Well, as to that,' Dulcie butted in, putting down her knife and fork as she stopped eating the potato and leftover minced-up joint and cabbage that Olive had fried up for their evening meal, 'today at the factory there was one girl that got scalped on account of her not tying her hair out of the way, like we're supposed to. The whole lot was ripped out,' Dulcie went on with obvious relish. 'Carted her off to hospital screaming her head off, they did.'

'Oh, Dulcie, how awful!' Agnes gasped.

Olive sighed under her breath before saying briskly, 'I don't think we really need to hear about that whilst we're eating, thank you, Dulcie.'

It was unseasonably cold for May, even though they were only a few days into the month, and since the previous Sunday, they had had what was being called 'Double Summer Time', which meant that it would be light until gone ten o'clock so that, even if Hitler did bomb them, it wouldn't be until after dark so no one needed to do down to the shelters before ten o'clock. The light evenings were something else of which Nancy didn't approve, announcing with some triumph to Olive that she had seen 'that boy the Dawsons took in out far later than anyone his age should be, and roaming all over the place with that riffraff he's taken up with. I've complained to Sergeant Dawson about the racket they make going into people's gardens without a by-your-leave, but of course he won't do anything about it.'

'It's only the gardens of the empty houses they go into, Nancy,' Olive had felt obliged to defend Barney, although in reality she herself wasn't very keen on having the two older boys around, especially after what Archie Dawson had told her, but she felt that had been said in confidence to her, and she certainly wasn't going to betray it to a troublemaker like Nancy.

Poor Archie Dawson. Olive felt sorry for him. He wanted to do his best for Barney but Barney seemed determined to ignore the police sergeant's warnings to steer clear of the Farley brothers.

'One of the other girls at the factory was telling me that in some of the big shelters, they've got dances going on some nights now, with music and everything,' Dulcie continued. 'I wouldn't mind a bit of a dance meself. It's been ages since I went to the Palais, what with you lot all paired up and Wilder flying his ruddy plane. Still, at least he's got leave this weekend, and he's going to take me out. I'll bet our Rick will be sorry that he isn't going to be here to watch the FA Cup Final. He's supported the Gunners since he was a kid. Mind you, there's a lot say that that Preston North End lot are going to win it.'

'Drew's going,' Tilly told her. 'One of the sports reporters has offered him a ticket. He's going to write about it for his American paper, to show that Londoners are getting on with their lives despite the bombs.'

Olive repressed a small sigh. Her refusal to allow Tilly to become engaged to Drew, never mind marry him, had only intensified their relationship.

'You shouldn't neglect your friends just because you're dating Drew,' Olive had tried to counsel her. 'You should still go out with Agnes, Sally and Dulcie. You used to have so much fun together.'

'I don't want fun any more, I just want to be with Drew,' Tilly had retaliated, adding, 'and, anyway, it isn't just me. Agnes wants to be with Ted, and Sally wants to be with George. You must have felt the same about

Dad – at least, you must have done if you loved him as much as I love Drew.'

Had there been an accusation in those words? Olive didn't know. She had loved Jim. She had loved him dearly. But not with the fierce turbulent passion she could sense in Tilly. She just wasn't the passionate type. Some women weren't. She had been grateful to Jim, and happy in the quiet gentleness of their love. Tilly's intensity worried her because she feared that where there was the capacity for so much love there was also the capacity for a great deal of pain. If only Tilly could see and accept that it was her mother's desire to protect her from that pain that motivated her instead of insisting that Olive didn't understand her and, even worse, was deliberately standing in the way of her happiness.

Finishing her tea, Tilly kept one eye on her watch. Drew would be coming round for her soon. They were going to go for a walk in Hyde Park, despite the chill in the air.

Thankfully they hadn't had heavy bombing since the two dreadful raids in April, and already some kind of order had been restored to the city.

Drew, who was interested in such things, had told Tilly that every brick, every piece of wood – everything, in fact, that could be salvaged to be used again – was being, whilst the ships that came over from America with much-needed supplies for a beleaguered Britain were returning to the United States carrying some of the rubble, which was also being used in Britain itself, to make runways. Nothing was to be wasted.

'How's Sally?' Tilly asked her mother.

They'd heard that Sally's home of Liverpool was being

targetted by the Luftwaffe, who had started bombing the city on 1 May, and now, six days later, were still doing so.

'She isn't saying very much,' Olive answered, 'but she's bound to be upset. Liverpool is where she grew up, after all.'

'But she hasn't got anyone there now, has she?' Dulcie pointed out. 'She hasn't got any family left.'

That was what the other girls thought, but Sally had told Olive in confidence that she did have family in Liverpool, though she had chosen to cut herself off from them. She had a father, a stepmother and a baby half-sister, and, knowing Sally as she did, Olive didn't believe that she didn't care about her father any more. She would be worrying about him.

Olive was right. Sally was thinking about her father, even though she kept telling herself that she mustn't and that she didn't owe him any concern after the speed with which he had rushed into marriage to Morag after her mother's death. It was just because she was a nurse, and trained to care, a nurse who had seen what bombs could do to human bodies and human lives, especially the bodies and the lives of small children, that her heart had hammered when she had first heard that Liverpool was suffering a dreadful blitz, nothing else. To allow herself to feel anything else, anything personal, especially for the child who was the result of her father's betrayal of her mother, would mean that she too was betraying her. She was the only custodian and guardian of her mother's precious memory now, the only one who really cared about her, and who hadn't betrayed her.

Not that there was very much news coming out of Liverpool. In fact, it was almost as though the Government didn't want anyone to know what was going on. Sally had asked Drew if he could find out what was happening, explaining away her concern as being for her old home city, and Drew had asked amongst the other reporters for her. Sally then learned that the city had experienced the most dreadful bombing.

'Excellent work, Sister,' the surgeon praised her, as he stood back from the operating table so that the patient on whom he had just operated was wheeled away. 'You run a good team.'

'Thank you, Mr Brett,' Sally responded.

It still gave her a small thrill to be addressed as 'Sister', but for some reason today that thrill was tempered by a sense of loss as well. Because she was thinking about her father? No. If she felt any sense of loss then it was because her mother couldn't share in her pride at being praised for her work. Her father meant nothing to her now. How could he when she so plainly meant nothing to him? She had begged him not to marry Morag . . .

As she walked into the canteen, a discarded newspaper headline caught her eye. 'An unnamed British city is cut off from the rest of the country by Hitler's bombs.'

She knew from what Drew had told her that that city was Liverpool, and she sank into a chair.

'Are you all right, Sister?' a fellow nurse asked her.

'Yes. Yes. I'm fine,' she responded.

'Heavy morning in theatre, was it?' another sister asked her sympathetically.

'It was,' Sally answered truthfully, even though she

knew that it wasn't the length of the operating list that was responsible for the sudden weakness in her limbs.

She'd be off duty soon. Then she could go back to number 13 and read through the newspapers properly. Drew would have got them for her.

Thinking of Drew made Sally smile. He was another gentle, kind man of the same type as her George. A thoroughly likeable, reliable, admirable man, even if poor Olive was desperately worried about the intensity of Tilly's love for him. Tilly could certainly have done a lot worse, Sally reflected.

She should get something to eat, she decided, but with that newspaper headline in front of her she found she had lost her appetite.

SIXTEEN

Alone in the kitchen of number 13, where she was about to paint her toenails, an activity forbidden anywhere than in their bedrooms, when the doorbell rang, Dulcie reluctantly slipped her still unpainted foot back into its open-toed shoe and went to open the front door.

Standing on the doorstep was a good-looking young man in naval uniform clutching a wriggling baby with a bruise on its forehead against his shoulder with one hand and carrying a battered leather case in the other.

Sally, who had gone up to write to George, was halfway down the stairs when she saw him. She'd been about to nip out to the post her letter, but now all thoughts of that were forgotten as she clung to the banister rail, her face drained of colour.

'Callum!' she exclaimed.

Here was an older, far more war-weary-looking Callum than the young man who had come to this very house to beg her to make things up with her father. Sally's whole body flinched at that memory and then flinched again as she focused on the child held tightly in Callum's arms, and clinging to his dust-soiled uniform.

It was *her*, the child, the result of the abhorrent betrayal of her mother by her father and her best friend.

Fury washed through her in a savage wave, but it was a fury that, despite its strength, could not entirely subdue the sick fear that was jolting her heart into a disjointed beat and crawling coldly through her veins. Logic told Sally that there could be only one reason why Callum was here with that child, but it was a logic that she didn't want to accept.

Instead she railed at him furiously. 'You have no right to come here. No right at all, and especially not with that . . . that child.'

'You know him?' Dulcie demanded, turning to look at her fellow lodger, her eyes narrowing as she saw the shock that had taken all the colour from Sally's face and left her staring from the good-looking naval officer to the child he was carrying and then back again.

'Yes, she does,' the man answered for Sally, stepping forward so that Dulcie was obliged to step back.

Once inside the hall he closed the door with his shoulder.

Callum. Callum was here and he was carrying *that* child. Agonising surges of angry pain burned into Sally.

'What are you doing here?' she demanded. 'Why have you brought that . . . her here?'

'You'd better come into the kitchen,' Dulcie invited, ushering the man – Callum, Sally had called him – along the hall and into that room, ignoring Sally's outburst. She was enjoying seeing Sally – who was always just that little bit superior, with her nurse's uniform and her closeness to Olive – so plainly caught off guard and uncomfortable. Besides, there was the exciting mystery of who the man was and, more important, the identity of the child. Dulcie had seen a lot of life in the raw, living with her parents, but this was the first time she had seen a single man turn up at someone's door carrying a child. A woman doing the same thing, yes, but a man, never.

'Come a long way, have you?' she asked chattily. 'I expect you'd like a nice cup of tea? Just park yourself here on this chair,' she told him as she pulled one out from the table for him.

The child eyed her with huge dark brown, thickly lashed eyes. A few wisps of dark curly hair had escaped from the knitted bonnet she was wearing. Since the bonnet was pink Dulcie surmised that the child must be female.

'Pretty little thing,' she commented. 'What's her name?'

'Alice.'

From the doorway Sally, who had followed them into the kitchen, gasped as though a knife had been twisted in her heart, which in a way it had. Alice had been her own mother's middle name.

'You can't stay here,' she told Callum. 'You've got to go. I don't want her here either. Take her away.'

Well, well, Sally was getting herself worked up and no mistake, Dulcie thought, recognising a bit of a mystery and, she hoped, a bit of a scandal with it.

'I can't do that, Sally,' Callum responded.

There was a small pause whilst he and Sally looked at one another and Dulcie pretended to busy herself making the tea, still agog and determined to find out what was going on.

283

'I had to bring her, Sally. She hasn't got anyone else anymore. You and I are all she's got now.'

Sally knew what that meant. It meant that the child's parents – her own father – were dead. Pain ripped through her. Inside her head she had a mental image of her father before Morag had destroyed their relationship, the tenderness of his love for her, his daughter, so clear to see in his expression. He had loved her so much – both her parents had – and she had loved them. Once she had thought that nothing could ever destroy that, but she had been wrong. The pain of her loss engulfed her, filling her with bitterness and angry resentment, against Morag for taking her father's love, against Callum for not siding with her in denouncing his sister, and for the child he was holding, who had taken what should have been hers – the love of their shared father. And was there also a feeling of agonised guilt somewhere in that mix, an anguished recognition that now there could never ever be a reconciliation between them? How could they have been reconciled, with the evidence of her father's betrayal there in the form of his and Morag's child? Their child, alive whilst they were dead. Alive whilst her father was dead . . .

'No.'

Sally didn't know whether the moan ripped from her throat was of denial against the claim Callum was making on her on the child's behalf, or of rejection of what she knew his words must mean.

She had known it, of course, from the minute she had seen him. There could be only one reason why Callum would bring this child here.

Out of nowhere an icy cold wave of weakness surged

through her. She swayed slightly, her hand going to her heart, her body crumpling.

Instantly Callum was on his feet, thrusting the child towards Dulcie, who took hold of her, and then going to Sally to place his hands on her arms to support her.

Callum was touching her; holding her; pretending to be concerned for her. His duplicity made Sally feel sick, and gave her the strength to thrust him off and then move to the sink, as far away from him as she could get. If only Dulcie hadn't been here and she had answered the door, she could have closed it against him, and locked him and that wretched child out. Then no one would have been any the wiser; no one would have known anything.

Against her will Sally's gaze was drawn to the baby, something painful swelling inside her chest as she watched the tenderness with which Callum took her from Dulcie. There was a familiarity about the baby's features and colouring. Sally had seen photographs of Callum and Morag as children, and this baby looked just like them. But then it should, seeing as Morag was its mother and Callum its uncle. She was glad that she couldn't see anything of her father or her own colouring in it, she told herself fiercely. That meant that she had no obligation to feel connected to it in any kind of way.

The baby was reaching for Callum's finger, closing her fat little baby hand around it and then smiling at him.

'Aaw, she's gorgeous,' Dulcie announced. 'That's a nasty bruise she's got there, though.'

'She's lucky to be alive,' Callum answered. 'The house

285

took a direct hit, Sally. Some wretched bomb crew discharging what was left of their bombs on their way back to Germany, according to the officials. It's a miracle that Alice was found. She was buried under the house. They found her in your father's arms. Morag was lying next to him. The ARP warden I spoke to said that they would both have died instantly.'

'Stop it!' Sally curled her hands into two angry fists. 'Do you really think that I want to know that my father gave his life to protect her? She should never have been born. Take her away. I don't know why you've come here. I'm sure the authorities would have found a way of letting me know about my father's death at some stage, even if somehow or other they managed to let you know first.'

'My ship had put into Liverpool and I'd been given leave to go and see my family – our family, Sally. I thought it was good timing, putting into Liverpool so close to Alice's first birthday.'

Sally's mouth tightened.

'You and I are all Alice has got now. She's your half-sister and my niece. She's our responsibility. I was there when they dug her out of what was left of the house. I'd gone straight there as soon as I could when my ship docked in Liverpool. The damage to the city is appalling, but even so, I hadn't expected . . .'

The grief Sally could hear in his voice caused her heart to thump painfully.

'Half the road had gone, even the cherry trees.'

There was a huge hard lump in Sally's throat. Her mother had loved the pink blossom that had filled the branches of the cherry trees in the spring. Whenever she thought of her home it was those trees she visualised.

'All of it flattened,' Callum was continuing grimly, 'but somehow Alice was saved. Someone had heard her crying beneath the rubble. They'd been digging for over two hours when I got there. I never thought . . . To find that she was unharmed . . . I've spoken with the authorities in Liverpool. They're overwhelmed with people to look after following the bombing, especially orphaned children. They were relieved when I told them that Alice had two close blood relatives, especially when I told them that one of them is a nurse.'

The baby was Sally's half-sister, and the handsome naval officer's sister had obviously been married to Sally's father, and not with Sally's approval, Dulcie reckoned.

Sally might be trembling inside with the pain that Callum's brief description of the scene of destruction caused her but she wasn't going to let him see that.

'The child is nothing to me,' she told him. 'I told my father when he married your sister that I no longer considered myself to be his daughter. The child is nothing to me. I want you both to leave.'

'You can't mean that. Alice has no one else. I've got to rejoin my ship tonight. They've only given me extra leave so that I could bring Alice to you. She's still a baby, Sally, unable to speak for herself. I can't believe that you mean to turn your back on her. Your mother would never have wanted you to do that.'

'You dare to mention my mother to me?'

Dulcie had never seen Sally so fired up.

'Your sister stole my father from my mother whilst

287

she was dying and this . . . this child is the result of that betrayal. Take her away, Callum. There's bound to be an orphanage that will take her.'

'I don't believe you mean that. You're in shock at the moment, and I'm sorry to have been the bearer of such bad news. I know how much your father meant to you.'

'Once, before he betrayed my mother, but not since then.'

As though Sally hadn't spoken Callum continued, 'I have to go.' He stood up and carried the baby over to Sally, almost forcing her into Sally's unwilling arms, and then bending his head briefly to kiss Alice, his voice soft as he told her, 'I'll be back, little one,' before straightening up to step back as though somehow he knew that, despite her anger and aversion, it would be impossible for Sally physically to reject someone so vulnerable, no matter what was in her heart.

By the time Sally's brain had taken on board that the soft warm weight she was holding was the child she desperately wanted to repudiate, Callum had reached the front door.

Hurrying after him, hampered by the fact that she was holding the baby, Sally could only watch as he opened the door and then walked out. She wanted to run after him and thrust the child at him as he had done her. She wanted to tell him to take it away and that he had no right to have done what he had done, but there was a huge, aching, raw place in her heart, like the bomb crater that she suspected must now be her childhood home, caused by the news that her father was dead.

The baby started to cry, her face growing red as huge

tears rolled down her cheeks and the sound of her wails grew in intensity.

Coming out of the kitchen, Dulcie closed the front door. 'Well, that's a turn-up for the book, isn't it?' she said. 'You having a baby sister, and not ever saying a word about it.'

Dulcie had to raise her voice over the frantic pitch of the baby's cries.

'Poor little mite's probably missing her mum and dad. Here, give her to me,' she ordered. 'No wonder she's yelling, you holding her like that. She's probably hungry as well. Let's hope that that Callum had the sense to put a bottle and some formula in that case he's left. Go and have a look, will you, Sally, whilst I try and settle her down a bit?'

'She's not staying,' Sally told Dulcie. 'She's nothing to do with me and I don't want her to be.' And yet she was still doing as Dulcie had suggested and opening the case, which was packed with baby clothes and nappies, all of them thick with brick dust. Inside her head Sally had an unwanted image of them being collected from the detritus of the destroyed house. She'd seen it so often, after all, here in London: people picking through the rubble looking for their belongings.

'Hurry up with that bottle, will you, Sally?' Dulcie urged her. 'There it is, look, and the formula with it.'

Numbly Sally put them on the worktop next to the sink, and then watched distantly as Dulcie deftly washed the bottle and the teat with hot water from the kettle, and then prepared a bottle of warm formula with one hand whilst holding the baby with the other. She expertly settled Alice in the crook of her one arm whilst testing

289

the heat of the formula on the bare skin of the crook of her elbow where she'd pushed up her cardigan sleeve.

Seeing Sally watching her, Dulcie scoffed, 'There's no need to look so surprised. You might be a nurse, but you can't grow up in the East End and not know how to look after a baby, which is more than you seem to know.'

Immediately she was given the bottle the baby started to suck hungrily. Settling herself in a chair, Dulcie took advantage of the situation to ask casually, 'Make us a fresh cup of tea, will you, Sally? I'm fair parched.' Adding, 'I'll tell you what, that Callum of yours is a good-looker. Mind you, I always think that a naval uniform makes a man look handsome.'

'He is not my Callum. He's nothing to do with me,' Sally denied.

'His sister was married to your dad, wasn't she, so that makes him related to you, doesn't it?' Dulcie challenged her, shifting Alice's weight to a more comfortable position and smiling back at her when the baby smiled up.

And that was how Olive, who had met Agnes walking up the street, found them when she walked into the kitchen after her WVS meeting.

'Don't look at me,' Dulcie told her. 'She's got nothing to do with me. I'm only giving her a bottle on account of Sally not knowing what to do. Oh, and I hope you can find a half-decent nappy in that case, Sally, 'cos she's going to need changing pretty soon and I'm not doing that.'

'Callum brought her,' Sally told Olive.

Olive knew all about her family history. Sally had confided in her when Callum had turned up on the doorstep on another occasion, hoping to persuade Sally to make her peace with her father.

'Her . . . my father and her mother are gone. The house was bombed.'

'Poor little mite almost bought it herself,' Dulcie told Olive. 'Only got saved because her dad's body was protecting her. Sally here and that Callum are all she's got left now.'

'She's nothing to do with me,' Sally insisted. 'I'm sorry about this, Olive. I'll find somewhere suitable for her as quickly as I can. Matron might know of a suitable orphanage.'

'An orphanage? Oh, Sally, no, please don't.'

They could all hear the shock in Agnes's voice, and Olive's tender heart ached for her, and for Sally. And if she was honest it ached for the small defenceless baby that was now drifting contently off to sleep in Dulcie's arms as well.

Olive looked from Agnes's anxious face, her eyes filled with tears, to Sally's, which was so set and yet, at the same time, so shocked, guessing just what both girls would be going through, and why, and decided that for now it was best that she took control.

'I think that the thing to do right now would be for the baby to stay here.'

'No!'

'Oh, yes.'

Sally and Agnes spoke together and then looked at one another.

'Alice isn't Olive's responsibility, Agnes,' said Sally

determinedly, 'and she isn't going to be mine either. If Callum wants to keep her then it's up to him to sort something out, not bring her here to me. How can I take care of her, even if I wanted to, which I don't? I'm a nurse. I'm working. There's nowhere for her to sleep. She's barely got any clothes or nappies. No, no, she—'

'As to that, Sally,' Olive stopped her, 'I'm sure between us all we can manage to find the time to look after her. For now she can sleep in my room, as I agree that it's not possible for you to look after her with the shifts you work. I'll turn out a drawer and we'll make her a bed in that. I'll have a word with Mrs Windle about sorting out some clothes for her. I dare say that Callum will come back for her as soon as he can. He obviously cares about her. No, Sally,' Olive insisted firmly when Sally looked as though she was about to protest again, 'I do know how you feel about . . . about what happened, and your father, but right now you're in no fit state to make any kind of proper decision. Not after the news you've just had,' Olive told her gently.

To her disgust, Sally discovered that she badly wanted to cry. That was the trouble when people were kind and nice to you when you had to harden your heart against those emotions. They were too much for you to bear. Her father, dead. It shocked her that she should feel so much pain and such an acute sense of loss, when since she had discovered his relationship with Morag, she had cut herself off from him emotionally. She didn't want to feel like this, just as she didn't want to feel that raw ache inside her that Agnes's emotional outburst had caused her. The baby – she refused to use her name – would be far better off in an orphanage and with people who could look after her properly. She could write to Callum, care of the navy, telling him where the baby was and he could then make his own arrangements for her. He had had no right to barge into her life in the way he had and dump the child on her. George would agree with her about that.

George. For the first time since she had seen Callum standing in the doorway holding Alice, Sally realised what problems the arrival of her half-sister were going to cause her. George, after all, knew nothing about Alice's existence, never mind the events that had led to Sally's alienation from her father.

'Dulcie, can you keep hold of the baby – does she have a name?'

'Alice.'

Sally looked at Dulcie as they both spoke the name together. She hadn't intended to say it but somehow she had.

'Oh, how pretty!' Olive smiled. 'If you can keep hold of Alice whilst I go upstairs and sort out somewhere for her to sleep that will be a help.'

'All right,' Dulcie agreed, 'but I can't sit here with her for long. I've got me toenails to varnish.'

Upstairs in her bedroom Olive removed a drawer from the mahogany chest and took the clothes from it. They smelled of lavender from the lavender seeds she had sewn into small scraps of cotton in the autumn after the flowers had finished flowering in the garden.

They could sew together some of the blanket squares the girls knitted in their spare time for the homeless to make a baby blanket, and a sheet folded over with a pillow underneath it would do for Alice's bed until they could sort out something else. Olive knew that she couldn't force Sally to keep the baby if she didn't want to, but she had to admit that, like Agnes, she didn't like the thought of her being handed over to an orphanage. Not when there was a houseful of women who could quite easily accommodate the needs of one very-much-in-need baby. Poor little thing. She must be feeling so confused, wondering who they were and what had happened to her mummy and daddy. Olive thought of how she would have felt as a young mother at the thought of her Tilly being orphaned at Alice's age, and handed over to strangers to bring up. The surge of protective maternal anxiety that filled her confirmed to her that, in insisting to Sally that Alice stayed, she was doing the right thing.

Of course, the situation had to be explained to Tilly and Drew when they came in, Tilly insisting on giving Alice her final feed of the night, once Drew had gone, under instruction from Dulcie. Agnes, well used to looking after the little ones from her time in the orphanage, volunteered to change her nappy, and did so expertly, whilst Olive kept a keen eye on what was going on.

'I'm really sorry about this,' Sally apologised to Olive when Olive went up to her bedroom with a cup of tea for her.

'It isn't your fault, Sally. How are you feeling?' Olive asked gently. 'It must have been a dreadful shock – to hear about your father.'

'I . . . I didn't think that I'd care, but I keep thinking about the way he was when I was growing up.' Tears filled her eyes. 'I know you mean to be kind, Olive, but she can't stay here. I don't think I could bear it.'

'It won't be for ever, Sally. Callum is bound to come back for her.'

'That could be months.'

Olive patted her gently on the arm. 'I do understand how you feel.'

'How I feel? That's the whole problem. I don't want to feel anything. I keep seeing him – my father – inside my head, teaching me to ride my first bicycle. I was so happy then . . .'

'You were lucky to have such loving parents, Sally,' Olive told her, opening the bedroom door to leave.

Olive didn't say any more, but Sally knew what she had been hinting at. She had had a happy childhood, but Alice wouldn't, especially if Sally insisted on sending her to an orphanage. But what else could she practically do? And what was she going to say to George?

But then why did she need to say anything? After all he didn't even know that Alice existed, and since she was going to send her to an orphanage there was no need for him to know, was there? It made good sense all round. She couldn't keep Alice, even if she wanted to do so. She worked shifts, and she lived in one room, which she rented. Olive was a kind and a generous landlady but even if she, Sally, wanted to keep her half-sister, she couldn't imagine that Olive or the other girls were going to be happy about having a baby around all the time, never mind be obliged to get involved in her care.

No, handing her over to the authorities was definitely

the right and the best thing to do – for everyone concerned.

In her own bed later that night, lying in the darkness, Agnes said a special prayer, begging that little Alice wouldn't be abandoned as she had been. They had been kind enough to her at the orphanage, but that hadn't stopped her always yearning for a family of her own, and since she had come here to number 13 she had realised even more just what she had missed out on. She would have loved to have had a mother like Olive, a loving, kind wise mother, who had loved her as much as Olive loved Tilly.

It had only been since she had come here and since she had met Ted that she had realised what maternal love actually was. Ted's mother loved her children every bit as much as Olive loved Tilly, even if Ted's mother's love for her son and her two daughters was a fiercely protective kind of love, which seemed to want to exclude Agnes from its magic circle.

Being orphaned was dreadfully lonely, more lonely than anyone who wasn't orphaned could ever imagine. So lonely that you could feel as though you were the only person in the world, even when you lived in an orphanage packed with other children. There was a coldness, an emptiness about not having anyone of your own, an envy of the happiness of families when you saw them together, a longing to be able to creep close to the warmth of their family life and an awareness that you never ever could because you didn't belong there.

Poor little Alice. Right now she knew nothing of this, but one day, if Sally handed her over to an orphanage, she would. But then Sally didn't understand what being orphaned was like. *She* did, though, and if she and Ted had already been married she'd have taken the baby in herself, Agnes thought sadly.

'You seem a bit preoccupied. Is everything OK?'

Sally nodded in response to her fellow sister's concerned question. 'We've got a full operating list for tonight already and I suspect that we'll have more emergencies coming in if there's more bombing tonight.'

It was the truth, and she hoped she was professional enough to give her full attention to the patients who needed it. But she also couldn't deny that her mind was also on what had happened at number 13 earlier. She couldn't possibly keep the child, even if she had wanted to, which she didn't. But Agnes's reaction to her announcement that Alice would have to go into an orphanage had touched a nerve within her that she hadn't realised existed.

And then there was George. It had been one thing not to tell him about her father when he had not been part of her life in any way, nor was likely to be, but now his death and the arrival of Alice complicated things.

Her father's death: his burial in a mass grave, because so many had been killed at once by the blitz in Liverpool. Sally closed her eyes to squeeze back her tears. Why should she want to cry for him, though, when she had lost the father she had once believed she had had over two years ago? Confusing, irrational, overemotional thoughts were threatening her normal self-control, and Sally didn't like that. She liked her life to be ordered and structured, calm and uncomplicated. She didn't care for drama and too much emotion.

She looked at the watch pinned to her uniform pocket and then went in search of one of her two juniors to ask her to fetch some cleaning fluid for the equipment trolley, before making her way to the theatre to make sure that everything was in order ahead of the first operation of her shift.

SEVENTEEN

On her way to her room Tilly paused on the landing as she heard her mother talking to Alice through the open door, as she walked up and down her bedroom floor with her.

'She was crying, poor little mite,' Olive told Tilly when she saw her. 'And no wonder. It must give her a fright when she wakes up in such unfamiliar surroundings and with so many strange faces around her.'

'Do you think that Sally really will put her in an orphanage?' Tilly asked, unable to resist smiling coaxingly at Alice's tear-dampened face.

'I don't know, Tilly. Are you and Drew going out after the football's over?' she asked, changing the subject. The truth was that in the few short days Alice had been with them, Olive had grown very attached to her. Once Olive had explained the situation to Audrey Windle and the other members of their local WVS group, they had all rallied round, and now Alice had a pram, a high chair, a playpen, several sets of clothes, some nappies, and a whole host of cooing admirers who were already offering to babysit, should their services be required.

'Seeing her reminds me of how much I want to be a grandmother,' Mrs Morrison had told Olive ruefully, 'and how much, at the same time, I don't want our Ian rushing into marriage whilst he's still in uniform.'

Hearing her WVS friend saying that had made Olive feel better about her refusal to allow Tilly to get married. But just like Mrs Morrison, she had discovered that Alice had made her realise how much she would enjoy being a grandmother – when the time was right.

'We aren't going out. Drew said that he'd probably end up going to the pub with the friend he's going to the match with, but he would come round afterwards. We decided London's bound to be busy with so many football supporters up for the FA Cup. I hope we don't have an air raid tonight.'

Alice was drifting off to sleep in Tilly's mother's arms. The arms that had held her as a baby, only then her mother had been very young.

'It must have been hard for you, Mum, without Dad, and having me,' said Tilly abruptly.

Olive looked at her. They had been at odds for so long that Tilly's comment had caught her off guard.

'Did you ever . . . did you ever wish that you hadn't had me? I mean, it would have been easier for you—'

'No. Tilly, you must never think that,' Olive protested, the sudden movement she made making Alice give a small baby protest before Olive settled her back comfortably in her arms.

'Well, I thought because you don't want me to get

married that perhaps it was because you regretted being left with me.'

'Oh, no, Tilly, never that. You were my strength, my reason for going on after I lost your dad,' Olive sighed. 'I know you think I'm being unfair and unkind in refusing to let you and Drew marry until you're older, but I promise you that I am doing it for your sake.'

'When Dad was sick,' Tilly persisted, 'did you worry then about him not being there and how you'd feel?'

'I couldn't believe it when the doctors told us. I suppose I didn't want to believe it. None of us did, even though we could all see how much weaker your dad was getting. Of course, we were living with your grandparents, and it was your grandmother who took charge and who did most of the nursing. I had you to look after, and he was her son, after all.'

Tilly tried to imagine how she would feel if she was prevented from spending that last precious time with a dying Drew – if she was relegated to the role of onlooker. She would hate it, she knew.

'That must have been hard for you.'

'Well, yes, it was, but I had you to look after as well, and your grandmother loved your dad so much. I'd hate you to be in the position that I was, Tilly, not wanted and even perhaps a little resented and blamed for some-one's ill health. Your grandmother wanted your father to herself, you see. He was her son, her child. She felt that marrying me had been too much for his health.'

'I worry so much about something happening to Drew,' Tilly admitted. 'He says it's silly. He says that nothing happens to reporters unless they're reporting from the front line, but I can't help it. Whenever he isn't with me I worry. Ever since that night when the incendiaries came down and I thought he was going to die . . . I don't feel frightened of the bombs for myself. Just for Drew. I'd rather we were both killed together than live without him.'

'Tilly . . .'

'I can't help it, Mum. I never realised that love could be like this and that I could feel so afraid. All I want is to be with Drew.'

'Marriage wouldn't take away your fear, Tilly,' Olive told her gently.

'No, but I'd have my memories, memories of being his wife.' Tilly's face went pink and Olive knew that she herself was colouring up a bit too. They both knew that Tilly meant memories of how it felt to be held close to the warm naked body of the man you loved, after he had loved you. Jim had been a gentle careful lover – when he had been able to be her lover. After Tilly's birth, when his health had started to get worse, the sight of him crying silently in their shared bed when he felt too weak to be a proper husband to her had hurt Olive far more than his inability to make love to her.

'I just hope that Sally doesn't put Alice in an orphanage, Ted. She's ever such a lovely little thing. As good as gold, hardly ever cries except when she wants her bottle. She's settled in so well at number 13, and when you think of what she's been through . . .'

'Now don't you go upsetting yourself,' Ted urged Agnes, recognising that she wasn't far from tears as they walked hand in hand towards Leicester Square and the Odeon in the early evening light. They weren't the only ones out and about: the city was busy with people making the most of the new Double Summer Time.

'I can't help it,' Agnes admitted. 'I can't bear the thought of poor little Alice growing up thinking that she's got no one of her own and that no one loves her.'

Ted squeezed Agnes's hand. He knew how much her own abandonment on the steps of the orphanage still hurt her.

'Well, you were the one who suggested coming to see a show instead of going dancing,' Dulcie reminded Wilder when he complained that the theatre just off Shaftsbury Avenue, in which they were now taking their seats, was small and 'nowhere near as good as anything you'd get on Broadway in New York'.

Dulcie felt that if anyone had the right to complain it should be her. After all, she already suspected that the only reason Wilder has initially chosen this particular review show was because the newspaper advertisement had claimed it had the highest kicking chorus line in London.

With the house lights still on, Dulcie could see that the red plush seats were faded, but then what wasn't looking the worse for wear in London these days?

The seats around them were certainly filling up, and many of the men were in uniform. At least Wilder had bought them good seats in the circle. She frowned again, though, when she saw him slipping a coin into the machine that dispensed a pair of opera glasses, the better to see the stage, but without offering to pay for a pair for her.

The lights dimmed, the curtains swishing open. The orchestra in the pit struck up a popular slightly saucy review number, the dinner-suited singer breaking off from singing it to tell the audience, 'Here come the girls', as the chorus came onto the stage from either side.

Dressed in fishnet tights, and a uniform of shorts, tightly fitted jackets and little hats perched on their curls, the chorus did a parade ground march to the shouted orders of their 'drill sergeant', much to the approval of some of the men in the audience.

The girls were all singing as they danced, and one of them in particular caught Dulcie's eye, her heart slamming into her chest as she stared at her in disbelief. She'd recognise that face anywhere, and that skinny body.

Edith. But it couldn't be. Edith was dead. Dulcie looked again, harder this time, as she focused on the blonde three in from the end of the line, who was making big eyes at the audience and wiggling her behind just that little bit more than the others, and then reached across and grabbed the binoculars with which Wilder had been studying the chorus line with far too much enthusiasm, ignoring his objecting, 'Hey,' to study closer the young woman who looked so like her sister.

Her mouth had gone dry, and her heart was racing. If it wasn't Edith then she had a double. Dulcie would have recognised those small pale blue eyes anywhere, even if she had tried to make them look bigger with all that bright blue eye shadow. Always been jealous of her own lovely eyes with their thick dark lashes, Edith had. How Dulcie had laughed at her for putting Vaseline into her own much sparser ones at night in the belief that it would make them grow.

She'd obviously peroxided her hair too. It had never been anything more than just short of mousy naturally, and she was probably wearing a hairpiece to thicken it up. Dulcie wasn't deceived, though. That was definitely her sister. Through the opera glasses she'd even been able to see that small chip out of one of her front teeth where she'd fallen as a ten-year-old. Never one to allow anything to get the better of her, Dulcie was already mastering her initial shock, even though her recognition of her supposedly dead sister had given her a really nasty turn. That was typical of Edith, it really was, not thinking about how someone who knew her was going to feel, seeing her like that, alive and large as life when she was supposed to be dead.

Hard on the heels of the initial shock that gripped her, Dulcie felt a fierce surge of anger.

Well, of all the . . . She was certainly going to have something to say to Edith the minute she got off that stage, letting their mother get herself in the state she had because she'd thought she was dead. Yes, and going on to her, Dulcie, about it like she had, Dulcie decided wrathfully.

The number was coming to an end. Dulcie stood up, putting the opera glasses down.

'Where are you going?' Wilder demanded when she made to get past him.

'I'm going backstage to see my sister wot's supposed to be dead, but isn't, since she's just been cavorting around and screeching on that stage down there, to find out what she thinks she's doing, pretending to be dead when she isn't. Mind you, I dare say I'd prefer to have people think I was dead than know that I was alive and working in a place like this.'

'Dulcie,' Wilder protested, but it was no good, Dulcie was already out in the aisle and making her way down towards the exit that led to the stairs.

"Ere, you can't come in 'ere,' a stagehand tried to stop her when she got backstage, but Dulcie ignored him, storming past and leaving Wilder to follow her. The babble of female voices led her down a short, dark, dank corridor smelling of cigarettes, stale air and dust, until she reached the open door at the end of it.

The narrow cramped room was filled with girls in various stages of undress, some of them merely wearing tiny diamante-encrusted G-strings, others in net costumes sewn with sequins who looked as though they were naked apart from the sequins, all of them wearing makeup that looked as though it had been trowelled on, in Dulcie's opinion, and all of them fighting for space in front of the wall of dressing tables and lit mirrors. Oblivious to the intruders' presence, some of them were pulling on tall feathered headpieces. One of them yelled out, 'Ow, Margot, that was me real hair you was pulling,' whilst another girl tried to pull off her headdress and a third pitched in with a sarcastic, 'Stop calling her Margot. Her real name is Maggie, as in Maggie may, and does.'

'Why you . . . you've got no room to talk, you bitch,' Margot defended her reputation, whirling round to drag her long red nails down the bare arm of her accuser.

'Al right, you lot, them of you what's in the next set

have got five minutes before you're back on stage. Them of you that's not on again until the second show had better scarper and leave a bit of room for them that is on stage to get changed. And remember, any girls found fighting will be sacked. I've told you that before.'

Until now Dulcie hadn't seen the small balding rotund harassed-sounding man, who had hidden in the middle of the packed dressing room.

The sight of another man in such close proximity to so many scantily clad and good-looking girls had Wilder, who had been eagerly staring into the room from Dulcie's side, move a bit closer in.

Dulcie, for once uninterested in her boyfriend's tendency to have a wandering eye where pretty girls were concerned, scanned the room for her sister. Her heart was thumping unusually fast and felt heavy in her chest. She *was* sure the girl she had seen was Edith, but right now, in these alien surroundings, she was suddenly experiencing an out-of-character wish that she had someone with her to support her, someone like their brother, Rick, or David. David? What possible use could he be to her? He didn't even know Edith. Rallying, Dulcie assured herself that she wasn't wrong. A sister like Edith, with all her nasty tricks, would never be forgotten, even if the Edith their mother had been so proud of had only appeared on stage as a singer, not a chorus girl. Dulcie wondered unkindly what her mother would have to say about that, and if she'd be as proud to boast about her talented 'star' of a daughter when she learned exactly how Edith was parading herself around now. But where was she? The small dressing room was packed, but then Dulcie saw her as one of the other girls moved and she

307

quickly claimed her empty seat in front of one of the mirrors whilst another girl, who had been hovering, obviously waiting for the space, complained, 'Hey, Edie, that's not fair. You aren't on again until the second show and I'm on in the next set.'

'Too bad. You should have been faster on your feet. Old man Parsons is always saying that your timing's out.'

'Oooo, don't try crossing swords with Edie, Fanny,' another girl chipped in. 'You'll not get the better of her. Got a tongue like a newly sharpened knife, she has.'

'Yeah, and a voice to match,' someone else called up from the back, her comment greeted with general and not very kind laughter.

Encouraged by the fact that her sister – and Dulcie was convinced now that it was Edith – was obviously not the most popular girl in the room, Dulcie pushed her way through the mass of hot female flesh, wrinkling her nose at the smell of sweat and greasepaint. Close up, she could see that it wasn't just the girls' faces that were covered in makeup; they were wearing it on their bodies as well to give themselves a tanned look, and the combination of hot skin and greasy makeup wasn't very appealing.

'Hey, what's going on?' one of the girls demanded, glaring at Dulcie.

'If you're after a job, auditions are held on Sunday afternoons and I warn you now there's already a waiting list your arm long. One of the best shows in London, this one is.'

'I wouldn't want to be seen dead prancing around in a few feathers and not much else,' Dulcie retorted sturdily, well aware that she was risking the dislike of every girl in the room with her criticism. But Dulcie was used to being disliked by her own sex and it didn't bother her. Besides, she had something more important to do than worry about a few other women, she acknowledged, as she focused on the reflection of her sister's face in the mirror and delivered the line, 'Unlike our Edith, who's supposed to be dead, and who has let her poor mother think that she is dead for going on for two years.'

There was a general gasp from the watching audience, as Dulcie had known there would be. Unlike the unfortunate Margot – apparently – Dulcie knew all about the importance of good timing and was a past mistress of its art.

Not that Edith seemed to think so. Beneath her makeup her face had drained of colour, her eyes reflecting her shocked disbelief as she swung round from the mirror just as the girls parted to allow Dulcie to walk right up to her.

Typically, though, Dulcie thought angrily, her younger sibling soon recovered herself and, patently oblivious to the fact that she was in the wrong and had been found out, just as she had always done as a child she tried to turn the situation around so that Dulcie got the blame.

'Well, I don't suppose you shed any tears over me, did you?' she said sharply. 'You were always jealous of me and my success.'

'You call this success?' Dulcie demanded, waving her hand around the dressing room.

'There's a war on, in case you've forgotten,' Edith retorted, 'and I'm doing my bit to keep our troops cheered up.'

A raucous yell of approval went up from the listening

girls, which spurred Edith on to demand, 'What are you doing – still working at Selfridges, nicking makeup samples?'

'No, as a matter of fact I'm not.'

'She's working in munitions.'

Dulcie turned round to find that Wilder had come into the room to stand beside her, his presence amongst them causing quite a stir amongst the girls – although not the kind of stir one might normally expect from a crowd of half-dressed young women who suddenly found a man in their midst.

'Oooh, look at what he's wearing,' one of them cooed. 'He's one of them American pilots. You know, like the one that you fancied, Arlene, only he didn't fancy you. Not once he'd got what he wanted off you and suddenly remembered that he'd got a wife and two kiddies back home.'

'Dulcie's working in munitions,' Wilder repeated to Edith.

'Munitions?'

Dulcie glared at Wilder as she saw the delight in Edith's eyes. 'My, that's posh, isn't it?' she mocked Dulcie. 'Munitions, and you always so keen to better yourself an' all, Dulce. I feel sorry for you, I really do.'

'And I feel sorry for our mum,' Dulcie told her, determined to change the subject. She'd have something to say to Wilder afterwards, and not just about what he'd said to Edith.

Dulcie didn't like the way her sister was smiling at Wilder all coy and downcast false eyelashes, as she told him in a soft little girl voice that Dulcie knew from the past was put on, 'Dulcie's always been mean to me, I don't know why. I know that our mum always thought I was the pretty one of the two of us, and the talented one as well, with my singing and that.'

As she wound a finger through her curls Dulcie felt like seizing her sister by the shoulders and giving her a good shake.

'Why haven't you let Mum know that you're all right?' she challenged her sister. 'You must have known how she'd be when you went missing that night the theatre was bombed. Broke her heart, it has, believing you're dead.'

'I would have told her if she hadn't moved away, and no one knowing where she'd gone, and then the whole street being blown up,' Edith defended herself.

'She didn't move away until weeks after you'd been reported missing, assumed dead.'

'Well, I couldn't do nothing about it at first, seeing as I was knocked clean out and then didn't know nothing about who I was or what had happened for weeks meself. The first thing I did as soon as I was well enough was go looking for Mum.'

'Doesn't sound to me like you tried very hard.'

'But with the houses being bombed what was I to think except that Mum and Dad had bought it?'

'You know where I live. You could have got in touch.'

'Why?' Edith demanded with brutal candour. 'We've never got on and I reckoned I'd be the last person you'd want to have back in your life, especially with me doing so well, and you only working at Selfridges. Mum always did say that it was because you were so jealous of me that you were the way you were with me.'

'One minute, girls. Oy, what are you two doing in

here? Dressing room is out of bounds to admirers,' the small rotund man announced, spotting Wilder.

'Well, you'd better get in touch with Mum now,' Dulcie told her sister, 'unless you want me to do it for you.'

'You've got to go. I'm on stage again soon.'

'Get in touch with Mum, Edith, or else. Look here's her address,' Dulcie threatened her before rummaging in her handbag to find a pencil and then using an empty cigarette packet from the dressing table in front of her to write down their parents' new address.

'Come on,' Dulcie told Wilder, turning her back on her sister, 'I've had enough of this place. Let's go somewhere else and have a bit of supper.'

'What? And miss the rest of the show when I've paid for the tickets?' Wilder protested angrily as they left the changing room. 'You can forget that. I want my money's worth.'

Dulcie knew what that angry hard look on Wilder's face meant. Sometimes she really didn't know why she bothered with a boyfriend who could be so difficult, she really didn't, except of course that they made a good-looking couple, and with him being American and everything other girls envied her. Unlike other boys who'd taken a shine to her, though, Wilder didn't know his place and kept on pestering her for the kind of favours she had no intention of giving him. Dulcie wasn't that sort. She didn't want the reputation a girl got when she was too free and easy in her ways.

Dulcie hadn't been particularly keen on going to watch the show in the first place. She'd much rather have gone dancing, but now that she knew that Edith was in it she liked watching it even less, especially when Wilder kept on nudging her and going on about what a good figure Edith had and how she knew how to show it off.

She was glad when the show finally came to an end. By then she was ready for the supper Wilder had promised her in a new nightclub he'd heard about from one of the other Eagle pilots. In the foyer to the theatre, though, he released her hand and told her that he needed to visit the 'washroom'.

Dulcie took advantage of his absence to visit the ladies' herself, but when she got back to their planned meeting spot Wilder wasn't there. Dulcie did not approve of men keeping her waiting. Then, as if that hadn't been bad enough, after several toe-tapping irritable moments when her irritation had only been mildly alleviated by the admiring smile of a man who had to be at least forty, and attached to a wife, when Wilder did turn up he had Edith in tow. Dulcie knew better than to let her sister know she was put out. That would be exactly what Edith would want.

'Look who I've just bumped into,' Wilder announced jovially.

Dulcie gave her sibling a false smile and told her, 'Such a pity that other girl, who was taller than you, blocked you out during that last number, and you was a bit out of step as well. I dunno what Mum is going to say when she hears that you've become a hoofer instead of a singer. What about that manager you were so friendly with? The one who was supposed to be going to turn you into the next Vera Lynn.'

Edith tossed her head but didn't answer, turning instead to Wilder and smiling at him flirtatiously.

'And remember, Wilder, any time you feel like coming

313

round to see the show, you just mention my name and they'll give you good seats at a reduced price. Especially if you bring some of your friends,' she told him.

'Thanks, Edith, I'll remember that. The guys are always talking about coming up to London.'

The enthusiasm in her boyfriend's voice caused Dulcie to narrow her eyes watchfully as she moved closer to him and put a firm hand on his arm.

'Pity we've got a second show. I could have come and had a bit of supper with you otherwise,' Edith announced quite plainly enjoying herself getting under her skin, Dulcie recognised.

But Dulcie brought their exchange to a determined end by stepping between them, blocking their view of one another. 'We've got to go, Edith. And don't forget to get in touch with Mum,' she said, before starting to walk away from her sister so that Wilder had no choice other than to follow her, since she was holding firmly to his arm.

'Of course, Edith was only flirting with you like she was to get at me,' Dulcie told Wilder once they were outside. 'She's always been jealous of me, with me being prettier than her.'

There! That should make it plain to Wilder what the situation was, Dulcie decided, as they joined the busy throng of entertainment seekers already moving through Leicester Square.

Although it was around eleven o'clock, the Square was still busy because it was Saturday night and because people had been taking advantage of the new Double Summer Time hours.

Wilder had stopped walking, determined to find a taxi

to take them to the nightclub he'd been told about, Dulcie standing at his side, when the first rising notes of the air-raid siren cracked off.

'Come on,' Dulcie told Wilder, grabbing his arm, and they started to hurry towards the nearest shelter.

At number 13 Olive was just about to get in to bed, after checking that Alice was asleep after her ten o'clock bottle, when she heard the siren.

'You take, Alice,' she instructed Tilly the moment her daughter appeared at her bedroom door, scooping the baby expertly from the cot that was on loan from another member of Olive's WVS group, and handing her to Tilly. 'You go straight down to the shelter. I'll get everything we need from the kitchen.'

'No, Mum, we'll go down together like we always do,' Tilly protested as they hurried downstairs. Tilly was still fully dressed because she'd been expecting Drew to call round on his way back to the Simpsons', but Olive was in her nightclothes and pulling on a dressing gown as she warned, 'Hurry, Tilly. The last thing I want is for you or Alice to be caught out of the shelter when the bombs start dropping. The Edwardses and some of the others are fire-watching tonight so I can come with you to the shelter.'

On her way downstairs, though, Tilly insisted on grabbing the old blankets they kept in the airing cupboard for use in the shelter, not leaving them there because of its dampness, ignoring Olive's pleas for her to go straight to the shelter, whilst she wondered anxiously where Drew was and how close he was to the safety of a shelter.

At the backs of both their minds, although neither of

them said so as they made their way to the Anderson shelter, was the knowledge of the terrible Blitz Liverpool had suffered and whether it was now their turn to endure the same.

By the early hours of the morning, though, Londoners' worst fears were confirmed. The city, and especially the docks, were being subjected to their worst bombing yet.

For Dulcie and Wilder, packed into a communal shelter along with hundreds of other people, the noise from the impromptu sing-a-longs that had started up to lift people's spirits was almost loud enough to drown out the sound of the approaching planes dropping their deadly cargo. Sally, though, at Barts in the relative silence of the operating theatre where they worked throughout the night on a constant stream of badly injured victims, discovered that a new and unexpected thread of anxiety was being woven into those she already had. Alice. It was not because she cared in the least little bit about the child that she felt that anxiety, because she didn't. No, what was making her anxious was the thought of something happening to her unwanted responsibility and Callum returning to blame her for it. Which surely was ridiculous when she hadn't asked for that responsibility and she certainly didn't want it. The sooner the child was packed off somewhere where it would be someone else's responsibility to keep her safe, the happier she would be, Sally told herself.

For Agnes and Ted, squashed into the small local shelter that served the needs of the flats where Ted's mother and sisters lived, the bombing raid passed relatively calmly.

Ted was busy comforting his mother and sisters whilst Agnes did her best to assist him by remaining calmly in the background. It hurt her that Ted's mother was still so obviously reluctant to accept her, but Agnes was becoming stoical about that hurt. In fact, deep down inside she felt that, because she had been an unwanted child, she actually deserved it. She was so lucky to have met Ted, who loved her despite the circumstances of her birth, she decided, as she tried not to mind that his mother, whilst drawing her daughters close, was keeping her back towards her as they all squeezed tightly into the shelter along with the other occupants of the Guinness flats.

To be allowed to rent a Guinness flat one had to be considered very respectable. Rental of a flat could be withdrawn and its occupants made homeless if an occupant was deemed to have transgressed against that rule of respectability, and so it was no wonder that people were withdrawing from the half-a-dozen or so shelterers who had grouped round a man with a penny whistle, who was encouraging them to sing. He was only trying to lift people's spirits, Agnes thought sympathetically, feeling sad for Ted's sisters, who, when asked if they wanted to join in with the other children gathering around him, looked at their mother and then shook their heads. Children should have some fun, Agnes thought sadly. Even in the orphanage they had had fun. Matron had encouraged it, although of course they had been expected to behave themselves as well.

For Tilly the relative safety of their own Anderson shelter couldn't offset her growing anxiety for Drew, the sound of every plane, the explosion of every bomb causing her to tense and stare fixedly toward the metal wall of the shelter, so fixedly that Olive, watching her, felt her daughter's gaze would burn through the metal in her need to find her boyfriend.

Tilly wasn't saying a word, but she didn't need to. Olive could see that she was being wrung out with the intensity of her emotions, and she was forced to acknowledge that she couldn't protect Tilly from the emotional pain that could come from love.

It was obvious from the sound of the bombs that the Germans were hitting the docks. But then a bomb exploded closer to them with an ear-splitting sound that woke Alice, who had been lying peacefully asleep in the washing basket Olive was using for a temporary bed. The baby starting to cry in obvious fear.

'Lift her out, Tilly,' Olive instructed. She could have reached for the baby herself but she was hoping that doing something for the baby might distract her daughter from her obvious fear for Drew.

Tilly reached for the crying baby. Alice was sweet, and so pretty, but right now Tilly didn't want to think about anyone other than Drew.

'What is it?' Olive asked her gently, seeing her frown.

'I was just thinking how hard it must be to have a baby who is totally dependent on you when you're worrying about the man you love.'

'Yes, it is,' Olive agreed, feeling closer to her daughter than she had done in a long time, 'but there is a great deal of comfort in having that responsibility, Tilly.'

Tilly shook her head as she handed the crying Alice to her mother.

'She's so frightened,' Olive said as she tried to soothe and comfort the baby. 'It makes me wonder how much her little mind might know of what she's been through with the death of her parents, poor little scrap.'

'What do you think will happen to her?' Tilly asked.

'I don't know, Tilly,' Olive admitted, both of them flinching as a bomb exploded close at hand, making it impossible for them to continue conversing above the dreadful sound.

She might be able to try to blot out the sound of the falling bombs but Tilly couldn't blot out her fears for Drew. The night she had seen the man from number 46 burned to death, and then witnessed Drew being separated from her by the same flames had left its mark on her. Over and over, inside her head she kept saying her prayers for him. He was everything to her, absolutely everything, and even though she knew her mother was afraid for her, she couldn't deny that feeling.

'It's definitely been the worst raid so far. They thought at one point that the Faraday Street telephone exchange would go up in the flames, and if we'd lost that, the country would have been completely cut off,' Olive heard Archie Dawson saying to the vicar outside church the next morning.

When he ended his conversation, though, to come over and join Mrs Dawson and Barney, who were standing a few yards away from Olive, she couldn't help but notice how Mrs Dawson grabbed Barney's hand and very firmly turned herself and the boy away so that they had their backs to him.

'I'm in the doghouse,' Archie Dawson admitted to

Olive, coming over to her rather than rejoin his wife. 'It's on account of me giving Barney a serious talking to when I found out that he's still palling up with those Farley lads. Mrs Dawson thinks I'm being too hard on him, even though I've told her that I'm only doing it for Barney's own good.'

Olive could hear the frustration in Archie Dawson's voice but, as much as she sympathised with him, her real concern just then was for Tilly.

At her mother's side Tilly couldn't concentrate on anything other than the fact that it was now morning and Drew wasn't here. Last night she had managed to convince herself that he would be sheltering somewhere, as her mother had told her. But now it was mid-morning and there was no sign of him. Tilly had wanted to go out searching for him, but her mother had said that it was too soon. Now Tilly felt sick with dread of her deepest fear: that Drew was dead. No! Surely she would know if that had happened. Surely the world would feel different? Surely she would have sensed his going?

'I heard about young Drew being missing. I'll do my best to find out what I can about him,' Archie Dawson assured Olive.

'That's really kind of you,' she thanked him. 'I did suggest to Tilly that she stayed at home instead of coming to church this morning, but she insisted that she wanted to come.' She looked towards Tilly, who was standing looking in the direction of Fleet Street, even though the street itself couldn't be seen from the church.

'. . . And to think Edith's been alive all this time and never said a word to Mum,' Dulcie was complaining to Tilly. 'Just goes to show how selfish she is. You'd never get me behaving like that. Always put others first, I have. Gave me ever such a turn seeing her there, I can tell you. It was like she'd come back from the dead, with us being told she'd gone.'

Dulcie frowned when Tilly made a small choking sound and pushed past her. What was up with her, acting all dramatic, like, when it was she, Dulcie, who had had the awful shock of seeing the sister she had thought dead was in fact very much alive. Very much alive and, by the sound of what she had said to Wilder, far too eager to get herself involved in Dulcie's life. Well, Dulcie had made it plain to Wilder last night when they had been in that shelter, just what a selfish person Edith was, and how he was lucky that he'd picked her, the much better sister.

Normally Tilly enjoyed Dulcie's chatter but today, when there was still no sign of Drew or any word from him, and with the air full of both the conversation about the devastation, and the dust and detritus from the damage, the very sound of Dulcie's voice felt like a saw on Tilly's raw nerves. All she wanted to do was escape to the privacy of a place where she could give way to her emotions, a dark room in which she could hide away with the pain and fear that was ripping into her. But at the same time, just having that pain when all around her people were being so brave and matter-of-fact, and getting on with their lives made her feel weak and worthless and ashamed of herself. She felt as though somehow she had become separated from a part of herself, as though she barely knew herself any more, such was the extent of her misery and fear.

'Tilly,' Olive began, wanting to offer her comfort and

reassurance and yet knowing that she couldn't. The truth was that the longer Drew remained missing the more likely it was that something had happened to him. Of course there were things they could do – like going round the hospitals to check if he had been admitted; like consulting the lists put up by each council of the missing and dead in their area to see if his name was on one of them – but Olive didn't want to think about how Tilly was likely to react if they were to do that.

As she held her daughter's arm with one hand Olive pushed the loaned perambulator with the other. Inside, Alice lay wide awake, her huge dark eyes gazing up. War was such a cruel thing, robbing people of those they loved, splitting up families, destroying lives and bodies . . .

The sound of Tilly suddenly saying, 'Drew', as though the word had been ripped from her throat, caused Olive to look up swiftly. Tilly's face was contorted with anguish, and she pulled free of Olive's hold and began to run toward her young American boyfriend as he ran toward her.

'It really is you! It really is. I was so afraid. I thought something must have happened to you. I thought I'd never see you again,' Tilly sobbed as Drew's arms closed round her. It might be Sunday morning, they might be within sight of the church and its worshippers, but Tilly was prepared to ignore convention as she clung to Drew and wept in her relief at discovering he was alive and whole.

'I'm sorry, Tilly, I'm sorry,' Drew tried to comfort her as he held her tightly. 'I got involved with several other reporters after the match. We went out for something to eat, and then we got caught in the bombing. The shelter we were in took a hit.'

Tilly gasped and trembled in his hold.

'We were lucky. It didn't effect the bit where we were, apart leaving us blocked inside from falling debris. It took them until this morning to get us out, but I've come straight here—'

'Drew, you must come back and have dinner with us and tell us all about it then,' Olive intervened.

Tilly's face was luminous with love but the strain of the night had had its effect on her, and it seemed to Olive as an anxious mother that her daughter had become thinner and more vulnerable-looking virtually overnight.

'Thank you, yes. That's a good idea,' Drew agreed, earning a smile of gratitude from Olive. 'I'll need to go home and have a bath first, though.'

Immediately Tilly's hand tightened on his arm. 'I'm so afraid if I let you go that you might disappear,' she told him emotionally.

From her bedroom window at number 13 Sally, who couldn't sleep despite the fact that she had worked so hard on her night shift, watched the small procession returning. Olive was pushing the pram and, as they approached the house, Sally could see one small pink fist waving from inside it. Something unfamiliar and unexpected gripped her hear: a feeling, an awareness, a sense of her mother's love for her and all that it had meant. Alice would never know that kind of love.

That wasn't her fault. Alice should never have been born, would never have been born if her father and her former best friend had remained loyal to her mother. It wasn't Sally's fault that Alice had been orphaned.

Sally turned away from the window. She felt as though the smell of blood and fear and death was still clinging to her. A long night in the operating theatre, working alongside the surgeons trying so desperately to repair the injured, did that to you. Inside her head, Sally had tried to lock away the unwanted images of the bodies of her father and Morag.

She had known from what Callum had not said, from the fact that they had not been individually recovered and buried, that there must not have been much of them left to bury. At least Alice would never know anything of those images, even if she had to grow up knowing she had lost the people who had loved her the most, and who had created her. They weren't here any more to love her and protect her. But it wasn't her job to do so in their stead, Sally defended her decision. She had a life of her own to live, a man who loved her and with whom she would have her own children. There was no place in her life for a child who could only ever be an unwanted reminder of a past betrayal.

Sunday dinner was over. Tilly and Drew were in the kitchen washing up. Sally was upstairs in bed asleep, Agnes and Dulcie were outside in the garden with Alice who was toddling on the grass.

Tilly had barely touched her lunch, her gaze fixed anxiously on Drew as though she was afraid that he might somehow disappear. Drew had insisted that they do the washing up, and Olive had let them, but now she felt that some fresh air and the sight of little Alice playing joyfully in the garden would do more to lift her daughter's spirits than washing up.

As she opened the door into the kitchen she could hear Tilly saying emotionally to Drew, 'Mum's right about me not being mature enough to be married. Last night, when I was so worried about you and all I could think about was you, I felt that if we had been married and we'd had a child, I'd have resented having to look after it when I wanted to be thinking about you. I'm such a coward, Drew.'

'Darling, please, you mustn't say that because it isn't true,' Drew protested.

'It is true,' Tilly insisted. 'Mum's right, I'm not fit to be married. I'd only drag you down with my worry and my cowardice. I'm not afraid for myself but I'm so afraid for you, so afraid of being without you. Last night . . .'

Drew put down the tea towel with which he had been drying the dinner plates and reached for Tilly's hand.

'It's the same for me, you know,' he told her gently. 'So if you worrying about me and not wanting to lose me makes you a coward, then me worrying about you and not wanting to lose you makes me one as well. But it isn't cowardice, my darling girl, it's love.'

'I can't bear the thought of losing you.'

'You could never lose me, Tilly. Never. My heart is yours for ever. My love will always be with you, and as for you being a coward, on the contrary, you have the courage of a lion, giving your love as you have done to a stranger from another land, trusting him, believing in him. That isn't cowardice. Only a very brave person can do that.'

'Oh, Drew, why is it that you always know just what to say to make me feel better?'

Standing on the threshold of the kitchen, Olive surveyed them both, her eyes damp with tears. Drew's words had caught at Olive's own emotions. There was no mistaking his sincerity.

Perhaps she had been too hard on the young couple, too fearful on Tilly's behalf. She wasn't going to change her mind about them getting married – she still felt that Tilly was too young for that – but there was some lenience and trust she could show that would help to restore her daughter to her old self and give her some respite from the horror of the Blitz.

Olive took a deep breath and then, before she could allow herself to change her mind, she stepped into the kitchen and announced calmly, 'I've been thinking about how much this dreadful Blitz is getting us all down, and I think it would be a good idea if you had a holiday, Tilly. You haven't had a proper holiday since you started work at the hospital, and now with summer coming . . .'

'A holiday?'

Tilly felt confused, and wary. Automatically she moved closer to Drew. If her mother was going to suggest parting them and sending her away from London and from Drew . . .

'Yes,' Olive agreed, looking steadfastly at her. 'I really do think that it would do you the world of good. I can't get away myself, unfortunately, so I was thinking that perhaps if Drew could go with you . . .'

Olive could hear Tilly's indrawn gasp of excitement and see the joy lighting up her eyes.

'Oh, Mum.' Releasing Drew's hand, Tilly almost flew

into Olive's arms, her voice breathless with delight and emotion as she told her shakily, 'Oh, I can't believe you really mean it. It would be wonderful. To be able to go away, and with Drew . . .'

'You can be sure that I'll take the very best care of her, Mrs Robbins,' Drew assured Olive.

'I know that, Drew. I wouldn't have suggested you go with Tilly if I didn't think that, and if I didn't feel completely able to trust you to do everything that is right.'

Quietly they looked at one another, and Olive could see from the seriousness of Drew's expression that he understood the promise she wanted from him and that he was willing to give it. He was everything any mother could want for her daughter, Olive knew.

To see Tilly's spirits restored so speedily and almost miraculously was wonderful, Olive had to admit later in the afternoon, as they all sat on the grass, Tilly's voice rising and falling excitedly as she chattered happily about the holiday.

'I'll have a word with some of the guys on the paper,' said Drew, 'find out where they recommend.'

'Well, if it was me I'd go to somewhere like Brighton where there's a bit of life,' Dulcie informed them.

'No, I want to go somewhere quiet and peaceful, a pretty little village with houses with thatched roofs, and a dear river with fishing boats,' Tilly said dreamily.

'I've never been to the seaside,' Agnes put in. 'We were going to go once with the orphanage, but I had to stay behind because I got some spots and they thought I was coming down with something.'

'I dare say the south coast itself will be out of bounds

because of the war,' Olive warned them, 'but Devon is supposed to be very pretty.'

'We could hire bicycles and explore the countryside,' said Tilly enthusiastically. The truth was that really she didn't care where they went as long as she and Drew were there together.

Dulcie pulled a face. 'That's not my idea of having a good time. I'd want to go dancing and be taken out for a posh meal.'

Seated at Drew's side, Tilly reached for his hand. She felt so happy, elated and buoyed up with a heady mixture of relief in his safety and joy at the unexpected gift her mother had given her that fizzed up inside her. Suddenly, despite the war, her world had turned from the darkness of fear into a place in which she could look forward to a special time for her and Drew to share together.

'We could go next month, in June,' she told Drew.

June, the wedding month. She and Drew might not be getting married, but that did not mean that she couldn't make their precious shared time away together something very special, and just for the two of them. A couple didn't have to be married for that. As *that* thought formed inside her head, Tilly deliberately avoided looking at her mother, knowing that what she had in mind right now as part of their special time together was not something of which her mother would approve at all.

'I'm going to go in and make us some tea,' Olive announced. 'You girls can keep an eye on Alice. Don't let her go too far, mind.'

'I'll come with you, Mum,' Tilly said, her conscience urging her to make the offer as though to make up both for the gulf that had existed between them in recent weeks, and the secret thoughts she had just had about how she would most like to spend her precious time with Drew.

The feeling of her daughter's arm through her own as they walked back towards the house together, the May breeze catching at the hems of the skirts of their floral dresses, filled Olive with relief. With just a few words she had brought Tilly back from that dark, frightening place she had gone to, and where Olive had really begun to fear she might lose her, and now she was her old optimistic sunny self again. She had made a mistake in judging her daughter's emotional makeup to be similar to her own, Olive acknowledged. Tilly loved fiercely and with everything in her, throwing herself into her emotions with unguarded intensity. Because of that she was vulnerable to her love in a way that Olive knew she herself was not. She might never have known the highs that love obviously brought Tilly, but she had never known the lows that were Tilly's either. As a mother all she wanted for her daughter was her happiness, a good steady ongoing happiness that came from a world at peace and a reliable, loving, living husband. At least in Drew Tilly had found a young man who did truly love her, Olive comforted herself as they walked into the kitchen. Not that she intended to say anything of what she was thinking to Tilly.

Instead she told her prosaically, 'You get the tea tray organised, Tilly, and I'll put the kettle on.'

Tilly reached for the tray, which was propped up at the back of the smart kitchen cabinet of which Olive was so proud, and then stopped, going over to where Olive was standing by the kitchen sink.

'Thanks, Mum,' she told her, reaching for her and hugging her tightly. 'This morning I thought that Drew was really gone and that I'd lost him, and now . . . I don't think I've ever felt so happy.'

The feeling of her daughter's young strong arms around her filled Olive's heart with emotion.

She hugged her in return then told her, 'You go back to Drew, Tilly, but remember, when you and he do go away—'

'I know, Mum. You don't have to tell me,' Tilly stopped her.

As she headed back to Drew she recognised that she hadn't crossed her fingers behind her back when she'd let her mother think she was giving her an assurance of 'good behaviour', but then crossing your fingers was a childhood thing and she wasn't a child any more. She was a woman on the verge of claiming that womanhood, and so very eager to do so, to give and share the reality of love with the man she loved.

June couldn't come soon enough.

Olive was just pouring the boiling water onto the tea leaves when Sally walked into the kitchen.

'You could have had a couple more hours in bed,' Olive told her. 'If we have another night like last night you'll be kept busy at the hospital.'

'I couldn't sleep. We had so many patients in last night that we just couldn't do anything for. Too many. You just lose count in the end, but to their families every one of them is someone loved who has been lost. You feel so guilty because you can't be more sympathetic, but there just isn't time.'

'I'm sure that people would much rather you were in the operating theatre helping people, Sally, than offering them cups of tea and sympathy. You're a trained nurse. Anyone can make a cup of tea.'

'That's exactly what my mum would have said,' Sally admitted, bending to pick up the tea tray. Olive had a way of saying things that were unexpectedly sympathetic and understanding. She couldn't have had a better landlady, Sally thought, and in her more fanciful moments she liked to think that her mother was looking down on her and thought the same thing.

Out in the garden Agnes was brushing her uniform hat free of the dust it had collected during the week's bombings, whilst Dulcie filed her nails. Tilly was showing Drew how to make a daisy chain, ostensibly for Alice, but since it gave her an opportunity to sit close to Drew and hold his hands whilst she showed him what to do, Olive suspected that the chain would be a long time in the making.

Alice herself, busy playing on the lawn spotted them, toddled towards them, stopped and then sat down and looked straight at Sally, holding out her arms to her.

For a moment there was silence. Olive held her breath. For Sally's sake as much as Alice's she really hoped that the two half-sisters could form a bond, and that Sally would find it in her heart to love her little sister, who needed her so much.

Sally, though, after the smallest hesitation, turned from the baby and walked away.

As she put down the tray Sally could feel her heart thumping so heavily that it was making her feel light-headed. She felt sick and shaky, angry inside, and yet guilty, in the same kind of way she had done as a child when she'd done something she'd known was 'wrong'.

When Sally turned from Alice, leaving the little girl to wail in rejected misery, the sound of her despair tore at Agnes's heart. Normally the last person to cause a confrontation of any kind, little Alice's plight touched such a raw place in Agnes that before she knew what she was doing she was on her feet and following Sally to the furthest end of the garden, telling her fiercely, 'I think it's a terrible cruel thing wot you're planning to do with little Alice, giving her away like she was just . . .' her gaze fell on the vegetable patch, '. . . just like she wasn't a baby and your own flesh and blood at all but a . . . a bag of veggies. I never thought you were the sort to do something like that, Sally.'

To be verbally attacked by Agnes, of all people, really caught Sally off guard, but she suspected that she should have expected it. After all, Agnes herself had been abandoned as a baby.

'I'm not planning to leave Alice on the steps of an orphanage, Agnes,' she informed her as calmly as she could. 'Far from it. She will be properly adopted and placed with a family who will love and care for her.'

'She has a family. She has you and her uncle.'

'Callum is in the Royal Navy, and I am a nurse. There is a war on, and both of us have duties to fulfil for which we have been trained. Alice will be much better off with a family.'

'No she won't. She'll spend the rest of her life wondering who her real family are, and why they gave her up. She'll worry that she wasn't good enough for them, and that they didn't love her enough. She'll grow up feeling that . . . that part of her is missing.'

Never in the whole time she had known Agnes had Sally heard such an impassioned speech from her. Agnes was normally so timid and quiet. Because she felt that, as an abandoned child, she didn't have the right to speak out or have an opinion? Was that what being rejected by one's family did to a child?

'I'm doing this for Alice's own benefit. Like I just said, I'm not going to abandon her, Agnes.'

'No you aren't. Doing it for Alice's sake, I mean. You're doing it for you're own because it hurts you too much to have her here because of what she means. You're punishing her for what you think her parents did, and that's wrong. I'd adopt her myself if I could, so I would.'

Without another word she turned round and ran back up the garden picking up her hat and then disappearing in the direction of the house.

'I'm sorry about the child being here, and about upsetting Agnes,' Sally apologised to Olive later when they were drinking their tea. 'It's not right that you should have to help out with her like this. She's nothing to you, after all. Callum should never have brought her here. She'd have been far better off in an orphanage in Liverpool.'

'I understand how you feel, Sally,' Olive told her gently, 'but I wouldn't be being fair to you if I didn't advise you not to rush into anything that you might one day regret, and as for Agnes, well, I think we both understand why she's so upset.'

'Yes. It's because of her being abandoned as a baby herself. It's all very well Agnes getting herself in an emotional state, but she doesn't appreciate the realities of the situation. Even if I wanted to keep Alice, which I don't, how could I? I've got George to think of. He doesn't even know she exists. How could I ask him to take her on? Besides, I'm not her only relative. She's got Callum. She's known him since she was born. She can't stay here, Olive. I'll have to do something.'

EIGHTEEN

'And we've booked to stay at this pub in a village on the River Otter, and—'

'Two rooms or one?' Clara demanded, interrupting Tilly in mid-sentence.

'Two,' Tilly responded. 'Mum wouldn't have let me go otherwise. She found out about the village for us from Mrs Windle, the vicar's wife. She knew about it from some friends of her family, and it was actually Mrs Windle who wrote to the pub on our behalf. They're a bit fussy about who they let stay, on account of not wanting to let rooms to RAF types who might be up to no good with their girlfriends.'

'Your mum told you that?'

'Not in so many words, but it was obvious what Mum was getting at when she gave me this lecture about not letting Mrs Windle down.'

'So when do you go then?' Clara asked, as they got ready for their day's work, removing the covers from their typewriters and folding them neatly away before sitting down at their machines.

'Just over two weeks. I can't wait.'

Clara nodded. Outside, the main streets of London might have been cleared of the worst of the debris from the dreadful blitz of 10 May, one might no longer have to literally crunch through ankle-deep broken glass on the pavements, the raw gaping awfulness of buildings ripped apart to show their most private interiors might have been softened by the herculean effort put in by people to restore the city to some semblance of normality, but London would never be the same. Too many buildings had been lost – too many buildings and too many lives. Rather than instil fear into people, though, the savagery of the May blitz had had the opposite effect, giving people a determination to see things through that was evident everywhere you went. Tilly now felt as though she was part of that courageous band. Knowing that she was going to have that precious personal time with Drew and that her mother finally accepted that she was old enough to do that had made such a difference to her, pulling her back from the edge of that awful fear that had dragged her down.

Her spirits had rebounded, her natural optimism reasserting itself. She and Drew had now survived three equally awful incidents: the bombing of St Paul's, the incendiary attack on Article Row, and finally the bombing of the city that had seen Fleet Street and the surrounding district on fire from end to end. Surely now they were safe now?

'I'd have liked to have stayed on the coast but, like Drew says, with the war on there's bound to be all sorts of restrictions about going near the beaches and that kind of thing, and this village where we're staying is on the river. Drew says he's going to teach me to fish.'

A happy smile curved Tilly's mouth. 'When he was growing up he and his family used to go to this lake every summer. He says it's something that Americans do.'

Once again Clara nodded. She was more interested in her own life than Tilly's, and wanted to talk about the effect the new law bringing in clothing coupons was likely to have on her ability to buy a wedding dress.

'I just wanted to say thank you, Sister, seeing as you were the one that was there when our Carole was operated on, after her being hurt in the bombing. Right as rain, she is now, thanks to everyone here, and her broken leg's mending a treat. Broke my heart, it would, if we'd lost her, aye and my hubby's as well. Funny how things turn out, isn't it? When we found out that our Betty had got herself into trouble with a seaman she'd been seeing, her dad was all for throwing her out he was that mad with her, showing us up and bringing shame on the family, and then when our Betty didn't survive the birth, well, my hubby said how it would be best if we were to give the baby up for adoption, her being illegitimate and everything. But flesh and blood is flesh and blood when all said and done, and it wasn't the poor little mite's fault that she'd been born the way that she had. You can't turn your back on your own. It weren't her fault what her mum did, bringing all that trouble on us and letting us down like she did.'

The woman shook her head and then told Sally, 'That was at the beginning of the war, and now you should see my Derek with her. Thinks the sun shines out of her, he does, and reckons she's the spitting image of his sister wot died of scarlet fever when she was a kiddy.'

Sally smiled politely and nodded. It wasn't unusual for the relatives of patients and patients themselves to come into the hospital to thank those who had helped them. Normally their thanks gave Sally a real lift, but listening to this woman, it wasn't a lift to her spirits she felt so much as a cold lump of unwanted guilt, which lay heavily in the pit of her stomach.

She knew the others at number 13 thought she was being cold-hearted and mean in ignoring Alice and refusing to have anything to do with her, but she couldn't help it. Every time she looked at the little girl she saw her father and her false friend, and every time she saw them she thought of her mother and what she had endured, the dreadful physical pain, the awfulness of her body wasting away as the cancer ate into her. Then, at a time when her father's thoughts should have been only for her mother, he had secretly been thinking of Morag.

Thinking of her, wanting her . . . betraying her mother with her. Sally could visualise her mother now, see her sweet loving smile, feel the gentle loving touch of her hand on her own head brushing her hair out of her eyes as she had done when she had been a child, loving her and protecting her. Now it was her turn to love and protect her mother, to be loyal to her.

Sally closed her eyes briefly and then opened them again when, as clearly as though she had been there with her, she could hear her mother's voice saying quietly, 'Sally, she's just a baby.'

'Morag's baby,' said Sally fiercely.

'Talking to yourself?' a fellow sister grinned as she passed Sally in the corridor. 'Bad sign that, you know.'

Sally smiled back dutifully, but in reality she didn't

feel like smiling. She wasn't sleeping and she was missing George, whom she hadn't been able to see since before the last air raid because of the shifts they were working. She really missed him, even though they wrote to one another every day. She wished desperately that she had been open with him right from the start about the situation with her father.

She had a day off in three days' time. She would go and see the vicar and ask him if he knew of a good orphanage that would take Alice. Olive might say that she was happy to have Alice living at number 13, and, even more generously, that she was prepared to look after her, but it wasn't right that she should have to do that. Alice wasn't Olive's responsibility, after all.

'Thanks for coming with me to take Mr Whittaker his tea,' said Agnes to Ted as they walked back from number 50 arm in arm in the late evening sunshine.

'I can't have someone scaring the living daylights out of my girl, especially when she's bin kind enough to take him a meal,' Ted smiled down at Agnes.

'Well, it isn't Mr Whittaker who frightens me, although he can be a bit gruff. Mind you, I think he's really taken to you, Ted. He was asking you ever so many questions, wasn't he?'

'He certainly was. Had me going right back to me granddad, wot worked down at the tannery he did. That took me back a bit, I can tell you. I can see Granddad now standing outside the Carter's Arms, smoking his pipe, waiting for it to open. If he was late back for his tea me nan used to go and give him a real dressing down,' Ted chuckled. 'Of course, Mum didn't really approve of

Dad's family, and she won't hear them spoken of now that she's got this Guinness Trust flat. Asked me about that too, Mr Whittaker did. And how I thought I was going to be able to support a wife. Told him that we'd agreed that we wouldn't get married until the girls are older. Anyway, if it isn't Mr Whittaker you're afraid of, what is it?'

'Number 49, the house next door, the one that the Lords used to live in. Mr Lord died there, you know, and Barney and those two lads he hangs around with swear that it's haunted.'

'They're having you on, Agnes, and just trying to scare you.'

'No, Ted. I've heard noises myself, after that bombing in May when I took Mr Whittaker his tea one night.'

'There's no such things as ghosts,' Ted assured her stoutly.

Agnes didn't say anything. Instead she moved closer to him.

It had been a difficult day at work. Sally had heard this afternoon that they'd lost a patient – a fireman – on whom they'd operated the night after the blitz. The surgeon had had to amputate both his legs and there had been wounds to his chest as well, caused by falling glass. They had all known that it would be a miracle if he did survive but that didn't make his death any easier to bear. Surgeons and those who worked with them took it as a personal affront if a patient didn't survive, and the atmosphere in the theatre after they'd had the news had been very prickly.

As an antidote to that loss Sally had changed into the

faded old dress she wore when she was working on the veggie plot and had come out to do some weeding.

Ten minutes ago Olive had come out with Alice, whom she'd placed on a blanket on the grass under the gnarled apple tree, and now Olive had gone inside, saying casually, 'Keep an eye on Alice for a minute for me, will you, Sally?' Sally was now alone in the garden with her baby half-sister.

Of course she had to watch her. She might not want her in her life but that did not mean that she was uncaring enough not to watch out for the baby's safety out of the corner of her eye whilst she got on with her weeding.

She could hear Alice talking to herself, half singing, half chattering as she did whenever she was trying very hard to do something, and as she turned round Sally saw she was crawling towards her at some speed.

Not that Sally was going to behave as the others did at this bit of baby cleverness. No. She certainly wasn't going to coo and smile and clap her hands, and then hold out her arms to the little girl. There was no point in encouraging her, after all.

But then Alice stopped crawling and sat back on her well-padded bottom and gave Sally the most beatific smile as she held out her arms to *her*, her fat little baby hands imploring Sally to hold her.

Inside her chest Sally felt as though something was cracking and then tearing apart, as though it were being ripped by strong hands, the sharpness of the pain making her catch her breath as she fought against both it and the instinct that urged her to go to the little girl. As she started to turn away from her she could see the happy smile fading from Alice's face, to

341

be replaced by a lost look of confusion and fear. The look of a child who knew even at that baby age how alone she was. She didn't cry or make any kind of sound at all, but Sally discovered that she wanted to cry. She had had such a happy childhood, filled with love and security. She had never needed to look like Alice was looking, or as Agnes sometimes did even now. She thought of her mother. No need to ask what she would think or what she would do; she had known the answer to those questions right from the moment she had seen Alice.

Putting down her hoe and removing her gardening gloves, Sally went towards the still silent baby.

When she reached her she crouched down beside her. Alice looked at her with a dark dense-eyed gaze that revealed uncertainty and anxiety. Inside her head Sally had a picture of Alice abandoned in an orphanage, whilst she walked away from her. Her heart was thumping heavily and fast, as though she had just escaped from the most awful kind of horrific accident, her relief at escaping it stabbed with the anxiety of how close she had come to succumbing to it. Sally felt as though she were waking from some kind of dangerous hypnotic dream that had, like a fast-flowing river, been carrying her towards some distant danger from which there could be no going back, and only just in time. What could have possessed her ever to think she could turn her back on Alice?

No baby should look like that, and least of all because of her. How could she have even thought of abandoning her? Her mother would have been horrified and disbelieving that the daughter she had raised with so much love could do such a thing to an innocent baby, and her own flesh and blood.

Quickly, as though she were afraid that someone might take her from her, Sally picked up her half-sister, and held her tight. How odd that holding her should feel so right, as though somehow she had always know her warmth and weight, and the small movements of her body as she kissed the top of the dark curls. Tears filled her eyes as she realised how close she had come to losing something very precious.

Olive, watching the small touching scene from the kitchen window, exhaled shakily in relief. She'd already made up her mind that if Sally had persisted in her plans to have Alice adopted she was going to offer to be the one to adopt her. And not just for Alice's sake. Olive knew her lodgers, she knew and understood what Sally had been through, but she also believed that if Sally had abandoned Alice ultimately she would have been torn apart by regret and guilt that would have completely overshadowed the happiness with George she so much deserved.

'Hello, little sister,' Sally whispered to Alice. How easy it was now to touch one rose petal cheek and marvel at the softness of skin that was the same tone as her own, the little nose surely the same elegant shape as their shared father's had been.

Was it foolish of her to feel that her mother had somehow had a hand in making her see not just what was right, but what true joy there could be in her loving Alice?

Sally looked up and saw Olive coming towards her carrying a tea tray.

'You knew this would happen, didn't you?' she accused her landlady ruefully as she settled herself in one of the deck chairs that had originally belonged to Olive's father-in-law, and which lived in the garden shed, which Sally now kept almost as spick and span as her operating theatre.

'I hoped that it would,' Olive agreed, watching Alice laugh and cuddle up to Sally as she sat in her half-sister's lap. 'For your sake as well as for Alice's, Sally. I understood how you felt, and the terrible shock you'd had, not just because of the arrival of Alice but also the news of the death of your father and Alice's mother. You loved them both very much, and love doesn't always die as conveniently as we want it to.'

'I've felt such a strong sense of my mother these last few days, as though she's watching over both of us and urging me to . . . to love Alice and look after her.'

Olive reached for Sally's hand. 'I'm sure that she is, Sally. I never met your mother, but from everything you've told me about her I don't doubt for one minute that she'd want Alice to be with you and that she would love her herself.'

'She would. She was like that. She loved people so much and they loved her. Everyone loved her.'

When Olive didn't say anything Sally challenged her shakily, 'You're thinking that my father and Morag must have loved her as well, aren't you?'

'Yes,' Olive acknowledged.

Sally gave a small sigh. 'I hope that one day I'll be ready to believe that, for Alice's sake.'

'I'm sure you will.'

'I don't know what I'm going to tell George, though,

Olive. That's part of the reason I didn't want her. I love George so much. I didn't want to sacrifice the happiness I know I'll have with him to look after Alice. I know that's selfish of me.'

'No it isn't. It's only natural. From what I know of George, though, I'm sure that he'll be as ready to take on Alice as you now are, Sally.'

Sally shook her head. 'I can't expect him to do that. It wouldn't be fair. Besides, once he knows how much I've kept from him . . . We've both always said that honesty between us is important, and now . . .'

In Sally's lap Alice made a small sad sound as though she sensed Sally's distress. Automatically Sally cuddled her closer to soothe her.

'I've got to go and see him and tell him everything. I've got to offer him his ring back, Olive. Anything less than that would be wrong.'

NINETEEN

'. . . and since then our Edith's started wanting to tag on with us when me and Wilder go out, and she's bin writing to him. The cheek of it,' Dulcie complained to David as they sat outside in the June sunshine, where she had wheeled him in his chair.

Whilst other amputees were getting to grips with their new false limbs, the complications David had had with his amputation wounds after he had first been operated on meant that it was likely that he would be in a wheelchair for the rest of his life. Not that Dulcie thought that should bother him.

'After all,' she'd told him on her first visit after the news had been broken to him that he would be wheelchair bound for the rest of his life, 'I dare say it's much more comfortable being pushed round in a chair than having to try to walk on them artificial legs. Ever so difficult, they look, and painful too. No, I think you're lucky that you can't manage them, David.'

'I expect you're right,' David had agreed, 'although it will mean me having to have ramps and the like put in when I move back to chambers and my rooms at Lincoln's

Inn, once I'm discharged from here. I'll have to find a decent-sized ground-floor flat, of course, and not too far from chambers either.'

Dulcie couldn't really understand why David was insisting on going back to work as a barrister, especially when it turned out that he had inherited so much money from Lydia after she had been killed, and her having all that money from her grandparents. But then men had their own funny ways, and right now it was Wilder's 'funny ways' that were occupying Dulcie's thoughts and exacerbating her ire.

'I've told Wilder that he's just got to ignore Edith, and that she's just making a play for him because he's going out with me. Always been like that, she has, wanting what I've got, and of course our mum always letting her get away with it. Well, I'm not going to.' She scowled as she thought of her sister and how aggravating she was being, writing to Wilder after he'd taken those friends of his to see her show, and actually daring to suggest that he took her out for dinner one night. The cheek of it! Of course, Wilder had agreed with her that Edith had had no right to suggest what she had. After all, he was her boyfriend, not Edith's. And just to prove that, Dulcie had allowed him to kiss her far more passionately than she normally did the last time he had taken her out. Just to let him know which side his bread was buttered on, so to speak.

'So you want to talk to me about something?'

Sally nodded, deliberately walking slightly apart from George as they set off on their favourite walk around East Grinstead, instead of tucking her arm through his.

The sunlight glinted on her engagement ring. The engagement ring she would be giving back to George before she left him today. Oh, she knew he would say that it didn't matter about Alice and that he loved her – he was that kind of man – but it did matter. It would certainly matter to George's family – to his mother, who had been so welcoming to her; how would they ever be able to feel they could trust her now, when she produced a half-sister she had never let them know existed? Last night when she had bathed Alice, the little girl had reached for her ring, her innocent delight in touching it tearing at Sally's heart. How could she ever have thought of George as just a pleasant young man? How could she not have known the minute she had met him how much she would love him and have told him everything there and then?

She looked at him now. His dear honest face was creased with concern – for her, she knew – and anxiety. He reached for her hand but she shook her head and, being George, he didn't fuss or object, simply watching her with even more concern.

She took a deep breath.

'I . . . I've lied to you, George. Deceived you. I'm so sorry. I wish that I hadn't. I didn't mean to. I didn't realise when we first met what would happen between us, and I was too . . . I didn't want . . . I let you think that both my parents were dead, because . . . because to me they were, but it wasn't the truth.'

Quietly she explained the events that had followed her mother's death and the anguish and anger they had caused her.

'I didn't mean to deceive you. I just didn't want to talk about what had happened – to anyone. Then when

Callum came to London to tell me . . . to tell me that there was to be a child, I had to explain to Olive what had happened but I didn't tell anyone else. To me, my father was dead – at least the father I had known and loved, the father I had thought I'd had was dead. I couldn't bear the thought of what he had done, of what they had done. I hated them both,' Sally admitted in a small guilty voice. 'I hated them and I hated the very thought of the child they were to have.'

'And Callum – did you hate him as well?'

For the first time in their relationship Sally could hear anger in George's voice and it confirmed everything she had known and feared would happen when she told him of her deception.

'Yes. If anything, I hated him even more than my father and his sister, because . . .'

'Because you loved him?'

Why were they talking about Callum? He wasn't important any more. The love she'd once thought she had had for Callum was nothing compared with the reality of the mature grown-up love she felt for George.

'I suppose so . . .' She brushed aside George's question. Her heart was thumping and it ached with the pain of the parting she knew must come. She was anxious to get to the end of her explanations, anxious to give him back his ring and walk away from him, leaving him free to find someone to love who would not be deceitful and who he could trust as she knew he would now never again be able to trust her, before she broke down completely, begged him to forgive her and never ever to leave her. That was how much he meant to her. He meant everything to her. *Everything*.

349

He was the very best of men, and he deserved the very best of fiancées.

'I thought it didn't matter that I hadn't told you about my father. After all, he wasn't part of my life any more, and as far as I was concerned he was dead to me, but then . . .' She stopped walking and so did George, so that she could turn towards him to stand in front of him and tell him what she must as bravely as she could.

'My father and Morag were killed in the May blitz on Liverpool, but Alice, their baby, survived. Callum brought her to me on his way to rejoin his ship. I'm all she's got, George. I wanted to have her adopted and never tell you about her. I was going to. I'd got it all planned, but I couldn't. She needs me. Please don't hate me.' She pulled off her engagement ring as she spoke, and held it out to him, her hand trembling. 'One day I hope you'll find a girl who's more worthy of this than I am.'

'And Callum, do you still love him? Are the two of you planning to bring up Alice together?' George demanded, as he took the ring from her.

'What? No, of course not.' Sally knew she couldn't cope with much more. 'I'm so sorry. I know you'd do the decent thing and take on Alice if I asked you to, but I can't do that to you or to your family. Not when she'd always be a reminder of my lack of honesty. Every time you looked at her – every time your mother looked at her – you'd both wonder if you could really trust me to be honest with you and I couldn't bear to have that barrier between us.'

'Sally . . .'

'No, please don't say anything, George. I can't abandon her. I couldn't live with myself if I did.'

And she didn't know how she would live without George and his love either, but somehow she must.

'I'm back on duty in ten minutes,' he told her. 'We can talk more about this later.'

Sally nodded, but she knew that 'later' she would be on her way back to London. What was there, after all, for them to say to one another that could put things right and miraculously give them back the security of the loving trust they had now lost?

'Oh, Drew, do look out of the window. How pretty the countryside looks, all these fields and trees.'

Drew smiled as he heard a city girl's wonder in Tilly's voice as she looked wide-eyed out of the window of their first-class compartment at the countryside through which they were passing. She was as excited as a little girl going on holiday for the first time, he thought indulgently, but of course she wasn't a little girl, and her pretty red cotton dress, with its bright pattern of black and white Scottie dogs and the sweetheart neckline, revealed a figure that most definitely did not belong to a little girl. A desire to take hold of her and kiss her gripped him, but Drew resisted it. He had promised Tilly's mother that his behaviour would be impeccable and irreproachable.

Tilly, though, seemed to have a sixth sense where his feelings for her were concerned because she suddenly looked at him and smiled.

'Since we've got the carriage to ourselves, why don't we pull down the blinds into the corridor and then you can kiss me – properly,' she suggested softly.

'Tilly,' Drew protested, 'you know what I promised your mother. Look,' he added quickly when she started to move towards him, it's nearly one o'clock – why don't we have our sandwiches?'

'Sandwiches? You'd rather eat sandwiches than kiss me?' Tilly protested.

'No,' Drew admitted ruefully, 'but I'm afraid that if I start kissing you now I won't want to stop.'

He had looked so handsome this morning when he had arrived to collect her, wearing a navy-blue blazer, which he had now taken off, over a pale blue V-necked sweater and white open-necked shirt, his smart grey trousers perfectly creased. Drew was always well dressed in good-quality clothes – clothes that in London, Tilly knew, were expensive, but she assumed that they must be less expensive in America because she knew also that Drew didn't earn an awful lot as a junior reporter.

Her own dress was new, made for her by a local dressmaker, one of two she'd saved up for and paid for herself, and a good buy now that clothes could be bought only with clothing coupons. She and her mother had got the fabric in a clearance sale from a warehouse that had been damaged in the April bombing. This red dress had a smart little white short-sleeved bolero, and her other dress, which was made from a lovely floral-patterned cotton sateen in shades of blues and lilacs and purples against a dark gold background, was smart enough with its halter-necked style to wear in the evening, as well as making a very pretty sundress for daytime wear, and it too had a matching bolero jacket.

Of course she'd brought more casual clothes with her in the small suitcase that Mrs Windle had lent her: shorts and a pretty blue and white spotted shirt-style top, which tied at the waist, a dirndl skirt in royal blue with a white scalloped hem she could wear with a white blouse and cardigan, and, very daringly, a pair of trousers, which had become all the fashion now that girls were having to take on men's jobs. Her mother had been a bit concerned they might be too modern for a quiet little village but Tilly had insisted they would be perfect for cycling in, and very sensible if the weather turned cold.

Drew had told her that he was packing his tennis whites in case there was a nearby court. Tilly didn't have a tennis dress, and nor could she play tennis, but Drew had said that he would teach her and that she could wear her white shorts, plimsolls and a white top and she would be fine.

The village where they were staying was several miles inland from the coast. They were to leave the train at Budleigh Salterton, and then take a branch-line train to the village of Astleigh Magna on the River Otter. Drew had planned the whole route, drawing diagrams and showing them all at number 13 the route they would take. Tilly had felt so proud of him for being so organised and manly.

Now, as Tilly unwrapped their egg and cress sandwiches from her mother's carefully hoarded greaseproof paper, the excitement fizzing up inside her felt as exhilarating as any champagne. Three whole days – and nights – completely alone with Drew. Well completely alone, that is, apart from the owners of the pub and their other patrons.

The sunlight streaming in through the carriage window lightened the shiny rich darkness of Tilly's curls and glinted on the gold of Drew's ring as it lay against her creamy skin revealed by the sweetheart neckline of her pretty dress. She was so wonderful, his Tilly, Drew thought as his heart swelled with love for her. So deserving of the very best of everything. It was excellent to see her restored to her old good spirits after the misery she had endured during the Blitz. All he wanted, all that really mattered to him now that he knew her, was Tilly's happiness. He was so lucky to have met her, and even luckier to have her love. She was so trusting, so giving, so adorable in every way.

'Was it like this when you and your family went on holiday to the lake when you were little?' Tilly asked him curiously, gesturing towards the landscape outside the window. 'How long did it take you to get there? Did you go by train?'

About to take a bite out of his sandwich, Drew stopped, his appetite gone as the guilt that was never very far away robbed him of his desire to eat. Like dark clouds on the horizon threatening the best of sunny days, the truth he had kept from Tilly threatened their happiness together.

He looked at her. She was so sweet and innocent, so trusting and unknowing. He tried to imagine her in the forbidding shuttered house in Chicago, which belonged to his father, but he couldn't. The life that was lived there would choke the joy out of her. But she didn't need to know about Chicago. He could stay here in England and protect her from it. Liar, liar, a contemptuous inner voice derided him. Tilly was looking at him now, her face radiant with her love for him, expectation and happiness shining from her.

She was still waiting for him to answer her question.

Drew looked away from her, through the carriage window.

'The lake's up in the mountains. There's lots of trees, but not fields.'

The heaviness of his voice and the sombreness of his expression made Tilly view him with concern. Lovingly she reached out and touched his hand.

'I'm sorry. I've made you sad, talking about your home, haven't I? You must miss it and your family, Drew. I know I would in your shoes.'

'I don't miss anything or anyone when I'm with you,' he assured her.

By the time they'd finished their egg sandwiches the train was slowing down as it approached their station.

Of course, the name of the station had been painted out to make it difficult for any Germans who might try to invade to know where they were. Prior to them setting out, though, Drew had counted the number of stops the train would make before reaching Budleigh Salterton, but he still checked with the uniformed guard as they alighted from the train to make sure they had the right stop.

A brisk nod of his head and a few words in an accent that had Tilly's eyes widening as she heard his Devon burr, and a porter was wheeling away their luggage, leaving them to follow him to the platform for their local train, after he had asked them, 'Do ee want the Astleigh Magna branch line, 'cos if ee do then him be this way?'

After exchanging a look with Drew and trying not to giggle, Tilly nudged Drew and said, 'Just look as these flowers. Everything is so pretty,' as she admired the flowerbeds bright with colourful bedding plants in red, white and blue.

'Won the best East Devon station prize four years running, us beds have,' the porter told them, overhearing.

It wasn't long before their train arrived, and half an hour later Drew was helping Tilly down off the train in a chocolate-box-pretty sleepy little village that was drowsing in the late afternoon sunshine.

From the station they could see the pub, which was at the far end of a row of thatched cottages, the first of which was a post office. As they walked past the cottages the air was filled with the sound of bees humming in the cottage gardens. Outside one of the cottages, an elderly lady sat knitting, a small fat dog snoring at her feet.

'I've got to take some photographs of this place,' Drew told Tilly.

As they approached the pub they could see that beyond it, in a dip in the land, lay the river, and a bridge that crossed it led to the church and a row of almshouses. Drew had read up about the village, which originally had been part of a large estate and had housed estate workers. Outside the pub three elderly men sat on wooden benches. Brief nods of their heads was the group's only acknowledgement of the newcomers' arrival, as Drew ducked his head under the low lintel of the pub's open door. Inside it was dark and cool after the warmth of the sunlight. It smelled of polish and beer.

A woman emerged from behind the bar. Plump and rosy-cheeked, she eyed them and then announced, 'You'll be that young couple as have come down from Lunnon. If you leave your cases here, I'll show you up to your rooms and John boots can take your cases up later for you. You'll get your tea served at five o'clock sharp, before we open, and then there'll be a bit of supper for you after last orders. With you not arriving until after opening time today, I've put a bit of cold pie and some salad to one side for you. Breakfast is at seven thirty, and you'll have to make your own arrangements for your dinners. It's this way.'

To Tilly's surprise she led them out of the pub via a back door and across a garden planted with vegetables to another building that made an L-shape to the pub.

'Used to be a barn, this did, in the days when there was coaches and horses,' the landlady explained as she opened the wide doors and led them up the steep stairs to a long narrow landing with several doors off it.

'These two rooms are yours,' she told them, indicating the two rooms that were furthest away from one another, one at one end of the corridor and the other at the other. 'Bathroom's here,' she opened the door in front of them, 'and there's a key in each of your doors. I'll thank you not to take the keys out with you on account of them getting lost. I'll leave you to settle in now. John boots will be up with your cases in a few minutes and then when you're ready if you come down to the bar I'll sort you out with your food.'

'Which room do you want?' Tilly asked Drew after they had waited to hear the door downstairs close on the landlady.

'I don't mind. Let's have a look at them both, shall we?' Drew suggested, 'and then you can choose.'

Half an hour later, when John 'boots' brought up their cases, they were both agreed that there was nothing much to choose between the rooms. Both were the same size, both possessed high old-fashioned double beds, small dormer windows with views over the surrounding countryside and large open fireplaces in which dried flowers had been placed since it was summer.

'I wish we'd been given rooms next to one another,' Tilly told Drew with a small sigh.

'I rather suspect that our landlady wouldn't have approved of that,' Drew smiled. 'Come on, let's unpack and then go down and have something to eat. Then we can go for a walk and explore.'

It was gone midnight. Tilly knew she ought to be asleep, but she wasn't. Her double bed was clean and comfy, the bed linen smelling of fresh air and summer. She and Drew had had a lovely long evening walk through the village and across the river to the church, closed for worship now, they had been told by the landlady, with worshippers having to travel to another local village to attend church since the death of their last vicar. Drew had shown her the fish basking beneath a rock in the river in the last rays of the dying sunlight, and she had picked him a nosegay of wild roses from the hedgerows as they had ambled arm in arm. It had been a long day, a wonderful day, and there was no reason for her to be lying here wide awake, on edge and unable to sleep. No reason except that Drew was in another bedroom separated from hers only by the length of corridor. She so much wanted to be with him.

Parting from him tonight had been such a wrench, and right now more than anything else she wanted to go to him, but they had promised her mother, and Drew would want to keep that promise, Tilly knew.

In London at number 13 Olive too was unable to sleep, worrying about the temptation she knew Tilly would be facing.

Sally was also lying wide awake, knowing that this was only the first of many nights when she would lie here aching for George and his love.

TWENTY

'I wanted to be with you so much last night.'

They'd picked up the cycles they'd arranged to hire from the post office that morning, where Drew had also enquired about obtaining a fishing licence and hiring a fishing rod so that he could show Tilly how to fish, and now, after a morning spent exploring the area, and stopping off at a teashop in another village, they were lying on a grassy embankment watching clouds drift across the sky.

'We can't, Tilly,' Drew reminded her.

'I know. Tell me more about your family, Drew,' she urged him. 'I know we aren't officially engaged but . . . well, it would be nice to be able to write to your sisters and your mother. What is it?' she demanded when she heard Drew's indrawn breath.

'Nothing,' he answered, but Tilly knew that he was concealing something from her, as surely as she knew that a cloud overhead had just obscured the sun.

'There is something, Drew,' she insisted. 'And I want to know what it is. You don't want me to write to your family, do you?'

'It isn't that, Tilly.'

'Then what is it? Will they think I'm too young, like Mum does, is that it?'

It was so unlike Drew not to answer her questions openly and immediately that instinctively she knew something was wrong.

This was the moment he had always known would come, and now it was here Drew's heart felt heavy with guilt and anxiety.

'Tilly, there's something I have to tell you . . . something I should have told you before . . .'

The heavy portent in his voice and his expression made Tilly feel as though someone had seized her heart in a vicelike grip.

'There's someone else?' she asked him, half stumbling over the words. 'Someone you loved in America before you loved me? Who is she, Drew? Tell me about her.'

Drew looked up at the sky and then back down at the ground. He reached for Tilly's hand and then stopped. Tears filmed her eyes. Right now she badly needed Drew to hold her hand. She was so afraid of what she was going to hear, so afraid of the dark uncertainty with its threat of heartache that had come out of nowhere. It was too late now, though, to wish her questions unasked.

'Let me explain to you a bit about my family background, Tilly. You know that my family live in Chicago and that I work for a Chicago paper as a reporter. All that's true, but what I haven't told you is that my father owns the paper. In fact, he owns several papers.' Drew exhaled. He was sitting up, his arms wrapped round his knees, and now he dropped his head toward them as he fought back the images and memories that were seething inside his head.

'My father had to work very hard to get where he has. He married late in life – my mother's family owned a rival newspaper he wanted to acquire. Her father, my grandfather, died of a heart attack after my father forced a buyout on him. My father desperately wanted several sons to mould in his own image to inherit from him, and after four girls my arrival . . . well, let's just say that my father had decided even before my birth what my life would be. He wanted more sons but an accident shortly after my birth meant that that couldn't happen. He's confined to a wheelchair, but woe betide anyone who thinks they can treat him as an invalid. My father rules his empire with an iron fist. And he rules us, his family, in the same way. I have never really been the son he wanted.'

'Drew . . .' Tilly protested, but Drew shook his head.

'No, it's true. I take after my mother's family. Her brother, who died of TB in his early twenties, wanted to be a writer, just like I do. My father doesn't understand why I would want to write. Writers, reporters – to him they are simply people who shape the news the way he wants them to shape it, so that he can control the opinions of the readers of his newspapers. The only reason my father allowed me to come to London in the first place was because of his vanity, his belief that having me based here, reporting back, would reflect well on him.

'I let him think that I agreed with his views of the way I should report back. That's something I'm ashamed of now, but it was the only way I could come here.

Somewhere in mid-Atlantic I deliberately jettisoned the Drew who was my father's heir and forced to go along with everything he wanted or risk seeing my mother half bullied to death by him for my sins of omission that were laid at her door, to become the Drew that I am today. But it was you who truly gave me the courage to be the person I've wanted to be, Tilly. You, with your love and your faith in me, your belief in me and your lack of concern for wealth and status. You allowed me to be myself, truly myself, for the first time in my life. You've allowed me to believe that money doesn't matter, that there are more important things, that being true to myself and my own dreams is the right thing for me to do.'

'And the girl? The girl you were to have married?'

'It was never anything formal. Just something my father wanted me to do – one day. We didn't even date. I never really even thought about her until I met you and I realised what love truly is. Can you forgive me, Tilly, for not telling you before? I can't promise you a life of financial comfort, I can't even promise you that I will make it as a published author, or even that I'll have a job once my father realises that I don't intend to go back. I can, though, promise you all my love for ever.'

Tilly could feel her heart thudding. Drew's revelations had shocked her. She had had no idea he was keeping such a secret from her, and hurt that he had. But she knew Drew.

She knew that he loved her and she knew that he would never want to hurt her. If he said that other girl had never meant anything to him and that he had never made a true commitment to her, then she, Tilly, was prepared to believe him.

'I don't care about your father's money. All I want is you, Drew. But what about your family, your mother? She must—'

Drew felt his eyes sting with tears. She was so true and honest, his Tilly.

'My mother isn't like yours, Tilly.' He looked away from her and then reached for her hand.

'Once my mother must have been a young woman who had dreams, or at least I hope that she was, but she was a very rich man's daughter, used to having the best of everything. When her own father died and my father proposed to her I think she felt it was easier to accept his proposal, with all that that would mean, rather than to risk suffering a drop in her standard of living. She loves all of us, her children, but her fear of our father means that she always has to put his wishes first.'

'She wouldn't approve of me, would she?' Tilly guessed.

Drew's grip on her hand tightened. 'I'll never let my father control our lives the way he has done the lives of my sisters. His wealth and his power, his need for that power, have corrupted him. That isn't going to happen to us. Our lives, mine and yours, will be lived here in England. If that's what you want. If I am what you want.'

'Oh, Drew, of course you are. I love you so much. Although you've said before that we'll live here, part of me was afraid that you might want to go back to America. I wouldn't mind for myself – wherever you are would be home for me – but there's Mum. She would miss me dreadfully although I know she'd never say so. She'd want me to be happy. I don't think we'd better tell her about your family, though, at least not yet. She'd only worry.'

They looked at one another in mutual understanding.

'I'm sorry,' Tilly told Drew a few minutes later.

'Sorry?'

'Sorry about your father, and your mother. It's so sad.'

'It did hurt, especially when I was a child and I didn't properly understand myself. To my father I shall always be a failure because I've chosen not to follow in his footsteps, but I know what's right for me, Tilly.'

'I am so proud of you, Drew,' Tilly told him, adding lovingly, 'so very proud of you, proud of everything that you are, and that you love me. No matter what happens we'll always have each other and our love, won't we?'

'Always,' Drew assured her. 'And if you ever do stop loving me, Tilly, then all you have to do is give me my ring back. I'll know then and I won't try to persuade you to change your mind.'

'I'll never change my mind, and I'll never stop loving you. I'll never give you your ring back, either. You'll have to ask me for it in person if you change your mind.'

'Then you'll be wearing it for ever, even when I place a wedding band on your finger, Tilly, because nothing will ever stop me loving you. Nothing and no one.'

Somehow Sally had managed to drag herself to work and, once there, being the professional that she was, she had concentrated fully on her work, putting her own heartache to one side. Now, though, she had finished work and was on her way back to number 13, where

Alice and their new lives together would be waiting for her. Alice needed her, and Sally would not desert her or let her down, not now. But how hard it was going to be to live without George, her quiet gentle hero, her one true love.

At least, as someone had said at work earlier, the Blitz seemed to be over. Over but never forgotten. Not by those who had lost anyone they loved.

Sunshine warmed the cobbles of Article Row as Sally turned in, her key turning easily in the lock to the front door of number 13.

The house was empty, but through the kitchen window she could see Alice's borrowed pram on the lawn under the apple tree. Olive was sitting in a nearby deck chair, talking, and Alice was laughing up into the smiling face of the man who was standing next to the deck chair holding her.

George. George was here, holding Alice. A wave of faintness had Sally grabbing hold of the cold stone of the kitchen sink. George was here. Holding Alice.

Her hands were shaking so much she could hardly open the back door. George and Olive watched her walking towards them and then, as she reached them, Olive stood up and said, 'I'll go in and put the kettle on.'

From George's arms Alice saw her and crowed with delight.

'What . . . what are you doing here?' Her voice sounded rusty and unsteady and her heart was pounding fiercely.

'I wanted to come and meet my new sister-in-law-to-be,' George told her calmly, adding, 'She's got your nose.'

'She's got my father's nose,' Sally corrected him automatically.

'How could you ever think that I wouldn't want you both, Sally?' There was pain in George's voice.

'I didn't think that. I just didn't . . . Don't want you to have to take us both on. What will your parents think, George – your mother? She won't want you marrying a girl who wasn't straight and honest with you, a girl who has a baby to bring up.'

'My mother will understand, Sally. I haven't said anything before, but her own circumstances . . . well, she was put in an orphanage after her mother died and her father remarried. She was adopted when she was ten years old by a couple who were emigrating to New Zealand. My mother won't think badly of you, far from it. I want you to put this back on,' he told her, producing her engagement ring from his pocket, 'and I want you to promise me that you will never ever take it off again, at least not until we're in church and I'm putting a wedding ring on your finger.'

'Oh, George.'

The kiss they exchanged was filled with tenderness and love.

'You wouldn't be my Sally if you hadn't decided to keep her,' George told Sally gruffly, 'and I wouldn't be the man you deserve if I didn't understand that.'

'I wanted to be able to turn my back on her. I wanted to be able to hate her but I couldn't,' Sally admitted. 'I just couldn't.'

They'd had the most wonderful day. As he had promised, Drew had shown Tilly how to fish, and had then pretended to be downcast when she'd managed to catch something and he hadn't, although Tilly had drawn the line at the thought of the small brown trout she'd hooked being cooked for their tea and had insisted on it being put back.

Now they were both in their bedrooms and Tilly was free to go over the events of the day. Funny how things could be. What Drew had told her had only strengthened her love for him. He had been so brave, standing up to his father in the way that he had. Tilly didn't care about his father's money and she was glad that Drew wanted them to make their own lives together here in England. And they would. Once the war was over they would rent a house not far from Fleet Street, perhaps even in Article Row. In the winter Drew would write his book in their little sitting room whilst she listened to the wireless, and in the summer perhaps they might even rent a little cottage here in Devon and Drew would write outside in the sunshine. They would be so happy together, and maybe one day, when the time was right, Drew would be able to persuade his mother to come over and see them. Darling Drew. He had been so afraid that he would lose her. She had seen that in his eyes when he had told her about his family. Darling, darling Drew. She wanted to be with him so much. Tilly looked at her closed bedroom door, a new determination filling her.

Pulling on her dressing gown, she opened the door. The corridor was empty, as she had known it would be. After all, they were the only two guests staying here. She padded along it to Drew's door, not allowing herself second thoughts as she knocked briefly on it and whispered, 'Drew, it's me, Tilly.'

It took him so long to open the door that she was beginning to think he hadn't heard her, and then he opened it only slightly so that she couldn't enter his room. He had obviously been getting ready for bed himself because his chest was bare and he was wearing a pair of pyjama bottoms. Tilly had seen Drew's bare chest already – or at least part of it, when they had sunbathed earlier in the day – and she had thought then how nice and manly it was, but now, in the shadowy darkness, she suddenly realised that seeing all of it was much more than 'nice', and that the feeling burning deep inside her was a very dangerous feeling indeed. Very dangerous and very exciting and . . . something she desperately wanted to share with him. She loved him and she wanted to show him that love. She wanted him to know that the words they had exchanged today where more than just words, the commitment they had made to one another a commitment that crossed a line from which there was to be no turning back.

'Let me in, Drew,' she urged him.

'No.' His voice was hoarse and harsh. 'No. You must go back to your own room, Tilly. Please . . .' he begged her.

Tilly shook her head and stepped towards him. Drew moved back. Tilly followed him in and closed the door.

'I love you and I want to be with you, Drew. I want us to be together. I want to show you how much I love you and how much I always will love you.'

'Oh, Tilly.'

The words were an anguished groan and then she was in his arms and he was kissing her and she was kissing him back, the feeling of his bare flesh beneath her hands heart-shiveringly exciting, but not as exciting as the way she felt when Drew cupped her naked breast beneath the flimsy cover of her open dressing gown and nightgown. Tilly gasped and suppressed a small sob as she moved closer to him, but Drew pushed her gently away.

'No, Tilly. No.'

'But, Drew, I want us to be together. I want this to be the night we show our love for one another so that nothing can ever part us.'

'We can't, Tilly. We can't take that risk. And you know what I mean. If you should become pregnant . . .'

'Then my mother would be forced to let us marry.'

The firm look that strengthened his face left Tilly in no doubts about Drew's stance when he told her emphatically, 'No. I admire and respect your mother, Tilly. She would be dreadfully upset by something like that. Nancy, for one, would have a field day, and that wouldn't be fair. Your mother loves you, Tilly. She is fiercely protective of you and fiercely proud of you. One day you will be exactly the same kind of mother to our children, our daughter. Just imagine how you would feel if she had to come to you to tell you that the man she believed loved her had allowed her to do something so potentially damaging . . . something that he had given you his word would not happen. More than that, family is important, Tilly, and your mother is part of the kind of family I want for our children.'

Drew's words were melting her heart, Tilly had to admit, but . . .

'We can be careful,' she told him. 'There's a girl at the hospital who says—'

'Careful?' Drew laughed. 'Tilly, you are far too loving

and passionate ever to be able to be careful, and I love you so much that I wouldn't be able to do a damn thing about that. No, my love, as difficult as it is, we must wait.'

'Oh, Drew.'

'There is something we can do, though,' he told her, seeing how downcast she was. 'Something that will bind us together, something that will belong to us alone and no one else, something that will be ours and of us, Tilly.'

His words mystified her.

Releasing her, he reached for the pale blue V-necked jumper he had been wearing when they had travelled down to Devon.

'Here, put this on,' he told her, whilst he reached for his own trousers and shirt, pulling the trousers on over his pyjama bottoms and then reaching for Tilly's hand.

'Come on . . .'

Outside, the village slept and the moon was high, lighting their path towards the river and then across it, Drew refusing to say anything when Tilly begged to know what he was doing.

It was only when they stood outside the church that she began to understand, her gaze meeting his in silence as he led her toward the unlocked door.

Inside the ancient building smelled of dust and disuse, but the moonlight pouring in through its stained-glass windows cast a soft shadowing of rich colours over the worn wooden pews and stone floor.

Picking up a dust-covered Bible from a pile, Drew guided Tilly over the stone flags to the bare altar where he reached for her left hand.

Without either of them needing to make any explanations, they began to speak the words of the marriage service, slowly, lingering over each solemn vow and promise as much as they had lingered over their passionate kisses and caresses earlier.

When Drew removed his ring from the chain around her neck to slip it onto her ring finger, Tilly curled her fingers tight so that it wouldn't slide off.

'I love you, Tilly, and I will always love you,' Drew told her.

'I love you too, Drew,' Tilly responded. 'And I will always love you.'

The kiss they exchanged was chaste and reverent.

Before they left the church Tilly kneeled to pray for Drew and for their love, and for her country and all those who served it; for peace and an end for ever to all wars.

There could surely be no greater joy than this, to have the love and the commitment of the man she herself loved so much.

'Nothing can ever part us now,' Tilly told Drew.

'Nothing,' he agreed, lifting her hand to his lips and kissing her closed fingers. 'We are one now, Tilly, and we have a bond between us that nothing and no one can ever break.'

'Those whom God hath joined together . . .' Tilly whispered.

'. . . let no man put asunder,' Drew completed.

As they walked together down the aisle a soft gentle sigh seemed to whisper round the church.

Drew had been right, Tilly admitted. She didn't want to hurt her mother, not really, and Drew's verbal picture of the future they would all share as a family had filled her with pride in him and yes, in her mother as well.

They may not have become physical lovers tonight but right now their private exchanging of their special vow was making her feel so very close to him that her heart was flooded with happiness.

'Our time will happen, Tilly,' Drew assured her as they stepped out of the church. 'I know it. You and I are destined to be together and bound together for all time now. I love you, and that love, my love, is yours for ever,' he told her huskily. 'Never forget that.'

'Oh, Drew, I love you too,' Tilly whispered as he gathered her close for the sweet precious intimacy of their shared kiss.